THE PROMISE OF TOMORROW

A SLOW-BURN ROMANTIC SUSPENSE

LOVE'S PROMISES
BOOK 1

SOPHIE BARTOW

CONTENTS

Dedicated to ...

My street team;
The Wall-Giennie Wicks-Delaney
Connector Inspectors- Cherie & Danette
Plot Catcher- Maggie Grimes
Sign Crew- Kate Semenyuk

And to my oldest, whose mischievousness gave me a terrific plot point.

Two Hearts Press
An imprint of LLIPSS, INC.
Copyright © 2025 by *Sophie Bartow*

Ingram Regular paperback ISBN: 978-1-965510-29-2

Cover Design by Kate Semenyuk

*Inspiration began
when a lost girl fell for a lost boy.*

*Blessed Children's Home –
a place where families are
created, not just by blood, but
also, by heart.*

MEET THE CHARACTERS

MADDY DAVIES - She's a social worker for the Blessed Children's Home in Dorchester, Mass. After her parents' death, the Blessed Children's Home raised Maddy. She has been best friends with Tina since they were seven.

Mason Weaver - He is a detective with the South Boston Precinct. Mason is partners with Darrin.

Darrin Anderson - He is a detective with the South Boston Precinct and best friends and partners with Mason.

Christina Stone - She's a dancer/dance instructor. When she was seven, Tina came to live at the Blessed Children's Home, where she became best friends with Maddy. Her story is told in **The Promise to Dance -Love's Promises Book 2 coming in summer 2026.**

Scott Weaver - He is the lieutenant at the South Boston Precinct. Scott's married to Joy, father to Rod, Mason, Brandon and Heather, and grandfather to Graham and Sierra. His story is told in The Promise of Home.

Joy Weaver - She is a psychologist at King's Castle General Hospital. Joy's married to Scott, mother to Rod, Mason, Brandon and Heather, and grandmother to Graham and Sierra. Her story is told in The Promise of Home.

Sister Maisie Blue – She's a social worker and the director of Blessed Children's Home. Sister Blue grew up in Swan Harbor.

Sister June Green – She's a special education teacher and works at Blessed Children's Home.

Sister Agatha Black – She's a special education teacher and works at Blessed Children's Home.

Ava King – The King family, and their corporation fund Blessed Children's Home by holding two events each year. Ava's story is told in **Kisses, Family & Hope.**

Natalie French – She's a student studying teaching and mother to Lucas.

Tori – She is two years old and lives at Blessed Children's Home. Her story is Love's Promises Book 3.

Abby – She is two years old and lives at Blessed Children's Home. Her story is Love's Promises Book 7

Welcome to Love's Promises

Where every story begins with hope.

ONE

*QUICK NOTE: IF YOU ENJOY LISTENING TO MUSIC WHILE reading, The Promise of Tomorrow has a playlist. It can be found here: **The Promise of Tomorrow.***

With that, enjoy!

Blessed Children's Home
Dorchester, Massachusetts
December 31, 1993
5:30 p.m.

SOCIAL WORKER MADDY DAVIES WANTED TO CHANGE LIVES ... NOT risk hers. At least, that's what the Sisters who raised her at Blessed Children's Home reminded her of daily. Yet, one desperate cry was all it took for her to throw caution aside and rush to help.

"Maddy, why are you here?"

Rats!

She glanced up to see Sister Masie Blue, the Director of Blessed Children's Home, leaning against the doorframe.

"I was just finishing the paperwork for the Connors' adoption." Maddy tapped the file. "Why? Is there something you need me to do?"

"No. I thought you were going to a party tonight. It is New Year's Eve, after all."

"So it is," Maddy sighed. "I was going …"

"Maddy," Blue, as everyone called her, scolded, "you're young. Go out and have a good time with your friends."

"But I …" Her argument faded when she noticed the indulgent look on the older woman's face. "Alright, Blue. You win. I'm going. I'm going."

"Good." Blue turned to leave and, at the last minute, stuck her head back in the door. "Happy New Year, Maddy. Have a good time."

Once Blue's footsteps faded, Maddy stashed the folder in her bottom drawer. The older woman was right about the New Year's Eve party. But with everyone paired up, she preferred to go straight home.

She slung her bag over her shoulder and was on the way out when the phone rang, causing her to hesitate. Her job as a social worker involved helping others navigate difficult times. If someone needed her …

The decision made, Maddy rushed to answer.

"Maddy," the woman on the other end cried. "He found me. I can hear him yelling. He's trying to get inside."

It took Maddy an extra second to weed through the crying and figure out who was on the other end. "Alisha?"

"Yes! Maddy, help! Tell me what to do!"

With every word the other woman uttered, there was a little more panic in her voice. Maddy's heart raced, and her mind searched for what to say. She could hear someone pounding on the door. Could hear the cries of Alisha's little girl.

"Call 911, Alisha," Maddy instructed. "I'm on my way."

"Hurry, Maddy. Hurry."

Maddy hung up, left her briefcase on her desk, and ran toward the front door.

"Maddy?" Blue questioned. "What's going on?"

"Call 911 to 15 Peach Street. Domestic situation," Maddy yelled on her way out. "I'll meet them there."

"But Maddy—"

The Home's front door slammed, shutting off whatever Blue was going to say. She'd apologize later. Right then, Alisha needed her.

She left the Home's grounds and took a right. Halfway there, she realized she'd forgotten her coat. Refusing to turn back, the memory of the young mother's cries propelled her forward.

Alisha Chapman had come to her attention one Saturday afternoon. Thin with dishwater blonde hair and an infant on her hip, Maddy recognized desperation when their eyes met. She'd immediately taken the other woman under her wing and helped her get back on her feet.

Unfortunately, the peacefulness lasted less than a year. That was when the man Alisha was seeing completely changed and wouldn't take no for an answer. With a restraining order in place and a subsequent move, they'd thought everything would be fine. However, if he'd found her ....

Maddy turned onto Peach Street and could hear sirens in the distance. A good sign, but sadly, right then, the negative outweighed the positive.

She ran up the steps of Alisha's home and found the door hanging open, shattered glass littering the floor. When she'd spoken to the young mother, someone was pounding on the door, and the child was crying. Now, there was only silence.

"Alisha," she called softly. "It's Maddy. Are you okay?"

There was a groan, then a shuffling sound, before it was quiet again. Something inside was saying, '*Run! Run!*' but the memory of the cry for help rang louder. She took one step and then another. Seeing blood drops littering the floor had her racing around the island to find Alisha sprawled on the ground.

Maddy dropped onto her knees, and what she needed to do raced through her head. In the distance, the sirens screamed, and urgency pressed down on her. With time rushing by, she checked for a pulse and began CPR. After the tenth pump, a noise alerted her she was no longer alone.

Hesitantly, she lifted her head to see a man holding a bloody knife and charging toward her.

Dorchester, Massachusetts
December 31

6:00 p.m.

Detective Mason Weaver's car radio blared to life: *Caucasian male reported running up Peach Street. He's armed and dangerous. Officers in pursuit.*

Mason turned away from the highway and started toward Peach Street. Technically, he was off duty, but ....

Officers on the scene of a domestic dispute at 15 Peach Street. Two females down. One deceased, the other on her way to King's Castle General Hospital. Social Services has been called for the little girl found unharmed.

"Damn!"

He and his partner had stopped by the house more than once in the last thirty days. They were looking for Parker Turner, a man whose name had come up multiple times in their current investigation. One that involved the drug ecstasy and high school parties.

Had he added murder to his repertoire?

When Mason reached Peach Street, he parked a few houses from the crime scene. Multiple law enforcement vehicles blocked the road—including several cruisers, one from the morgue, and another that belonged to his lieutenant.

He sat still for a moment, contemplating the scene. His date was expecting him at a New Year's Eve party. If he didn't show, she would be pissed. It forced him to decide—which was more important?

Ultimately, the reason they'd visited the home won out. It pushed him through the sea of officers and onto the porch.

"Weaver," Mason's lieutenant greeted him. "I wasn't aware you were on the duty roster tonight."

"I could say the same for you," Mason returned.

The lieutenant brushed back his salt-and-pepper hair and gave him a self-deprecating smile. "My wife's still out of town. Now, it's your turn."

"Dad, I'm not fifteen any longer."

Scott Weaver, Mason's father and Lieutenant, stepped aside to allow room for the medical examiner's gurney to exit the house.

"Anything else, Lieutenant?"

"TOD?" Scott asked.

"Less than an hour."

"COD?"

"Looks like exsanguination secondary to multiple stab wounds," the medical examiner replied. "I'll know more once I complete the autopsy."

"What about the second woman?" Mason questioned. "Do you have a name?"

"She didn't have any identification on her."

"And the child?" Mason followed up.

The medical examiner shrugged. "She's at King's Castle General, waiting for the social worker."

Mason nodded his thanks and followed his father inside.

"Why are you watching this house again, Mason?" Scott asked quietly.

"Drugs."

"Is there a connection between this and the recent teen hospitalizations?"

Instead of answering immediately, Mason wandered deeper into the house and took in the scene. There were multiple smells—blood, urine, fried foods, and ... was that powder?

"Is the woman who lives here your suspect?" Scott asked.

"No."

"Then why are you here?"

"It's possible the drug dealer we're looking for has a connection to this house."

"With the woman?"

"I don't know," Mason snapped, just sharply enough to earn a look from his father.

"Sorry," he sighed. "For some reason, this case frustrates me more than normal."

"Does it remind you of another time?" Scott put him on the spot.

"It reminds me of how careless high school kids can be."

"You'll figure it out," Scott assured him. "I know you will."

Mason gave his father a half-smile and then wandered around the room. It was small, utilitarian almost. The furniture was old but looked comfortable. There was a kitchen to the right and two bedrooms to the left.

The crime scene technicians were working in the kitchen, which was the only reason he stopped at the threshold.

"Did you find any ID?" he asked the tech.

"Purse is in that bag." The tech nodded toward the table. "Do you need some gloves?"

Mason slipped on the gloves, opened the clear plastic bag, and took out a backpack-style purse. Inside, he found two diapers, some wipes, an extra pair of child's socks, and a snowsuit. At the very bottom, he found a wallet.

"Alisha Chapman, age 21," he read from the Boston license. "She was young."

"And the man you're looking for?" Scott asked. "What's his name?"

"Parker," Mason answered. "Parker Turner."

"Had you spoken to Ms. Chapman?"

"Not yet. She wouldn't answer the door," Mason sighed. "Either that, or she wasn't home."

He continued sorting through the wallet. Besides the license, he found three photos: one of a child, one of a woman and child, and one of an older couple. On the back of the child's photo was a date.

"Anything about the child?"

"She's almost two, but I can't find a name."

"And the other woman?"

"Nothing," Mason stated. "Do you know what happened?" he asked the tech.

"I can give you my current working theory," the tech answered. "Just don't hold me to it."

"Go on," Mason encouraged.

"The male kicked down the door and chased the woman through the house." The tech pointed to several broken or displaced items. He then indicated a butcher's block on the counter. "Either she grabbed one of those knives, and he took it away, or the assailant took the knife and went after the victim."

"What about the other female?" Mason asked.

A little smile spread across the tech's lips, making him wonder what he'd missed.

"My working theory," the tech began, "is she came into the house and interrupted the killer. He knocked her down, but she went right back at him."

"How did she get away?" Mason frowned. "How did she not end up the second victim?"

The tech showed them another evidence bag. Inside was a cast-iron skillet.

"She hit him with a skillet?" Scott grinned. "Really?"

"I think so," the tech hummed. "It's the only way to explain how the second female's still living."

"Was the visitor a neighbor? A friend?" Mason murmured. "Did Alisha call them when she heard someone outside?"

"Haven't gotten there yet," the tech answered. "But you could hit *69 on the phone and see who she called last."

"Good idea. Thanks."

King's Castle General Hospital
December 31, 1993
8:30 p.m.

WHEN THE NURSE FINISHED WRAPPING HER ARM, MADDY SAT UP, ready to leave.

"Hold on," the nurse stopped her. "You aren't going anywhere right now."

"Why not? I need to find Tori."

"Tori?"

"The little girl whose mom died tonight. Have you heard anything?"

"Nothing, I'm sorry. But I can try to find out."

"I'd appreciate it."

"While I'm gone, rest," the nurse instructed. "You have quite the shiner where your head bounced on the floor. We need to make sure you don't have a concussion."

Hearing the word reminded Maddy of her pounding head—a pain she'd been able to ignore until right then.

"Why did you say that?" she grumbled.

"Does your head hurt?"

"I hadn't noticed until you said the word concussion," Maddy sighed. "Now, there are jackhammers in there."

"Let me get you something for the pain. In the meantime, close your eyes and put this cold cloth over them." The nurse handed her a wet rag. "I'll be right back."

Maddy laid the cloth over her eyes and tried to relax. However, each time she heard a child cry, she thought about Tori. Each time it was too quiet, she remembered the silence in Alisha's house. When she shut her eyes, she saw the flash of the knife and felt the pain as it tore into her arm. With that, her heart raced, and fear climbed a little higher.

A handful of minutes later, she heard her name spoken in a baritone voice that caused her heart to race, but not from fear. This time, it was all about the connection between a woman and a man.

"Are you family?" one nurse asked.

"No."

"Then I can't let you go in there."

The nurse's response was definitive, bringing a smile to Maddy's lips.

"I only have a few questions," the man pressed.

"Sir," the nurse said irritably. "I said no."

"Will this change your mind?"

Maddy wondered what he'd said or done because the nurse returned less than a minute later.

"Maddy," she whispered. "Do you feel up to a visitor?"

"Who?"

The nurse placed a business card in her hand. "He said his name is Detective Mason Weaver. He has some questions."

Maddy lifted the cloth, and the bright light immediately made her stomach churn. She fought the feeling and tried to focus on the nurse's words.

"If you don't feel up to it …?"

"I'll see him," she whispered. "Maybe he can explain what happened. In the meantime—"

"—Find out about the child," the nurse guessed.

"Please."

"I'll see what I can do."

Maddy replaced the cloth and waited for the Detective to enter. When he did, a sense of heat stretched between them. It warmed her from the outside in, and his smell—a combination of soap and cologne—caused her head to swim.

"Miss Davies," he purred in a sexy-as-sin voice. "I'm Detective Mason Weaver. Do you have time for a few questions?"

His voice shouldn't have affected her, but it slid across her skin like velvet

—too smooth, too warm, too much. She wasn't supposed to notice things like that. Not tonight. Not after what she'd seen.

She told herself it was just adrenaline. A trick of her exhausted, overtaxed mind. But the way her breath caught when he spoke? That wasn't imagined.

Maddy held off for another heartbeat or two before she couldn't stand it any longer. She slowly removed the cloth. Her gaze clashed with the detective's, and her breath caught.

He was tall, his eyes were dark, dark brown, and his hair was short. His stare was intense but not scary intense. More in an *'I wasn't ready for this—whatever this is' kind of way.*

"Do you feel up to answering a few questions?" he asked after a moment.

She tried to answer, but couldn't get the words to form.

"Would you care for a drink?"

"Please."

He hit the control to elevate her head and handed her a cup of water. "Do you need help?"

"I can do it." Her hand shook when she took the proffered cup, forcing her to support it with the other.

"Don't drink too much," Mason cautioned. "You don't want to get sick to your stomach."

He was watching her like he saw more than just bruises and a bandage. Like he could read what she was trying to hide beneath the calm.

And worse—he made her want to say it out loud. To tell someone what it felt like to kneel in blood, trying to save a woman who'd trusted her.

That was dangerous. Wanting comfort was dangerous. Wanting *his* comfort was unthinkable.

"How did you know Miss Chapman?" Mason began.

"How did you find me?" Maddy countered.

"*69."

Maddy sighed. "I was too late to save her."

"You're damn lucky you aren't lying in the morgue next to her," Mason snapped. "Why didn't you wait for the police?"

"Because she called me!" Maddy barked right back. "She'd lost faith in your kind."

"My kind?" Mason's brows rose. "You're telling me she didn't trust the police?"

"She didn't."

"Why?"

"I don't know all the reasons," Maddy answered. "What I can say is, at my insistence, Alisha reported her boyfriend's behavior more than once, and look how much good that did for her and Tori. Speaking of the little girl, where is she?"

"Tori is the child?"

"Yes! She's almost two."

"I see," Mason replied. "Social Services was called in, so you don't need to worry about her."

"I'm Social Services," Maddy retorted. "The child is now my responsibility."

The combination of her frustration on top of her pounding head caused her stomach to churn even more. She swallowed several times, trying to force down the bile, not wanting to appear weak in front of him.

"I'm," Maddy could feel it rushing up and barely had time to lean over before everything bubbled up and out.

TWO

King's Castle General Hospital
December 31, 1993
9:00 p.m.

MASON SET ASIDE THE TRASH CAN HE'D PICKED UP AND HANDED
Maddy a wet cloth. When she covered her face with it, he took a few seconds
to observe her.

Thanks to her comments, he knew her name, age, where she lived, and
occupation. Yet nothing had prepared him for the impact of her silver-blue
eyes. Nothing had prepared him for the sadness in them when she referred to
the deceased as having called her. Nor for the way they flashed when she
hadn't liked his questions. But what hit him hardest was just how vulnerable
she looked before she'd gotten sick.

"Can I get you anything else?"

Maddy held up the cloth. "Would, would you wet this again for me?"

The tremor in her voice hadn't been there before. It made him want to
back away and not cause her any more pain.

"Cold water?"

"Please."

When he turned to re-wet the cloth, the nurse returned.

"Physically, Tori is fine," the nurse relayed. "She's with an aide until someone arrives for her."

"I told you," Maddy muttered. "I'm the social worker. Her mother would want me to take responsibility."

"Yes, you did say that."

"I work for the Blessed Children's Home," Maddy grumbled. "We'll become Tori's support system. Now, when can I leave?"

"You threw up, Maddy," the nurse murmured. "Are you sure you don't need to stay overnight?"

Maddy thumbed in his direction. "It's only because he upset me."

"Hey," Mason frowned. "What did I say?"

"Maddy?" the nurse pressed. "How do you feel?"

Mason watched several expressions flit across Maddy's face. She was embarrassed, which explained why she wouldn't look at him. But with a killer out there, he needed her cooperation.

"Miss Davies, Maddy," said Mason. "I still need to ask you some questions."

"But ..."

"Once you're discharged, I can take you and Tori wherever you need."

Only when he mentioned the child did she look at him. Just as before, her stare hit him harder than he liked.

He told himself he was just observing a witness—but that wasn't true.

Something about her got under his skin. The way she winced without complaint. The grief behind her steady stare.

She reminded him of himself.

And that was the problem.

"Okay."

Mason let go of the breath he hadn't realized he'd been holding and waited for the nurse to leave.

"Alright, detective, ask away."

"Were you Alisha's social worker?"

"Not in a professional sense."

"Friends?"

"I don't think you could even say we were friends."

"Yet, you said she called you."

"She did."

Her stubbornness had him clinching his jaw.

"Go on."

"I've helped Alisha out of a bind a time or two."

"Such as?"

"The first time I met her, Tori was only a few months old. I helped Alisha get back on her feet."

"And the next time?"

"Her boyfriend was stalking her. I assisted with the restraining order."

"Was that against Parker Turner?" Mason followed up.

"Parker Turner?"

"He's wanted for questioning in Alisha's death."

"I don't know him, but he's not the ex-boyfriend."

"Are you sure?"

"No."

"Who did she have the restraining order against?" Mason asked, attempting to regain the upper hand.

"Brian Lloyd."

The name triggered a memory. One Mason filed away to explore later.

"You said Alisha called you tonight, right?"

"Yes. While on the phone, I heard someone pounding on the door and yelling her name. I thought it was the ex. In fact, ..."

"In fact?" Mason prodded.

"She said, 'He found me.'"

"So you assumed it was the ex?"

Maddy nodded. "I could hear a man yelling in the background, and I—"

"Took off without waiting for help."

His tone was sharper than he'd meant, and it showed in the way her eyes flashed.

"I told someone to call 911," she snapped. "When I arrived at Alisha's home, I could hear them coming and knew they weren't far away."

"Then what happened?"

Maddy looked down at her hands. When she started speaking again, her voice was low and shaky.

"I found her on the ground and started CPR. Then I heard a sound and saw someone running toward me."

"Was it Brian?"

"Maybe. It happened so fast."

"Then you grabbed the frying pan?"

She almost smiled. "It was handy."

"Then what happened?"

"What do you mean, what happened? I went after him."

The woman in the bed might have an angelic face, but he'd bet she'd be pure spitfire if she felt better.

"Tell me what you remember about the man."

WITH EACH QUESTION, MADDY'S HEAD POUNDED HARDER. SHE wanted to close her eyes, shut out the glaring lights, and the man whose chocolate brown eyes made her heart race.

"Look, detective. Can we—?"

Blue rushed into the room. "Maddy, dear!" "I heard you were here. What happened?"

"I—"

Lieutenant Scott appeared right behind her.

"I told you to wait for me," Scott grunted.

"Dad?" Mason frowned. "I thought you—?"

"He was," Blue asserted. "But as soon as I heard what happened to Maddy, I made him bring me to the hospital. If you'll excuse us, Maddy needs to get dressed."

"Wait. I still need—"

"Give it up, son," Scott murmured. "When Blue makes up her mind, there's no changing it."

Maddy blinked, trying to catch up. Her thoughts felt scrambled, like puzzle pieces dropped on the floor.

"We'll wait for you in the lobby, Blue," Lieutenant Scott replied. "Alright?"

"Perfect. We'll be there as soon as possible."

Once the door shut, the air felt lighter, and she could breathe. But that was something she expected, as Blue always had that effect on her.

"I brought you a change of clothes," Blue told her, setting a small bag on the bed. "While you are changing, I will take care of Tori."

Maddy side-eyed the older woman. "Why was Lieutenant Scott with you? Why didn't I know his son was a detective?"

"We'll talk about it later," Blue replied. "Now get dressed. It's late."

A sentiment Maddy appreciated. There was too much uncertainty on the highway, one reason she didn't drive.

With Blue gone, Maddy swung her legs over the side of the bed. Her head swam, and her stomach churned. *Deep breath in.* Moments later, she felt well enough to untie the hospital gown and pull on the clean sweatshirt. Everything hurt, but sleep would only bring memories.

As a social worker, she dealt with people down on their luck. People who had gone through tragedies and who needed to start over. She'd even rushed into situations where she probably shouldn't have to save people—from others and themselves. Yet, she'd never had to fight for her own life. That was new and something she was still trying to understand.

She slipped on her boots, only then, realizing Blue was standing inside the door, watching her. Her stare was all-encompassing, almost painful to see. Especially knowing how much the entire ordeal had to have hurt her.

"Where's Tori?"

"Mason has her," Blue whispered in a husky voice. "She went to him easily."

"The detective? Really?"

"You've seen his father with kids. He'll be fine."

"Oh, okay."

"How are you really?"

"I have a headache."

Blue brushed Maddy's hair off her forehead. "You're going to have quite the shiner."

"You don't think it's my color?"

"Oh, Maddy." Blue touched the bruise on her forehead, then the bandage on her arm. "Don't make light of these. I was worried sick. Are you hurt in just these two places?"

"I have a scratch on my side." Blue's expression didn't change, and that was worse. "I'm okay. Really. But I wish ..."

"You'd gotten there earlier?"

"Yes."

"And what if he'd still been at the door?"

"I'm not—"

"Don't do that, Maddy. We don't get to rewrite what already happened. You might have been able to change the outcome. But then again, maybe not."

"Meaning I might not have been so lucky."

"That's right. How often have I told you not to rush in where angels fear to tread?"

"Too many times to count."

"And you're still not listening."

Tears rushed to Maddy's eyes, and she spontaneously hugged Blue.

"Thanks for coming to get me," she whispered. "I don't know what I would do without you."

"Right back at you, Maddy. I have your discharge paperwork. Ready to leave?"

"I'm ready."

"Let me help you."

Maddy almost brushed aside the help. But her head was still spinning, and ending up on the floor wasn't something she wanted.

"If you insist."

"Don't be so cheeky, young lady."

"I'll do my best."

"You've said that before."

"I know. I'm sorry."

"It's okay, Maddy. Shall we? Mason's waiting for us."

Hearing his name had her heart skipping a beat. She couldn't afford to notice him, but apparently, she was no longer the one in charge.

King's Castle General Hospital
December 31, 1993
10:00 p.m.

Mason brushed back the toddler's golden curls and contemplated her solemn expression. She'd just lost her mother, and Miss Davies had been injured. Whether it would affect Tori in the future, only time would tell.

When he lifted his head, it was to find Sister Blue and Maddy Davies watching him. The older woman's expression was affectionate, familiar. The same quiet connection his father seemed to share with her. But his gaze drifted straight to the younger woman. From a distance, she was pretty. Up close, when her silver-blue eyes locked with his, she was unforgettable.

He stood. "Ladies. Is everything alright?"

"It's time to take Maddy and Tori home," Blue replied. "Where did Scott go?"

"To get the car. He should pull up any minute."

"Oh, that's lovely. I'm so happy he thought of it. Are we ready?"

"I'll give this one to you." Mason gently handed Tori to Blue. "Then I'll get my car and take Maddy wherever—"

"She's coming home with me," Blue cut in.

"I don't need—" Maddy began.

"You shouldn't be alone tonight," Blue said firmly.

Mason almost suggested he could stay with her. Except that allowed room for thoughts he shouldn't be having.

"I feel fine."

"You may feel fine, but you still need to be watched."

"Oh, but ..."

"It's only for one night. There's Scott now. I'll ride with him, and you two can follow. Will that work?"

"We'll be right behind you." Mason stepped aside and indicated the chair he'd just vacated. "Sit. I'll get the car."

He walked with Blue to the curb and held the car door while she strapped in Tori. When the older woman stepped back, she held his gaze for an extra second. It was thoughtful and made him feel like he'd missed something only she could see.

"We'll see you in a minute, right?" she asked.

"Yes."

With Tori and Sister Blue in his father's care, Mason jogged to his car. By the time he reached the drop-off area, Maddy was already there—waiting. Before he could offer to help, she'd climbed inside.

"Are you okay?"

"I'm not going to throw up. Is that what you wanted to know?"

Mason studied her a little longer. Was she still upset about the trashcan? Or was she deflecting?

"It wasn't. But it's good to know."

Maddy smiled, but it never reached her eyes. Those were haunted.

"Can we go? Please?"

He gave a nod and pulled into the traffic. "I need an address."

"You don't know where the Home is?"

"Should I?"

"Your dad's a regular," she murmured before giving him the information.

The address explained why she'd not worn a coat to Peach Street. The Home wasn't far. A few blocks, maybe. Dorchester, if he remembered correctly. A big old Victorian.

While he drove, Mason's thoughts wandered. There was something he was missing. Not just about his father, Blue, and Maddy. But there were threads he hadn't yet connected.

His mind drifted in another direction.

... Blood, urine, fried foods, and ... was that powder?

He could still smell it. Slowly, he lifted his hand and sniffed his fingers. Not from Tori.

Mason glanced to his right. Maddy shifted, her eyes still closed.

It was her.

The soft scent washed over him, settling something deep inside. It brought him back to his thoughts of trying to decide if he'd wanted to go to the party. Loud music, cold drinks, meaningless conversation, and a much stronger perfume.

Now that he was sitting next to a woman who smelled like quiet strength and trouble he knew he was exactly where he was meant to be.

THREE

Blessed Children's Home
December 31, 1993
11:00 p.m.

MADDY SHIFTED SIDEWAYS IN THE SEAT AND STARED OUT THE window. She searched the darkness for something to capture her attention. Something to keep her awake. Something to keep her from slipping into a light sleep where all she saw was ....

Once again, she readjusted, searching for a place where the haunting images didn't follow. Where she wouldn't close her eyes and see Alisha lying on the ground. Where she couldn't smell blood, or feel it coating her hands as she tried to pump life back into the young mother.

Yet the images persisted. Each time they reappeared, they lasted a little longer. Burned a little brighter.

She was tired. Tired of trying not to scream. Tired of holding on to the tears that threatened. Tired of fighting to keep the pain inside.

The pain had started as a small kernel, and every time she pushed it back down, it grew until a sound escaped. It was haunting and made her feel weak.

Maddy pressed her lips together, determined to stay silent. *Later, when you're alone. Later.*

Once more, she moved around. Except that time, she realized her hands weren't as cold. Realized she wasn't as alone.

"Don't fight it, Maddy." Mason squeezed her hand in support.

"I have to. If I don't, then—" Her voice wobbled. She immediately slammed the door on those feelings and focused on the sound of the tires as they slid across the road. The quiet noise lulled her into a semi-relaxed state. Once there, she fought to remain. Fought to stay in control. It didn't seem to matter, though, as the pain inside continued to grow. Before she could stop it, another whimper escaped.

When the car exited the highway, Maddy pressed her hands against her mouth, determined not to fall apart. But the feelings inside had grown so much she could no longer contain them.

"Why? Why couldn't I have—?"

"Come here." Mason loosened her seatbelt and forcefully pulled her into his arms. "Let it go. You've held it inside too long."

Letting go wasn't part of her skill set. Not when people were counting on her to stay strong.

But something about the way he held her—like he wasn't afraid of the mess she was in—broke down her last wall.

She hadn't asked for a rescue. And yet, here he was. How dangerous was it to need someone like that?

Maddy gripped his dress shirt, needing to be closer, needing to share some of what she was feeling.

When he wrapped his big hand around hers and held on, she began to settle.

Long minutes passed. Her tears dried, leaving her emotionally drained. That's when she noticed the steady beat of his heart under her hand.

Mason brushed his fingers over her cheek, wiping away the last of her tears. It left behind a lethargy she hadn't known before.

She drew a deep breath and sat back, unable to meet his gaze. Instead, she wiped her nose with his handkerchief and settled into her seat.

"I'm sorr—"

His long finger closed off her words of apology and, with a bit of pressure under her chin, he forced her to look at him.

"Where are we?" she asked hesitantly.

"In my apartment building parking lot."

"Why?"

"Come on, Maddy. Don't make light of what happened just now."

"Nothing happened just now."

Mason chuckled, and the sound sent a shiver straight up her spine. "I was comforting you. Is that so bad?"

"Why, though? You don't even know me."

He brushed his finger down her cheek. "That doesn't mean I can't feel your pain. That I don't understand what you're feeling. After all, I see crime scenes all the time."

"But how often are they someone you know?"

"Not very often," he murmured. "But it has happened."

A tone in his last statement had Maddy studying him closely, wondering what she'd heard behind the simple comment.

"Are you ready to go? I don't want to worry Blue—or give her and my father a reason to come looking for us."

The teasing note in his voice made her smile. Somehow, she could imagine just that happening.

"I'm ready."

Maddy waited until they were back on the road. Then, as hard as it was, she offered, "I'm sorry and ... thank you."

Mason squeezed her fingers before turning his attention back to the road. "Anytime, Spitfire. Anytime."

"What did you say?"

He flashed another smile. "I said anytime, Maddy. Why? What did you think I said?"

"Noth—nothing," Maddy stuttered. "But thank you."

"My pleasure." Mason side-eyed her. "My shoulder is available if you need it again."

"We'll see," she whispered as he stopped in front of the old Victorian.

⚜

Blessed Children's Home
December 31, 1993
11:15 p.m.

MASON SLOWED TO A STOP, YET NEITHER OF THEM MOVED. HE wanted to say something profound, but when nothing came, he chanced a look in her direction. She was staring at her clenched hands, looking so alone he nearly reached for her.

"Maddy, I—"

The Home's porch light flipped on, illuminating the entire yard. It stole whatever he'd been about to say—and nearly made him laugh.

"Does that remind you of something?" he asked.

"Of dates bringing me home when I was a teen. You too?"

"Oh, yeah."

"I'm not..." Her voice faded, and sadness replaced her smile.

"Maddy?" He hesitated. "Are you ready?"

"I guess."

"Okay. Stay right there."

When Mason opened the passenger door, Maddy didn't move at first. After a pause, she swung her legs out—but that's as far as she got.

He crouched beside her. "Do you need some help?"

"No."

"Are you dizzy?"

"No."

"What's going on?"

She sighed. "When I go inside, the Sisters will cluck around me."

"And what's wrong with that?"

"I don't want anyone to cluck around me," Maddy grumbled. "If they do, I might ..."

"You might fall apart?"

"Yeah."

"Do you want to go home?"

Maddy's breath hitched. "You would do that?"

"If I did, would Sister Blue come after me?"

"Don't think she wouldn't be tempted." Maddy grinned. "She can be fierce, even if I'm no longer sixteen."

"What's the story between my father and Sister Blue?"

"You mean you don't know?"

"I don't know."

"He's known her since she was a child."

The comment surprised him so much it had him taking a step back. Had anything ever been said about Blessed Children's Home? He didn't think so—which had him wondering why?

"Come on, Maddy."

When he held out his hand, she hesitated. Then she slid hers into his and a spark zipped up his arm.

Maddy's eyes flared. Slowly, she stood. One hand still in his, and the other holding the door.

"You okay?"

"I was a little dizzy, that's all."

He wanted to say they could wait until she felt like taking the next step.

"I could carry you."

"What did you say?"

Mason pulled her closer and reached around to shut the door. "I said I could carry you."

"Oh, that would go over well."

There was something behind the words he didn't understand. However, he wouldn't dig into it right then. Instead, he situated Maddy next to him, wrapped his arm around her waist, and started toward the Home.

Her first few steps were hesitant, labored even. But halfway there, she seemed to accept the inevitable and walked a little faster. Maddy turned the doorknob, and before she stepped over the threshold, sent him a look. It said, '*Don't say I didn't warn you.*'

"Maddy, dear, we've been waiting for you. How are you feeling?"

"I have a headache, Green," Maddy sighed.

"Green, Black." Scott appeared from the right, eating a cookie. "Meet my son. Mason, these lovely women are Sisters Green and Black."

"Blue, Green, and Black?" Mason muttered, tongue in cheek. "Really?"

"We've been looking for a red and yellow, but so far," Green shrugged, "We've had no luck."

Mason cleared his throat to keep from laughing. "I'll be ... I'll be sure and let you know if I meet them first."

Black's eyes twinkled. "We'd appreciate it, but now, Maddy needs her rest."

"But," Mason sputtered. "I still have a few questions for her."

Maddy straightened her shoulders and stood a little taller. When she turned to face him, her look was one of quiet resignation—an expression he had no difficulty reading. Part of her understood she needed to talk about what happened. The other part wanted to push away the pain.

"Will you give me a few minutes?" she murmured. "I'd like to check on Tori and maybe change clothes."

Mason glanced at his watch. It was almost midnight. What was a little longer?

"Go ahead. I'll be right here."

She flashed him a quick grin and, flanked by the Sisters, headed up the stairs.

Once they were out of sight, Mason turned his attention to his father. He had a cookie halfway to his mouth, and a couple of crumbs had landed on his tie.

"You've known Sister Blue since she was a child?"

"I have." Scott held out a cookie. "Are you hungry?"

Mason's stomach rumbled, reminding him he was supposed to have eaten at the party. "Are they any good?"

"Are they any good?" Scott scoffed. "They're better than good." He cupped his hand next to his mouth as if telling a secret. "Don't tell your mother, but they might be better than hers."

"Wow, dad," Mason exclaimed. "Don't let mom hear you say that."

"Your mom knows where she stands with me."

"She does." Mason hesitated a beat. "Why don't I know anything about this part of your life?"

"Do I know everything about yours?" Scott returned.

"Probably not."

"And you don't know everything about mine." Scott stuffed the rest of the cookie into his mouth. "Let's get some more."

Mason watched his father move through the dining room, comfortable in his surroundings. He had a lot of questions to ask several people. However, since he had to wait, he'd deal with the easiest issue—his hunger.

Blessed Children's Home
December 31, 1993

11:30 p.m.

MADDY WAITED UNTIL BLUE LAY TORI DOWN BEFORE SHE STEPPED across the threshold. The bedroom was large enough for four cribs, but only two were occupied. In one, an eighteen-month-old Abigail, Abby, who arrived in the fall, and now Tori.

They'd be a comfort to each other. And maybe someday, something more than that—sisters not by blood, but by bond.

"She's asleep, finally," Blue whispered. "Do you know if she slept with a special blanket or animal?"

"A pink cat," Maddy smiled. "But how did you know?"

Blue's eyes twinkled. "Practice."

Maddy arched her brows to relay a '*That's all you're giving me*' look.

"Tori wouldn't settle until I gave her a blanket and a stuffed animal," Blue capitulated. "I just assumed."

"Hopefully, it's in her crib, and we can get it soon," Maddy returned. "I wish ..." The words lodged in her throat, and once again, her eyes filled with tears.

"Come on." Blue cupped her elbow and led her from the room. "Are Scott and Mason still downstairs?"

"Yes. I know I need to talk about what happened, but ..."

"I'll be right there with you." Blue hesitated. "You know that, right?"

"I do, and I appreciate it."

"I wouldn't be anywhere else." Blue gently touched the bandage on her arm. "Are you ready?"

The butterflies in Maddy's stomach had her making an excuse and closing herself in the bathroom. It wasn't until after she'd washed her hands she decided she had to look. However, what she saw in the mirror had her grabbing hold of the sink to keep from sliding onto the floor.

The area surrounding her left eye was red and puffy and already bruising. Her hair hung limp, and she was pale.

Her eyes drifted closed, and Alisha's face appeared. "Stop! Just stop!"

"Maddy." Blue knocked on the door. "Are you okay?"

The social worker wanted to get this over with in hopes of finding Alisha's killer. However, the woman was scared for the child left behind.

Before she could change her mind, Maddy stepped into the hallway. "I'm ready."

They descended the stairs and started toward the great room. Before she crossed the threshold, Maddy hesitated and studied Lieutenant Scott and his detective son. However, after falling apart on his shoulder, that no longer felt right. Somehow, he'd become Mason.

They were looking at the wall of photos, and Scott was pointing to one and laughing. It had her wondering why he'd never told his son about his connection to the Blessed Children's Home.

"Mason said he didn't know about you," Maddy whispered. "Or about your connection to his father. Do you know why?"

"I don't," Blue returned. "When we're meant to know, we'll know."

Maddy side-eyed the older woman and shook her head. She was always full of wise words and sayings. Ones that could annoy in the moment but later made sense.

Blue cleared her throat to alert the men of their presence. "Can I get you anything before we start?"

"We helped ourselves to cookies." Scott grinned. "I'm good. Mason?"

"I'm good." Mason's dark eyes clashed with Maddy's, causing her heart to race. "I have a few questions, and then we'll get out of your hair."

"Okay. Where do you want to talk?"

"Wherever you're most comfortable."

Usually, she would suggest they go to the morning room, but something held her back.

"Here's fine."

"Shall we?" He indicated a group of chairs.

Maddy pressed her hands against her stomach, needing to still the butterflies. She took a seat and crossed her ankles.

"You told me you helped Alisha out of a few binds, right?" Mason began.

"Yes."

"How often did you see her?"

"Before she called today, it had been a month or more."

"I saw her right before Christmas," Blue added. "She appeared happy and healthy."

"When you saw her, was she alone?" Mason followed up.

"Do you mean, was Tori with her?" Blue asked.

"No," Mason denied. "I mean, was she with a man?"

"She was with her friend, Natalie," Blue explained. "They were Christmas shopping."

"Natalie?" Mason repeated.

"Natalie French," Maddy supplied.

"How did they know each other?" Mason asked another question.

"Natalie and Alisha were taking courses at the local junior college," Blue explained. "They both had young children. When one was in class, the other stayed behind to watch them."

Mason nodded. "I see. Do you know how I can get in touch with Natalie?"

"I don't have her number," Maddy replied. "But I know Alisha had an address book beside her phone."

"Okay." He flipped through the notebook he'd been writing in, then returned with another question. The nature of it said she needed to be 'on.'

"You told me you heard yelling when you were on the phone with Alisha," he stated. "Then you ran over there, right?"

"Yes."

"It's what? Three or four blocks?"

"About that, yes."

"Do you think we can walk in your footsteps?"

Maddy closed her eyes and clenched her fingers together. When she opened them, it was to find Mason watching her intently. It warmed her. Even with others in the room, his gaze felt intimate.

"I can try."

"I know this won't be easy," he murmured. "Why don't you try this? Imagine you're watching it happen on a TV or movie screen. Pull yourself out of the scene. Sometimes, it helps to put a little distance between you and what happened."

"Okay."

"Start with the phone call," he instructed.

Maddy explained what had happened—from returning to the office, answering the phone, and then running out the door. She shared a little about how it felt to arrive and find only silence.

"It was so quiet," she whispered. "My sixth sense was telling me to run, but then I heard a groan."

Her stomach rolled. She dropped her head and covered her eyes. That internal fear was back. If she continued forward, she knew what she'd run into.

"I'll just get you a glass of cold water," Blue murmured.

Maddy fought to keep her breathing steady. Fought to use Mason's suggestion and pretend she was watching TV. She glanced up, and their eyes met. There was such empathy—and heat—in his, it warmed her.

"Take your time," he whispered. "I'm right here, and you're safe."

FOUR

Blessed Children's Home
December 31, 1993
11:45 p.m.

WHILE MADDY WAS TELLING HER STORY, THERE WERE MORE THAN a handful of times Mason had to stop from taking her hand. That she was holding onto her emotions by the skin of her teeth was evident in the tenseness around her mouth. Evident by the haunted look in her eyes.

"Here, Maddy." Blue handed her a glass of water. "Drink slowly."

Maddy took a sip of the liquid and set it on the table. She laced her fingers together and leaned forward to rest her elbows on her knees.

"Alisha was lying on the far side of the kitchen," she went on. "When I couldn't get a pulse, I started CPR, and then I heard a noise."

"What kind of noise?" Mason murmured.

"What do you mean, what kind of noise?"

Mason exchanged looks with his father and Blue before continuing, "Was it a door closing?"

"I, I don't think so."

"You said you heard a groan. Right?"

"Yes. But not then. That was when I first walked inside."

Her response had Mason thinking back over the layout of Alisha's home. Based on Maddy's reaction, the killer could have been in the bedrooms when she arrived. Or they could have been in the bathroom, located close to the kitchen. The realization of how easily the story could have ended differently caused the acid in his stomach to churn. But he'd already barked at her once for her foolishness and was determined not to do so again.

"You heard a sound," Mason chose not to give it a *name*, "and turned around, right?"

"Yes."

"Is that when you grabbed the skillet?"

Blue gasped. She crossed herself, and her lips tightened as if determined not to say anything.

"I don't think I grabbed it right then," Maddy whispered. "The person knocked me backward, away from Alisha. That's when he cut my arm."

"Had you lifted your arm for protection?"

"Maybe." Maddy shrugged. "It's all just a blur."

"He knocked you backward." Mason pushed her story forward. "Then what happened?"

"I jumped up to run," Maddy intoned. "That's when I saw the skillet."

"And you grabbed it?"

"I think so." Maddy hesitated for several seconds, and the frown between her brows said she was working through something. "I missed him the first time, but the next time, I hit him. Then the police arrived, and he ran out the back door."

"Let's back up," Mason returned to when she'd first arrived. "When you first walked into the house, did you hear anything besides a groan?"

"No."

"And you didn't go check on Tori? You just followed the sound?"

"Yes."

Before he dove into more painful memories, Mason backed away from the event to ask about the ex-boyfriend.

"You said you helped Alisha with her restraining order, right?"

"Yes."

"How so?"

Maddy glanced at Blue, who exchanged looks with his father. It pushed Mason to ask, "Did you help, dad?"

"I might have," Scott admitted. "I didn't even think about that when we were at the house."

"But Scott," Blue comforted him. "It wasn't like you spent time with Alisha."

"True," Scott replied. "I passed it on."

Mason sent his father a look meant to say, '*We might have to reopen this conversation*,' and then moved on. "Had you ever seen the ex-boyfriend? Brian …"

"Lloyd," Maddy supplied. "The only time I ever saw Brian Lloyd was from a distance."

"Go on."

"The day I took Alisha to make her report, Brian followed us," Maddy admitted. "When we left the police department, he was gone."

"But you never saw him close up?"

"No."

"I understand this won't be easy, but I need to see if you can describe the killer. Okay?"

Maddy wrinkled her nose, but then gave him a resigned sigh. "I can try."

"Think back on when you turned around," Mason began. When she tensed up, he backed off. "Don't look directly at him or the knife. Pretend he's frozen in time. Can you do that?"

"I'll do my best."

"That's a good girl. Now, you heard a noise and glanced over your shoulder, right?"

"Yes."

Her voice grew softer, making him wish there was another way.

"Look up, Maddy," he crooned. "Can you see his hair?"

She closed her eyes and was quiet for a handful of seconds. Then she surprised him by saying, "I can see a little hair."

Mason exchanged another look with his father before prodding some more. "Why? Did he have a shaved head?"

"He was wearing a hat."

"What kind of hat?"

"What do you mean, what kind of hat?" Maddy murmured, her voice tight and tired. "It was a hat."

Mason studied Maddy's expression. He wanted to push her as far as possible, yet not too far. It was like walking on a tightrope.

"Was it a stocking cap?"

"I, I don't think so."

When her voice broke, he softened his. "Keep your eyes on the hat, Maddy. Just the hat. Do you see it?"

"Yes."

"You said it wasn't a stocking cap, right?"

"No. It's not pulled down over his ears."

While it could have been folded up, Mason went with his instinct. "Was it a baseball cap?"

Maddy started to shake her head, but then, at the last second, her eyes flew open. "It was red."

He grinned. "Red? Really?"

"It was red," Maddy repeated, this time with confidence. "It was a red baseball cap."

Mason hadn't read the reports yet, making him wonder if the killer had left anything behind when he was running away.

"You're doing very well, Maddy," he murmured. "The man was wearing a red hat. Does it say anything?"

"I …"

Mason didn't think, just reacted. He reached for Maddy's fingers and squeezed. "I know this is difficult. Just a little longer, okay?"

Maddy's gaze locked on where Mason held her hand. Before he'd squeezed her fingers, she could feel a wall rising, shutting down her memories. Whether it was instinct or self-preservation, she didn't know. But his touch warmed her, settling her insides, and gave her strength to continue.

"Can you stay focused a little longer?" he murmured. "This time, you're not alone."

Her gaze drifted up, moving an inch at a time, until she had the hat in her sight. But something prevented her from seeing the writing.

"What does it say?"

"It doesn't *say* anything."

"Nothing?"

"No." Her eyes drifted open and locked with Mason's. "There's only a letter on it."

Mason's eyes flared, and his lips curled into a little smile. "What letter can you see?"

"An F." She frowned. "Does that mean anything?"

"It might. It just might."

"So, that's good, right?"

"It's very good, Maddy," he went on. "Earlier, you mentioned not seeing much hair, correct?"

"Right."

"Of the hair you could see, what color was it?"

Maddy closed her eyes and returned to the exercise. The longer she stared, the harder it was to stay focused on the hat and not let her gaze drift down. She ended up having to clear her mind and then repeating the process.

In her mind's eye, she could see herself kneeling next to Alisha's prone body, then slowly turning around. Up, up, her gaze drifted to the ceiling, then right back down. There was the red hat, the white F, and ....

"Brown. Just brown."

"His hair was brown?" Mason repeated. "How much, and where could you see it?"

"Here." Maddy touched the side of her head. "I could see a little hair hanging over his ear."

"Brown hair that was barely long enough to hang over his ear, out from under a baseball cap," Mason murmured. "Right?"

"Yes."

"Mason, can't you see she's exhausted?" Blue broke in. "Can't this wait until tomorrow or the next day?"

He turned his dark-eyed gaze on her, and just like earlier, there was heat in them. They warmed her in such a way she wanted to bask for a while.

"I'm okay, Blue," Maddy reassured the older woman. "My memories are probably stronger now than they will be later."

"Well, *if* you're sure."

Maddy squeezed Blue's hand. "I'm positive. Why don't you go to bed? I know you're always up early."

"I'm where I need to be for now."

"Go on, Mason," Maddy whispered. "Let's finish."

He smiled, and his eyes heated even more. It took her breath and had her looking down lest she say—or do—something she shouldn't.

"Go back to when you heard the sound," Mason instructed. "When you turn around this time, focus on the floor in front of him."

Her attention landed on the man's shoes, and a chill raced up her spine.

"What is it?"

"Blood. There's blood on his shoes."

"Good, but don't stop there. Keep sliding your gaze upward. What kind of pants?"

"Jeans."

"What color of blue?"

"They're black jeans," she clarified.

"And up top?"

Maddy frowned because every time she tried to move up, something held her back.

"I can't."

"Why not?"

"I just can't." Maddy shrugged. "It's like ... a barrier or something is keeping me from seeing his jacket—"

"What did you say?" Mason interrupted.

"There's a barrier that keeps me from seeing his," her eyes widened, and she whispered, "jacket. He had on a jacket."

"That's terrific," Mason grinned. "Now, just a little more. What kind of jacket?"

"Like, like an exercise one."

"Was it the kind you slip over your head? Or did it have a zipper?"

Maddy closed her eyes and tried again to picture the jacket. But the image refused to form, making her head ache just a little more. She reached for her water and pressed the cold glass against her forehead. It wasn't much, but just enough to allow her to catch her breath.

"Can I get you something for your head, honey?" Blue asked.

"Please."

Blue pointed her finger at Mason. "Don't move on until I get back."

"Okay," he agreed. "I'll wait."

"Since we're waiting," Scott added, "I'm going to use the facilities."

With the older adults gone, the quietness was even more noticeable, and the intimacy of the evening pressed in.

"I bet this isn't how you planned to spend New Year's Eve," Maddy guessed.

"Not exactly," Mason admitted. "I was supposed to go to a party at the Waterfront. It was nothing much. What about you?"

"I was supposed to go to a party, as well."

"You don't appear to be very upset you missed it," he pointed out.

"I could say the same for you," Maddy teased. "Why is that?"

"Let's just say this case is important to me and move on."

She tilted her head and studied him. Something told her there was more to the story. Before she could figure it out, Blue returned and handed her two tablets.

"Take these."

Maddy wanted to grumble. Instead, she tossed back the medication and willed it to take her headache away. The jackhammers were pounding and had started messing with the juice in her stomach.

"Can you try again?" Mason asked. "Do you see what color the jacket is?"

Maddy repeated the process from different angles, but every time she reached where the jacket would start, the barrier reappeared.

"I'm sorry, Mason. I can't."

"Mason," Scott jumped in. "Why don't you give it a rest for a few hours? You can come back tomorrow or the next day."

Mason's eyes bore into hers for a handful of seconds. Then he gave a subtle nod and closed his notebook.

"Okay, dad. May I come by tomorrow?" he asked Blue.

Maddy wanted to be petulant and remind him she was the one he wanted to see. That he should be asking her. However, when he turned his attention to her, the look in his eyes said he knew exactly what he was doing. It had her letting it go ... right then, anyway.

"That would be fine, Mason," Blue replied.

"Maddy?"

"That's fine."

"Let us walk you out," Blue spoke up. "We'll expect you tomorrow."

Mason nodded once more and stood. He handed Maddy a business card. "Call me if you remember anything."

"I will."

"Cookies," Scott broke in. "Think I can snag a few more cookies before we leave?"

MASON WAITED UNTIL HIS FATHER AND BLUE WERE GONE BEFORE turning back to Maddy. She was pale, and the area around her eye had bloomed into various shades of purple.

"You'll call if you remember anything new?"

"I will."

"Good." He stepped closer to her and tapped the business card. "I'll see you tomorrow."

"Okay." Maddy was quiet for an extra heartbeat, then came back with, "Do you know if they found Parker?"

"The last I heard, they hadn't. Why?"

"Do you think he knows me?"

Mason's heart raced at what he was being asked. Not just because he was worried about her. It was more because he hadn't considered the possibility.

"You said you didn't recognize him, right?"

"Right."

"If I find any sign you were recognized, you'll have a guard."

"Oh, but I can't ..."

"Don't, Maddy," he whispered.

Blue and Scott returned shortly after, and Mason met them at the front door.

"Thank you again," he murmured. "I'll be in touch."

When the door closed behind them, there was a finality about it that made him uncomfortable, but he couldn't say why.

"What's the matter, son?"

Mason met Scott's questioning gaze with one of his own. "Maddy asked if the killer recognized her."

"What did you tell her?"

"That I saw no reason to think she had been."

"But you're not sure?"

"Am I 100% sure? No. I didn't lie to her, though. There isn't any reason to think she might be."

"One step at a time, Mason," Scott cautioned him. "Do you have time for a nightcap?"

He side-eyed his father. "Are you going to tell me about your connection to the Home?"

"If you want to hear it."

"Your place?"

"I'll see you there."

They separated, each climbing into their cars, but headed in the same direction. When they arrived, Mason met his father inside. "You realize you'll have to clean before mom comes home, right?"

"Maybe." Scott propped his hands on his hips and looked around. "Okay, probably. But your mom will expect it to be messy."

"Which is your way of saying you'll clean if you have to?"

"Probably." Scott nodded toward a chair. "I'll grab a couple of beers. Do you want a glass?"

"As opposed to?"

"A bottle."

"Bottle's fine."

"Be right back."

Instead of immediately dropping into a chair, Mason wandered around the room. His mother had gone to Swan Harbor right after Christmas to care for his grandmother, who'd suffered a stroke. In the week since she'd been gone, his father had been working longer hours—and not cleaning.

"Here you are."

Mason clinked his bottle against his dad's. "To answers."

"To promises," his father countered. "Have a seat."

Mason left his suit coat draped over the back of a chair and settled on the sofa. He was a patient man—had always been a patient man—but his father was even more so.

"You have questions?" Scott guessed.

"I do."

"Ask away."

"What's the story with you and Maddy?" The words slipped out, even though they weren't what he'd intended to say.

Scott's eyes twinkled. "That wasn't the first question I expected."

"Wasn't the first question I'd planned on asking."

"I first met Maddy one stormy night almost twenty-three years ago," Scott began.

"She was around three, wasn't she?"

"I believe so."

"What happened?"

"There was a wreck," Scott murmured. "It occurred right before midnight and instantly killed her parents. When my partner and I arrived at the scene, I didn't think anyone could be alive."

"But you found Maddy?"

"I did. When she looked up, something in her eyes caused my heart to twist. Right then, while I knew I couldn't bring back her parents, I could promise her tomorrow."

Mason's gut tightened at the thought of what had transpired between his father and the woman with the piercing silver-blue eyes. Something told him she'd made the most of the days she'd been given.

"Then what happened?"

Scott smiled. "I followed her to the hospital that night. There was no next of kin, meaning she needed a place to go. Blue's father and I grew up together."

"In Swan Harbor?" Mason asked. "Why have I never met him?"

"Matt died in Vietnam," Scott replied. "Right after that was when we moved away from Swan Harbor. Missy—his wife—took the kids and left town. After that, it was easy to lose touch with that part of our life."

"So how did you know about Blue and Blessed Children's Home?"

"Your mother," Scott admitted quietly.

"Mom?"

"Joy reminded me Blue's brother ran a home for wayward boys in Swan Harbor. And in Dorchester, Blue ..."

"So, you made a phone call and took Maddy to Blue?"

"I did."

"Maddy said you were a frequent visitor at the Home," Mason pressed. "Why didn't I know about it?"

"I never meant to keep it a secret." Scott shrugged. "But yes, I made a point of stopping by the Home a few times a month. In fact," he laughed, "you can thank me for her quick thinking with the skillet."

"You taught Maddy self-defense?"

"I did."

Silence followed as Mason absorbed the information. There had been a connection between him and Maddy from the beginning—one he didn't understand. He told himself it was just empathy. But now ... he knew better.

"Mason," Scott brushed his hair back before taking a sip of beer. "Maddy is ..."

"What is Maddy?"

"Reckless," Scott answered, "with a heart of gold."

"Which explains why she ran to help after Alisha called."

"And why she can be her own worst enemy," Scott added. "She means well, but—"

"Don't expect her to sit back and wait?"

"Well," Scott stretched the word out. "Do I think she'll investigate on her own? Not in a traditional sense."

"But you don't expect her to wait calmly for answers?"

"No."

"She's a spitfire," Mason said with a huff.

Scott grinned. "That's as good a word as any. Just ... keep an eye on her."

Mason dropped his head against the sofa cushion. Just what he needed. A killer on the loose and a woman with a foggy memory. Were answers possible with no more bloodshed? Only time would tell.

FIVE

Blessed Children's Home
January 1, 1994
6:30 a.m.

MADDY SAT STRAIGHT UP IN BED. HER HEART RACED, AND THE sound of her screams echoed around her. If she'd just been a little faster …

Don't do that, Maddy. You don't get to rewrite what already happened. Maybe you could have changed the outcome. But maybe not.

It took several deep breaths for her pulse to settle, and another minute to shift from the *what ifs* to the *what now*. Was there something she'd missed? Some detail that could help Mason find whoever had killed Alisha?

Mason.

Just the thought of him caused a funny feeling in the pit of her stomach. She'd even slept in the sweatshirt from the night before. It still smelled of his cologne, making her feel as if his arms were around her.

She had so many questions. Especially about his marital status.

He hadn't been wearing a ring.

Which wasn't necessarily an answer.

When he'd mentioned the party at the Waterfront, he hadn't said anything about a wife. Or of a girlfriend.

And he hadn't seemed particularly upset about missing the event. Did that mean something?

She rolled over and buried her head in the pillow. *What am I doing? What am I thinking?* Alisha was dead, leaving her child alone. Were there family members who might take Tori in?

The need to check on the little girl pushed her out of bed. She tiptoed down the hall and peeked inside. Abby was still asleep, but Tori was standing in her crib. Her blanket and stuffed dog lay directly on the floor beneath her.

"Would you like these?"

Tori refused the blanket and reached for the dog. She studied the toy carefully, before frowing.

She wants her pink cat—the one she'd slept with from the beginning.

Worried they might wake Abby, Maddy whispered, "Are you hungry? Come with me?"

The little girl held up her arms, making the first step easy. But as Maddy turned to leave, Tori reached toward the crib.

"Do you want this?" Maddy offered the stuffed dog.

Tori shook her head and tossed it on the floor, then clutched the blanket tightly.

Maddy sighed softly and adjusted her hold. "Okay then. Let's get some breakfast."

She wanted to say it surprised her to find both Green and Black baking in the kitchen. It would have been a lie, though, as that was normal for them during times of stress.

"Something smells good." Maddy sat Tori in a highchair and tossed some cereal on the tray. "What are you making?"

"Cinnamon rolls," Black murmured while Green said, "Biscuits."

"Both of you baking," Maddy clucked. "I told you I was fine."

"You did." Black nodded once.

"Doesn't mean we aren't worried about you." Green gave her a pointed look. "What if...?"

"Mason doesn't think I need to worry," Maddy explained. "He doesn't think the person knew who I was."

Black turned from the bowl of dough she'd been punching and propped her hands on her hips. "He doesn't think? That's not a guarantee."

"There are no guarantees in life," Maddy whispered.

"Says the woman who runs in where angels fear to tread," Blue said, appearing from her quarters.

Maddy poured a cup of coffee and dumped a splash of milk into the cup. She leaned back against the counter and took several sips, attempting to wake up a little more. Three against one were not good odds.

"Look," she finally offered. "I realize I shouldn't have run off alone, but I—"

"—Needed to help," Green said gently.

"I did," Maddy sighed. "But now, there's not much I can do except help with Tori."

"She'll be fine," Blue assured her. "Which, if you're honest with yourself, you know."

"I know. I just wish …"

Green held up her hand in the universal way of saying stop, and Maddy's words trailed off.

"You know, wishing won't fix things."

"I know."

"And deep down," Green continued. "You know how you can help."

"See if I can find any of Alisha's family," Maddy murmured.

"Do you know anything about where she was from?" Blue asked.

Maddy thought back to the first time she'd seen Alisha at the Boston Public Market, then to the other times they'd spoken of the past.

"I don't know why I think this, but I got the feeling she was from the Boston area."

Blue hummed, but saying nothing fixed Tori some bananas and cereal. Then she settled at the table with a cup of coffee.

"What's hum?" Maddy prompted when Blue didn't offer.

"Do you think Natalie knows?"

"Maybe?" Maddy shrugged. "I only met Natalie twice."

"What about when Alisha decided to take classes at the community college? Didn't she have to transfer grades?"

Maddy took another sip of coffee and thought back to the previous summer. "She had to take her GED to get her diploma."

"Did you help her with that?"

"I sent her the link," Maddy replied. "Alisha handled the rest."

"Maybe Scott or Mason can get us copies of her records," Blue offered.

"That's a possibility." Maddy stretched slightly. "But right now, I'm going to head home and clean up."

"You know you can shower here." Blue gave her a pointed look.

"Oh, I know." Maddy tugged the sweatshirt away from her chest and struggled to maintain a neutral expression. It still smelled of Mason's cologne.

"But I don't have any clothes here," she reminded them. "I'll shower, change, and come back. Okay?"

Blue, Green, and Black exchanged looks, making Maddy wish she could read their minds.

"If that's what you want to do, dear," Blue murmured. "We'll be here."

Maddy rinsed her cup, put it in the dishwasher, and headed for the door. *Something* had transpired between the three Sisters, she just didn't know what.

15 Peach Street
January 1, 1994
12:30 p.m.

MASON WAS STILL WORKING ON PIECING TOGETHER THE EVENTS of the night before. He'd gone over his notes twice already, hoping something —anything—might stand out. Something that might tie everything to Parker Turner.

He'd found the address book Maddy had mentioned. It was underneath the phone, making him wonder why they hadn't looked through it the day before. What he found inside saddened him, as it painted a picture of someone who had potential. Yet, whose life seemed lonely.

There were multiple phone numbers written inside the book in a loopy scrawl. They reminded him of being fifteen again and finding a note left by a girlfriend.

Most of the numbers were of places. Restaurants she liked, stores where she shopped, the pediatrician's office, and the junior college. Other than that, there were only a few names: Natalie, Maddy, Becky, Joni, TG, and Brian, the latter no longer legible.

Mason jotted Natalie's address and phone number and made a mental note to visit her during the week. The other three names in the book—Becky,

Joni, and TG—didn't have last names or addresses. He made note of those numbers as well. That he'd found no indication or mention of Parker didn't go unnoticed.

From there, Mason wandered toward the other side of the house. There was nothing in the bathroom worth a second look. In Alisha's bedroom, he discovered she was taking basic classes at the junior college and liked to doodle on her notes. The drawings seemed random—shapes and swirls with no clear meaning.

He found a brush, a mirror, and a small jewelry box on the dresser. Inside the box, he found a locket and a man's identification bracelet with the name scratched off. Was it anger, jealousy, or maybe both?

Mason peered into the closet, but the few pieces of clothing barely made a dent in the small space. When he shut the door, a sense of sadness overwhelmed him. It had him wishing he'd been able to save the woman.

The feeling propelled him from her room to the little girl's. As soon as he stepped over the threshold, the atmosphere changed. Alisha didn't have much money, yet what she *did* have was spent on her daughter.

Tori's room was pink and princessy, and he wanted to scoop up everything to take to the Home. There were stuffed animals in a corner, and a few in the crib. The closet was full of clothing, and the shelves were overflowing with books. On the chest of drawers were three disposable cameras, a little white brush, and a small bracelet.

Mason stepped into the hallway and turned on his flashlight. He backtracked and found drops of blood halfway down the hall, then more in the bathroom. Had he been correct in thinking the killer was hiding in there when Maddy arrived?

The thought of the danger she'd been in sent a shiver racing up his spine. A feeling not normal for him when investigating a crime scene. Yet, one more thing about the mystery that set it apart.

A sound from the other room stopped his investigation. He ducked behind the bathroom door and listened.

The footsteps grew fainter, likely going toward the kitchen. Then silence. It was so quiet he began to wonder what the person was doing.

When the footsteps returned, heading in his direction, Mason tensed. Fifteen seconds passed. Sweat beads popped out on his forehead. He fought the need to wipe them off and stayed still.

The intruder moved without hesitation, like someone familiar with the house's layout. Before he got a glimpse, his nose gave him his answer.

Mason stepped into the hallway. "Just what the hell do you think you're doing here?"

Maddy froze, but didn't immediately turn around. For a moment, he thought she might ignore his question. But then she looked at him, and her expression was not what he expected.

"Mason!" she exclaimed. "What are you doing here?"

"What am I—?" he fought the edge in his voice. "No, no, no. That's not how this works!"

Maddy frowned. "What do you mean, '*That's not how it works?*' How can you say that? In a conversation, I ask a question, you answer, then vice versa."

Mason felt like bouncing his head against the wall. She wasn't this dense, but was deflecting, and he knew it. That realization only irritated him more.

"Maddy." Mason advanced on her slowly. When only a foot separated them, she took a step backward, but not out of fear. "Why are you here?" he asked again, this time quietly, deliberately.

"I—I'm here for Tori," she stuttered.

"Tori?"

"Yes, Tori." She pointed to the large bag hanging over her shoulder. "I'm here for Tori."

He squinted a little and took another step closer, so close he could have touched her. "How does being here for Tori keep you from trespassing? Didn't you see the tape across the porch?"

"The tape?" Maddy frowned. "What tape?"

"The bright yellow tape," Mason returned, his voice clipped. "The one that reads crime scene. Do not cross."

"There's no tape," Maddy stated.

"There most certainly is."

"Go look."

"Don't think I won't."

Mason spun on his heel and marched toward the front door to prove her wrong. He knew there was tape, as he'd stepped over it when he'd entered.

· · ·

MADDY WAITED UNTIL MASON HAD TAKEN OFF TOWARD THE front door, and then hesitated. Should she show him the tape wasn't stretched across the porch? Or should she slip into Tori's room and get what she'd come for?

Mason decided for her when he bellowed. Before he could shout again, she inched his way, stopping right inside the front room.

"Do you see this?" He held up the strip of tape.

"I'm not blind, Mason," she said coolly. "Of course, I can see it."

"Yet, you crossed it."

"No, I didn't."

Mason blew out a breath. "How can you say that?"

"It was blowing in the wind, not stretched across the steps." Maddy shrugged. "Besides, I didn't think it was meant for me."

"Not meant for you?" He hesitated, his exasperation obvious. "Maddy, you almost ..." Mason tossed the crime scene tape aside and rushed toward her.

She told herself she was going to hold her ground. But as he drew closer, her bravado slipped, and she took a step backward. He intimidated her. Not because she was scared *of* him. It was because of her reaction *to* him.

For every step Mason took toward her, Maddy retreated—until she bumped against the wall and had nowhere else to go.

But Mason kept coming.

His smile was predatory. His eyes, like twin black coals of heat, aimed directly at her. They drifted lazily around her face, then slid down, igniting little prickles of fire everywhere his gaze touched.

"Mason?" she whispered. "I'm sorry. I just needed ..."

"What was it you needed, Maddy?" he murmured. "Tell me what couldn't wait."

She pressed her palms against the wall behind her. If she didn't, she wasn't sure where they might land.

"Tori's cat."

Mason frowned. "Tori's cat?"

"Yes."

"Go on."

"She needs it for bedtime." Maddy's voice steadied as she explained why she thought that to be true. "I was on my way back to the Home, and when I passed by—"

"—You thought you would help yourself?"

"Well, yes."

Mason reached up and cupped her jaw. He brushed his thumb across her left cheekbone—his touch gentle.

"Have you forgotten what happened here?"

Tears immediately sprang to her eyes. "No! How can you ask me that? Tori lost her mother."

"I'm talking about what happened to you," Mason replied, his voice rough. "Have you forgotten? Because if you have, look in the mirror. It's written right here on your face."

The warmth of his touch made it hard to breathe. Maddy wanted to lean into his hand. To lean into *him*. He made her feel things she'd never felt before. Things she couldn't name.

"Of course I haven't," she whispered. "But Tori ..."

Mason's expression shifted. "Do you need a caretaker?"

The question had her standing a little taller. She was 5'9" without heels, yet he topped her by several inches. Where she should have been feeling intimidated, she was anything but.

"I've been taking care of myself for quite a while," she snapped. "Let me grab Tori's blanket and cat, then I'll get out of your way."

Without waiting for his okay, Maddy slid past him and started down the hallway. She'd taken a handful of steps when Mason caught her elbow and turned her to face him.

"Maddy," he whispered in a shaky voice. "When you came in here yesterday, the killer was still inside. He was in the bathroom."

A zip of fear raced through her, causing her to sink into Mason's firm body. "I'm sorry. I—" The words clogged her throat, and without thinking, she pressed her face against his chest.

For a moment, neither moved. Then, slowly, Mason wrapped one long arm around her waist. Then the other.

"My father warned me about you."

"He warned you about me? What did he say?"

"That you have a heart of gold but—"

"I rush in where angels fear to tread?"

Mason chuckled. "Those weren't quite the words he used, but they fit."

"I'm sorry."

"Did you lose my card?"

"No. Why?"

"Because I told you to call me."

"You told me to call you if I remembered anything," Maddy corrected. "I didn't. Why? Do you have more questions?"

"Just a couple."

"Do you want to ask me?"

His arms tightened around her, just a little, and she was almost certain he kissed her head before stepping back.

"Let's find Tori's things," he murmured. "Then I'll walk you back to the Home. Okay?"

A little thrill rushed through her. Spending more time with Mason wasn't a hardship.

"Okay."

On their way to Tori's room, Maddy peeked into Alisha's bedroom.

"What happens to her things?"

"If we can't find someone else, they'll go to Tori. Why?"

"No reason."

Tori's well-loved pink cat was in her crib underneath a pink and white blanket with bunnies. With Mason's permission, Maddy grabbed the large diaper bag and stuffed some clothes, diapers, and a little pair of boots inside. From there, she opened the bag she'd brought, swept everything from the top of the chest into it, and added socks, sleepers, a few books, and Tori's winter coat.

"This will suffice until I can pack everything else."

"Are you sure?"

"Positive."

Mason led the way out and shut the door behind him.

"Who fixed the door?"

"The patrolmen who showed up first. Why?"

"I just wondered."

With the door locked, Mason slipped both bags over his shoulder. A part of her wanted to laugh, as it should have looked funny. Instead, somehow, it added to his masculinity.

While they walked, their arms brushed against each other. It made her want to tuck her arm inside his. A thought that had her taking a step in the other direction.

"Were you at the house for a specific reason? I didn't think you'd work today. Especially New Year's Day. I thought you'd be watching football."

Mason shrugged. "I wanted to do a walkthrough since I didn't get to do one yesterday. I'm still looking for a connection to Parker Turner."

"I'm sorry," Maddy replied. "I've never heard that name—from Alisha or anyone else."

"I found the address book," he explained. "There were only a few names in it, and yours was one."

"I told you I helped her."

"You did. You said Natalie took classes with her, right?"

"Yes."

"Do you know the name Becky?"

"Becky's name was in the book?"

"Yes. Who is she?"

"The woman who cuts my hair."

"Did Alisha use her?"

"I don't know," Maddy sighed. "Maybe Natalie will know."

"I plan to talk to her tomorrow."

"Okay."

It was quiet for the next few minutes. Maddy glanced sideways to find Mason watching her. She crammed her hands into her coat pockets and looked away.

"My father told me about you last night," he surprised her by saying.

"Scott told you he saved me?"

"He did."

"What else did he say?"

"That he's to thank for your quick thinking with the skillet."

Maddy winced. "He is."

"I can't see my father teaching self-defense classes. Can you tell me about it?"

Maddy laughed at the memory. "It was Blue's idea," she began. "There were four of us, and we were sixteen ..."

SIX

Scott & Joy Weaver's Home
January 3, 1994
1:00 p.m.

MASON RECLINED ON HIS PARENTS' SOFA, STARING AT THE TV where a bowl game blared. His thoughts, though, were miles away.

"Who's winning?" Rod, his brother, asked, dropping into the chair beside the sofa.

"What?"

"Who's winning?"

"No clue."

Rod side-eyed him, but before he could say anything, his five-year-old son, Graham, beat him to it.

"Uncle Mason, what have you been doing?"

Mason frowned. "What have I been doing?"

"Yes," Graham nodded.

"Thinking."

"About a girl?"

Rod laughed. "Where did that question come from, Graham?"

"Grandpa."

"Who was Grandpa talking to?" Mason asked. "And when did you hear this?"

"He was on the phone," Graham answered. "He said, 'She looked good, hon. Mason had a lot of questions about her.'"

"And from that, you assumed I was thinking about a girl?"

Graham grinned, showing off his missing teeth. "Well, was I right?"

"Yeah, Uncle Mason," Rod teased. "Was he right?"

Mason sent his brother a dirty look and considered ignoring him. Knowing Rod, though, he'd pester until he had an answer.

"Let's hear it. I'm too tired for twenty questions."

"Rough night?"

"Sierra cried all night," Graham explained of his two-month-old sister. "Mom said she probably had gas."

"Your mother had gas?" Mason deadpanned.

"No, silly," Graham giggled. "Sierra had gas. That's why she couldn't go to sleep."

"I see."

"No, you don't," Rod retorted. "But maybe someday."

"You never know," Mason murmured absently.

"You usually run when that topic comes up." Rod grinned. "What changed?"

His father stuck his head around the corner before he could respond. "Graham, grandma wants to talk to you."

"Yeah." Graham ran off, leaving the adults alone.

"Did you know dad has a connection to the Blessed Children's Home?"

"What's the Blessed Children's Home?"

Mason briefly explained, then added, "You've never heard about the place either, have you?"

"No. Did you ask him why he hadn't said anything?"

"He said it was because I didn't know everything about him." Mason frowned. "Not exactly a satisfying answer."

"Not even close. How did it come up?"

"A murder, an almost murder, and a little girl."

Rod's brow lifted. "Parker Turner?"

Rod Weaver was also a detective, but worked in a different precinct. There were moments when that was beneficial, as he could bounce things off someone who wasn't involved in the case.

Mason nodded.

"What's bothering you?"

Mason ran his hand through his short hair. "Honestly, I don't know."

"But something is?"

"Yes."

"Who was killed?"

"Alisha Chapman. Her daughter's at Blessed Children's Home."

"And the almost murder?"

"Blessed Children's Home's social worker."

"I see."

"You see?" Mason arched a brow. "What is it you think you see?"

"I'm not making light of the murder," Rod assured him. "But that's not the biggest problem. It's the social worker. Right?"

"How the hell did you know that?"

"Dad told me."

"You asshole." Mason threw a decorative pillow at his brother. "You could have said something."

"Sorry." Rod gave him a cheeky grin. "I wanted to see if I'd learn more from you."

"And did you?"

"You're worried about her."

"Of course I am. Anyone in her situation would worry me."

"Dad says she's reckless."

"She showed up at the scene yesterday," Mason explained. "Told me she was getting a stuffed cat and a blanket for the little girl, Tori."

"Does that mean you'll have to keep a close eye on her?" Rod wiggled his brows suggestively. "Is she hot?"

"She has the most amazing blue eyes." Mason cleared his throat. "Don't be a dick."

Rod chuckled. "It sounds like she's already gotten under your skin."

"Maybe." Mason shrugged. "I don't want to see her get hurt."

"Which goes without saying."

"True. But ..."

"Here I am." Graham ran back into the room and flopped on the sofa. "What did I miss?"

"Not much." Mason ruffled his hair. "What was grandma doing?"

"She had lunch with her friend Terri Patterson."

"I thought grandma was there to care for Grandma Lillian," Rod hummed. "What happened?"

Graham cupped his hand around his mouth and whispered, "Grandma Joy said she needed a break because her mother was driving her crazy. What did she mean?"

Mason left Rod to answer the question and slipped into the kitchen, where he found the stash of cookies Blue had sent home with his father.

His thoughts drifted to the day before. After walking Maddy back to the Home, he'd stayed for lunch. The time had flown by, and five hours had passed before he'd known it. When he'd gotten home, he'd tried to remember the last time he'd spent more than a couple of hours with a woman—just talking.

He couldn't. Which left him wondering. What was it that made Miss Davies different? Was it only the case pulling him toward her? Or something else entirely?

Maddy's Apartment
January 3, 1994
2:00 p.m.

Maddy leaned close to the mirror and gently touched the bruise beneath her eye. It throbbed and was multiple shades of purple. But she was alive—Alisha wasn't.

Like every other time she thought about that night, Detective Mason Weaver's face rose in her mind. At first, she'd blamed it on the investigation. Then on the fact he'd been there when she'd thrown up. Reluctantly, she'd stopped lying to herself.

When he'd touched her, a current had zipped between them. A connection. One unsettling and undeniable.

The kettle whistled, pulling her from the bathroom. She'd just reached for a cup when someone knocked on the door.

Maddy's heart raced.

Mason?

Except he didn't know where she lived.

He's a cop and could easily find out.

Or worse. What if it's the killer?

She took a deep breath and cracked the door.

"Maddy!" Her best friend, Tina Stone, swept inside, blue eyes blazing. "I'm tired of waiting."

"For what?"

"Well, duh. What do you think?"

Their blue eyes clashed, and as always, Maddy caved first. Tina never lost stare-downs.

"Does it hurt?" Tina gently touched the bandage on Maddy's arm.

"It itches."

"And your eye?"

"It hurts if I squint or touch it too hard."

Tina tilted her head, examining her from different angles.

"Stop it, Tina. Ask questions, but no staring."

"I can ask questions?"

"Yes."

"Anything?"

"Sure. Just be nice. I'm injured."

"I'm always nice."

Maddy set out the tea and some cookies, then settled on the sofa and wrapped both hands around her teacup, needing some of its warmth.

"Don't forget. Be nice."

"Tell me what happened."

The memory of that night sent a shiver up Maddy's spine. "I was too late."

"Too late for what?"

"Too late to save Alisha."

Maddy nodded.

"But you weren't too late to be there for her daughter. You weren't too late to save yourself."

"Meaning?"

"Maybe you were there to save the little girl, just like someone saved you all those years ago."

"Lieutenant Scott."

"Yes."

Maddy hesitated. "Mason said the killer was still in the house."

Tina sat up a little straighter. "Who's Mason?"

"The detective looking into the case. He's Scott's son."

"Interesting," Tina hummed. "There's something in your voice when you say his name. What is that?"

"Gratitude?"

"Mmm. More than that."

Maddy took a sip of her tea and ignored the comment.

"Fine," Tina huffed. "We'll circle back. What's really worrying you?"

Maddy blew out a breath. Of course, Tina would get straight to the heart of it.

"I asked Mason if the killer might come after me."

"What did he say?"

"He said no—but I don't think he believed what he was saying."

"You didn't recognize the killer?"

"No. They mentioned the name Parker Turner. Except if it was him, I don't know of any connection to Alisha."

"Maybe now's the time to play the damsel in distress." Tina gave her a coy smile. "*Mason* just might ride to your rescue."

"What's that supposed to mean?"

Tina pressed her lips together, and her blue eyes twinkled. "It seems it's time to circle back."

"He said his father warned him about me."

"That you're reckless?"

"I tend to rush in—yes. I've heard that before."

"You care. No one can fault you for that."

"I do care. I also don't want to die."

"Then be careful and keep Mason's number close."

Maddy rubbed her finger between her brows, where a slight throb had started. "Can we change the subject? Tell me about the party. Meet anyone new?"

A grin bloomed on Tina's face. "I did."

"From your tone, I'd say you met a man. What about Eli?"

"Yes, Eli came as my date. Turns out, he worked with the guy's date I hit it off with."

"So, you switched dates? That sounds like a soap opera."

"Maybe. He's 6'3", has slightly curly blond hair, and blue eyes. When our eyes met, it felt like I'd been stuck by lightning."

Maddy tilted her head. Something about Tina was different. Still flirty—but softer. Grounded.

"You like him."

"I do."

"And this feels different?"

"It does. We talked all night. He kissed me at midnight and left with his date."

"Was it as awkward as it sounds?"

"Surprisingly, no. It felt ... right."

Maddy understood, as she'd felt the same way with Mason. Except her *meet-cute* came with blood, trauma, and questions she couldn't answer.

Mason's Apartment

January 3, 1994

8:30 p.m.

Instead of taking the most direct route, Mason left his parents' house and drove the long way to his apartment. It took him past 15 Peach Street, where all was quiet. From there, he angled past the Home, then drove by Maddy's apartment complex.

Almost unconsciously, he pulled into her building's parking lot and slid into a space. Maddy's apartment was lit up, telling him she was home.

What was she doing? Watching TV? Reading? Soaking in a warm bath? A part of him wanted to knock on her door and find out. The excuse, 'I was in the neighborhood,' was handy, but it didn't feel right.

He'd decided to leave when a door opened, and someone came out with a trash bag. They were wearing coat, but he could see them clearly when they walked under the light. It was Maddy. What would she say if she knew he was close by?

She tossed the trash bag into the dumpster and started back toward the building. Halfway there, she stopped and glanced around. Mason considered ducking down, but the shadows kept him hidden. When she finally went inside, he crawled out of his car and walked around. It wasn't until he'd assured himself there was no one there he drove home.

Except once home, he couldn't settle. He kept seeing Maddy stopping in the middle of a dark parking lot. Kept imagining what could have happened someone had been there. While he'd not lied to her about the probability of Parker seeing her, he couldn't stop worrying—which was new and unexpected.

Mason turned on the TV and tried to get interested in the football game. Instead of seeing the field, he saw the parking lot. Instead of seeing the players, he saw Maddy frozen mid-step, fear written on her face. He should have told her he was in the area and thinking about her.

Except would that give her the wrong idea? If he'd done so, would she assume he hadn't given her the whole truth? Would it make her worry more? Would it make it more difficult for her to be alone?

His gaze drifted to the phone, and with quick, almost angry motions, Mason pulled out his notebook and punched in her number. It rang three times before her answering machine picked up.

"Hi. You've reached Maddy. I'm not home right now. Please leave your name and number, and I'll get back to you as soon as possible."

"Hi, Maddy. This is Mason Weaver. I'm calling to ... ugh, check on you. If you need anything, call me. My home number is (617) 555-0705."

He'd just hung up when the phone rang. "Hello!" Mason barked.

"Muh, Mason," Maddy's soft voice crossed the line. "It's Mad—"

"—Maddy," Mason breathed. "I didn't catch you at a bad time, did I?"

"No, I ..." She hesitated, and there was uncertainty there.

"Are you okay?"

"I'm okay. I didn't answer because ..."

Once again, her voice faded. .

"Why, honey? Why didn't you answer?"

"It's silly, really."

"Were you worried about who might be on the other end?"

She blew out a breath, and although he couldn't feel it, goosebumps skated along his skin.

"I know you said you didn't think Parker knew who I was. But I'm still—"

"Jumpy?"

"Yes."

"I'm sorry. I've not found anything connecting Parker to Alisha and, in turn, to you. If I do, I'll tell you."

"You will?"

"I promise. Just continue to be careful. Okay?"

"I always am." She paused for a few seconds, then returned with, "Was there something specific you needed?"

"Not really. I just ..."

"Well, okay. Thank you for calling to check on me, Mason."

"You're welcome. Have a good evening. I'll talk to you soon."

"Bye, Mason."

"Goodnight, Maddy."

As soon as she cut their connection, feelings rushed through Mason he hadn't experienced in a long time. The question was, would it be dangerous for Maddy if he expressed interest in her? Or would it be more dangerous if he didn't?

SEVEN

Blessed Children's Home
January 4, 1994
10:00 a.m.

MADDY WOKE LATE AND MISSED THE FIRST TRAIN. BY THE TIME she raced into the Home, frustration simmered just under the surface—not because she'd missed her ride, but because of *why* she'd missed it.

Mason!

She shouldn't have kept the message. Shouldn't have listened to it twice. But hearing his voice made her feel anchored, like the world hadn't entirely spun off its axis.

That wasn't normal. It wasn't safe.

She'd only known him a few days. Why did it feel like he saw right through her?

When she arrived at the Home, it smelled of cereal, pancakes, and coffee. She found Green in the kitchen, cleaning the breakfast mess.

"Did you draw the short straw?"

"You know that's not how it's done, Maddy dear," Green clucked. "It's my week."

"Where's everyone else?"

Green finished wiping the table, then leaned back against the counter with a contemplative expression.

"Let's see. Blue took Tori to the pediatrician. Black is upstairs with Abby, and everyone else is at school."

"Tori's at the doctor? Is she alright?"

"She's right as rain." Green smiled. "But you know Blue."

"I do," Maddy laughed. "Blue wants to ensure she's crossed all her Ts and dotted her Is. Does Blue think Tori has something going on?"

"Oh, no! I believe she was talking about vitamins."

"Oh, okay." Maddy poured a cup of coffee and added a dash of milk. "I'm going to see if I can find out where Alisha was from. I'm just not sure how far I'll get."

Green gave her a sympathetic smile. "You could always ask Scott's son, Mason. He's quite the charmer."

Maddy agreed but had to be careful when saying so and not to protest too much. It was a balancing act—one she'd not dealt with too many times in her life.

"I'll keep it in mind," she settled on. "In the meantime, I'll be in my office if you need me."

"Okay, honey. Good luck."

Once in her office, Maddy tossed her coat on an empty chair and settled behind her desk. It had been almost four days since Alisha had called. Nearly four days since she'd rushed to help. Was there anything else she could have done?

"We don't get to rewrite what already happened. You might have been able to change the outcome. But then again, maybe not."

Blue's words crashed against Tina's.

"You weren't too late to be there for her daughter. You weren't too late to save yourself."

"Meaning?"

"Meaning, maybe you were there to save the little girl, just like someone saved you all those years ago."

If Maddy looked at it like that, she felt better. While it didn't erase the uncomfortable thoughts—nothing did—it eased the guilt a little. And, as long as she focused on work, she could keep the negative feelings away ... at least temporarily.

For the next hour, she steadily worked through her morning tasks. Once finished, though, she couldn't hold off any longer, and took out the thin folder she'd started on Alisha Chapman. It listed the basics—name, date of birth, address, and the hospital where she'd delivered Tori.

On a whim, Maddy looked up the number for St. Brigid's Medical Center, in Sturbridge, Massachusetts. After five rings, someone picked up.

"Hello. Can I help you?" a hurried voice asked.

Maddy frowned. "Is this St. Brigid's Medical Center?"

"Oh, I'm sorry," the woman apologized. "This is Sister Gretchen. Things are a bit chaotic today. How can I help you?"

Maddy quickly explained what she was looking for.

"May I put you on hold for a moment?"

"Of course."

While she waited, Maddy's heart raced—both from anticipation and nervousness. Could she have found a clue to a few answers?

After a minute, the nun returned. "I'm sorry, Maddy. The social worker is out today, and our head, Sister Margaret, is in a meeting. But just so you know, Sister M can be a little hesitant about sharing patient information."

"Meaning?"

"She might require some legal paperwork before she says anything."

"Thank you. I'll keep that in mind."

Maddy hung up and reached for a notepad. She made note of what she wanted, then wrote the hospital's name, Tori's date of birth, the Sister's name, and phone number. In this situation, Blue's tenacity was needed.

She left the note with Green to pass along and then rushed to the subway. Her original destination was the library, but at the last second, she jumped off at Haymarket station. Fritz's, her favorite diner, was nearby, and she could walk to the library afterward.

But first—Clip & Snip. If she were lucky, Becky could answer a few questions.

At just after noon, the salon was quiet. Becky, her longtime hairdresser, was at her station reading. When she glanced up, her smile was immediate.

"Maddy! What brings you to Faneuil Hall? Fritz's?"

Maddy laughed. "You know me too well. In fact, do you have time to join me for a bite to eat? I have some questions."

"Sure." Becky stuck her book into her purse and slung it over her shoulder. "I'm *supposed* to be dieting, but a burger and fries sounds way better than a salad."

"And Fritz's has the best."

"Agreed." They walked a few feet before Becky gave her a side-eye glance. "What's going on, Maddy? There's a sadness in your eyes that wasn't there the last time I saw you."

"I've had a lot on my mind."

"I can tell."

Maddy hesitated, then asked, "Becky, do you know the name Alisha Chapman?"

"Sure. I cut her hair just last week. Why?"

Her breath caught, and once again, her heart felt heavy. "There's no good way to say this, but Alisha died Friday evening."

Becky froze. "Whuh—what?"

The color drained from her face. She swayed, and Maddy caught her before she fell.

"Sit." Maddy guided her to a bench.

Becky sat heavily and was silent for a long moment. Then, in a whisper, she turned toward Maddy, "I just remembered something."

"What was it?"

"While I was cutting her hair, Alisha seemed nervous, and kept looking out the front window." Becky swallowed, her tone thick with unshed tears. "When I asked if I could help, she said, 'I thought I saw someone I knew… someone from back when.' But she wouldn't explain."

"Back when?"

"I assumed she meant before she had Tori. Honestly, though, I didn't press her—she was jumpy enough."

Maddy tucked that away to share with Mason. But before she could say more, Becky blinked several times as if trying to make sense of everything.

"What happened to Alisha, Maddy?"

South Boston Police Precinct
January 4, 1994
2:30 p.m.

MASON FOLLOWED HIS PARTNER, DARRIN ANDERSON, INTO THE precinct and went straight to the coffeepot. Their attempt to talk to Alisha's friend, Natalie, had been a bust. It reminded him of the times they'd gone by 15 Peach Street. Were they dealing with a similar situation? One where the person they wanted to talk to didn't trust *his kind*?

He poured two cups of coffee, set one on his partner's desk, and settled at his own. Before they'd left, he'd asked for several follow-up reports. After giving half to Darrin, Mason opened the first.

Someone had spotted Parker Turner near Franklin Park the previous evening. However, when the patrolman had gone looking for him, he'd vanished.

The time stamp sent a little chill up Mason's spine. The sighting had occurred not long before he stopped by Maddy's apartment building, which wasn't far from the park.

Had he been wrong about Maddy's safety? Had Parker Turner recognized her from Friday night? Or was he trying to fit pieces together that didn't belong?

"What's put that look on your face, Weaver?" Darrin asked.

Mason tossed the report onto his partner's desk. "Another Parker sighting."

"Okay."

"What do you mean, okay?"

"Franklin Park's big. Parker was spotted—not caught. It doesn't do us much good."

"True." Mason hesitated, not ready to admit where his journey had taken him the night before. "It still feels like something is off. We've blanketed the entire area with Parker's photo, and no one can catch him. Something's going on."

Darrin tossed another folder onto Mason's desk. "You're right. Take a look."

Mason opened the file, and his stomach churned. Another high school party. More ecstasy, but this time, three teens ended up in the hospital. Unlike the last two cases, the report included a photo of a pill. Blue with a smudged stamp.

"I can't tell what the image on the pill is. Can you?"

Darrin pulled a magnifying glass from his top drawer and studied the photo. "I can tell you what it *isn't*. Does that help?"

"What do you think?"

"No, huh?"

"Anything else?"

"Brian Lloyd hasn't turned up. The officer who stopped by his apartment heard two stories. One—he'd just disappeared. Two—he'd moved and didn't leave a forwarding address."

"Did they speak to the landlord? Or check Brian's work?"

"It doesn't look like it." Darrin flipped through a few more pages. "I'll track down the landlord and see if I can find out where he worked."

"Good. I think I'll swing by Natalie's again tonight. You never know. She might answer if there's only one of us."

"Maybe I should go then," Darrin quipped. "After all, I'm the better-looking one."

"Bite me," Mason muttered. "What are those last two reports?"

"One's from the officers who chased the assailant down the street the night of the murder. The consensus is—a male who's in shape."

"So ... not helpful?"

"Not helpful," Darrin confirmed.

"And the last report? Maddy remembers seeing blood on his shoes. And, when I did the walkthrough, I saw drops of blood on the floor between the bathroom and bedrooms.

"That's in the report," Darrin murmured.

"Were they able to ID the blood as Parker's?"

Darrin opened the last folder and studied it. Halfway through, his frown piqued Mason's curiosity.

"What is it?"

"In the kitchen, they found blood from three different individuals—the victim's, Miss Davies', and a male's."

"A male's? They didn't identify it as Parker's?" Mason exclaimed. "Wouldn't his DNA be in the system?"

"You would think so. After all, isn't that how we found him?"

"Was it?" Mason removed Parker Turner's file from his desk drawer and flipped through the first few pages. "Not only did several people mention his name, but he was seen at multiple high schools."

"That's right," Darrin hummed. "Then someone spotted him at the Field's Corner station, and on a security camera or two."

"All of which led us to 15 Peach Street, where Alisha's neighbors claimed to have seen a male fitting Parker's description hanging around," Mason added.

"Leaving us to watch 15 Peach Street hoping to question him," Darrin murmured. "But we didn't get anywhere."

There was more they needed to learn about Parker, but Mason set his folder aside and circled back to the blood spatters found at 15 Peach Street.

"What does it say about the male?"

"They couldn't identify the male DNA," Darrin read off the report. "Why?"

Mason pushed away from his desk and stretched out his long legs.

"Why, Mason?" Darrin repeated. "Why does that bother you?"

"I feel like we're missing an important piece of the puzzle." He frowned. "What it is, though ..."

"Is that the truth, or are you holding back?"

"Why would you think so?"

Darrin rolled his eyes. "Look, I know I wasn't with you Friday evening. Nor have I met Miss Davies. But the way you say her name makes me think you're worried about her."

"I'm worried I've given her a false sense of security," he finally admitted.

"Okay, go on."

"She asked if Parker might have recognized her."

"Do you think it's possible?"

Mason blew out a breath. "Do I have concrete evidence? No."

"But your gut is telling you something?"

"It is. Maddy doesn't live far from Franklin Park."

Darrin's brows rose. When he didn't offer an opinion, Mason explained about driving by her apartment building.

"You're worried somehow Parker knew who she was and will go after Maddy next, aren't you?"

"Yes. No. Ah, hell, I don't know!" Mason brushed his hand through his hair. "I'm trying to decide if I should warn her."

Darrin's blue eyes twinkled. "You're just looking for an excuse to see her again."

"I'm ..."

"Don't deny it," Darrin tsked. "I haven't seen you this tongue-tied since we were in college."

"So, old wise one," Mason retorted. "What do you suggest I do?"

"That's easy. Go talk to her."

Mason glanced at the time. He would—once he'd finished his paperwork.

To Blessed Children's Home

January 4, 1994

4:30 p.m.

WHEN THE TRAIN PULLED INTO THE STATION CLOSEST TO THE Home, Maddy slung her bag over her shoulder and followed the crowd onto the platform. As usual, she was jostled a few times, but not enough to bring her focus back to the present.

Her mind was still on her conversation with Becky—and the pages of notes she'd taken at the library. She just didn't know what to *do* with the information.

The crowd began to thin as people split off in different directions. Maddy was following the crowd to the street-level exit when a man stepped in front of her. Something about him unsettled her.

"Excuse me," he whispered.

Before she could respond, someone pushed her from behind. She stumbled, and a hand caught her elbow, steadying her.

Even without looking, she knew. It was the man.

She rushed ahead, and once clear of the building, glanced over her shoulder. There was nothing out of the ordinary. No one was watching her, and the uneasy feeling was gone.

It's nothing. It's probably nothing.

Maddy started toward the Blessed Children's Home—an early twentieth-century Victorian. Originally, the old home had five bedrooms, five bathrooms, and a three-car garage. However, with some remodeling, it currently had seven bedrooms, six bathrooms, office space, and the garage had been converted into a small one-bedroom apartment for Blue.

Maddy's earliest memories were of stories before a roaring fire and the smell of baking goods. It was of children's laughter and secrets whispered between friends. Of family.

Maybe that was unusual for just any group home, but it was the life to strive for. Then, once it was built, it was meant to be celebrated.

With only a few blocks to go, Maddy's insides alerted her she was no longer alone. Before her flight-or-fight instinct kicked in, a car cut in front of her, and slid to a stop.

Mason crawled out and gave her a jaunty wave. Then he smiled—one so sexy her knees grew weak.

"You're just the person I was looking for."

Maddy started to laugh, and then their eyes met. The way he was looking at her and the tenor of his voice caused her breath to catch.

"You were looking for me?"

"I was looking for you," he confirmed.

"Looks like you found me."

Mason's smile grew as he started toward her. Should she hold her ground and make him come to her? Or ... did she meet him halfway?

"Heading back to the Home?"

"I am."

"Dare I ask where you've been?"

"Faneuil Hall."

One of Mason's dark brows rose. "You went by Clip & Snip, didn't you?"

"Maybe."

Mason blew out a breath. "Are you okay?"

"Why wouldn't I be?"

"The look on your face," he said softly. "Before you realized it was me, you looked ... well, distracted."

"I was." She adjusted her bag a little higher on her shoulder, then gave up pretending. "What do you want, Mason? It's been a long day."

"Do I have to want something?"

His surprise in his voice mirrored her own.

"Well, no ..."

"Good. Then let me give you a ride. I want to run a few things by you."

"A ride would be nice." Maddy narrowed her eyes. "Just as long as there's no lecture involved."

"No lecture." He paused, and his grin returned. "At least, not *this* time."

The atmosphere in the car was relaxed for the short ride to the Home. It wasn't until Mason pulled into the driveway, the mood shifted.

"Why did you go see Becky?" He hesitated. "Why didn't you call me first? Why didn't you ask if it was a good idea?"

Maddy blinked. "Ask you if it was a good idea? Why would I do that?"

Mason sighed. "Because I don't want you to get hurt."

"How would I get hurt?" When he didn't immediately answer, she added, "I didn't *plan* to see Becky."

"No?"

"No. I was headed to the library."

"And you *just* happened to pick a library close to Becky's salon?" He snorted. "Is that your story?"

His voice was low, dangerous, and a tad overbearing. It made her want to push back.

"There was no happening to it," she snapped. "It's the library closest to my home. I know it best."

Mason's dark-eyed gaze locked with hers, and for a moment, she thought he was weighing her truthfulness. Finally, he tapped her bag.

"Did you learn anything?"

"Maybe."

"Go on."

"When Becky cut Alisha's hair last Thursday, she kept glancing out the window. Does that mean anything?"

"Maybe." Mason shrugged. "Then again, maybe not."

Maddy fought the urge to stick out her tongue. He could be maddening.

Mason raised a brow. "Is there something else?"

"My job is to help Tori, right?"

"It is."

"That's what I was doing today. Trying to learn more about Alisha's family."

"And?"

"Becky said something that made me hesitate." "She said, 'Alisha was a runaway. What if she was running away from something bad?' Do you think that's a possibility?"

"With runaways?" Mason's expression sobered. It's always a possibility. But you don't have to take on this alone. You know that, right?"

"Meaning?"

"We've already started searching for Alisha's family."

"Really?"

"Yes."

A weight lifted from Maddy's shoulders. "Thank you."

"You're welcome. But I'm not doing it for you."

"Oh, I know," she said softy. "You're doing this for Tori."

"And Alisha," he added.

"Will you keep me posted?"

"Maybe."

Maybe? she grunted. "How can you say that?"

"Well ...," He stretched out the word with a grin. "If I do a favor for you, will you do a favor for me?"

"You want a favor from me?"

"I do."

"What?"

Mason grinned. "You haven't said yes."

"You haven't told me what you want me to do," she countered.

Mason gave a playful grown. "You drive a hard bargain, Maddy Davies. Fine ... would you go with me to talk to Natalie?"

Her pulse quickened. "You need my help with Natalie?"

"I'd like *your* help with Natalie," he corrected. "Will you come with me?"

"I will."

"Really? Great. What time should I pick you up?"

"I don't have any appointments tomorrow. Whatever works for you."

"Late morning?"

"That's fine."

"Perfect! It's a date."

EIGHT

South Boston Police Precinct
January 5, 1994
9:00 a.m.

The following day, Mason buried his head in a folder and pretended to stay busy. He wasn't. The words *"It's a date,"* kept bouncing around in his head, dragging him back into the *Should he?* or *Shouldn't he?* spiral where Maddy was concerned.

"You're smiling." Darrin propped a hip on the corner of Mason's desk. "This wouldn't have anything to do with the social worker, would it?"

Mason let Darrin's teasing roll off his back. His mood was too good.

"Can a guy just enjoy a beautiful Wednesday?"

Darrin snorted. "Do you need your eyes checked, Weaver? It's gray, freezing, and it's supposed to snow."

"Well, when you put it like that ...," Mason shrugged. "I see your point."

"Have you asked her out?"

"Maddy?"

"No, the mail carrier. Yes, Maddy."

"No."

"Why not?"

"She's a case."

"*She's* not the case," Darrin scoffed. "She's connected to it, sure. But don't pretend that's the real reason."

Mason bounced his pen between his thumb and finger for a few seconds. "I saw her last night."

"Oh?"

"There's no *oh*."

"Then, by all means," Darrin smirked, "fill me in."

"Maddy went to Clip & Snip and talked to the hairdresser."

"Your dad said she might need to be watched. Looks like you've got the perfect excuse."

"But wait, there's more."

"Of course there is," Darrin sighed.

Mason ignored his partner's theatrics and explained what happened, including why Maddy hadn't answered her phone.

"You *called* her?" Darrin's brow rose. "And I'm just now finding this out?"

"It was a phone call. Stay with me here."

"I'm with you," Darrin grumbled. "But you're rambling. Think you can get to the point?"

Mason leaned back in his desk chair, took out the timeline he'd created, and flipped it around so Darrin could see.

"The first time we heard about the blue ecstasy being sold at the local high schools was November 5th. Then, after talking to the students and teachers, we started looking for Parker Turner. Right?"

"Okay." Darrin tapped the sheet of paper. "To the timeline, we can add our visits to 15 Peach Street—November 30, December 14, and December 28 —all dead ends."

"According to Maddy, Alisha didn't like *our kind*," Mason murmured. "That could explain why she never answered the door."

"It could."

"But here's the thing," Mason went on. "The hairdresser said Alisha was nervous on December 30. Why?"

Darrin shrugged. "A phone call? She saw Lloyd? Or maybe she was worried she'd run into *us* again."

"I hadn't thought of that," Mason admitted. "But yeah—it's possible."

"Where was the child while Alisha was having her hair cut?" Darrin murmured.

"Natalie was watching her," Mason guessed. "I wonder if she noticed anything different that day?"

"Maybe." Darrin frowned. "Then, a day later, Alisha was dead. We really need to talk to Lloyd."

"Agreed. It would help narrow our search. And that brings me back to Parker. If *he's* the killer, what's his connection to Alisha?"

"Another question we need answered."

Mason's voice softened. "I also want to know what Parker was doing so close to Maddy's apartment."

"Again, Franklin Park covers a lot of space. It's as close to Dorchester and Roxbury as it is to Maddy's apartment in Jamaica Plains," Darrin pointed out. "You're making leaps you wouldn't normally make."

Mason blew out a breath. A part of him agreed. The other part, though ....

"Stop making excuses, Weaver. Just face it—you're interested. And that worries you."

"Who said I was interested?"

Darrin raised a blond brow. "It's written all over your face."

Mason thought about denying it. But what was the point? Darrin would believe what he wanted. Besides, his partner was right. Maddy *did* interest him. He just hadn't decided if that was a good thing yet.

"I'll think about it," he finally offered. "That's as far as I'm willing to go right now."

"It's something," Darrin grinned. "You're getting braver."

"Bite me. I'm not twelve."

"Maybe not, but you're acting like you're twelve."

Fifteen, Mason thought. *More like fifteen*. He glanced at the clock and began organizing the files on his desk.

"I told you I'd think about it. But right now ..."

"Where are you going?"

"To talk to Natalie."

"But I'm your partner," Darrin protested. "Shouldn't I come too?"

"Normally, yes. This time, I thought, I'd try something different. I'll see you later."

He pushed in his desk chair, but before he'd gotten far, Darrin called out, "You're taking the social worker, aren't you?"

Great! It's a date.

"Maybe."

"Wait! Why do *you* get to go on a date in the middle of the day?"

"It's not a date. I'm following up with a witness. Later."

Darrin flipped him a rude hand gesture, but the smirk on his face said he wasn't really mad. That was a good thing—he could ignore it.

He left the department, and the wind whipped around, chilling him to the bone. Who was he kidding? His partner had been right. It wasn't a beautiful morning, but damn cold.

On the drive to the Home, Mason fought to stay within the speed limit. He *knew* it wasn't a date. But that didn't change how he felt about seeing Maddy again.

Fifteen.

He definitely felt fifteen all over again.

Blessed Children's Home
January 5, 1994
11:00 a.m.

Maddy's morning had been a bust. The anticipation of seeing Mason played havoc with her concentration.

When the doorbell finally rang, she jumped—and felt her cheeks grow warm.

Calm down. It's just Mason.

That didn't keep her from pressing her hands against her stomach, to still the butterflies when she opened the door.

"Hi," she breathed.

"Hi yourself," Mason said with a grin. "Are you ready?"

"I'll just grab my coat."

"Let me help."

"I can—"

Her words faded when Mason stepped closer and reached for her coat. His warmth surrounded her, and her breath stuttered.

She turned ... and their gazes clashed.

His gaze traveled over her face, slow and watchful. Then, gently, he cupped her jaw and brushed his thumb across her left cheekbone.

"Does it hurt?"

"Not really," she whispered. "But I'm glad the bruises are fading."

He sobered, and a look she couldn't decipher flickered in his eyes. The longer they stood there, the more intense his stare ... so intense it almost had her turning away.

"I don't want you to get hurt," she thought she heard him say. Except his voice was so soft she couldn't be sure.

Maddy tried to smile. Tried to come up with something light and witty. But nothing felt right. Instead, she offered the same words she'd given to the Sisters.

"I'm fine."

"I'm glad." He offered his arm. "Shall we?"

Once they were in the car and on the way, Maddy found herself tongue-tied. Every topic she thought of felt too light, too unimportant. Finally, she kept it simple.

"Have you learned anything new about Alisha's case?"

"Nothing solid," he admitted. "I'm hoping Natalie can fill in a few blanks."

"That would be nice."

Mason glanced at her. "You said the other night you'd only met Natalie a few times. Right?"

"About that, yes."

"Did Blue say anything more about Alisha and Natalie's friendship?"

"Not really. To be honest, though, I haven't pushed for details."

"And Blue has volunteered nothing new?"

Maddy winced. "Not really. I wish I had asked more ..."

Before she could finish, Mason's hand closed around hers.

"Don't beat yourself up, Maddy. You were there for Alisha. She trusted you."

"But if I—"

"Don't."

He gently squeezed her fingers. His touch calmed her, soothing her negative thoughts.

"I'm sorry."

"No apology necessary."

Silence settled between them as Mason pulled into a parking space in front of Natalie's apartment complex. Just like before, he got out first, and opened her door.

"I'm perfectly capable of opening my own door. You know that, right?" she said, lifting a brow. But that didn't keep her from placing her hand in his and letting him help her out.

Mason grinned down at her. "I know you are."

"Good."

He tipped her chin until they were eye to eye. "What if I want to open your door next time?"

His gaze was so dark, so direct, it nearly unraveled her.

"Do you?" she whispered.

"Yes." Mason hesitated a beat. "I am a gentleman, after all."

Maddy swallowed, but it wasn't easy. "You are?"

"Most of the time." He winked and continued toward the complex.

For a moment, Maddy felt as if she needed to run to catch up. Mason's behavior was all over the place. One minute warm and teasing, the next distant. What had she missed?

By the time she caught up with him, he'd already knocked on Natalie's apartment door.

They waited. Five seconds. Then ten.

Mason exhaled sharply, frustration rolling off him in waves.

"Natalie." Maddy knocked again. "It's Alisha's friend, Maddy Davies. We need to talk to you."

A heartbeat later, the chain rattled, and the door opened a few inches.

"Natalie." Maddy stood so the younger woman could see her. "Do you remember me?"

"Yes."

"Please help us find who did this."

"I don't know."

Mason glanced at her. Then, using his soft, sexy baritone, tried again.

"You might know more than you think."

"Please?" Maddy added gently.

After a long moment, Natalie stepped aside and invited them in. She led them into a small living room, then excused herself briefly to close a bedroom door.

"My son's," she explained. "He's not feeling well."

"I'll try to keep this short." Mason's tone was professional, but kind. "But in cases like this, time can be a factor."

"I understand."

Maddy watched Natalie carefully, noting she was pale, and the sparkle in her eyes was gone. The changes were subtle—but telling.

"Sit wherever you're most comfortable," Mason murmured. "Then we'll get started."

Natalie settled on the couch, tucked one leg underneath her, and leaned back. She looked like she was trying to appear calm, but failing miserably. It had Maddy wanting to take her hand and promise everything would work out. Instead, she let Mason lead.

"When did you first meet Alisha?" he began.

A wistful smile crossed Natalie's face. "Last September."

"At school?"

"Kind of."

"Go on."

"I work part-time for King Industries," Natalie explained. "One of the women introduced me to her daughter, Joni."

THE NAME HAD MASON LIFTING HIS HEAD FROM THE NOTE HE'D written. "You said Joni?"

"Yes."

"Who's Joni?"

"Her name is Joni Gardner, and she's a college counselor. Joni matched Alisha and me because we were single mothers and lived fairly close together."

"Do the initials TG sound familiar?"

Natalie frowned. "No. Should they?"

"It was a contact in Alisha's address book."

"Oh." Natalie hesitated. "I'm sorry, but I don't know them."

"Did you know Alisha had a restraining order against someone?" Mason took the questions in another direction.

"I did."

"Did you ever see him hanging around? Or know if he tried to contact her?"

"No."

That wasn't the answer Mason had been expecting. However, it sent him in a different direction than he'd planned.

"Alisha had her hair cut last Thursday. Is that right?"

"Yes."

"Were you watching Tori while Alisha was gone?"

"Yes."

Mason side-eyed Maddy and almost grinned at the way she was watching Natalie. It reminded him of a mother cat protecting her kittens. That told him if he didn't behave, her claws would come out.

"According to the hairdresser, Alisha was nervous. Did you notice anything off?"

Natalie's gaze flitted from his to Maddy's, then back again. Whatever she was going to say made her visibly uneasy.

"I did."

"Do you know why?"

"Did she tell me why? No."

"Meaning?"

"One day, when we were shopping, Alisha kept looking over her shoulder. I asked her what was going on, but she brushed it off. Said it was nothing."

Mason blew out a slow breath and shifted directions. "Did Alisha avoid anyone? Or seem wary around certain people?"

"Not that I know of."

"And you never saw her using anything?"

Natalie's eyes sharpened. "No. Alisha was a good mother."

He considered explaining the context, but in the end, decided it didn't matter. "Did Alisha have other friends that you know of?"

Natalie's expression softened. "She told me more than once I was the only person she could count on."

"I'm sorry to ask this, Natalie, but did Alisha ever mention the police trying to contact her?"

"No."

He'd questioned enough people to tell Natalie was holding back. The question was, why?

"Does the name Parker Turner sound familiar?"

Natalie hesitated. "I've heard it before. I'm just not sure where."

"Could it have been from Alisha?"

"Maybe. Alisha didn't name names much. We mostly talked about school and the kids." She paused, then added, "What about Tori? Is she okay?"

"Tori's at the Blessed Children's home," Maddy murmured. "You can visit anytime. Just call me first."

"Really?"

Maddy gave her a card. "If you have any problems, my number is there."

"Thank you."

Mason brought the focus back to his questions. "You said Alisha was watching over her shoulder during that shopping trip. Did she say anything else?"

"Not really, but ..." A child's cry interrupted her. Natalie sighed. "I'm sorry. I should check on him."

Maddy stepped in. "We'll see ourselves out. Please call if you need anything."

Mason shot Maddy a disgruntled look, annoyed she hadn't asked if he was done. But one glance at her expression told him she'd decided he'd pushed Natalie far enough for one day.

Maddy lifted a dark brow, and her silver-blue eyes dared him to argue. "Do you have a card for Natalie?"

He handed over his card, then added, "If I have more questions, you'll be available. Right?"

Natalie glanced at Maddy before returning to him. "I'll be around. Now, I'd better ..."

"We're going." Maddy said, nudging him toward the door. "I hope your little boy feels better."

The door had barely clicked shut when Mason turned, pinning Maddy with a hard stare. "Just what the hell was that? I wasn't done."

"Yes, you were."

Mason caught her elbow before she could walk away. "It is my case."

Maddy's silver-blue eyes narrowed. She lifted her chin, her mouth tightening just slightly. "It might be your case, but you pushed Natalie too far."

"No, I didn't. I hadn't leaned on her enough. She knows more than she's saying."

"Maybe," Maddy allowed. "Or maybe not. But she just lost her best friend, and the only person who helped with her son. Natalie needs a few days to get her feet back under her."

Their eyes locked in a silent duel, and Mason's thoughts from earlier returned ... *the way she watched Natalie reminded him of a mother cat protecting its kittens.* Apparently, he'd just seen her claws.

"Do you think she knows more?"

"I think," Maddy said with a sigh. "I think she was choosing her words carefully. And no, before you ask, I don't know why."

Mason cupped Maddy's elbow as they walked toward his car. "You're not going to stay away from Natalie and let me do my job, are you?"

"I have no intention of getting between you and your job."

"But?"

"I won't let you run over Natalie. She's in a delicate place and needs a softer touch."

Mason pressed his lips together, swallowing the retort that rose to the surface. "Promise me you won't do anything dangerous."

"I'm not a masochist, Mason. I only want to help."

Exactly what his father had warned him about. It also added another layer to 'Should he?' or 'Shouldn't he?' when it came to Maddy Davies.

You were feeling like you were fifteen again.

He'd spent much of his fifteenth year hopelessly confused by the female population. So why would the second time around be any different?

NINE

Blessed Children's Home
January 7, 1994
11:30 a.m.

Two days later, Maddy struggled to maintain her focus. Instead of finishing the report, her thoughts kept drifting to the conversation with Natalie. She agreed with Mason—the younger woman hadn't told them the entire story. What was she hiding, though? Was it something that would put her in danger?

"Maddy?" Blue tapped lightly on the door. "Are you busy?"

"Not really. Did you need something?"

Blue tilted her head and studied her for several seconds. When she'd been younger, that dark-eyed stare had made her nervous—especially if she was trying to keep a secret. Now ... not so much.

"Just ask," Maddy grinned. "I can tell you have a question or two."

Blue's dark eyes sparkled. "I heard you went somewhere with Mason the other day."

"Who told you? Green?"

"Of course. You know Sister Green can't keep secrets."

"No, she never could." Maddy paused a moment. "Anything else you're dying to know?"

"Anything you want to tell me?"

"Now that you mention it ...," Maddy's tone shifted. "I wanted to ask what you know about Natalie?"

Blue's smirk softened into something knowing. "Natalie? Why? Does this have something to do with Alisha?"

"Maybe. Mason's convinced Natalie knows more than she shared."

"And what do you think?"

"I think it's possible. But her behavior could also be grief."

"Possibly."

"Tell me about Natalie. I know she never lived here."

"No, she didn't," Blue murmured. "I met her late last summer."

"How?"

"Sue Gardner told me about her."

"Gardner?" Maddy hummed. "Her daughter is the one who introduced Alisha and Natalie. Right?"

Blue nodded.

"And Sue Gardner works for King Industries?"

"She does."

"How come her name is familiar?"

"Sue is in charge of King Industries' fundraisers," Blue reminded her. "Didn't you meet her last year?"

Blessed Children's Home ran solely on donations. Events put on by Leo King, his daughter Ava, and their corporation funded the Home's operating expenses. The year's first event was at the end of the month.

"Remember, I had the flu last year."

"Oh, that's right." Blue's dark eyes twinkled, and Maddy knew exactly was coming. "Perhaps you could ask Mason to accompany you this year."

"Where did that come from?"

Blue shrugged. "There's a connection between you two."

"Right now, he's focused on the case."

"Hmm. If you say so." Blue's tone was unconvinced, but she let it go. "Now, let's see what I can tell you about Natalie. Her grandmother worked at King Industries for years. When she died unexpectedly, Sue stepped in to help —but there was only so much she could do."

"Where's Natalie from?"

"Minnesota, I think. I gather Natalie was a good student and planned to attend college until she found out she was pregnant."

"Oh, dear. What happened?"

"The day after she graduated, her stepfather kicked her out. She stayed with her grandmother until her death."

"Let me guess. No will, and Natalie was out in the cold again."

"Sadly, that's what happened. And this time, it was her mother who made sure of it."

"That's awful. She was lucky Sue was there."

"Very lucky. However, Sue had only a few resources, so I stepped in."

"You helped Natalie get on her feet."

"I tried." A little pucker developed between Blue's brows. "By the way, did Natalie mention who's watching Lucas while she works?"

"No."

"Maybe I'll call her. There's a woman who lives in her building who might help."

"I'm sure Natalie would appreciate it."

"Do you want me to ask her if she remembered anything new?"

Maddy blew out a breath. "No. Mason might get all bent out of shape."

Blue laughed. "What happened?"

"Oh, nothing really." Maddy rolled her eyes. "I just stopped him from pushing Natalie too far."

"He'll get over it." Blue slid a piece of paper across the desk. "Sister Margaret, the head of St. Brigid's, and I go way back. For a time, we were in the same order."

"You didn't find anything new?"

Blue sighed. " Sister Margaret wasn't there—she's away at a conference, but I'll call again next week. Still, I learned something interesting."

"Go on."

"I explained everything to the woman who answered the phone—Margaret's assistant—and she thinks she remembers Alisha."

Maddy's heart skipped, and a ripple of excitement roared to life inside. "Did, did she give you anything that might help?"

"She said Alisha was sweet, but her behavior was quite curious."

"How so?"

"On the outside, she appeared quite polished. But in certain ways, she behaved much younger—almost as if someone older had sheltered her."

"Any ideas what that could mean?"

"Not yet." Blue's tone was thoughtful. "But I'll let you know when I talk to Sister Margaret."

"Well, it's something." Maddy hesitated. "Was there anything specific you needed?"

Blue laid two 3" x 5" cards on her desk, and Maddy had to bite her lip to keep from laughing. As the Home's director, she was required to schmooze—but she didn't care for it. She'd rather work quietly in the background and let others take the credit.

"You designed these, didn't you?" Maddy teased. "I don't see your picture anywhere."

"I don't need to be on there," Blue humphed. "And for privacy reasons, I didn't want the children's faces on the invitations."

"So, you settled for the house or the back of the children?"

"That's right, dear. Now, which do you like best—the exterior or the interior photo?" Blue pointed to the corresponding card.

Maddy studied the cards, trying to be objective. She could see the advantages and disadvantages of both.

"Which one do you like best?"

"I think you know. I just need to have my choice validated."

"This one's my favorite. It says 'family.'" Maddy handed Blue the card showing the interior of the Home. A warm fire was burning, and several older kids were reading in front of it.

Blue beamed. "I knew you'd agree with me. Now, I'll let you get back to work."

Once Blue was gone, Maddy pulled a folder from her drawer and several intake forms. Alisha's death had created a hole in Natalie's life. If she wasn't ready to talk, there were other ways she could help.

South Boston Police Precinct
January 7, 1994
1:30 p.m.

As soon as Mason returned from lunch, his phone rang.

"Weaver."

"Get your ass over here, Weaver," Rod grumbled. "I have something for you."

"Rod?"

"Of course, it's Rod. Now, are you listening?"

"What's going on?"

"You're certainly grumpy," Rod returned. "And you don't even have a child to blame it on."

Mason exhaled. "Sorry. This case has too many missing pieces, and something tells me it just started."

"Well, I might've found you a piece."

His brother's comment had Mason sitting up a little straighter. Was this the break they needed?

"What do you have?"

"Just come to Franklin Park," Rod replied. "You'll want to see for yourself."

Mason jotted down their meeting place, then hung up and tapped his partner's desk. "Wheels up. Rod claims he found a piece of our puzzle."

Darrin glanced up from the file he was working on. "Where are we going?"

"Franklin Park."

"As in Franklin Park, where Parker was last seen."

Mason sighed. "The very one."

"Are you sure they're related, or are you grasping?"

"Grasping," Mason admitted. "But I need a few pieces to fit together rather than a bigger puzzle."

"Picky, picky."

"Let's go."

They grabbed their coats and had only been in the car for a few minutes, when Darrin tossed out, "We're still on for tonight, right?"

Mason frowned. "On for what?"

"The Brass Chord."

The Brass Chord was a club in Davis Square featuring live bands several nights a week. The food and music were good, and the atmosphere was comfortable, whether you were alone or with friends.

"I thought I'd order a pizza and stay in tonight," Mason replied. "Maybe tomorrow night?"

"Come on, Mason," Darrin wheedled. "I promised Tom I'd be there to hear them sing."

"Tom?"

"My neighbor, remember?"

He didn't, but why quibble? "I thought you had a date."

"She said she might stop by."

"But in case she doesn't," Mason grinned. "You don't want to seem desperate?"

"Exactly."

"I'll try to stop by for one drink. Just know you owe me."

"I'll keep it in mind." Darrin was quiet for a beat, then circled back to their case. "It's not a body, right?"

"I don't think so. If it were, Rod would have said so."

"Not a body, so evidence," Darrin surmised. "What could it be?"

"The knife?" Mason guessed.

"Wishful thinking."

"Still, it would be nice."

"I'm not arguing. Do you believe in coincidences?"

"Usually, no. This time? Maybe so."

They found Rod waiting, arms crossed, wearing a disgruntled expression. "It's about time," he said when Mason climbed from the car. "It's damn cold out here."

"We don't live right next door," Mason shot back. "We're here now. The question is, why?"

"Come see for yourself," Rod said, already turning away.

They took a winding path deeper into the park, and hadn't gone far when Mason heard voices. "Tech's already here?"

"Just a few minutes ago," Rod murmured.

"What was found?"

"A bloody jacket."

Mason stopped. "You're telling me someone found a bloody jacket?"

"Yes."

"But how do you know the bloody jacket belongs to our crime scene?" Mason followed up.

"You always were impatient," Rod grunted.

"I've been trying to hold him back," Darrin chimed in. "I think it's because of Maddy."

Rod grinned. "Oh? What's happening with Maddy?"

"Why don't you ask dad," Mason sighed. "Isn't he the one who shares news with you?"

Rod barked out a laugh. "True. However, this time, he was the one who asked me."

"Mason *claims* nothing is going on with Maddy," Darrin added, not bothering to hide his grin.

"Which explains why he's grumpy," Rod mused. "Would you like dating advice?"

"I don't need any dating advice," Mason snapped. "I have no difficulty getting a date."

"Uh-huh," Rod sighed. "Well, the offer is out there."

"I'll remember that."

"How was the evidence found?" Darrin questioned. "And why did it take a week?"

"A little hanky panky behind the bushes," Rod snickered.

"What?" Mason cut in.

"Just hold on," Rod muttered. "We're almost there."

Mason gave his brother an annoyed look, but since they were at the crime scene, bit his tongue.

"To the southwest is Forest Hill High School," Rod continued. "Two teachers took a walk during their lunch hour. I'm guessing they wanted a little privacy and slipped into that grove of trees."

"They stumbled on the jacket?" Mason murmured. "And probably trampled all over the scene."

"It gets worse," Rod grimaced. "The woman was carrying a mug with coffee. When she saw the blood—"

"She dropped it?" Mason finished.

"Got it in one." Rod nodded.

"The teachers didn't wait?" Darrin asked, frowning.

"Refused," Rod said. "Said they had to get back to class."

"Tell me you got their names, at least," Mason snapped.

"I've been doing this longer than you, little brother," Rod smirked. "Play nice."

Darrin snorted. "Told you he was grumpy. I'm making him meet me at the Brass Chord tonight. The Minors are playing."

"Dating advice is still available," Rod offered.

"I told you I didn't need advice," Mason grumbled.

"Do you want to walk through before I pick up?" the tech interrupted to ask.

Mason stopped about five feet from the evidence and took in the scene. A black jacket with white stripes was lying in the center. The rust-colored stains stood stark against the white background.

"Blood?" Mason asked the tech.

"Yes," the tech confirmed. "And yes, it's human."

Mason slipped on gloves, then stepped closer to the jacket. One side of the material was folded to reveal a blue sticky note.

"Damn!"

"That's how we knew it was from your crime scene," Rod murmured.

"Where was the note?" Mason asked.

"Right pocket."

Mason sighed. "You were right. It's a piece of the puzzle."

"Told you so," Rod quipped. "I'm just that good."

The sticky note had been inside the jacket pocket for a week and exposed to the elements. While smeared, the writing on the note was still legible. It said *15 Peach Street*—Alisha Chapman's address.

Blessed Children's Home
January 7, 1994
6:00 p.m.

MADDY SAT CROSS-LEGGED ON THE FLOOR, ENTERTAINING ABBY and Tori. One was stacking rings, the other pushing shapes into a container. It wasn't her regular Friday evening activity, but it kept her away from her empty apartment—and close to the little girl whose loss mirrored her own.

Tori didn't understand what she'd lost, not yet anyway. But Maddy did, and that knowledge made her want to spend as much time with the little girl as possible. Something she knew Blue, Green, and Black had done for her when she'd first arrived. It was important to the Sisters that each child feel safe as if they were part of a *family*.

"Maddy, dear," Sister Green interrupted her musings. "Is everything okay?"

"It's fine. Why?"

"Well," Green went on. "It's a Friday night, and you're not out with your young friends."

"Are you trying to get rid of me?"

"Now, Maddy," Green scolded lightly. "You know that's not the case."

"I just thought the girls could use a little extra attention."

Green smiled, a touch of melancholy in her expression. "You're seeing yourself in Tori's situation, aren't you?"

"Maybe a little. It would be nice to find out Tori had family waiting for her."

"It would," Green agreed. "That's not always the case, though."

"True."

"Any luck with your search?"

"I've gone as far as I can. Mason said they were working on it from their end."

"Well, maybe ..." The doorbell rang, cutting off what Green had been about to say. "I wonder who that could be."

"Do you want me to get it?"

"No, dear. You stay there with those babies. I'll be right back."

A part of Maddy wished the person at the door was for her. Wished it was Mason coming to sweep her off her feet for an evening out. Except, if he wanted to be with her, he would have asked. Since he hadn't ... that spoke volumes.

"Maddy, look who's here." Green returned to the room, followed closely by Tina. "Do you two need anything?"

"We're fine, Green. Thank you," Maddy answered. "I'll let you know if there's a problem."

"Okay. I'll be in the kitchen."

As soon as they were alone, Maddy turned to Tina. "What's up?"

"What's up with *you*?" Tina shot back.

"Not much," Maddy hummed. "Why?"

"I stopped by your apartment."

"You did?"

"I even waited about ten minutes for you to get home," Tina admitted.

Maddy leaned back on her hands and studied her friend. "Did I forget something?"

"No. I did."

"What did you forget?"

"What was going on tonight."

"Don't you usually teach on Friday nights?"

"I did in the fall, but not this session."

"That still doesn't explain what's going on tonight. Nor does it tell me why you're here."

Tina dropped into a chair and propped her elbows on her legs. "I'm making a mess of this, aren't I?"

"Since I have *zero* clue what you're talking about, I can't say either way."

"I told you about the guy I met at the New Year's party, right?"

"Yes."

"What have I told you about him?"

"His height, eye, and hair color," Maddy replied. "Not much else."

And because she'd been so caught up with Alisha's death, and with Tori, she hadn't asked any questions.

Tina winced. "I'm sorry."

"No, Tina, I'm the one who's sorry. This week has been ... different."

"Maddy," Tina exclaimed. "Stop. Your situation is completely understandable."

Maddy knew her friend well enough to realize she was working her way around to the real reason for her visit—and it involved a man.

"Tell me about the man you met," Maddy prompted. "What's his name?"

"Darrin." Tina paused, her expression saying the name should mean something. "You don't know, do you?"

"Know what?"

"You don't recognize his name."

"Should I?"

"Yes!" Tina exclaimed. "Maddy, *Darrin* is Mason's *partner*."

Maddy had to fight to keep her mouth closed. "*Darrin* is Mason's partner? He's a detective?"

"He is."

Maddy passed another block to Tori while she tried to process the new information. "What are you getting at?"

"Will you go to the Brass Chord with me tonight?"

"Why?"

"Because Darrin and Mason are there."

Maddy shook her head. "Does Mason know you're my friend?"

"Well ... not exactly."

The news that Tina's new boyfriend was friends with Mason was exciting. So was hearing they were at the Brass Chord. But just *showing* up?

"Why don't you go alone?"

"Mason's interested in you."

"Right. Mason's so interested he's been knocking down my door to ask me out."

"This is your chance to see if something is there," Tina pressed. "At least you won't have to worry about carrying the conversation all on your own."

Which hadn't been a worry the few times she'd been with Mason. But showing up with her friend, knowing he would be there? That was terrifying and a little underhanded.

"Tina, I don't know."

"Come on, Maddy," Tina pleaded. "I *really* want to spend time with Darrin."

"Then go. Alone."

"Maddy ... please."

TEN

The Brass Chord
January 7, 1994
7:30 p.m.

When Darrin told the Brass Chord hostess, there were four in their party, Mason side-eyed his partner. However, he held his tongue until they were seated and had placed their order. Then he leaned in and called him out.

"Okay. What gives?"

"Stop it," Darrin smirked. "You'll thank me before the night is over."

"Really? Should I thank you for dragging me here under false pretenses? Or is there something else I should thank you for?"

"I didn't lie," Darrin replied with mock innocence. "My neighbor *is* singing tonight, *and* I told him I'd come and listen."

"So, it's the *something else*," Mason sighed. "Who are you trying to fix me up with?"

"Maddy."

Mason's breath caught, and his heart rate ticked up a notch. Spending time with Maddy—especially somewhere low pressure, like a music club—had crossed his mind more than once. But being *fixed up?* That didn't sit right.

"Darrin," he sighed. "I told you I'd think about asking Maddy out."

"Just listen," Darrin cut in. "Yes, I think you should ask Maddy out. Yes, you told me you were going to think about it. But when this situation presented itself ..."

"You couldn't say no?" Mason muttered.

Darrin winced. "It turns out the woman I met on New Year's Eve is Maddy's best friend."

"Your Tina is ..." A movement from the corner of Mason's eye had his voice fading. Maddy was standing next to the club door beside a petite blonde. "How long have you been planning this?"

"Just a day," Darrin murmured. "It hasn't been that long."

"So that '*Are we still on for tonight*?' wasn't because I'd forgotten something?"

"Not exactly," Darrin smirked. "But you can't tell me you aren't happy."

"I can't?"

"No." Darrin pushed back his chair as the women approached. "You're practically jumping up and down with excitement."

"Now, who needs their eyes checked?" Mason muttered just before the women were within earshot.

"Mason." Darrin greeted the blonde with a smile and pulled her gently into his arms. "This is Tina Stone."

While Darrin was introducing Tina, Mason struggled to keep his gaze off Maddy. He wanted to talk to her. Wanted to ask her if this was okay.

"This is Maddy Davies," Tina added, turning to Mason. "I think you two know each other."

"Maddy," Mason whispered. "It's nice to see you again."

Her silver-blue eyes locked with his, and he could see she had questions. Would she understand his reasons for not exploring their connection on his own?

"If you two will excuse us." Darrin tightened his hold on Tina. "We're going to dance."

As they walked away, Mason blinked once, then twice, before he remembered what to do. "I'm sorry. Here, have a seat. Can I get you something to drink?" It wasn't what he wanted to say, but it was all he had.

"I can wait until Tina gets back," Maddy replied softly.

Mason glanced briefly toward the dance floor. When he turned back, it was just in time to see the uncomfortable expression on Maddy's face.

"I hope this is okay?"

Maddy tilted her head. "I was going to ask you the same thing."

"Why wouldn't it be?"

"Come on, Mason," she scoffed. "You know exactly what I mean."

Instead of answering, he asked, "Did you know I was going to be here?"

"Tina explained who you were when she tracked me down earlier."

"Yet you still came."

"Should I have stayed home?"

"No, I should've ..." Mason dropped his head, attempting to reset, then looked back up. "I've thought about asking you out more than once," he confessed, surprising himself.

Maddy smiled, her silver-blue eyes twinkling in the low light. "Why didn't you?"

How could he explain his feelings about her? Not only was she involved in the case, but she was also important to his father, and to Blue—a complication he didn't need.

"I ..."

"Mason." Maddy leaned a little closer and laid her hand on his arm. "Don't you think I feel it, too?"

"What?"

"The pressure."

"The pressure?"

She rolled her eyes. "Yes, the pressure. The pressure of disappointing your dad. Or the Sisters. Or of getting it wrong."

"My thoughts exactly," Mason admitted. "If I hurt you, I'd never hear the end of it."

Maddy grinned. "I'm a big girl, Mason. Just like I can open a car door by myself, so can I fight my own battles. I don't need Blue or your father there to fight them."

"I know that, and so do they," he murmured. "It's just ..."

"Mason."

"What?"

"Can I ask you a question?"

"Anything, Maddy. You should know that."

"I do," she answered, her smile not quite reaching her eyes.

"But?"

"Will you tell me the truth?"

His gut tightened, and Parker's name flashed across his mind. But he didn't think this had to do with the case.

"If I can," he promised.

"If your father or Blue weren't in the picture, would you want to ask me out?"

"In a heartbeat."

She raised a brow. "That's good, right?"

"Maddy."

"Yes, Mason?"

"Now, you answer my question." He hesitated, then put it out there. "If I had asked you out, what would you have said?"

"Oh, that's easy."

"Really?"

"I would have said yes."

He exhaled, only then realizing he'd been holding his breath. Now all he needed was a reset to strip away everything but their feelings. Anything that would allow them to be a man and a woman spending time with friends.

The smile on Mason's face took Maddy's breath, and that scared her. Somehow, she knew falling in love with him would be easy. Almost too easy. But that terrified her. She wanted nothing to complicate her relationship with Scott—or with the Sisters.

"Friends?" Maddy offered, holding out her hand.

The moment he wrapped his fingers around hers, electricity zipped up her arm. Awareness simmered right below the surface, and all she wanted was to be held.

"Would—?"

"Would you like to dance?" he asked before she could finish the question.

"I would like that very much."

Mason cupped her elbow and guided her to the small dance floor. When he put his arms around her and tucked her against his chest, it was a fight not to lean into him.

"Relax, Maddy," Mason purred against her temple. "I don't bite ... much."

Maddy chuckled, but it proved to be what she needed to allow herself to melt against him.

"There," he whispered. "That's better, isn't it?"

It's heaven.

A part of her wanted to slow down. To be smart. To be careful. While the other part wanted to close her eyes and hold on for as long as the moment lasted.

One song morphed into another, and couples came and went, but Mason never acted as if he was ready to let her go. In fact, the longer they danced, the tighter his hold.

"How's Tori?" he murmured. "Any problems with her?"

"None," Maddy assured him. "Especially now that she has her cat and blanket."

"Maddy," Mason growled. "Don't even—"

"I'm sorry," she giggled. "I couldn't resist."

"My father was right about you."

She leaned her head back enough to look him in the eyes.

"What are you doing?" Mason asked.

"I was reading your expressions."

"Why?"

"To see what was behind the comment."

Mason nuzzled her temple, causing her breath to catch. "And what did you see?"

"That you're not mad," Maddy murmured. "That you're unsure of what's going on between us."

"You could say that again."

She started to say she was sorry, but was she really? No, Maddy Davies could only be Maddy Davies. If Mason didn't like it ....

"Have you ...?"

Mason placed his finger over her lips. "No more shop talk," he murmured.

"But ..."

"No more shop talk," Mason repeated. "Let's just enjoy the dance. Can you do that?"

"I can."

"Good."

His eyes twinkled, and before she caught her breath, the music picked up speed, and Mason swung her around. The feeling was exhilarating, and she wanted nothing more than to do it all night.

"Who taught you how to dance?"

"My mother." Mason laughed. "I was fifteen and wanted to ask someone to the homecoming dance."

"I'll have to compliment her the next time I see her."

Mason slowed a little, and his smile grew curious. "Do you know my mother?"

"Of course I do. Why?"

"I asked my brother, Rod, if he knew about Blessed Children's Home," Mason explained. "He didn't."

"Like you didn't?"

"Yes."

For the next few heartbeats, Maddy stared at the button on the top of Mason's shirt. That Scott and his wife hadn't told their family about the Home was strange.

"Does it bother you?"

"I'm not sure bother me is the right word," he sighed. "It makes me curious." Mason's dark eyes dove into hers. "Doesn't it make you wonder why?"

"Blue would say, 'We'll know when we're meant to know.'"

Mason chuckled. "That sounds like my mother."

"By the way, how is Joy?" asked Maddy. "She's visiting her mother, right?"

"Yes, Grandma Lillian. I'm not exactly sure when she'll be back."

"Scott must miss her."

"He does. He'll need to clean before mom comes home."

"That bad, huh?"

"That bad."

As the song ended, he swung her around in a couple of flashy moves. They made her breathless—or was that because she was in his arms?

"Are you hungry?" he asked on the way back to their table. "We ordered pizza."

"I could eat."

"Good."

Mason pulled out her chair and settled next to her. There was curiosity in both Tina and Darrin's eyes, and while she had questions, she let them slide. She wasn't one to look a gift horse in the mouth.

"How long have you and Tina been friends?" Darrin asked.

Maddy glanced in Tina's direction, wondering what Darrin knew about her past. Her expression was closed, making it a little more difficult to be completely honest.

"Forever," she grinned. "We met when we were seven. Tina talked me into taking a dance class with her, and I've never forgiven her."

"Dance class?" Mason repeated. "Is that where you learned to dance?"

"Hardly!"

"No?" Mason prodded.

"I had two left feet when I was seven," Maddy exclaimed.

"No, you didn't, Maddy," Tina scoffed. "You just thought you did."

Maddy glanced at Mason. "I did."

"She did not," Tina interjected again.

"Okay, okay," Maddy sighed. "Maybe not two left feet. But I wasn't nearly as graceful as this one here. Tina ended up exactly where she belongs."

"What about you two?" Tina glanced between Mason and Darrin. "How long have you known each other?"

"Since college," Darrin supplied. "We were roommates."

"And you both ended up at the BPD?" Tina smiled. "Was that planned?"

"He was always getting me in trouble," Mason grinned. "My dad warned him. Told him it's either join the force or end up in jail."

"No, he didn't," Darrin laughed. "Besides, it wasn't me who was the troublemaker. You had your fair share of escapades."

Mason put his finger on his lips. "That's our secret."

"That's really not fair," Maddy grumbled. "You don't start a story, then let it die before spilling all the good stuff."

"Maybe someday," Mason murmured.

Maddy glanced in Mason's direction to find he was watching her. What did '*Maybe someday*' mean? Did it mean he wanted to spend more time with her so she could *know* him? Or was it just a line—one of those easy, empty things people say?

The Brass Chord
January 7, 1994
11:00 p.m.

MASON LEANED BACK AND PROPPED HIS ARM ON MADDY'S CHAIR. The evening had zipped by, and a part of him didn't want it to end. But the other part couldn't help but wonder what was next.

"Would anyone like dessert?" the server appeared.

"No, thank you," both Tina and Maddy replied.

"More drinks?" their server followed up.

"Just the check," Darrin responded.

Once she walked away, the music started again, and Darrin's friend, Tom, stepped up to the microphone.

"One more slow song for the evening. Fellas, grab your girl and tell her to hold on."

"Sounds like our dance." Darrin took Tina's hand, and they disappeared into the crowd.

"Would you like to dance?" Mason whispered.

Maddy turned to answer, and she was so close he could see the silver flecks in her eyes. So close he could feel her breath every time she breathed out. So close, he could ....

"Mason?"

He forced his gaze up until their eyes met. "Yes?"

"Do you really want to dance? Or did you ask to be nice?"

"I really want to dance."

"Okay."

Mason guided her to the dance floor, and unlike the first time, she melted against him. Although he'd only known her for a week, he felt like he'd known her forever. It made no sense.

"How do you typically spend your weekends?" he asked.

"Usually at the Home. There's always something going on around there."

"Oh?"

"Yes. Tomorrow is the birthday party for one of the boys. He's turning fifteen."

Mason laughed, which made it a little tricky to explain why he'd done so.

"How about you?" Maddy followed up. "How do you spend your weekends?"

"It depends. Tomorrow, I'm going over to my parents' house."

"Are you going to help Scott clean?"

"Hardly," Mason grinned. "Although we probably should. I'm going to help my dad watch my older brother's kids. He's taking his wife to a concert."

"You're babysitting? No wonder you didn't have any issues when you were holding Tori at the hospital."

"I have a younger brother and a younger sister," he replied. "I used to help my parents with them."

"You're a good man, Mason Weaver," Maddy murmured.

A rosy tint colored her cheekbones when their eyes met, and Mason couldn't help but wonder if she'd meant to say it aloud.

"Right back at you, Maddy Davies."

Maddy snuggled a little closer, allowing him to tighten his arms even more. He rested his head against hers and couldn't believe how soft her hair felt under his jaw. It made him think thoughts he probably shouldn't be thinking. Not only was it the first time they'd been out together, but he hadn't even done the asking. Add in the situation between his father and Blue, and suddenly things felt more complicated than they should.

When the music ended, Mason reluctantly led Maddy back to the table. They found Darrin and Tina slipping into their coats, and the check already paid. Their night was ending. Was it what he wanted?

"How did you two get here?" Mason asked.

"We took the train." Maddy glanced at her watch. "In fact, I should—"

He didn't think—just reacted. "You'll ride with me."

Maddy's brows shot up in surprise. "Excuse me?"

The tone of her voice had him rephrasing his comment. "Can I see you home?"

She grinned, but before she answered, he turned to Darin. "I'm assuming Tina is riding with you?"

"She is," Darrin confirmed.

"Is that okay, Maddy?" asked Tina.

Mason caught the look Maddy exchanged with Tina and had to wonder what it meant. Although he didn't think she would make a big deal of it, especially since she didn't seem ready for the night to end either.

"It's fine, Tina. You'll be there tomorrow for the party, right?"

Tina grinned. "I wouldn't miss it."

"The birthday party?" Mason murmured.

"Yes!" laughed Maddy. "Theo has a huge crush on Tina."

"Do I need to worry?" Darrin teased.

Tina linked her arm through Darrin's and whispered something in his ear. "We'll see you later."

Mason and Maddy followed Darrin and Tina out the door. Once outside, the wind whipped around them, making him glad he'd not parked far away.

"Are you cold?" He slid his arm around Maddy's waist and waited to see if she would stiffen.

When she glanced up, her smile was shy. "Not anymore."

Somehow, her response made him feel ten feet tall.

On the way toward Maddy's apartment, Mason found his thoughts traveling to the end of the journey. He didn't plan on allowing her to go in alone. But did he offer to double-check her place or ....

"Thank you for the ride, Mason," Maddy murmured as soon as he pulled into her parking lot. "I hope it wasn't out of your way."

"Even if it were, I would have offered to bring you home," he told her when he opened her door.

"Then thank you again."

"Shall we?" Mason directed her toward the building.

"You don't—"

"I'm walking you to the damn door, Maddy," Mason grumbled.

"Okay, fine."

Her apartment was on the second floor, and habit had him cataloging the building's safety.

She unlocked her door and turned, questions flickering in her eyes. Before he could speak, Maddy went up on her toes and kissed his cheek. Just like when they'd touched earlier, the spark was there.

"I'll see you later."

She slipped inside, leaving him frozen in place.

Mason stood there for another beat, waiting for his thoughts to clear. His friend might have set up tonight, but next time, the pleasure would be all his.

ELEVEN

Blessed Children's Home
January 8, 1994
1:00 p.m.

MADDY RUSHED UP THE STEPS OF THE HOME, JUGGLING SEVERAL bags of party decorations in one hand and fifteen helium-filled balloons with the other. Just as she set the bags down, a car door slammed.

"You look like you could use some help," Mason's teasing voice came from behind her.

Her breath caught as she turned. Mason stood a few feet away, a mysterious light in his eyes—and hooked over one arm, an infant seat with a sleeping baby inside.

Multiple questions bubbled up, but a sudden gust of wind yanked at the balloons, and she decided some things could wait.

"Help would be great." With Mason holding the balloons, Maddy pushed open the door and set the bags in the hallway.

"Where do you want these?"

"Let me," she began before a little boy and Scott came from the kitchen to join them.

"I'll take those." Scott took the balloons from Mason. "You can help Maddy with the other decorations."

"And Sierra?" Mason held up the infant seat.

"Take her into the kitchen," Scott suggested. "Green and Black are in there."

"Does that work?" Mason asked Maddy.

"It does."

"Maddy." Scott put his free hand on the little boy's shoulder. "Have you met my grandson, Graham?"

"It's nice to meet you." Maddy grinned at the little boy. "Is your grandpa keeping you busy?"

Graham side-eyed his grandfather. "So far, we've just eaten cookies."

Mason started laughing. "That sounds about right. Did you save one or two for me?"

"Do you want a cookie, Uncle Mason?"

"Since I need to take Sierra into the kitchen, maybe you can show me where they keep the cookies?"

"Alright. Come on." Graham took off toward the kitchen, then, with a shrug, Mason followed.

"What's wrong, Maddy?" Scott asked. "You look a bit ... I guess confused is the only word I can come up with."

Maddy hesitated for a few minutes, uncertain if Scott knew she'd spent time with Mason the previous evening.

"I wasn't expecting so much help," she finally settled on. "It caught me off guard."

"It was a last-minute decision," Scott admitted. "I'd forgotten about the party until Mason said something."

Which answered one of her questions. If Mason had said something, he could only have gotten the information from her.

"So you packed up the car and headed over to help?" She grinned. "That sounds just like you."

His face reddened slightly. "You never said where you want the balloons."

"You can either tie them to the backs of the chairs or let them hang. Whichever is fine."

"That should be easy." Scott nodded toward the bags on the floor. "Do you need help with those?"

"I'm going to spread these out and divvy up jobs." Maddy picked up the bags. "But first, I need my helpers. Any ideas?"

"They should be down any min—" Scott's reply was cut off when it sounded like a herd of cattle running down the stairs.

"Boys, boys," Blue called over the noise. "We just had this talk."

"Sorry, Blue," the taller of the two apologized. But then he rushed toward Maddy. "Hi. Where's Tina?"

Maddy laughed. "She's not here yet, Theo. But I'm here."

"Okay." He shrugged. "Is Tina coming?"

"She's on her way. But right now, can you and Jimmy help me with these bags? Everything goes on the table. Okay?"

"Sure, Maddy."

"I'll take care of my job," Scott said, trailing after the boys.

Maddy hung her coat in the closet. When she shut the door, Blue was waiting, holding Tori's hand on one side and Abby's on the other.

"It looks like your hands are full."

Blue smiled indulgently. "You could say that again. I'm delighted you asked Scott and Mason to come help."

"I didn't ask them," Maddy admitted. "I'm just as surprised as you are."

"Really?" Blue frowned. "I thought Scott said you had."

Maddy shrugged. "I can't take the credit. It seems this one's all Mason."

Blue's smile deepened. "I'll have to thank him."

"Good idea. Now, I'd better make sure the boys haven't taken over my decorations."

"Good luck," Blue chuckled. "They've probably unpacked everything already."

Maddy stopped in the dining room's doorway. As she'd expected, Theo and Jimmy had already dumped the contents of the bags haphazardly across the table.

"Theo," Maddy jumped in before he could tear into his gift. "Is it time to open that?"

A dejected look crossed Theo's face, and his shoulders drooped. "I'm sorry, Maddy."

She smiled fondly at the boy. After three years at the Home, he'd recently been diagnosed with Asperger's Syndrome. With Blue's background in social work, and Green and Black's in special education, the Home always had room for children with special needs.

"Where does this go?" Theo asked, regarding his gift.

"For now, why don't you set it over there?" She nodded toward the sideboard. "We need to put up a table for the gifts."

"Okay. What can we do?"

"Do you think you can set the table and put the decorations on it?"

"Of course." Theo nodded. "I can even show Jimmy how."

"Come find me if you have any questions."

Maddy gathered the streamers and banner she'd purchased and had started toward the great room when Mason came out of the kitchen. He was wearing black jeans and a black cotton sweater that molded to his nicely defined chest. It looked soft enough to touch and caused her breath to stutter.

"Where do you need me?" Mason purred in his sexy baritone.

Multiple, not-so-pure thoughts raced through her head. Mason's gaze slowly drifted down her body, then back up, making her extra glad Blue hadn't followed her. The electricity in the air was palpable. If they weren't careful, they might get burned.

"Mason?" Maddy questioned. "Are you okay?"

Mason forced his attention back to her words. "Fine? Why?"

"Because for a second there, you reminded me of those boys." Maddy thumbed over her shoulder at the lanky teens. "Especially when they're playing Pokémon."

Once again, Mason's gaze drifted down Maddy's body, then slowly back up. Her leggings molded her long legs, and her sweater hit mid-hip. He took a step closer, and as he'd expected, her signature scent surrounded them.

"I was enjoying the view."

"Oh? Oh!" Maddy exclaimed. "I guess I should say thank you."

"You're welcome. Now, what can I do?"

She indicated the items spilling from her arms. "Streamers or the banner?"

"Well," he drawled. "Since both are two people's jobs, why don't we work together?"

"Together?" Maddy echoed softly. "I'd like that. Follow me."

In the great room, Maddy dumped the streamers she was holding onto a chair and handed him one end of the banner.

"We need a blank wall. This is 5' long."

Mason glanced around, and while there were several places higher up that might work, anything lower didn't give them enough room.

"What do you plan to do with the banner?"

"Why?"

"Is it just decorative," Mason clarified, "or does it have another purpose?"

"Oh! Everyone who comes to the party will sign it," Maddy explained. "Then we'll roll it up and save it for Theo."

"How about the hallway?" he suggested. "Or would you rather put it in the dining room?"

"The hallway works."

He held the banner while Maddy pressed the adhesive putty against the wall in two places. Once she made sure one side was stuck, she moved closer to work on his end. Her powdery scent tickled his senses, and for one reckless second, all he wanted was to bury his nose against her neck.

Later, he promised himself. *Later*.

"Do you think it will hold?" she whispered.

"It will until someone touches it." Mason chuckled at her expression. "Hey, sorry, but you asked."

"You could have lied," she said with a mock pout.

"I could have." He stepped closer, and when she licked her bottom lip, a bolt of heat shot straight through him. Right then, he wanted nothing more than a taste.

"Mason?"

"I'm right here."

"You are," she hummed. "But why?"

It took him a second to ferret out what she was asking ... or at least what he thought she was asking. "Why do you think?"

"I, I don't know."

Mason dropped his voice an octave. "Are you sure you don't know?"

Theo burst into the room, causing Maddy to take a step back. He felt the loss immediately and reached to pull her closer—but then he stopped. Not here. Not like this. Not now. Instead, he let her go.

"Not yet, Theo," Maddy pointed to the sign. "But we hung up your banner. What do you think?"

Theo studied the banner, tilting his head one way, and then the other. "I like it. Can I sign it?"

"Well, Theo," Maddy whispered. "You *could*. But usually, it's just the guests who sign. And you're—"

"—The birthday boy." He wrinkled his nose. "I don't like being the birthday boy."

"No?" Mason grinned. "Would you rather be the birthday man?"

"No," Theo laughed. "I'm the birthday King."

"The King, huh?" Maddy murmured. "Why the King?"

"Because then everyone has to listen to me," Theo glanced from one to the other. "Right?"

"Well, Theo," Maddy responded. "You might have to discuss that idea with Blue."

Theo frowned. "I'll think about it."

"For now, though," Maddy changed the direction of the conversation. "We need to finish the decorations. Are you coming, Mason?"

"Do you want me to come?" he asked in a voice that sounded huskier than he'd anticipated.

Maddy lifted a brow. "What do you think?"

"I'm asking, Maddy."

"Hurry up, Mason," Theo giggled. "We need to finish before the guests arrive."

"Yeah, Mason," Maddy laughed. "Hurry up."

Knowing that was the best he was going to get right then, Mason helped Maddy and Theo with the streamers. Once more, he was presented with a different side of her. One that showed her patient, playful, completely in her element with the kids. It stirred something in him he couldn't quite name.

They'd just finished when the doorbell rang, and Theo's face lit up.

"Do you think it's Tina?"

"Maybe so," Maddy replied. "Do you want to go see?"

"Okay!" He shoved the wrappers he'd been gathering into Mason's arms and scurried off.

Maddy laughed. "Would you like me to take those?"

"Either that or tell me where the trash goes."

Before Maddy could respond, Theo came back into the front room, followed by Tina … and Darrin.

"This place looks great," Tina exclaimed. "I'm sorry I didn't make it earlier. But we …" Her voice faded, and the look she exchanged with Maddy had him curious.

"We're not completely done." Mason nodded toward the wrappers. "There's still trash detail."

"I'll take it!" Theo jumped in. "Tina, do you want to help?"

She glanced back and forth between Maddy and Darrin before giving Theo her attention. "I would love to help."

Mason watched several expressions cross Maddy's face. Her attention wasn't on Tina or Darrin—it was on Theo. Protective, maybe even a little anxious. It had him wondering what he'd missed.

Blessed Children's Home
January 8, 1994
4:00 p.m.

WITH THE PARTY IN FULL SWING, MADDY LEANED AGAINST THE wall and watched the boys play Twister. Theo was the tallest of the bunch, but he wasn't as flexible. Something that proved to be his downfall in a couple of games. The first time, he'd laughed it off. The second, he'd become frustrated. She held her breath, bracing for a potential outburst. Then, one boy fell over, and the moment passed.

"Punch?" Mason held out a cup.

Her gaze drifted up from the cup to meet his dark eyes. He was watching her closely, and his expression reminded her of their interrupted conversation.

"Thanks. Didn't you want one?"

"I'm good." Mason nodded toward the empty spot on the other side of her. "Is that reserved for someone?"

"You."

Mason's eyes twinkled. "That's the right answer."

"Then why'd you ask?"

"I thought I'd be nice. But I'm glad you gave me the answer I wanted."

Maddy side-eyed him. A part of her wanted to pick up on the conversation from earlier.

"I'm right here."

"You are. But why?"

"Why do you think?"

"I, I don't know."

"Are you sure you don't know?"

She knew what she wanted him to say. But after last night, she didn't want to assume.

"Are you okay?" he surprised her by asking.

"Fine. Why?"

Mason nodded toward the rowdy game. "You looked worried earlier."

"Theo has difficulty reading social cues." She let the previous conversation go for the time being. "He's come a long way, but he can get territorial. Especially where Tina's concerned."

"And you were afraid Darrin would trigger something?"

"A little." Maddy glanced across the room to see Darrin playing a game with Graham, then to Tina, in charge of the Twister spinner. "It seems the potential crisis has been averted ... for now, anyway."

"Did you talk to Tina?"

"Yes."

"What did she say to calm you down?"

"She introduced Darrin as a 'friend.'" Maddy grinned. "So far, everyone looks to be having fun."

"They do," Mason agreed.

"Where's Scott?"

"Last I saw, he was on the floor with Tori and the other little girl."

"Abby," Maddy offered.

"The girls were chattering. Sounded like an interesting conversation."

Without thinking, Maddy playfully backhanded Mason in the stomach. "Hey, be nice."

He caught her hand and brushed his thumb across the outside of hers. His touch sent tingles racing up her arm and threatened to bring back those impure thoughts she'd been having earlier.

"Did you figure out why I'm here?" Mason whispered in his husky baritone.

"Buh-Because your father wanted to come?"

"He did." Mason leaned in. "*After* I reminded him."

"Why?"

Mason's gaze drifted around her face, his gaze full of heat.

"You, Maddy. I'm here for you."

His raw honesty sent a shiver straight up her spine, waking her goosebumps.

"There you go again," she murmured. "Starting something that has to stop before it gets to the good parts."

"I'm sorry."

The not-so-contrite look on Mason's face made Maddy laugh. That it lessened some of the tension building between them was both a blessing and a curse.

"Your expression says you really aren't sorry."

"I'm sorry it has to stop. I don't want you to feel uncomfortable."

"And you're not?"

The pink tint on his face told her he'd realized what he'd said. He adjusted his stance, making her press her lips together to keep from laughing.

"I can see that twitch."

"Twitch?" Maddy widened her eyes. "Where?"

"Here." Mason touched her bottom lip, right in the center. It was only a fleeting moment, but one that left a lasting impression on her mouth.

"I'm sorry."

"No, you're not." Mason plucked the empty cup from her hands. "I'm going to get something cold to drink."

"Okay."

"Do you want anything?"

Maddy studied his expression. Everything felt surreal. She'd had parties at the Home when she was young. Yet, she'd never flirted with a man the same way she was flirting with Mason. What was it about him that made her feel shy one minute, then want to jump into his arms the next?

"That's it." Mason nodded toward where he was standing. "Just remember, that's my space."

When he walked away, something told her she was wearing a bemused expression. Before she could give it much thought, she saw Graham heading her way.

"Did you win?" she asked when he reached her side.

"I did," Graham exclaimed. "Do you know where Uncle Mason went?"

He went to cool off.

Which Graham wouldn't understand, but if he repeated it, well ....

"I'm not sure, Graham," Maddy answered. "Did you need him for something?"

"I wanted him to play Trouble with me," he murmured. "But ... do you want to play instead?"

Maddy laughed at the mischievous smile on the little boy's face. She'd seen the same look on his Uncle Mason's.

"I've not played Trouble in a long time. If I play, you might have to tell me the rules again."

"Okay." Graham grabbed her hand and started across the room. "What color do you want?"

"What are my choices?"

"Yellow, Red, or Green."

"There are only three colors?" Maddy grinned. "I could have sworn there were more."

"Well," he shrugged. "There are four, but I'm blue. It's my lucky color."

"Then, by all means, you should be blue. Which one do you think I should use?"

Graham rested his chin on his hand for several minutes and studied the board. "I think you should be yellow."

"Yellow, it is. Now what?"

He handed her the yellow pieces. "Now, put them ..."

TWELVE

Blessed Children's Home
January 8, 1994
5:30 p.m.

WITH MADDY BUSY, MASON WANDERED DOWN A NARROW hallway leading to a door and out onto a covered patio. Even though he didn't have his jacket, the view had him stepping outside.

There was a large tree with a tire swing hanging from a branch. Off to one side was a fire pit anchored by a couple of benches and, just beyond, a double swing for adults. It was quiet, calming even.

He'd turned to go back inside when the door opened, and Sister Blue stepped out. Her expression made him feel like he was fifteen and wanted approval from his girlfriend's mother.

"Was it too noisy in there?" Blue asked.

"Not really. Once I looked out the door, I had to get closer."

"Most of the time, it is peaceful out here." Blue turned on the outdoor heater in deference to the winter day. "It usually only takes a few minutes."

"That's handy."

Blue chuckled. "It is, and quite the indulgence."

"But allows you to enjoy the patio year-round."

"It does."

"Why do you think my dad never shared this with his children?" he blurted.

"Did you ask him?"

"I did. He didn't give a direct answer."

Blue sighed. It was a weighted sound, making him even more curious.

"While I don't know for sure," she murmured. "I've always thought he was trying to atone for something."

"Atone for something? Like what?"

"I don't know." Blue hesitated a second, then came back with, "He's not said anything. My thoughts are based on observations of his behavior through the years."

"Maddy was the first child he brought here, wasn't she?"

"She was. Even then, she had those mesmerizing blue eyes."

That was the first thing he'd noticed, but he kept that piece of information to himself.

"Since then," Blue went on. "Your father makes it a point to stop by once or twice a week. He even built the fire pit."

"My dad built the fire pit?" Mason asked in disbelief. "My mother has a hard time getting him to do those types of things at their house."

"See what I mean," Blue murmured. "When it comes to the Home, he puts himself out there."

"I wonder if my mother knows."

"She does."

Mason thought about pursuing the topic, but at the last minute, let it go. It left him waiting. For what, he wasn't sure.

"Thank you for coming today. Maddy told me you were responsible for the extra hands."

"It was nothing. I wanted ... I mean, my dad jumped at the chance. Probably because he knew it would keep Graham entertained."

"Maddy enjoyed seeing you, too," Blue grinned. "She's a wonderful person. Sometimes, though, she gets a little zealous."

Mason barked out a laugh. "My father says she's reckless, with a heart of gold."

"That she is," Blue agreed. "But if not treated with care, even gold can bruise."

There it was, the warning he'd expected from his father that hadn't come —or at least, it hadn't come yet.

"I …" he barely got out before Blue turned her dark eyes in his direction. "Take care of her, Mason. Now, if you'll excuse me, I should check on the chaos. Just turn off the heater when you come inside."

Mason took a deep breath and tried to make sense of what she'd said. He'd been given a warning—something he understood. Blue's other statement, though, he wasn't sure of its meaning. Had he been given her blessing?

The door opened again, and without turning around, he knew who it was.

"Did you win?"

Maddy chuckled. "No, Graham won."

"Did you cheat so he could win?"

"Who, me?" She leaned on the railing. "Did you get the talk?"

"The talk?"

Maddy took a step closer to him. She'd not worn her coat, but had her arms around her waist, trying to keep warm. Mason didn't ask, but cupped her elbows and pulled her against his chest.

"You're so warm."

And getting warmer by the minute.

"The talk," Maddy repeated. "The one we discussed last night."

"She didn't tell me to leave you alone. Mainly, we talked about my father."

"Scott? Why?"

"I asked her why he hadn't told his children about this place."

Maddy tilted her head back until their gazes met. The position was almost too tempting.

"What did she say?"

"Blue doesn't know for sure."

"But knowing Blue, she has an idea."

"Atonement."

"For?"

"No clue."

"Maybe someday." Maddy's words reminded him he'd said the same to her the night before.

"Yes, maybe someday. Right now, though, there's something else I want."

"Something else you want?"

"Yes."

Maddy licked her lips, and her gaze dropped to his mouth, then back up. "What is it you want, Mason?"

"I want …" Mason leaned down to where his lips hovered just above hers. He wanted to kiss her. Had wanted to kiss her for a few days. His heart raced and an almost giddy feeling rushed up inside.

Maddy's eyes drifted shut as he narrowed the distance between them. He was so close he could feel her breath. So close he could count her eyelashes. Right before their lips touched, a loud sound caused Maddy to jump backward.

"Uncle Mason!" Graham burst through the door, as only a five-year-old can do. "It's time for cake."

Mason clenched his jaw to keep from rattling off a string of words he shouldn't say in the presence of a child or a lady. He gave Maddy another look meant to mean, '*Later*,' and turned his attention to his nephew.

"It's cake time?"

"It is." Graham nodded vigorously. "Grandpa sent me to find you."

"Oh, he did, did he?" Mason grumbled. "What did he promise you?"

Graham dimpled. "A bite of his cake. Come on."

"Wasn't that what you wanted, Mason?" Maddy teased. "A piece of cake?"

"I wanted something sweet, alright, and it wasn't cake."

"Maddy, do you want cake too?" Graham asked.

"That works … for now." On her way inside, Maddy brushed by close enough that he could feel her heat. He barely had time to turn the heater off before she disappeared around a corner, leaving him to follow.

Blessed Children's Home
January 8, 1994
6:30 p.m.

MADDY WAS ON HER WAY TO FIND MASON WHEN TINA PULLED HER aside.

"Spill."

"Spill?"

Tina rolled her eyes. "You know exactly what I'm talking about, Maddy Davies. What's the deal with you and Mason?"

"We're ..." Maddy paused, searching for the right word. "Flirting."

"Yeah, I caught some of the flirting," Tina smirked. "The temperature in the room went up several notches."

Maddy fanned herself. "Tell me about it. I didn't even recognize myself."

"Did you invite him in last night?"

"No."

"No? Why not?"

"Being with him at the club was easy. But I think I was waiting for some sort of sign."

"A sign from him? You know, some guys need to be hit over the head."

"Oh, I know. Because of who we are, though, there's extra pressure. We both feel it. I just needed to know he was interested in me—*because* of me."

"And not because of the case?" Tina guessed.

"Yes."

"What about today?"

Maddy giggled. "Today, he was here for me."

"I told you he was interested," Tina reminded her. "Now, go—before he gets away."

"What about you and Darrin?" Maddy turned the tables. "It seems like you two are getting along well."

"So well, it scares me," Tina whispered.

"Take it slowly. I don't want you to get hurt."

"I don't want me to get hurt either," Tina sighed. "And believe me, I'm trying to take it slowly, and then ..."

"He looks at you in a certain way, and you want to jump him."

Tina laughed. "I see we're back to talking about you and Mason."

"Sorry." Maddy gave Tina a sheepish smile.

"No problem. But I think Darrin and I are going to take off now."

"I'm glad you came."

"You know I wouldn't miss one of Green's birthday cakes," Tina replied. "I'll talk to you later."

They walked into the front room, and Maddy handed Tina and Darrin their coats. That Mason wasn't there to say goodbye surprised her.

"Looking for Mason?" Darrin grinned.

Maddy felt the heat climbing. "I thought …"

Darrin nodded toward the library. "He's in there."

"Okay, thanks."

"Go get him." Darrin winked.

She closed the door behind them and started toward the library. Her knees grew weak, forcing her to grab hold of the door frame as tears rushed to her eyes.

Mason was sitting in a chair with Tori on his lap. He was holding a book, and every time he turned a page, the little girl would show him something, to which he patiently answered. Maddy sighed, and her heart did a little flip.

"Watching them reminds you of when Scott used to visit, doesn't it?" Blue joined her.

"I don't remember those times," Maddy murmured. "I just know what I've been told."

"Scott used to stop by weekly and read to you. I was almost envious of your relationship with him."

Maddy frowned. "Why?"

A melancholy smile crossed Blue's face. "When my father left for Vietnam, I was a teen. For several years after that, Scott became the 'father figure' in my life. It hurt when we lost touch."

"Does he know that?"

Blue side-eyed her. "What do you think?"

"No," Maddy murmured. "You kept it inside."

"It was a long time ago."

"What was a long time ago?" Scott joined them, carrying Sierra's infant seat.

"Nothing important," Blue responded a little too quickly. "I see you pried Sierra away from Green."

"It was difficult, but I did it." Scott nodded toward where Graham was dancing with Theo and Jimmy. "Someone is going to sleep well tonight. I thank you for that."

"You know you're always welcome here, Scott," Blue smiled. "Let me take Tori from Mason, and you can go."

"Did you get extra cake to take home?" Blue asked.

"Extra cake?" Scott's attention went to Maddy. "Would—?"

"I'll get it."

"You might want to get some for Mason, too," Scott called. "Then I don't have to share."

"What about Graham?" Maddy questioned. "Do you think he'll want more?"

"If he doesn't, I'll eat it." Scott winked. "Thank you."

Maddy left the older adults and went looking for Scott's extra cake. She found a bag on the counter with his name on it, and when she peered inside, there were three foil wrappings.

"Did you find what you needed, Maddy dear?" Green asked, wiping her hands on a dishtowel. "Do I need to cut a piece for you as well?"

"An extra piece of cake would be great." Maddy smiled. "I'll have it for breakfast."

Green wrinkled her nose. "That's no breakfast, Maddy. Remember, it's the most important meal of the day."

Maddy laughed. "So you've said more than once."

"And I'm not about to change my mind, either. Go on and take that to Scott. When you get back, I'll have yours ready to go."

"Thanks, Green."

Maddy returned to the front room in time to see Scott putting on his coat. Mason and Graham were already wearing theirs.

"It was nice seeing you again, Maddy." Scott buzzed her cheek. "You take care of yourself."

"Bye, now."

"Bye, Maddy," Graham yelled. "See you soon." He tugged on Mason's hand. "Come on. Let's go."

Her eyes met Mason's, and his look of frustration said they were thinking the same thing. However, with the little boy ready to go, there wasn't much he could do about it.

Mason handed the child his keys. "Can you unlock the doors for me? I'll be right there."

Graham's eyes grew wide. He grabbed the keys and took off.

"That was awfully brave of you."

"Probably."

"Thank you for coming today. It was a nice surprise."

"It was *my* pleasure." Mason glanced over his shoulder. When he turned back around, there was an expression on his face she couldn't interpret.

"Night, Maddy. I'll be in touch." Then, just as she had the night before, he kissed her cheek.

Long after she'd closed the door behind him, her face continued to tingle from where his lips had touched. It was an exhilarating experience, and one she knew she'd never forget.

Scott & Joy Weaver's Home
January 8, 1994
9:00 p.m.

MASON CLOSED THE '*I Spy*' BOOK AND SET IT ON THE NIGHTSTAND. He tossed Graham his stuffed dog and adjusted the pillows before tucking in the blankets.

"Uncle Mason, can I ask you something?"

Considering it had only been a week since his nephew had asked him if he was thinking about a girl, a slight feeling of discomfort settled in the pit of Mason's stomach. He was tempted to say no, but he couldn't do that to the little boy.

"Sure. What is it?"

"Why do those kids live at the Home?"

For a second, Mason wished he'd chosen to put Sierra to bed. However, since he hadn't, he needed to come up with an answer that didn't generate more questions.

"For a variety of reasons."

"Like what?" Graham came back.

"Most of the kids who live there don't have parents they can live with."

"Why can't they live with their parents?"

Mason blew out a breath. "Sometimes their parents can't take care of them, and they have nowhere else to live."

"You mean they don't have a grandpa or grandma they can stay with?"

"Or an aunt or uncle," Mason added.

"Oh." Graham paused, and his frown said he was mulling something over. "Maddy told me she used to live there. Did you know that?"

"I did. Do you know why she had to live there?"

"I do," Graham murmured. "It's 'cause her mommy and daddy are up in heaven."

"That's right. Did she tell you anything else?"

He might have asked for personal reasons, but he told himself it was just curiosity about how open Maddy had been with his nephew.

"Maddy said Grandpa took her there. That was nice of him, wasn't it?"

"Very nice," Mason agreed. "Now, you really—"

"One more," Graham jumped in.

"Go on."

"Do you like Maddy?"

Mason pressed his lips together and wondered who he'd heard talking.

"Maddy is very nice."

"No, Uncle Mason," Graham prodded. "Do you *like* her?"

"Do I *like* her?"

"Yeah. Like mommy and daddy. Are you going to marry her and live in the same house?"

An image of Maddy's face, as he bent toward her, bloomed in his head. He'd not even kissed her. Yet, the idea of living in the same house with her wasn't like a punch in the gut.

"Maddy and I just met. I think we have a way to go before we consider those things."

"Okay. But when you decide, will you tell me?"

"I'll do my best," was the only answer he could give right then. "Now, you need to go to bed. Is there anything else?"

"My music."

Mason started the CD player and, with a Mozart concerto playing softly, left Graham and wandered downstairs. He found his father in the kitchen with his piece of cake and a glass of milk.

"Yours is over there." Scott pointed toward the counter next to the refrigerator. "And you know where the milk's kept."

It took Mason a handful of seconds to decide he wanted milk and cake. Then, another few minutes before, he sat down. He'd just taken his first bite when his father leaned his crossed arms on the table.

Here it comes, Mason thought. *The conversation he'd been expecting.*

"You like Maddy, don't you?"

"Maddy is a nice person."

"You know that's not what I'm asking."

Mason chuckled. "You don't need to tell me not to hurt her. Blue already took care of that."

"She told me." Scott grinned. "I know you'll heed her advice."

A part of Mason considered reminding his father he was no longer fifteen. But the other part wanted to hear more.

While contemplating his next move, he took a bite of cake and chewed it slowly, followed by a drink of milk. He could tell his father was getting antsy, but surprisingly, he remained quiet.

Finally, once he'd finished his snack, Mason pushed aside his plate and mimicked his father's position.

"Maddy and I talked about this."

Scott's brows rose. "You talked about what?"

"The pressure."

"Go on."

Mason studied the crumbs on his plate for a beat, then came back with, "There's been a connection between Maddy and me since we first spoke. But I tried to ignore it."

"Yet, it was impossible, because she was always there," Scott guessed.

"In a way," Mason conceded. "It's more likely I kept putting myself in front of her."

"When did the conversation about pressure happen?"

"Darrin and Tina set us up." Mason let go of a light laugh. "But I'm glad they did. It was the push I needed."

"Has she done anything reckless lately?" Scott murmured. "At least reckless, so she needed to be rescued."

Mason skipped right over the trip to see the hairdresser and briefly touched on asking her to help with Natalie.

"I really don't think she has any information that could lead her to danger. She's been looking for Tori's family, but she could only go so far. And Natalie didn't have any information. The only thing Maddy has said about the case lately is to ask when she can pack up Alisha's things."

"Who owns the house?"

"The tax records say Frank and Beatrice Kennedy," Mason imparted. "They're both dead."

"Who pays the taxes?" Scott came back with the expected question.

"Their estate."

Scott's brows went up in surprise. "How did Alisha end up there?"

"That's what we're trying to figure out. We have an appointment with the bank manager next week."

"Did you ask Blue about the house? Maybe she's heard of the family."

"It's worth a try. I'll do that next week."

"What about the jacket you found in the park?" Scott brought back their latest piece of evidence. "Is it from your crime scene?"

"Results on the blood should be in on Monday."

"Go on," Scott prodded. "Tell me about the scene."

Mason grinned. "The jacket was found …"

THIRTEEN

Blessed Children's Home
January 10, 1994
9:00 a.m.

Maddy stepped off the train and automatically scanned the station. Since that man had stepped in front of her the previous week, she'd tried to be more aware of her surroundings. Once she was sure no one was nearby who shouldn't be, she started toward the Home. The wind whipped around her, causing her to duck her head and pull her scarf a little higher.

She turned onto Mill Street and rushed toward the sprawling old Victorian. It wasn't until she was halfway up the sidewalk she noticed someone was waiting on the porch.

A chill raced up her spine, and the words, '*He found me*' reared up. Maddy's breath caught. Then, the person looked over their shoulder, and she relaxed.

"Natalie?" she called when she was close enough. "How long have you been waiting out here?"

"Not long." Natalie's expression had Maddy running up the stairs to unlock the door.

"Go on," she encouraged. "It's freezing out here."

"Thank you."

Maddy hung Natalie's coat on a hook and led the way into the kitchen, where they were treated to coffee and cinnamon rolls.

"Do you want to sit in here? Or do you want to go to my office?"

"Your office, please."

"Then right this way."

Once inside her office, Maddy set her large bag on the floor behind her desk and directed Natalie to a small table. She waited for a few minutes, and then tossed out a softball question.

"Did Blue help you find someone to watch Lucas?"

A smile flitted across Natalie's face. "She did. Mrs. McMurtry has been very helpful.

"Blue said she lives in your building."

"The third floor," Natalie grinned. "It makes it very easy."

Maddy paused for a moment before continuing, "I'm glad to hear that. How's school going?"

"Good."

"What are you studying?"

"Teaching." Natalie's dark eyes sparkled when she said the word. "I really want to teach elementary school."

"That takes a lot of patience."

"It does. But I've wanted to be a teacher forever."

"Do you want to stay in this area once you graduate?"

"Maybe." Natalie hesitated. "Sometimes I want to flip a coin and see where it lands on the map. Other times, I want to move to a small town where 'everyone knows your name.'"

"Usually, those places come with an 'everyone knows your business' as well. Do you really think you could be happy in a small town after living in Boston?"

"I just want to find a place that feels like home. Does that make any sense?"

"I know exactly what you mean." Maddy took a breath. She didn't want to push Natalie. However, she wasn't patient enough to wait much longer to find out the reason behind the visit. "Did you come by the Home to see Tori?"

"I would like to see Tori," Natalie murmured, "but in a minute."

"Is there something I can do to help?"

"I saw him."

"You saw him? Natalie, who did you see? Was it Brian Lloyd?"

"Brian Llo—?" Natalie began, only to stop. "Not him. The one Detective Weaver mentioned." She reached into her bag and laid a piece of paper on the table. "Him."

Maddy unfolded the dirty, ripped piece of paper that looked like someone had stepped on it multiple times. On it was an artist's sketch of a man, and underneath the words.

Have you seen this man? His name is Parker Turner, and he's wanted for questioning.

"You told the detective you'd heard his name. Did you mean you'd seen him before?"

"No," Natalie denied. "I wasn't lying."

"Go on."

"I was on the train yesterday, and two girls were sitting behind me. They were talking about a party on Saturday evening. One of them said, 'Did you see what Parker Turner left?' Then the other one said, 'I heard about it, but I missed the party. My folks wouldn't let me go.'"

"Did they ever say what this Parker Turner 'left' for them?"

"No."

"Where did you find this poster?"

"Franklin Park."

Maddy remembered Mason telling her they were looking to question Parker. She also recalled him saying they'd distributed flyers, but so far, nothing had come of it.

"Was it hanging on a building?" She pushed for more information.

"It was on the ground," Natalie admitted. "Almost as if someone had dropped it when walking through the park."

"You didn't see anymore?"

"No."

"So, you heard these girls talking about the party?" Maddy organized the information in her head. "Then you walked through Franklin Park and saw this man?"

"Yes."

"Was he also in Franklin Park?"

"He was standing next to the pond."

"What caused you to notice him?"

"I'm not sure. He looked sad, though."

Which didn't fit Mason's idea of Parker being a killer. Unless he was sad because he wasn't as free to come and go.

"There's more, isn't there?"

"Yes." Natalie took a breath, and when she started speaking, her voice shook with emotion. "Remember, I told the detective Alisha had acted weird one day when we were shopping?"

"Yes." Maddy nodded. "You said she kept looking behind her."

"I thought her ex-boyfriend was following us," Natalie replied. "Now, I know I was wrong."

"How so?"

"It wasn't her ex-boyfriend who was behind us. It was this guy." She tapped the page. "I saw him while we were shopping but thought nothing of it."

"Why didn't you call Detective Weaver?"

Natalie dropped her head and played with her cinnamon roll crumbs for several seconds. "I thought maybe you could talk to him for me. Will you? Please. Will you talk to him for me?"

Maddy nibbled her lip for a second, then came back with an option. "If I tell him, but he needs more information from you, will you talk to him? It can even be here in my office."

"Okay," Natalie agreed, albeit reluctantly. "I can do that."

"I'm sure Mason appreciates your help." Maddy took a last drink of her coffee and pushed back her chair. "Would you like to visit with Tori before you leave?"

"Yes, please."

"Then, let's go."

Forest Hills High School
January 10, 1994
11:45 a.m.

MASON PINCHED THE BRIDGE OF HIS NOSE. THE MORNING WASN'T even over, yet it had already been hectic. They'd met with the bank president, hoping to find out who owned the home on Peach Street. What they'd discovered would fit on the top half of a piece of paper. Nothing that helped them find out how Alisha ended up living in the house. The only thing of value they had was the name of the law firm that managed the estate.

Cook and Sons was in downtown Boston, and the senior partner, Darrel Cook, was meeting with them later in the week.

From there, they'd stopped by the crime lab to pick up the report on the jacket. As he'd expected, the blood was from the 15 Peach Street crime scene and the same three individuals. Two females—Alisha and Maddy, and a male, yet unknown.

That information brought them to where they were now. At Forest Hills High School to speak with the principal, and the teachers who'd found the jacket on Friday.

"Think this is going to be a waste?" Darrin asked once they'd parked.

"I'm not sure," Mason sighed. "I wish I would have looked to see where Parker was spotted last week."

"Near Franklin Park."

"I know. I mean, *where*? Was it on this side of the park or the other?"

"You're trying to decide if Parker ran straight toward the park from Peach Street, aren't you?"

"I am."

"How far from Forest Hills High was the jacket found?"

Mason glanced at the notes he'd gotten from Rod.

"About half a mile."

"That's not far."

"Not far at all. Ready to go back to school?"

"Not even a little," Darrin grunted. "I was fine the first time around. There is no way I'd want to do it again."

They ran up the steps to the building and then went straight to the office.

"Principal Stan Marsh," a man about his father's age, introduced himself.

"Detectives Mason Weaver and Darrin Anderson." Mason pointed to himself, then to his partner. "We'll try not to take up much of your time, Mr. Marsh."

The principal assessed them for a few seconds, his steely gray eyes curious. "Is this about the party this weekend?"

"The party?" Mason frowned. "What party?"

"There was a party at one of the football player's homes this weekend," Mr. Marsh explained. "He's in the hospital."

"Drugs?" As soon as he'd heard about the party, Mason started connecting a few dots.

"I'm afraid so," Mr. Marsh replied.

"Was there only one individual sent to the hospital?" Darrin followed up.

"If there were more, I've not heard," Mr. Marsh stated.

"What type of drug was it?" Mason questioned. "Was it ecstasy?"

The principal frowned. "How did you know?"

"It's happened before," Mason explained. "Did the parent find any of the drugs?"

"He did." Mr. Marsh opened his top drawer and tossed a small bag across the desk. "Said he found it next to where his son had passed out."

"Before we leave, we'd like the information to contact the parent," said Mason. "I'd like to know where the pills came from."

"I'll have it ready for you," Mr. Marsh assured them.

Mason took one look at the bag with the blue pill inside and knew it matched the other one they had. Just like those, the stamp was smeared.

"If this isn't about the party, then what's it about?" Mr. Marsh brought them back to the reason for their visit.

"Gerry Hines and Trina Smith were in the park on Friday and found evidence from a crime in Dorchester," Mason briefly explained. "We just have a few questions."

"Alright," Mr. Marsh nodded. "They're on their lunch period right now. Do you want me to have them brought to the office?"

"Actually," Mason came back with another option. "Would it be alright if we talk to them in their classrooms?"

"Certainly." Mr. Marsh pushed his chair back. "Let me take you there."

"Thank you."

They followed the principal down the hallway. When they passed a trophy cabinet, Mason's attention landed on a red baseball cap, complete with the letter F.

"Mr. Marsh." Mason pointed toward the cap. "Does the F stand for Forest Hills?"

"It does," Mr. Marsh nodded. "I'm afraid it's not very original."

"Meaning?"

"The employees at Franklin Park Zoo wear those caps. As do the kids at Fenway High, a little league baseball team or two, and—"

"—Froggy Pond," Mason grumbled.

"Can I ask why you're interested in the hat?" Mr. Marsh questioned.

"No real reason, sir," Mason denied. "I was just curious."

"Oh, okay." Mr. Marsh glanced from him to Darrin and back. "If you're ready, shall we?"

They continued until they reached a fork in the hallway. "Mr. Hines's room is to the left. Ms. Smith's to the right. Which would you like to speak to first?"

"We'll separate," Mason responded. "I'll go this way."

Darrin and Mr. Marsh went right. Mason took the left hallway and began looking for 123. He found it at the far end. When he peered through the small window, he could see the teacher was alone.

Mason opened the door, causing the teacher to jump. "Gerry Hines?"

"Yes, who's asking?"

"I'm Detective Weaver. I have a few questions about your walk on Friday."

Gerry Hines sighed. "Come on in."

Mason let the door close behind him. Hines was in his mid-50s and had taught for thirty years. He had brown hair, blue eyes, and was in good shape.

"You took a walk in Franklin Park on Friday, right?"

"Yes."

"While you were walking, did you see anyone else?"

Gerry shrugged. "I think we saw a maintenance man or two."

"That's it?"

"Yes."

Mason took out a copy of a Franklin Park map and handed it to the teacher. "Can you show me where you walked?"

Blessed Children's Home
January 10, 1994
1:00 p.m.

Since she'd said goodbye to Natalie, Maddy hadn't been able to get the visit out of her head. She'd tried for several hours before giving up and pressing the paper flat on her desk. This time, though, she focused on the man.

The drawing was rough, which was probably the reason he hadn't been caught. His face was too generic, his clothing too typical. However, the longer she stared at his image, the more familiar he looked. Why was that? Was it because she'd seen him somewhere? Or was it because she'd been looking at the picture for so long?

Her phone rang before she could decide which answer fit best.

"Hello, this is Maddy Davies."

"Well, hello, Maddy Davies." Mason's smooth baritone came across the line. "Are you busy?"

"No." He was quiet for a handful of seconds, but she could hear road sounds and had to wonder why he'd called. "Where are you?"

"You don't think I'm sitting at my desk?"

"No, Mason, you aren't sitting at your desk. It sounds like you're outside."

"Very good, Miss Davies," he purred. "Darrin and I are following up on a few things."

"And you decided you needed to talk to me?"

"I wanted to ask you a question."

Maddy's heart rate took off, and her hand started to shake.

"What?"

"I know it's short notice, but what are you doing tonight?"

"Tonight?"

"Yes, tonight. Darrin and I bowl in a league on Monday nights, and he told me Tina was coming."

A part of her wanted to tell him she was busy. To let him know she wasn't sitting around waiting for him to call. However, on the other hand, who was she kidding? Especially when she wanted to see him.

"Are you afraid of being the third wheel?" Maddy teased.

"It has nothing to do with being the third wheel, Maddy. I really do want to see you again. But just so you know, I *will* take you home."

"Oh?"

"And I *will* walk you to your door."

"You will?" Her heart jumped into her throat, causing her voice to be breathy and almost made her light-headed.

"And this time," Mason went on. "There *will* be no interruptions when I kiss you goodnight."

"Oh?"

Mason chuckled. "Is that all you can say?"

"Sorry. I'm ..." Her gaze landed on the flyer. She should say something. "Mason, I—" was all she got out when his radio went off.

"I need to go now, honey. I hope to see you later." Then the phone went dead.

Maddy slowly hung up and debated with herself for a second before picking up the phone and calling her friend.

"Tina," she exclaimed before saying hello. "I understand you're going to watch Darrin bowl tonight."

"I am, and I have instructions to bring you."

"Mason just called."

"Did you say yes?"

"No."

"What? Why not?"

"Should I go?"

"Well, duh? Don't you want to see him?"

"That's a given."

"Then what's the deal?"

"I don't want him to think I'm sitting around waiting for him," Maddy huffed.

Tina laughed. "But aren't you?"

"No!"

"This is the first time Darrin has asked me. Does that help?"

"This is the first non-holiday Monday in January," Maddy pointed out. "That doesn't work."

"Normally, it's just the guys. But since I don't teach on Monday nights,

Darrin invited me. Then he called a few minutes ago and told me to bring you. Come on, Maddy. It will be fun."

"Watching them bowl?"

"Oh, yeah," Tina hummed. "We can stare at their butts when they bend over to throw the ball."

"That is true," Maddy conceded.

"See, you really want to go. Shall I meet you at the train station?"

As soon as Tina uttered those words, flashes of something floated by. But it wouldn't coalesce enough for her to figure out what it was.

"Maddy? Do you want to meet me at the train station?"

Maddy debated with herself for half a second, before she surrendered. "Okay. I'll meet you at the train station."

"Great! I'll see you then."

Maddy hung up, and once more, her attention went to the drawing of the man.

"Then you walked through Franklin Park and saw this man?"

"Yes."

"Was he also in Franklin Park?"

"He was standing next to the pond."

A memory of getting off the train when she'd returned from Faneuil Hall formed. She was on her way toward the exit when a man stepped in front of her.

"Excuse me."

He'd unsettled her, but she couldn't put her finger on why that had been so.

"Excuse me."

Maddy pulled the poster closer and pressed it flat. This time, she focused only on the man's eyes.

"Excuse me."

It was him. Parker Turner had tried to talk to her at the train station. How had he known where she was? Did that mean he'd been following her? Since the incident, she'd been more vigilant. Besides that one time, nothing had seemed out of the ordinary. No one had seemed out of place.

"I got off the train ..."

Which train?

Maddy took out a subway map and traced the green line first and then the orange line. Both lines ran through Franklin Park, but which one had she taken?

Where had Natalie been going? She hadn't asked. Nor had the destination been offered.

What time of day was it? Another question that needed an answer.

Maddy wanted to give Mason as much information as possible. With those questions in mind, she picked up the phone.

FOURTEEN

Franklin Park
January 10, 1994
2:00 p.m.

WHEN THEY COMPARED THE TEACHERS' STORIES, THE discrepancies were minimal. However, the more he thought about what they'd said, the more curious Mason became. He wanted to put himself in their shoes.

Not that he *just* wanted to walk into Franklin Park from Forest Hills High. He also wanted to know about the assailant's trail the night of the murder. Did those two paths cross? If so, where?

In order to track those, they needed copies of reports they'd left back in the South Boston Precinct. That had them taking a shortcut and dropping in on his brother, who worked in Dorchester. With that taken care of, they drove back to Forest Hills High and spread the map of Franklin Park on the hood of the car.

"What do you think?" Mason asked Darrin. "Do you think the paths cross?"

Darrin looked up at him from under his brows. "The look on your face says it's possible."

"Show me what you would do." Mason slid the map so they both could see it.

"Here's Peach Street." Darrin traced a thin line from Dorchester north toward Franklin Park. Once inside, the path angled west. "According to the report, the officers who were chasing him lost him after about seven blocks, right?"

"Yes." Mason pointed to a section on the map. "Which means our perp was either hiding or cut across someone's yard."

"He had to stay out of the lights, though," Darrin reminded him. "There was blood all over his jacket and probably on his person as well."

Mason took another look at the streets that were easily accessed from Peach Street. "What about here?" He pointed to a route that would have had the perp running, not only toward the park, but also toward the edge of the park closest to the high school.

"I wonder if any of those businesses have security cameras," Darrin murmured.

"Maybe we can get the Lieutenant to call in some favors with the Dorchester guys."

"Worth a shot." Darrin tapped a road that ended on the border of Dorchester and the park. "Let's say he entered near this pizza shop. If he'd done that, the trip west would have been easy."

"But dark."

"But dark," Darrin agreed.

Mason folded the map and stuck it into his pocket. He pulled on warmer gloves, and they started toward the path the teachers had taken.

"Why do you think the teachers walked this far away from school? It seems a little out of the way, especially since their lunch hour isn't very long."

"True," Mason hummed. "However, if you want to engage in a little something something, I doubt you want to be caught."

"Hines didn't strike me as someone who couldn't keep it in his pants," Darrin retorted. "What's the attraction?"

"You're the one who spoke to Trina Smith," Mason reminded him. "Did you ask?"

"What do you think?"

Mason laughed. "Yeah, I wouldn't have asked either."

The path they were taking took them northeast, around Ellicott Arch, then started back south where it crossed the bridge. The clump of trees where they found the jacket was located right before the path turned east once again.

"That took about fifteen minutes," Mason murmured. "Then another fifteen minutes back."

"Certainly doesn't give them long for hanky panky."

"True." Mason stopped on the path and looked around. There was still snow on the ground, and it was cold. However, an image of walking hand in hand with Maddy kept flashing in his head. "Do you want to head back or push forward?"

"Let's keep going. We can add to our timeline."

They'd gone less than half a mile when a woman walked around a bend. She wasn't watching where she was going, but was looking down at a map.

"Well, hell," Mason muttered.

Darrin snickered. "This should be interesting."

It was then Maddy looked up, and the frightened expression on her face softened his response ... just barely.

"Do I even want to know?" Mason asked, his voice laced with frustration.

"Mason!" Maddy's face lit up. "And Darrin, too. What are you doing out here?"

"No, Maddy," Mason growled. "The question is, what are *you* doing out here?"

"Helping," she replied with a flash of defiance—or was it just confidence?

Mason frowned. "Excuse me?"

"No, really," Maddy returned. "I am helping."

Mason exchanged glances with Darrin, then turned his attention back to his reckless Spitfire. That he was already referring to her as '*his*' wasn't something he chose to acknowledge ... then, anyway.

"Go on."

Her silver-blue eyes clashed with his for several seconds, but she held her ground.

"Natalie was waiting for me when I got to work today."

"Natalie?" Mason questioned. "Why?"

"She remembered something."

"Go on."

Maddy dug through her bag and handed him a folded page. Before he'd opened it, he knew what it was—one of the flyers they'd put up with the sketch of Parker Turner.

"Natalie had this?"

"She did."

"Where did she get it?" Mason groused. "Why do you have it?"

Maddy quickly explained what Natalie had shared about hearing the girls talk, as well as about seeing Parker. When she got to the part where the perp was seen next to the pond, a chill raced up Mason's spine, and he had to hold his tongue to keep from making a biting remark.

"I wanted to be able to tell you where she was going, and which train she'd been on." Maddy shrugged. "So I called her."

"You called her?" Mason gave her a pointed look. "I don't see a phone anywhere."

"I called her from my office," Maddy replied. "When she wasn't home, I stopped by on my way to the park. After a few quick questions, here I am."

"I just talked to you a short time ago. Why didn't you say anything?"

"Well, I was going to."

"You were going to?" His voice dropped an octave. "But you didn't."

"Your radio went off, and you hung up," Maddy answered as if it was the most obvious response.

"Damn!" Mason spit. How could he be angry with her, and at the same time want to pull her into his arms and kiss her like there was no tomorrow?

MADDY GLANCED AT DARRIN AND COULDN'T HELP BUT SEE THE twinkle in his eyes. She was sorry Mason was upset. However, just like she'd decided when they were at the Brass Chord, she couldn't be anyone but who she was.

"You know what?" Darrin suddenly spoke up. "I'm sure you're going to walk Maddy back to the Home, right?"

"Right."

"Oh, but you—" Maddy began.

"I'm not letting you walk alone out here," Mason snapped.

Maddy narrowed her eyes and clenched her jaw, not wanting to say something she might regret.

"I'll go get the car and meet you at the Home," Darrin suggested. "Have fun you two."

Once he'd walked away, Mason took a step closer. One look at his expression told her if she didn't put her foot down, he would try to run over her.

"Look," she pounced verbally. "There is no reason for you to go all he-man on me. I'm perfectly capable of taking care of myself."

Mason blew out a breath. "Maddy." He took a half step toward her. "You're going to be the death of me. You know that, don't you?"

Her breath caught. She wasn't sure if it was his tone, the look in his eyes, or the truth behind the words.

"Mason, it's daylight. There's no one else around."

He dropped his head and toed the ground for a heartbeat, then another, and another. Finally, he held out his hand. "Let's start back, and we can talk."

She tilted her head in one direction, then in the other, trying to decipher his mood. He wouldn't hurt her—something she knew for sure. What he was thinking, though, was a little more difficult to read.

"I'll walk with you," Maddy murmured. "*If* you promise not to lecture me."

First, his dark eyes softened, then his lips twitched. "If I promise not to lecture, will you hold my hand?"

She glanced down to see he was still holding out one hand, then back up to read the expression in his eyes once more.

"I guess I can do that."

When she slipped her hand into his, just like those other times when they'd touched, the spark inside ignited. It sent a streak of heat straight up her spine to lodge deeply in her heart. *Oh, boy,* she thought. *I might be screwed.*

"Thank you."

Maddy side-eyed him but didn't say anything right then. She'd reached a point where she wasn't sure exactly what to say.

"Besides the conversation Natalie overheard and seeing Parker beside the pond, was there anything else?"

"She said Parker looked sad," Maddy offered. "Why would he be sad? I don't understand that."

"Remember, Parker didn't have a violent youth record," Mason replied. "Just petty stuff. Something had to have pushed him over the edge."

Maddy chewed on that piece of information but looked at it through the lens of a social worker. Selling drugs, especially ecstasy, wouldn't be that big of a stretch from his pranks in juvie. Murder, though, didn't fit.

"Have you considered the fact that maybe Parker isn't the one you're looking for? It doesn't fit the typical profile."

"Desperate people," Mason reminded her. "Perhaps he was sad he had to kill someone. Or maybe he's sad because we're closing in on him, and his income is drying up."

"That sounds more like it."

Mason didn't offer a response, making her wonder if he was just being patient, or if he was mulling through something. She still needed to tell him her last piece of news.

"Just spit it out."

"How did you know I had more?"

"Your expression telegraphs all." Mason squeezed her fingers. "You wouldn't be good at bluffing."

"Why do you say that?"

Mason chuckled. "Play poker with me sometime, and I'll show you."

"Remember last week when you took me back to the Home after I got off the train?"

"When you returned from talking to the hairdresser?"

"Yes. You said something about the look on my face."

"You looked distracted," Mason replied. "Why?"

"You know how it's always crazy when you get off the subway?"

"Yes."

"Well, that day, I was jostled but following the crowd. Just before I exited the station, a man stepped in front of me."

"Let me guess," Mason growled. "It was Turner?"

"I think so."

"But you're not absolutely certain?"

"No. I remembered his eyes when I was staring at the drawing."

"And he only said, 'Excuse me?'"

"Yes." She paused for a handful of steps, replaying the encounter in her head. "I think he would have said more if it hadn't been so crowded."

"Did he look angry?"

Maddy thought back, but couldn't come up with the perfect description.

"I don't think he looked angry," she began. "Nor did he look sad. More … more confused."

"Confused?" Mason murmured. "I wonder why."

"If I see him again, I'll ask," Mason growled, making Maddy snicker. "You're so easy."

He glanced down at her, and his eyes said if they were anywhere else, he would have backed her against a wall and kissed her. The thought caused her pulse to race and made her wish he'd just go with his feelings. Instead, he was holding back. How much longer would that go on?

"Why were you in the park, Mason?" Maddy whispered. "Were you tracing Parker's potential steps?"

"We were tracing the teachers' footsteps—the ones who found the bloody jacket."

Maddy's breath hitched, and a shiver worked its way through her system. "You're telling me someone found the jacket I remembered off the same trail we were walking on?"

"The teachers found it on the southwest end of the pond on Friday."

"So you think Parker—or the killer—ran away from 15 Peach Street and eventually made their way into the park, where they tossed the bloody jacket?"

"That's what we think."

"The person took off the jacket because it was bloody," Maddy murmured. "It was freezing that night, though. Did they have a coat stashed somewhere? Plus, the paths aren't lighted. How did they see where they were going?"

☙❧

Damn, if she wasn't asking the same kind of questions he'd been wondering about. But how did he get her to stop jumping in with both feet, when she should have pondered first?

"Those are all good questions," Mason acknowledged.

"But you have no answers," Maddy guessed.

"Not yet." He glanced in her direction, then returned his attention to the street they were walking down. "What street are we on?"

She named a street he wasn't familiar with, but one that had him taking out the map he'd stuffed into his back pocket. He spread it out and had

Maddy show him where they were. There was a main thoroughfare on one side and another on the left. However, it angled in such a way, it would have crossed Peach Street.

Maddy pushed down the map so she could see what he was looking at. "That's ..." Then her voice faded, as if she'd just put two and two together. "Is that the getaway route?"

"It could be. We're hoping some businesses on the other side have security cameras."

"I told you I had some information that could help. See, now, aren't you glad I came?"

Mason folded the map and crammed it into his pocket. He took her hand, and once again, they started walking.

"Am I happy you were out there all alone? No. Am I happy you jumped in without thinking things through? No. However, am I happy you gave us some news we didn't have? Yes. And am I happy we had this time to walk together? Very much so."

When Maddy looked up, and their eyes met, the smile on her face nearly took his breath. He pulled her into his arms and swooped down for a kiss. Before their lips met, he felt the presence of others. Slowly, he turned his head to find he'd been right. They were being stared at ... by Theo.

"Hi, Mason!" Theo bounced toward them. "Did you come to see me?"

It was only then Mason realized how close they were to the Home. He dropped his forehead against Maddy's and took a deep breath.

"Hi, Theo. No, I didn't come to see you today. I walked Maddy home and thought I'd talk to Blue. Is she around?"

"She is! Come on. I'll show you."

"I think it's a conspiracy," Mason muttered on their way inside. "What do you think?"

"A conspiracy?" Maddy repeated. "What are you talking about?"

"A conspiracy to keep us apart. Every time I get close, there's always someone around."

Maddy giggled. "That's pretty much true. But no, no conspiracy."

"Then what is it?"

She looked up at him with an impish grin. "It's just bad luck. I'll see you later. I have some work to do before I leave." Then she handed him the map she'd drawn on, the flyer, and a page of notes before disappearing down a hall.

Mason glanced in the mirror hanging in the hallway and wasn't surprised to see the dazed look on his face. Practical Maddy had taken over again—efficient, maddening, and entirely unforgettable.

"Mason," Theo appeared from the direction of the kitchen. "Blue said she'll be here in a minute. Okay?"

"That's fine. I'll just wait here for her."

But Theo's mannerisms made him think there was more the boy wanted to tell him.

"What's going on, Theo?"

"Is it okay to ask you?"

Mason swallowed hard, as he didn't know where the boy was going, but he'd already agreed.

"What do you need to tell me?

"Last night, when I looked out my window, I saw a bad man standing out front."

Mason's breath caught. "You saw someone standing outside last night?"

Theo nodded.

"Do you know what he looked like?"

"No." Theo frowned. "But he had on a hat."

"Could you see the color?"

"It was too dark. Sorry."

Mason assured the boy that he'd look into the problem, but it didn't give him a good feeling.

"Mason?" Blue appeared from the direction of the dining room. "Theo said you were looking for me. Is everything okay?"

"Theo just told me he saw someone outside last night. Have you seen anyone watching the Home that shouldn't be?"

Blue's eyes widened with worry. "No. But I will tell Green and Black to watch more closely. Is there anything else?"

"As you know," Mason continued, with the real reason behind his visit. "I'm investigating Alisha's death. My dad thought you might be able to answer a question or two."

"I'll try. I'm not sure how I can help, though."

"It won't take long."

"Would you like a cup of coffee? We can sit in the morning room."

"That sounds nice. Thank you."

Mason followed Blue to the small nook, where she set a steaming cup of coffee and cookies in front of him.

"I'm sure Scott has told you there are always cookies around here." Blue's eyes twinkled. "Both Green and Black love to bake."

"My father said they were even better than my mother's."

"But swore you to secrecy?" Blue guessed.

"He didn't quite say that. However, it was implied."

She chuckled. "That sounds like Scott. My grandmother Ruby used to .... Never mind. I'm sure you have a few questions for me."

It was a challenge not to ask her about her grandmother. Not to ask her if she'd been going to say something about their fathers when they'd been boys. Instead, he took out the notes he hoped she could help answer.

"I have some questions about the house Alisha lived in," Mason began. "Do you know how she came to be staying there?"

Blue frowned. "No. Did you ask Maddy?"

He couldn't remember if he'd asked her or not, but moved on. "The tax records for the house show the owners as Frank and Beatrice Kennedy. Did you know them? Or know of them?"

"I knew Bea, but not Doctor Kennedy."

"Doctor Kennedy?" Mason wrote the name. "Do you know what kind of doctor he was? Or where he practiced?"

"He was a surgeon. I think he worked at King's Castle."

"And his wife?"

"Bea used to stop by once or twice a week and help the kids with homework," Blue murmured. "I think she missed her family."

"Did she have a big family?"

"Not big," Blue went on. "She only had one child—a daughter. Her name was Angel."

"Angel?"

"Well, that's what Bea called her." Blue paused and took a sip of her coffee. "I guess it could have been a nickname for Angela as well."

"But you never met Angel?"

"No. In fact, Bea only volunteered for a few years," Blue explained. "And then they moved."

"They moved?"

"I believe Frank was involved in some medical invention, and they came into quite a bit of money."

"Would you have any idea why they didn't sell the house?"

"I don't. But if the Kennedys still own it, who pays the taxes and upkeep?"

"That's what I'm trying to find out," Mason sighed. "So far, all I have to go on is the name of the attorney who's managing the estate."

"I'm sorry. I wish I could be of more help. Is there anything else?"

"No, not right now." He paused when a car horn honked. "I bet that's Darrin. Thank you again. I'll let myself out."

Mason took a couple of steps, then backtracked and grabbed a handful of cookies. "For the road," he winked. "Kudos to the cooks."

FIFTEEN

Maddy's Apartment
January 10, 1994
6:30 p.m.

MADDY RUSHED INTO HER APARTMENT AND, ON HER WAY BY, HIT play on her answering machine. It beeped once, and then there was a click.

Good, it was only a hang-up.

She tossed her coat over a chair and dropped her bag on the floor.

"And this time, there will be no interruptions when I kiss you goodnight."

The memory of his husky baritone making a promise to kiss her caused a little thrill to race up and down her spine. She wanted to pick out the perfect outfit. One that was sexy, but not too sexy. Flattering, but not too flattering. One that was ... perfect.

"Being with him at the club was easy," Maddy sighed. "But I think I was waiting for some sort of sign."

He'd given her more than one sign. Not only had he shown up at Theo's birthday party, but when he'd asked her to watch him bowl, he'd made a promise—one she couldn't wait to accept.

The phone rang, bringing her back to the here and now. On the third ring, she grabbed it. Before she could say hello, there was a distinct click.

Two hang-ups in one day were a bit strange. However, with time counting down, she brushed aside the little niggle of fear and raced to get ready.

"It's not a date, date, Maddy," she reminded herself when she couldn't decide what to wear. "It's just an evening at the bowling alley."

Except whom was she kidding? She still wanted Mason to look at her with heat in his eyes. Something that made finding the right outfit imperative.

In the end, she threw on her favorite sweater, grabbed her coat, and was on her way. The phone rang before the door had closed completely.

She hesitated long enough to wait for the answering machine to come on. When all she heard was a click, she took off running. If she hadn't, she would have missed her train.

Maddy found Tina waiting right inside the station. "You're late. Is everything okay?"

"It's fine." Maddy gave her friend a sheepish smile. "I lost track of time."

"Oh?" Tina's blue eyes twinkled. "Any specific reason?"

Maddy shrugged nonchalantly. "Not really."

Tina snickered.

"Besides, I wasn't sure what to wear."

"You weren't sure what to wear to a bowling alley? Really?"

"Stop it," Maddy scolded. "There have been a few times I've seen you nervous before a date."

They boarded the subway and settled into seats before Tina answered. "It's nice to see the tables turned for once. I'm usually the basket case, and you're the calm one."

Maddy contemplated her friend's words for several seconds. "Why am I nervous? I've spent time with him before. I even saw him earlier today."

"Oh?" Tina side-eyed her. "How did that come about? When we talked, you said he'd called."

"He did."

"Maddy, what aren't you saying?"

"Alisha's friend, Natalie, came to visit me today. I was following up on something."

"Maddy, Maddy, Maddy," Tina tsked. "What did Mason say?"

Maddy laughed. "Oh, he was a little irritated. But he got over it."

"Just be careful. Okay?"

"I'm fine. Really."

"Here's our stop." Tina led the way off the subway and to the red line. "It's too cold to walk the rest of the way."

"Where are we going? Apparently, it's not the place I thought."

"Fortune's Alley."

"Fortune's Alley?" Maddy repeated. "Is that new?"

"Relatively. I think it's closest to the South Boston Precinct. Also, there's more than bowling."

"Really?"

"It has three floors," Tina continued. "The bottom floor has pool tables, dart boards, and dining. There's dancing on the second, and a bowling alley on the top floor."

Less than fifteen minutes later, they reached their stop and took the steps to the exit. Fortune's Alley was directly across the street.

Purple, pink, turquoise, and yellow neon stripes lit the front of the building. Above the doors, a massive sign with the business's name flashed in neon green to the beat of the music.

"Wow!"

"I agree. It's ... colorful."

"That's one way to describe it," Maddy murmured. "Is it just me, or do you expect to walk in and hear nothing but 70s music?"

"And everyone's doing the hustle." Tina hip-bumped her. "We should have worn tie-dye and bellbottoms."

When they walked inside, the atmosphere completely changed. It was sedate, calming even, with soft music playing in the background. Over it all, they could hear the clicking of the balls from the pool tables, and the low rumble of conversation.

"This way." Tina started up the stairs. "They're on the third floor."

Maddy followed Tina, and with each step, her nerves climbed a little higher.

Fortune's Alley Arcade
January 10, 1994
8:20 p.m.

"Haven't you heard a watched pot never boils?" Darrin teased.

Mason gave his partner a rude hand gesture and continued watching the staircase. She was late.

"Where do you think they are? Do you think they changed their minds?"

"Take a deep breath, Mason," Darrin replied. "They're female. There are a million reasons why they're late."

"Maddy is coming, right?"

Darrin's brows rose. "You mean you didn't ask her on the walk back to the Home?"

"No. She just said she'd see me later."

"It means the same thing. Relax."

"You're up, Weaver," Tim, one of the other team members, called.

Mason collected his ball and lined up for the shot. He took a step, and from the corner of his eye, someone wearing bright blue distracted him. His foot faltered, and the ball fell from his hand ... behind him, instead of in front.

"Did you forget how to bowl, Weaver?" Tim snickered.

"Bite me."

Mason ignored his teammates' ribbing and took his second turn, knocking down eight of the ten pins. When he started back toward his seat, she was there, and his heart almost stopped.

Her blue sweater matched her eyes, and somehow, he knew that's what he'd seen earlier. Black jeans molded her slim hips, and around her neck, she was wearing a long, silver heart pendant.

"Mason." Darrin elbowed him out of the way. "Go tell her hello, then get your head in the game. We can't lose to Dorchester."

With every step Mason took toward Maddy, his heart beat a little harder. Especially when she seemed just as eager to see him by cutting the distance in half. How was he going to focus on his game with her so close?

"I wasn't sure you were going to come," he murmured, and not what he'd intended.

"Why?"

"Never mind," Mason grinned. "You're here now."

"I am." She smiled. "Am I going to distract you?"

"Probably. I'm sure I'll get teased more than once."

"I'm sorry."

"Don't be sorry, honey." He squeezed her fingers. "I want you here."

"Good. But now," Maddy glanced around him. "Your friends are waving you over."

"A man's work is never done." He gave her a long-suffering sigh. "I'll see you in a minute."

Mason contemplated kissing her on the cheek, but knew he wouldn't be able to resist her mouth, especially if he were that close. He considered kissing her hand. However, that wasn't what he wanted. In the end, he squeezed her fingers once more and watched until she sat down.

Determined not to make a fool of himself a second time, Mason found his ball and sent it flying down the lane. It crashed into the pins, causing them to scatter.

"Whoa, Weaver!" Stu, the fourth member of their group, exclaimed. "If you're going to bowl like that, then I'm going to insist you bring your girlfriend all the time."

Mason grinned, amazed the connotation didn't bother him. Nor did the idea of Maddy watching him bowl every week. In fact, the idea was exciting, and he couldn't help but hope it happened.

Once more, he picked up his ball and sent it down the lane. Again, he bowled a strike, giving him the highest score.

"That won't last," Tim grumbled. "I still have a chance."

Mason let Tim's comments roll off his back. If he won, it would be nice. If he didn't, he didn't care. There was only one thing he wanted right then, and he couldn't have it while he was bowling.

For the next forty-five minutes, Mason found his attention torn. Every time he turned around, Maddy was watching. But if he gave her too much of his time, his friends ribbed him. It was a challenge not to make a fool of himself.

It felt strange, as usually he enjoyed Monday night bowling league. The guys on his team had been friends for years, and it was always nice to chat and not think of anything else.

However, he'd found his exception. He'd never invited a date to watch before. It was different ... not bad different, just different.

"Last frame," Stu finally called.

Like he'd done before, Mason stuck his fingers in the bowling ball holes and set up. He almost glanced over his shoulder to make sure Maddy was still watching, but at the last minute refrained.

"Hurry up, Weaver," Tim teased. "We don't have all night."

One step, then another, and Mason let go of the ball. It zipped up the lane and crashed into the pins, scattering all but one.

"Oh, tough luck, Weaver," Tim continued to chatter. "Looks like I'm going to win."

Mason easily knocked down the remaining pin and backed away toward the chairs. He'd ended up with a 256, a score he'd never gotten close to. Maddy had proven to be his lucky charm.

"You're up, Timmy," Mason quipped. "See if you can top that."

"Feeling good, I see," Darrin murmured. "Much better than grumpy Mason."

"We're no longer in high school," Mason retorted.

Darrin laughed. "No? Who couldn't focus on his game until the object of his desire walked in?"

"And she proved to be a good luck talisman, didn't she?" Mason pointed out. "You're just jealous you didn't beat my score."

"True," Darrin grumbled.

With the game over, Mason's attention turned to what lay ahead. Meaning the faster he was ready to go, the quicker he could pursue what he wanted.

He changed his shoes, and when he sat up, the game was over. For the first time all season, he'd won.

"Good game, Mason." Tim shook his hand. "I'll get you next week."

"Probably," Mason conceded. "It was fun while it lasted, though."

Darrin and Stu offered to store their bags, leaving Mason free to join the women ... finally.

When he was about eight feet away, Maddy jumped up and threw her arms around him. "You won," she exclaimed. "Congratulations."

Mason was so shocked it took him an extra minute to hug her back. He hadn't expected her exuberance. It wasn't the first time her excitement over something he did made him feel ten feet tall.

THE REALIZATION SHE'D SQUEALED LIKE A TEEN IN THE MIDDLE OF a bowling alley had Maddy taking a step back. When she did, her gaze crashed into Mason's. There was heat in his eyes, and suddenly, the only thing that mattered was what was happening between them.

Her breath lodged in her throat, and her heart took off, beating a little faster every second.

"I'm so—"

Mason placed his finger over her mouth. "You were my good luck charm. Celebrating is a must."

"Oh?"

"It is."

"What did you have in mind?" She paused. "Do you want a drink?"

"No."

"Do you want to dance?"

"No."

"Then what do you want?"

"I told you my plans when I invited you to come tonight," Mason practically purred. "Do you remember what that was?"

She forced down the lump in her throat but, not trusting her voice, just nodded.

"Good. Then let's go." Mason slipped his arm around her and pressed her against his body from hip to shoulder.

"We're going to take off," he told their friends. "Winning has taken something out of me."

Darrin laughed. "Don't let it go to your head."

Maddy slung her bag over her shoulder. "I'll talk to you later, T."

"Behave, you two," Darrin called on their way out. "Don't do anything I wouldn't do."

"Sorry about that." Mason grinned down at her. "For some reason, my partner thinks I'm fifteen."

Maddy laughed, but it sounded forced, as she felt the same way. Like she was fifteen and waiting for her first kiss.

They collected their coats, and when she climbed into his car, it was just as before. His cologne surrounded her, and it was a fight to stay on her side.

The ride was relatively quiet. Not because she had nothing to say, but because she was anticipating what came next. She licked her lips to assure herself they weren't chapped. Then she surreptitiously put her hand close to her mouth to check her breath.

A short time later, Mason pulled into her apartment complex parking lot, and her stomach started doing somersaults. It was crazy, really, as he'd brought her home before.

On the way inside, he wrapped his arm around her. With every step, the tension between them climbed a little higher. From the first floor to the elevator, then to her apartment door, it continued to increase, bringing her heart rate along with it.

"Do you remember what I said about tonight?" Mason nuzzled her temple, and the feel of his hot breath against her cheek gave her goosebumps.

"What you said?" Maddy tipped her chin until their eyes met. "You said a lot of things tonight."

Mason playfully tapped her chin. "Don't play coy, honey."

His smile was dark and sexy. It caused her knees to weaken and her breath to catch. He backed her against the wall, and his mouth hovered close. So close, it wouldn't take much for the space between them to disappear.

Their gazes clashed, and with every second they dueled, the heat climbed inside. It burned until it threatened to consume her.

"Maddy," Mason whispered against her mouth. "I'm going to kiss you now."

Maddy tightened her hold on his jacket, not to push him away but to bring him closer and closer. "What are you waiting for?"

A corner of his mouth went up. "What do you think I'm waiting for?"

"I don't know."

"Are you sure about that?"

"No, I ..."

"You," Mason whispered. "I'm waiting for you."

Maddy tugged him toward her until their lips met in a heated exchange. One that stole her breath and pulled her along on a ride, making her feel like she was free-falling.

Mason's kiss was nothing like any she'd experienced in her lifetime. He cupped her jaw, covered her entire mouth, and his tongue demanded entry. It was forceful, almost to where she couldn't help but think he was trying to leave an imprint.

One of them groaned, but instead of letting her go, Mason angled his head in the other direction and dove back in. The kiss was hot, hard, and caused her knees to buckle. If he hadn't been holding her so tightly, she would have melted into a puddle.

Time ceased to exist, and the only thing that mattered was the way she felt wrapped in Mason's arms. The way her mouth felt under his. The way he smelled, and what he did to her. He undid her in so many ways, she had a difficult time knowing what was up … and what was down.

With every second their mouths touched, she fell a little more under Mason's spell. Wanted a little more of whatever he was willing to give. Wanted to give him a little more of whatever he wanted from her.

The kiss threatened to consume, to overwhelm, and then, suddenly, it changed. No longer was it hot and hard, but a soft and sensual meeting of their lips. One where there was no doubt in her mind that if they had been inside, could have easily burned out of control.

Mason slowly lifted his head and leaned his forehead against hers. He was breathing heavily, and his fists were still wrapped in her coat.

"I'm not going to apologize."

"Did I ask you to?"

"No."

She tightened her hold on him even more and pulled him down for another kiss. This one, however, didn't burn out of control. It was soft, sweet, and she could feel the heat simmering beneath the surface.

"Do you want to come in?"

Mason lifted his head. His face was flushed, and there was a tenseness in his jaw that hadn't been there before.

"I'd better not … tonight."

That Mason had a hold of her coat, and was still breathing harder than normal, told her more than he was saying. It wasn't that he didn't want to come inside. It was the opposite. He wanted to be with her *too* much, and the complexity of their situation was holding him back. Somehow, that made her care for him even more.

"I understand."

Maddy unlocked her door, and before she could tell him goodbye, he swung her around and kissed her once more. It was powerful, and way too short. Yet, it left her breathing heavily, and her lips tingling.

"Lock up, honey. I'll be in touch." Then he was gone. Her knees practically gave out, causing her to fall back against the door. Slowly, she touched her bottom lip. She could still feel Mason's mouth and had no doubt her dreams wouldn't be tame.

On her way into the bedroom, her phone rang. Maddy grabbed it even before it rang a second time. "Hello."

"Maddy," someone whispered. "Is this Maddy?"

A chill raced up Maddy's spine. She slammed the phone down and looked around wildly for what, she wasn't sure. Seconds later, the phone rang again, and something told her it was the same person. Rather than answering, she pulled the plug. If she had any say, her dreams were going to be of kissing and not of whispered voices.

SIXTEEN

South Boston Police Precinct.
January 13, 1994
9:00 p.m.

Three days later, every time Mason closed his eyes, the kiss replayed in his head. He could still feel the imprint of her mouth. Still feel her body pressing against his. Still smell her powdery scent each time he climbed into his car.

Her kiss had triggered dreams he'd not had since he was ... well, fifteen. They turned him on. However, they also tied him into knots, because their situation hadn't gotten easier. In fact, it was more difficult.

"Earth to Mason." Darrin snapped his fingers. "Where were you?"

"I think Maddy is keeping something from me," Mason blurted.

Darrin frowned. "Say that again."

"I think Maddy is hiding something."

"What did you do to her?"

Mason tossed a paperclip at his partner. "Stop it. I didn't do anything to her."

Darrin laughed. "Sorry, it was too easy."

"Everything was fine when I dropped her off on Monday evening. Then, when I called her on Tuesday, it was like she was holding back."

"But you have no idea what?"

"None. Has Tina said anything?"

"No."

"Both my father and Sister Blue told me Maddy is reckless," Mason sighed. "Hell, I've even experienced it."

"You're talking about finding her in the house and the park, right?"

"And going to see the hairdresser. Although I didn't catch her until afterward."

"Are you afraid she might do something?"

"Her heart leads her, which is what makes her Maddy," Mason murmured. "But I would worry less if she would think first."

"I know you're concerned. I can see it on your face. However, a relationship won't go anywhere unless you trust her."

"But—"

"There isn't a but, in this case," Darrin shut him down. "Yes, she leaps before looking. Yes, you've found her in a couple of not-so-great situations."

Mason raised his brows at his partner's comments, but it didn't do any good as he continued.

"Tina agrees your social worker can be impulsive when it comes to helping people. However, she also said Maddy isn't dumb. Nor is she suicidal. They've been friends for over fifteen years. She thinks if Maddy needs you, you'll know."

"You and Tina have discussed Maddy?"

"I had to make sure she was good enough for you." Darrin laughed. "I'm surprised you haven't gone behind my back to check up on Tina."

"How do you know I haven't?" Mason quipped.

"Because you've been too busy chasing after Maddy. Otherwise, you'd have interrogated Tina ... or questioned Maddy. Now, are you ready to do non-Maddy work?"

"Not really. But lay it on me."

"Principal Marsh told us about the football player who was in the hospital, right?"

"What about him?"

"I spoke to the father," Darrin said. "While his son is out of danger, the dad is still pretty shaken."

"I don't blame him. Did the dad know anything else?"

"Not really," Darrin continued. "He did, however, say we could talk to his son. There could be a problem, though."

"A problem? What kind?"

"He said he doesn't think his son remembers much."

"When do we leave?"

"Now."

"Damn, Darrin. You're just as big a pain in my ass as you were in college."

"Are you going to tell your father on me?"

"Don't tempt me. Shall we?"

They signed out and headed towards King's Castle General Hospital.

"Where are we supposed to meet the dad?" Mason asked once they'd parked.

Darrin pulled out the notebook he used for notes and flipped through several pages.

"The father's name is Allen Bracket, and the son is Greg. He said he would meet us in the lobby, right inside the hospital."

"What feeling did you get from speaking with Bracket?" Mason asked on the way across the parking lot.

"He's angry."

"Dangerous?" Mason tossed back. "Do you think he would go off on his own?"

"That, I don't know. With a little luck, we'll know before we leave."

When they walked into the hospital, Mason immediately spotted the father. Darrin had been right in saying he was angry. So angry, in fact, that it came off him in waves.

"He's wound tight."

"You can say that again."

They introduced themselves, and when Bracket turned his stare on him, Mason had a difficult time maintaining eye contact. Something about the look in the other man's eyes left a bad taste in his mouth.

"How's your son feeling?" Mason asked once they were on the elevator.

"Better." Bracket relaxed a little. "The doctor said, as long as nothing changes, we can take him home in a few days."

"That's good to hear," Darrin replied. "Did you tell him we were coming?"

"I did." Allen let go of a light laugh. "He claims he remembers nothing about that night."

Mason immediately followed up with, "Do you believe him?"

Allen shrugged. "Honestly, I don't know. This incident has me wondering if I truly know my son."

"Would you let us talk to him alone?" Mason asked. "Maybe he'll be more open."

"It's worth a try," Bracket answered. "I'll wait right here."

Mason thanked him and followed his partner into the hospital room. The teen was pale and looked much younger than his age.

"What do you remember about that night, Greg?" Darrin asked once they'd introduced themselves. "Anything?"

"Not much," Greg admitted. "I remember Travis, Kara, and Hannah arriving. Everything else is fuzzy."

"Who are they?" Darrin followed up.

"Travis is my best friend, and Kara is his girlfriend," Greg supplied. "Hannah is the girl I'm dating."

"There was booze?" Mason assumed.

"A lot," Greg winced. "We took it from our parents."

"And they don't know, do they?"

Greg shrugged.

"Have you talked to Travis or either of the girls since you've been in here?" asked Darrin.

"Not yet."

"Do you remember how many people were at the party?" Darrin backed away a little.

"A lot. But I only hung with Travis and the girls."

"Can your father give us the information about contacting your friends?" Mason asked.

"Probably."

Darrin laid one of his cards on the nightstand. "If you remember something else, call us. Okay?"

"I will." They'd turned to go when Greg called them back, "My dad told me I had a reaction to some drug."

"You did," Mason replied. "Ecstasy."

"I don't do drugs," Greg murmured. "Where did they come from?"

"That's what we're trying to find out," Darrin answered. "We'll keep in touch."

"You know what this means, don't you?" Mason asked on the way to the car. "It means another visit to Forest Hills High."

"Without the parents there?" Darrin winced. "I can't imagine it going over really well."

"I can't either," Mason agreed. "Maybe the principal will set something up for us."

They'd question the students and then compare those answers to the other high school situations. From there, they'd see.

To Blessed Children's Home
January 13, 1994
12:30 p.m.

MADDY SPENT THE MORNING OUTSIDE OF THE OFFICE AND WAS anxious to get back to the Home. After a post-case visit with the Connors, and an intake with a new family, she barely made it onto the train before the doors hissed shut behind her. She'd just found a seat when a commotion pulled her attention outside the window.

Her gaze clashed with Parker Turner's as he pushed toward the door. Had he been following her? Fear zipped up her spine, and she shrank back against the seat. When the subway took off, she let go of the breath she'd been holding, and couldn't help but think—at least he was out there.

For the past few days, she'd been looking over her shoulder more often. More than once, she'd seen someone immediately turn a corner. But since there wasn't anything concrete for her to tell Mason, she'd kept quiet. In a way, it left her exposed—and that unsettled her more than she wanted to admit.

Parker's interest in her was both scary and curious. If he was Alisha's killer like everyone thought, it would make more sense for him to leave town. On the other hand, if he wasn't the killer, then how was he involved?

Since the hang-up calls on Monday night, she'd screened everything and adjusted her schedule. She varied her routes. Sometimes she'd switch from the red to the orange, and other times, she'd detour onto the silver line. She was trying to stay one step ahead of whoever might be watching. It was exhausting, and somehow, she realized the time to stop running had come ... from Mason, anyway.

When she arrived at the Home, she heard giggles and peeked into the library to find the source of the laughter. Abby had Tori's pink cat and was playing keep away. The smiles on the girls' faces said it all, and the entire picture touched a place deep inside. Unwilling to dissect it right then, Maddy ignored it.

"I'm exhausted just watching them." Maddy grinned at Blue. "How long has this game been going on?"

Blue smiled. "Since they finished lunch. I'm hoping they wind down soon."

"Do you need help?"

"Would you mind watching the girls for me? I'd like to make another call to St. Brigid's." Blue's dark eyes scrutinized her. "How was your visit with the Connors?"

"Perfect." Maddy tossed a pillow onto the floor to sit on and leaned back against a chair. "Julie and Andrew are making themselves at home."

"Toddlers have a way of doing that," Blue said, nodding toward the chaos. " Then her gaze sharpened. "But that's not what's on your mind."

Maddy heard it for what it was. Blue had noticed her behavior the last few days and knew something was wrong. Not only knew, but expected it to be shared.

"What do you mean?" she tried to ward off her confession.

"Your poker face reminds me of that stuffed bear you patched up when you were twelve—bless your heart—but the stuffing still showed."

"Hey, be nice. Bean might have been lumpy, but he was a good listener."

A corner of Blue's mouth curled. "And that's important, isn't it?"

"Very."

"Did Mason do something?"

It didn't surprise Maddy when Blue returned to her earlier question.

He kissed me senseless!

Except that wasn't something to be shared, at least not with Blue.

"No. Why would you ask?"

Blue shrugged.

"Did you give him 'the talk'?"

"Me?" Blue placed her hand on her chest with feigned outrage.

"You don't need to worry about Mason, Blue," Maddy assured the older woman. "I think we're both on the same page."

"That's good." Blue paused long enough to close the folder she was holding. "Then what's going on?"

Maddy's thoughts scattered for what, and how much to say, to pacify a concerned Blue. She finally decided on, "Last week, I had an unsettling encounter with this man, and I saw him again today."

"Are you okay?"

"Besides being a little jumpy, you mean?" Maddy sighed. "I'm fine."

"And annoyed?"

"Maybe a little. I don't like having to change my routine to avoid this man."

Since she didn't know what, if anything, Blue knew about Parker Turner, Maddy kept his name out of the conversation. She didn't want to worry the older woman unnecessarily.

"You're going out of your way?" Blue frowned. "How?"

Maddy shrugged, wanting to convey the idea it wasn't a big deal. However, Blue's expression said she wasn't doing a good job.

"It's nothing, really. I'm getting on and off at different stops. I'm sure everything will be fine."

"I think you need to tell Mason."

"He'll just worry."

"Maddy."

"How about this?" Maddy opted for. "When I see him again, I'll tell him."

Blue held her stare for several long minutes. Finally, she gave a slight nod. "I'm going to hold you to that."

"I know you will." Maddy turned her attention to Abby and Tori, who were showing signs of tiring. "Why don't I take the girls upstairs and see if they'll go down for a little nap?"

"That would be a big help." Blue gathered her files. "I'll let you know what I find out."

"Abby, Tori. Let's clean." Maddy tossed a couple of the toys into the toy box. "Come on, help me."

Abby shook her head. "No."

"Yes, please." Maddy handed Abby a rubber duck. "Put it into here." She pushed the box closer.

"No."

"Watch me." Maddy picked up several items off the floor and, one by one, put them back into the box. "Now, your turn." Then, once again, she handed Abby a toy.

This time, Abby gave the block to Tori, who took off running.

Okay, this won't be as easy as I thought, Maddy sighed. Hoping to evade an accident, she left the girls alone and quickly picked up the toys. When she finished, Abby patted her arm and then pointed at the box.

"Good job." Then the chase resumed.

"Good job," Maddy muttered. "Two toddlers outsmarted you."

Maddy's Apartment
January 13, 1994
9:30 p.m.

AFTER MORE THAN TWO HOURS OF TALKING TO THE STUDENTS from Forest Hills High, Mason was tired and had a headache. However, he knew there was no way he'd completely relax until he'd talked to Maddy. Something was going on. He could feel it.

A quick stop by the supermarket netted him a yellow rose, and he was ready for the confrontation.

Mason pulled into Maddy's apartment complex parking lot and carefully examined the area. Nothing seemed out of place, but with Turner still on the loose, he wanted to be ready.

When he climbed from the car and started toward her building, he was feeling confident. He took the stairs two at a time, and the moment his foot hit the top step, his nerves climbed. Was he making a mistake? Had she decided she didn't want to spend time with him? Was that why she'd put him off?

"You're an adult, Weaver," he muttered. "Just ask her."

The pep talk carried him down the hall to her door. While he waited for her to answer, he began having doubts again. Should he have called?

But if he'd called, she might have told him not to come. Then he wouldn't be able to read her expression.

Mason thought about knocking again, but before he did, Maddy opened the door. Her appearance shocked him so much that he took a step backward.

"Did I get you at a bad time?"

"Bad time? Why would you think that?"

He dropped his gaze and took in her clothing. She was wearing a long-sleeved t-shirt, too-large fleece pants, and fuzzy pink slippers. A towel covered her hair, and she'd smeared what looked like mud on her beautiful face.

How to respond to her alluded him for several seconds. She hadn't smiled at him like she always did. Nor had she shut the door in his face and told him to go away. Instead, she stood there silently, watching him, almost as if she was unsure what his next move would be.

Mason brushed the rose down Maddy's cheek, thankful when it didn't come away brown. Her eyes widened as if she'd not expected that action.

"For you."

Their gazes clashed for several seconds, before she relaxed and took the rose from him.

"It's pretty. Thank you."

His lips twitched. "I could say, the age-old line, 'just not as pretty as you,' but ..."

Her smile started with a slight uptick of her lips before spreading to eye crinkles, then her cheeks.

"Ouch." She laid her hand on her face. "Don't make me laugh. It hurts."

"Your face hurts when you smile? Really?"

"Really. Would you like to see?" Hesitantly, he brushed his knuckles down her cheek. Whatever she was wearing felt rough and crusty under his fingers.

"Not like that."

"Then how else ...?" However, it clicked what she'd been saying.

"No, thank you. I don't want that ... whatever it is ... on my face."

"You don't know what you're missing." Maddy pulled her door open a little wider, inviting him into her inner sanctum for the first time.

"I'm going to wash this off. Get comfortable."

While he waited, Mason wandered around her living area. There were photos on one wall, many taken at the Home and others, from what he could tell, at college.

When Maddy returned, her face was clean, and the look in her eyes was hesitant.

"Did something happen?"

"Why do you ask?"

She tilted her head in one direction, then in another, while studying him carefully, closely. "I just wondered why ..."

"Why I'd barge in?" That it had come out sounding a bit defensive wasn't something he liked.

"Mason," Maddy murmured. "You're welcome to come by anytime."

"I am?"

"Yes."

His plan hadn't been to push. It had been to stand back and let her dictate the action. Then she took a step closer, and everything he thought was going to happen flew out the window.

Mason brushed his thumb across her cheekbone where the bruise had been. "It's gone."

"It is. I don't think that's why you're here, though."

"It's not."

He tipped her chin, and when their eyes met, Maddy's flared slightly. What he read in her expression didn't match his fears. The look on her face didn't say, '*Go away*.' In fact, unless he was totally off base, it said the opposite.

Their lips touched, and it was like coming home. It so surprised him he lifted his head slightly and stared down into her blue eyes.

There was a dreamy look on her face, causing his heart to race. In a single motion, one arm went around her waist, the other behind her head, and their mouths connected.

Maddy pressed her body against his and wrapped her arms around him. With their mouths fused, she showed no sign of moving. For that, he was thankful.

The longer they kissed, the higher his temperature climbed. His body hardened and shouted for attention. Mason tightened his hold and pulled her hips into the cradle of his. The feeling was so intense, he wasn't sure how much more he could take. He wanted to be closer—and frottage was not what he had in mind. But if his choices were that or letting her go, then he'd take the heaven with the hell.

"Mason. Wait."

He rested his head against hers and fought to bring his breathing under control. Fought to cool off.

"What's going on, Maddy? What happened after I left on Monday evening that you're holding back? Trust me."

"I do trust you." She leaned her head against his chest for a second, then stepped out of his arms. "I really didn't want to have to tell you."

"Why?"

"I didn't want you to worry."

Those words were the bucket of cold water he needed. Mason put a little more distance between them and dropped onto the sofa. "Sit." He patted the cushion next to him. "Tell me what's going on."

Their gazes met and held. Finally, Maddy sat down. "No lectures, please."

"Just tell me."

"Okay. It started Monday night when ... "

SEVENTEEN

Blessed Children's Home
January 14, 1994
1:00 p.m.

MADDY'S CONCENTRATION HAD BEEN OFF ALL DAY. TELLING Mason about her encounters with Parker had been easier than she'd anticipated. What worried her was, had he taken on the weight she'd released?

He'd been wonderful and attentive while they'd discussed the situation. Once everything was out in the open, she'd been more than willing to resume their activities. But Mason had proved to be the stronger of the two. They'd laid on the sofa and, while watching a movie, kept their hands to themselves ... mostly.

She loved being with Mason. He made her feel things she wasn't sure how to name. When they touched, the spark was still there, simmering, growing hotter and hotter. Soon a fire would rage—and when it did, it would consume her. Was she ready for what came next?

The memory of being in his arms heated her body and had her pressing her forehead against the window. It was snowing again. Weather made to sit in front of a nice fire with a warm glass of tea and a good book.

"Maddy?"

She took a deep breath and turned to face Blue. The older woman was watching her carefully. Her dark eyes so intense, Maddy couldn't help but hope she wasn't reading her mind.

"Did I forget something?"

Blue smiled. "I just got off the phone with Sister Margaret."

"You did?" Maddy asked almost hesitantly. "Did you learn anything?"

Blue pulled a piece of paper from her pocket and handed it to Maddy. There was more written on it than she'd expected.

"Sister Margaret said Alisha had been in town for several months before she gave birth. She'd worked at the local diner and was friendly to everyone."

"It sounds like when Alisha arrived in town, she was already pregnant."

"My thoughts as well," Blue murmured. "While I didn't get to speak to the social worker, I gather he helped Alisha find a place to live in Jamaica Planes."

"What was his name?"

"Thomas Gilbert."

"Did you talk to Thomas?"

Blue shook her head. "He's fishin,' Sister Margaret's words, not mine. But she's going to give him the Home's number."

"Alisha never mentioned being helped by another social worker," Maddy murmured. "I wonder why?"

"We'll probably never know," Blue sighed.

"Sad, but true."

"Very much so. You'll give the note to Mason, right?"

Maddy nodded. "I will."

"That's good. Now, one other thing before I go. Have you decided about the fundraiser?"

"Decided?"

"Whether you're going—and is Mason going with you?"

"Oh, that."

"Maddy?" Blue hesitated a second. "You are planning on attending, right?"

"Of course, I'm coming. I know how important it is for the Home. I've—"

"—Had other things on your mind," Blue grinned. "Other things, like

Mason, perhaps? You look more relaxed today. Did you tell him about your encounter?"

Maddy felt the heat creeping up her face and settled back at her desk. "I did. Mason stopped by last night."

"Did he say anything specific?"

"He grumbled a lot. However, he said I was doing the right things. That as long as my movements weren't repetitive, it would make it more difficult for the man to catch me alone."

"Is that it?"

"That's it. Honestly, I expected him to say more."

"And the fundraiser?" Blue prodded. "The RSVPs are coming in."

"I'll ask him the next time I see him."

"Okay, dear. I'll let you get back to work." A mischievous grin crossed Blue's face. "You looked quite busy when I arrived."

If only she knew, Maddy couldn't help but think.

She'd just taken out the notes from the Connors' post-case home visit when the phone rang.

Maddy reached to answer, and for a beat, she hesitated, worried it was Parker. Then it rang once more, and she couldn't stand it.

"Hello. This is Maddy Davies." Mason's husky chuckle came through the line, causing her heart to flip. "Mason!" Her voice came out breathy, but right then, she didn't care.

"Are you busy?"

"No, why?"

"Because I didn't want to bother you if you were."

"Bother me! Please, please, bother me!" Maddy gave a light laugh. "Anything to keep me from paperwork. Did you need something?"

"Besides you, you mean?"

"There you go again," she forced out through a tight throat, "saying something that can't go anywhere."

"Sorry," he practically purred. "I'll make it up to you later."

"Oh?"

"Maddy," Mason muttered, "behave."

"Hey, you called me," she pointed out. "Are you going to cancel our date?"

"Not at all. I promised to cook for you, and I will. The reason I called is to ask if you're ready to pack Alisha's things."

"It's time to do that? Already?"

"What is it?" he followed up, which she should have expected.

"Nothing, really."

"Maddy."

She took a deep breath. "While I want to collect Tori's things, the thought of going back inside the house is …"

"I'll be right there with you," Mason promised. "Feel free to hold on to me."

"I might take you up on that."

"You'd better," he growled.

"Any leads?"

"Concrete? No. Why do you ask?"

"Just wondering."

"You didn't see Parker on your way to work today, did you?"

"No."

"Don't worry, honey. We'll find him," he murmured in a husky voice.

Maddy closed her eyes and let his words roll over her. "I know you will."

"Now," Mason circled back. "You never gave me an answer."

"About packing Tori's things? Sure. We can store them here. Do you want me to meet you there?"

"No."

"No?"

"I'll pick you up."

"Okay. Do I need to bring some boxes?"

"That would probably be a good idea. I'll be there at 4:00 p.m."

"Is it going to cost me?"

Mason chuckled. "Are you willing to pay?"

His voice sounded dark, dangerous and did things to her she hadn't expected. If he had been standing in front of her, she would have shown him exactly how he affected her.

"If I was," Maddy murmured. "What would you want?"

"I think you know."

"Tell me, Mason."

"You, Maddy," Mason purred. "I just want you."

Maddy swallowed hard, pushing down the lump in her throat. "Soon, Mason."

She heard his breath quicken, and he groaned, "You're killing me, honey."

"I'll see you at 4:00 p.m."

"Yes, you will."

She hung up and fought the goofy grin she knew was on her face. "Be calm, Maddy. Just be calm."

South Boston Precinct
January 14, 1994
2:00 p.m.

MASON STARED AT THE SPREADSHEETS ON THE TABLE AND TRIED to organize the information they'd gathered. To date, they knew of four 'parties' where blue ecstasy had been found. So far, they'd added four high schools to their list. The last was the party Greg Bracket had attended.

With the information Allen Bracket had given them, they called upon Principal Marsh and questioned the students. Then, he spent the morning creating spreadsheets with all the information. He planned to compare the answers between the schools.

He lined up the spreadsheets in order of the reported party dates—Fenway High, Dorchester High, Franklin High, and Forest Hills High. Once finished with that, Mason grabbed his yellow highlighter and started looking for similarities. With that completed, he wasn't sure what he was looking at.

The door to the conference room opened, and Darrin walked in carrying folders and a stack of red baseball caps.

"You've been shopping."

Darrin grinned. "What was your first clue?"

"I'm good." Mason nodded toward the caps. "What did you find?"

"The principal of Forest Hills High was correct when he said multiple organizations used these." Darrin laid out the caps across the top of the table. "However, there are a few subtle differences."

"The letter." Mason noticed that while only the letter F was on each hat, it wasn't always the same font. Nor was it the same color. Most of them were plain white; one had red piping around it, and two had blue.

"The letter," Darrin agreed. "Besides the high schools," he separated three hats from the others, "there are maintenance workers," he pushed aside three more, "and the rest are employees of various places."

Mason pointed to the first three. "The high schools are Fenway, Forest Hills, and Franklin. Two Fs are plain, and one has blue around the edges."

"Right," Darrin nodded. "Franklin is the one with the blue."

"And the others?"

"The groundskeepers at Franklin Park, Froggy Pond, and Fenway Park all wear red hats with white Fs." Darrin touched the two with plain white letters. "These are for Franklin Park and Froggy Pond."

"So the white F with the blue piping is for Fenway Park staff?"

"Right. And this one," Darrin tapped the cap with the white letter edged with red, "is for a bar in Fenway Park. The rest are plain white."

Mason chewed on the information for a minute. He thought back to when he'd questioned Maddy about what she'd seen. Then traveled to the discovery of the jacket in Franklin Park.

"What did the assailant do with his hat, pants, shoes, and the knife?"

"You would think he dumped them at the same time," Darrin murmured. "But it was a cold night. If you shed something, you need to be prepared."

"True. Prepared takes the murder into premeditation, as opposed to an act of passion."

"I want to say we should canvass again. Except it's been two weeks. If someone tossed them into a dumpster, then—"

"—They're already landfill."

"Exactly." Darrin gathered the red caps and pushed those aside. "What do you have?"

"Honestly?" Mason ran his hand through his short hair. "We have too many puzzle pieces still missing."

"Go on."

Mason turned the spreadsheets upside down so his partner could see them. "The yellow ones are common answers across the groups."

It was quiet for several moments while Darrin looked through the responses. When he was done, Mason could tell they had similar questions.

"I'll be damned. It's like a secret."

"And not just figuratively."

"Which makes our job more difficult."

"Yes."

Mason had realized at each high school, the host's girlfriend had taken the pills to the party, and not Parker Turner. For Greg's party, Hannah had unknowingly ended up with them.

"You questioned Hannah, right?" Darrin asked.

"She said on the Friday before the party, she found a large bag on her porch with a note. '*Sorry, I can't make the party tomorrow. Can you take this for me? Parker Turner.*' When she looked inside, Hannah found two boxes of beer but didn't take them out."

"Because she didn't want her parents to see?" Darrin guessed.

"Most likely."

"The pills were in a baggie and stuffed through the handles, weren't they?" Darrin quipped.

"That's the only thing I can think of. Once at the party, the beer is flowing, and they find the pills."

Darrin frowned. "Why didn't any of the girls ask who Parker was?"

"Either because it was free beer, or they didn't care. Or they thought their boyfriend knew Parker Turner."

"Did we follow up to find out if Parker Turner had really attended these schools?" Darrin rifled through the paperwork. "Here it is. Parker was at Fenway High from November 8 to November 22."

"What was his attendance record like?" Mason wanted to know.

"It doesn't say," Darrin murmured. "Question is, does he have a connection to the other high schools?"

Mason skimmed through the information from Dorchester High and Franklin High. "There's no mention of him at either of these schools. Did we ask Marsh?"

"We didn't. I'll put in a call to the principal and see what he says."

"How about the Cook law firm?" Mason brought up the ownership of 15 Peach Street. Another piece of information they were still missing.

"They manage the estate, however, not the money," Darrin sighed. "That comes from the estate administrator."

"And?"

"The administrator is another law firm, this one in Burlington. I put in a call. Depending on what we find out from them, we might need to go to probate court and get a copy of the Kennedy's will."

Mason blew out a breath. "It's progress ... I guess. What about the last folder you brought in?"

"Brian Lloyd hasn't returned to his apartment, but several individuals have seen him a handful of times."

"Moved with no forwarding address?"

"Seems to be the best answer. Unless ..."

"Unless?" Mason pushed.

"Unless he's shacked up with someone new."

"That's all we need."

"You said it."

Mason couldn't help but think the case reminded him of a set of stacking dolls. The ones where you start with the big picture—or the largest doll—and need to pull off one doll to get to the next. It had him wondering how many more dolls they had to discover before they reached the core.

Blessed Children's Home
January 14, 1994
3:45 p.m.

THE SMELL OF MASON'S COLOGNE TICKLED MADDY'S SENSES AND pulled her focus away from her notes. When she glanced up, he was leaning against the doorframe, watching her closely. There was something so intimate in the way he looked at her, it was a struggle to sit still. He literally took her breath.

"You're early."

"I finished what I was doing and ... wanted to see you. Are you done?"

Maddy glanced down at what she'd been working on and realized she had a way to go. But they would wait until Monday.

"Done enough for today."

"Good." Mason sauntered toward her, and Maddy couldn't decide what she was supposed to do. Should she stay seated, or should she stand?

"Are you ready to go?"

"I'm ready. Just not to go ... yet."

The look in his eyes telegraphed everything—that this wasn't just a simple kiss hello.

"Mason!" she squealed when he tugged her into his arms.

"Come here," he barely got out before his mouth was on hers in a swoonworthy kiss. "There."

Maddy forced her eyes open. Her lips still tingled from his kiss, and she wanted nothing more than to fall back into another. That was why she took a step backward, almost using her desk as a shield.

"That was nice."

Mason chuckled. "If it were just nice, I might have to try again."

"It was more than nice." Maddy blew out a breath. "But feel free to try to outdo it later."

"I like a challenge." His dark eyes sparkled. "This is going to be fun."

For a second, her thoughts spun, and she couldn't remember what she needed to do. It finally came back around, allowing her to close the folders and store them in her drawer.

"Okay, I'm done. Are you ready to go now?"

"In a minute." Mason sat on the edge of her desk and gently pulled her between his thighs, his hands settling at her waist. "I need to ask you something first."

"Mason," Maddy frowned. "What's going on? Does it have to do with the case?"

"There is something about the case you might be able to help with," he admitted. "What I was going to ask, though, doesn't. I heard this from a little birdie."

"A little birdie? Now, you're being silly."

Mason shrugged. "Sorry."

"And?" she prodded. "What is it?"

"I heard you needed a date for the fundraiser. I want to take you."

Maddy dropped her head against his chest. "Who told you?" she grumbled. "Was it Blue?"

"Blue? Why would you ask that?"

"Because she was in here earlier asking."

"Well? Will you go with me?"

"Who else would I go with?"

If possible, his eyes darkened even more. "That's the right answer," he purred.

"Who did you hear it from?"

"Darrin," he admitted. "He's taking Tina."

"I *was* going to ask you," Maddy assured him. "Really."

"Good answer." Mason placed a light kiss on her lips, then put some distance between them. "Shall we?"

"Before we go, I have something for you."

Mason lifted a brow. "Is it about Parker?"

"No, it's about Alisha and Tori."

"Go on."

Maddy quickly explained what Blue had discovered, and then handed him the note.

"Is that anything new?"

"It might be." Mason tugged her against his chest. "I'll follow up on this later. Right now, I'm just glad you're safe."

Maddy rolled her eyes and led Mason from her office to collect a few boxes. Then they started the drive toward 15 Peach Street. With every house they passed, bringing her closer, Maddy's stomach tightened a little more.

"Maddy." Mason wrapped his hand around hers. "I'm right here."

"I know."

She turned her hand over and linked their fingers. Just the small connection settled some of the wild feelings inside. So much so, she was ready by the time he pulled up in front of the house.

They climbed from the car, each carrying a couple of boxes. Maddy was fine until they reached the stairs, but she couldn't make herself take the first step.

"Honey, are you alright?" He tossed the boxes they were carrying onto the porch and tugged her into his arms. "You don't have to do this."

"Yes, I do. I need to do it for Tori."

"Are you sure?" Mason kissed her forehead. "You don't have to do it alone."

"I know." Maddy took a deep breath and moved away from his warmth. "You'll be with me, right?"

"Every step of the way." He smiled, and his eyes crinkled at the corners.

"Now, let's get done. There are other activities on the agenda that are much more fun."

Maddy laughed. "Like what?"

Mason wiggled his brows. "I think you know." He handed her a keychain and picked up the boxes. "I'll carry. You unlock."

She studied the keychain for several seconds. It was a large A with a picture frame attached. "This was Alisha's, wasn't it?"

"It was."

"Which means the photo is Tori."

"I would guess so," Mason replied softly. "Go on."

Maddy blinked away her tears and unlocked the door for Mason to enter. It wasn't until she heard his colorful language she got a good look at the living area.

Someone had tipped over and ripped apart the furniture. Everything on the shelves was now on the floor, including Tori's toys, which were spread all around.

Mason tossed the boxes, pulled his gun, and pushed her behind him. "Stay close while I make sure we're alone."

Maddy followed when he took off toward the kitchen. Every room they looked in had been torn apart, leaving behind nothing but destruction.

"Why?" she cried. "Why did someone do this?"

Mason stuck his gun back into its holster and pulled her into his arms. "They were looking for something."

"Parker?"

"Possibly."

"Do you think they found it?"

"If they did, it wasn't until the last room. Otherwise, they wouldn't need to trash the entire house."

"What were they looking for?"

"I don't know." Mason tucked her closer and led her back outside. "Whatever it was, though, I'd bet my life it's what got her killed."

"Don't say that!"

"I'm sorry." He placed a firm kiss on her mouth. "Are you okay?"

"I'm okay."

"I'm taking you back to the Home, then I'll call this in. It looks like our evening plans just got pushed back."

Maddy went up on her toes and kissed him again. This one softer than the previous one.

"Do what you need to do. Just promise me you'll catch the person who did this."

EIGHTEEN

South Boston Precinct
January 17, 1994
10:00 a.m.

Mason laid the stack of folders he'd created for the Turner case in the center of his desk. He separated them into color-coded piles and flipped open the one he'd yet to label. It was the latest forensic report for the house on 15 Peach Street.

"Anything interesting?" Darrin asked softly.

"They jimmied the locks on the back door," Mason read. "Once inside, they searched every nook and cranny. There were also signs they'd checked to make sure the floorboards were tight."

"Why? Was something hidden underneath one of them?"

"That sounds plausible."

"What else?"

"The crib mattress and clothing were about the only things they didn't destroy."

"Was anything taken?" Darrin followed up.

"I don't think so—at least based on my recollection from my first visit right after Alisha's death." Mason flipped through a couple more pages and came to the summary. "Here's something curious, and apparently, the forensics team thought so as well. Curious enough to comment on, anyway."

Darrin's brows arched in surprise. "Really? What?"

"Whoever it was, ripped every book apart," Mason murmured. "They even destroyed Alisha's school notebooks."

"As if they were looking for something inside one of them?" Darrin surmised.

"That's my guess, as well as the working theory. What that does, though, is possibly distance Alisha's death from the drugs case."

Darrin blew out a breath. "Any more sightings of Turner?"

"No." Mason sorted through the files, finally located the one he wanted, and handed Darrin Blue's note. "There's the TG mentioned in Alisha's address book."

Darrin lifted a brow. "A social worker?"

"Yes. He helped Alisha get settled in Jamaica Planes."

"Are you going to follow up?"

"Sister Blue's waiting for a call back. I'll see what that brings."

"How about Maddy? Everything quiet on her end?"

"As far as I know. She's still jumpy. Even more so when we're out in the open."

"You're staying close, though, aren't you?" Darrin smirked. "Very close?"

Mason ignored the comment and continued reading. "There were no finger, palm, hand, or footprints found. Nor new hairs. It's like a ghost destroyed the house."

"How do we know one didn't?" Darrin laughed. "You never know."

"I can just imagine the Lieutenant's expression if we tossed that at him."

"I could if you'd like me to."

"It's all good. Ready for our meeting with the guys upstairs?"

"Lead on."

Mason collected the files he'd sorted, and they took the stairs to the second-floor offices. Their Captain and Sergeant were waiting in the small conference room with his father.

"Detectives." Scott ushered them in. "We've been waiting for you."

"We're hoping you have some news," the Sergeant added. "Preferably good news."

Mason handed each a file with copies of their notes. "What we have," he began, "is a lot of information. While we've answered many questions, more still exist."

"Explain," the Captain prodded.

Since the Captain hadn't been in the loop for the last few briefings, Mason gave him a quick rundown of where they were, emphasizing what they knew.

"And the child's okay?" the Captain followed up.

"Tori is fine," Mason assured them.

"She's at Blessed Children's Home," Scott added, "with the Sisters—Blue, Green, and Black."

When Mason caught the Sergeant pressing her lips together in response to the Sisters' names, he had to look away to keep a straight face.

"They do good work," the Captain murmured.

"The best," Scott agreed.

"Where does the case stand now?" the Captain moved on.

Mason blew out a breath. "That's a little more difficult to figure out." He hesitated a second before continuing, "Our prime suspect is Parker Turner. We can place him at Fenway High School, which is where everything starts— or at least we think that's where everything starts."

"Meaning?" Scott asked. "Are you wondering if there were other incidents prior to the November 5 one?"

"Not so much incidents," Mason clarified. "I'm still trying to fit Parker Turner into the puzzle. It's like he's the square piece, and the hole is round."

"Go on."

"His name is the commonality at all four schools," Darrin picked up. "Yet we can't place him at Dorchester High or Franklin High. We're also waiting for a call back from the principal from Forest Hills High."

Scott opened the folder in front of him and studied it for several seconds. "No one claims to know Turner at the other schools either. These spreadsheets are extensive, but they don't list the entire student body, right?"

"No," Mason answered. "Those are only the names of the students who were at the parties. Or at least the ones we've learned about."

"Another thing," Scott added. "Based on your report, the reaction to the drug is a little worse each place it's seen, right?"

"Seems to be the case," Mason agreed.

"What if the pills were available in September or October?" The Sergeant took their timeline back a little. "Yet the side effects didn't send anyone to the hospital. Did you check with the other high schools?"

"There wouldn't have been a police report, so we didn't consider it," Mason responded. "But this angle might give us that excuse. We'll just have to figure out a way to find out about any parties that occurred before November 5."

Suddenly, the Sergeant opened her file and began rifling through the notes.

"Start with the coaches," she instructed after a few moments of silence. "See where that leads you."

"Coaches?" Mason echoed. "What did we miss?"

"These 'parties,'" the Sergeant added air quotes, "were 'hosted' by a person who played sports. The ones in the fall were by 'football players.'"

"Whereas the one most recently was a basketball player," Darrin added.

"We'll get right on this." Mason and Darrin stood to go. "We'll keep you posted."

"Thank you, Detectives."

"Which task do you want?" Darrin asked on the way back to their desks.

"I'm going to talk to Natalie again. I have a few questions about Alisha's house."

"Do you need me to come with you?" Darrin smirked. "Or are you taking Maddy?"

"What do you think?" Mason grinned. "Why don't you follow up with some of the other high schools while I'm gone? Maybe we can get a better picture formulated when I return."

"There you go again," Darrin grumbled. "Going on a date during work hours."

"A date? Hardly." Then he added, "However, you never know."

Sal's Sandwich Shop
January 17, 1994
12:00 p.m.

Maddy rushed into Sal's Sandwich Shop and found Natalie waiting at a table in the corner.

"Thank you for meeting me," she began. "I hope this place is okay."

"It's not a problem." Natalie grinned. "No one makes a meatball sub like Sal."

"On that, we agree."

"What's going on, Maddy?" Natalie prodded for information. "Is everything alright with Tori?"

"Tori's fine. Mason is still trying to figure out what happened to Alisha."

Natalie sighed. "I miss her. She was a good friend."

Maddy's heart twisted for the younger woman. "I'm sorry," she murmured. "I can't imagine."

"I'll be fine ..."

Maddy glanced over her shoulder to see what caused Natalie's voice to fade. Mason had arrived, and the look in his eyes made her fight not to throw herself into his arms. However, they were here for business, which meant a little decorum, right?

He greeted her with a kiss and then turned his attention to Natalie. It surprised her so much it took an extra minute to settle her jumbled thoughts and tune back into what was being said.

"Thank you for meeting me here today." Mason smiled. "I'll not keep you long."

"It's not a problem." Natalie tilted her head in question. "What's going on?"

"Have you ordered?" Mason asked instead of answering.

"No, we were waiting for you," Maddy replied.

"Let's order." He glanced up from the menu. "Alright?"

"It, it's fine." Natalie nodded.

"Maddy?"

She studied him for several heartbeats before agreeing. Once they'd ordered, he took out his notebook.

"Natalie, you met Alisha last September, right?" Mason began.

"Yes," Natalie confirmed. "It was just after fall classes started. We were both living in Jamaica Plains."

"That was not long after I helped Alisha get the restraining order against Brian Lloyd," Maddy added.

Mason turned his attention to her. There was a slight pucker between his brows she wanted to smooth.

"Did you help her move after she got the restraining order?"

"No, why?"

"Did you?" Mason asked Natalie.

"Help her find the house? No. Why?"

Instead of answering, he deflected once again.

"Maddy, did Blue help Alisha find a new place to live?"

"I don't think so. Why? Where are you going with this?"

Mason's lips turned up slightly, reminding her of his kiss when he'd arrived. He'd not kissed her in front of others before, and while she didn't mind, it threw her.

"We've been trying to find out who owns the home on 15 Peach Street. The amount Alisha paid was minimal when compared to what the renters could have gotten."

"I always wondered about that," Natalie murmured. "In Jamaica Plains, we lived in the same apartment building. Then, one evening last October, she stopped by my apartment and told me she was moving."

"No advance notice?"

"None."

"Alisha didn't say why or where she found the house?" Mason tossed out a couple more questions.

"Nothing. Even when I asked her how she'd found such a great deal, she put me off."

"How long after she moved did you follow?" Mason pressed forward.

"A month or so," Natalie answered. "After Alisha moved, we realized how much easier it was to have someone we knew who would watch our kids. She asked if there was any way I could find a place in Dorchester."

"Blue helped you find your apartment, didn't she?" Maddy guessed.

Natalie smiled. "She did."

"Did you have a lot to move?" Mason questioned.

"What do you mean?"

"Is the furniture in your apartment yours? Or did you only have clothing?"

"Oh." Natalie frowned. "Alisha helped me move."

"Go on."

"She showed up in an old truck." Natalie laughed. "Getting everything from the truck to my apartment was a challenge."

"Alisha showed up in a truck?" Mason repeated. "Did she say where she'd gotten it?"

"No."

Mason turned his attention to Maddy. "Any ideas?"

"None." She hesitated a bit. "Natalie, you said you knew Alisha was friendly with a few people from class, right?"

"Yes. Why?"

"Do any of the students you know have old trucks?"

"I have no idea."

"Can you give me the names of the students you think Alisha was friendly with?" Mason pushed his notebook across the table.

While Natalie was writing the names down, Maddy nibbled on a potato chip. She felt Mason watching her, and when she turned her head slightly, discovered she'd been right.

"Do you want a chip?"

He surprised her by opening his mouth. When she stuck the chip between his lips, he wrapped his fingers around her wrist. Her breath caught. The look in his eyes ratcheted the heat up a few notches, and suddenly it was a struggle to look away.

"I don't know all the last names," Natalie admitted. "Joni might have them."

"Thank you." He returned the notebook to his pocket. "You've been a big help."

"I hope so," Natalie sighed. "I really want you to find out who did this."

"Me too, Natalie. Me too. And now, if you ladies will excuse me, I need to run."

"Oh?"

Mason grinned that crooked smile of his that made her heart beat a little faster.

"I have a pushy partner."

Maddy laughed. "I won't tell Darrin what you said."

"Don't worry about it," Mason chuckled. "I'll tell him to his face."

Once again, he surprised her by kissing her. It was a possessive kiss, and it made her head spin.

"I'll pick you up at 7:00 p.m." Mason collected the check and, on his way out, winked.

Maddy fought the silly grin that kept wanting to bloom on her face. When she looked up, Natalie was watching her.

"You like him."

"I do."

"But it worries you."

That the younger woman could read her so well was disconcerting, especially when she spoke nothing but the truth.

"A little."

"Why?"

"You know I grew up in Blessed Children's Home, right?"

"Yes."

"Well, the way I ended up there was ..."

South Boston Precinct

January 17, 1994

2:30 p.m.

Mason strolled back into the precinct, whistling some song he'd heard on the radio. It reminded him of Maddy.

"You sound happy. Did you get lucky?"

"In a way," Mason quipped. The surprised look on Darrin's face had him adding, "Just not the way you're hinting at."

"I'm sorry," Darrin sighed. "Perhaps next time."

"What about you?" Mason ignored the personal and moved back to business. "Did you have any luck?"

Darrin nodded. "We have an appointment with the principal of Newton High School at 4:00 p.m."

"Did you find out something? Or are we going fishing?"

"Some of both."

"Go on."

"I spoke to the school secretary," Darrin began. "She was hesitant to give out any information. However, my charm—"

"Skip to the good parts," Mason cut him off.

Darrin sighed. "You take the fun out of everything."

"Sorry."

"No, you're not. Anyway, the only thing I could get out of the secretary was a confirmation that Parker Turner had gone there."

"She wouldn't tell you when?"

"No. Which is why we get to drive to Newton to see the principal."

"And most likely get stuck in rush hour traffic on the way back."

Darrin shrugged as if to say, '*There wasn't anything I could do.*' "Anyway, I also followed up with the other high schools and updated the timeline."

Mason noted his partner's puzzled expression. "But you have a question."

Darrin smirked. "You'll be asking the same one in a minute." He pulled out the timeline and set it on Mason's desk. "The first police report was from November 5 at Fenway High. Parker Turner was a student there from November 8 - November 22. The Saturday night before, November 20, there was a party at Dorchester High. They don't know Parker. On December 10, there was a party at Franklin High. Again, Parker was not a student. The last party was January 4 at Forest Hills."

"Did you talk to Principal Marsh?"

"He sent me to the secretary, who said they didn't have a Parker Turner on the roll."

Mason frowned. "So, there's a possibility three of the five schools we're looking at have no listing for a student named Parker Turner." He paused to let the words roll around in his head. "Then how did Turner's name get involved?"

"We're missing a connection, aren't we?"

"More than likely," Mason blew out a breath. "I also have a few questions I'd like answered."

"Such as?"

"Where did Parker get the pills? Did he make them?"

"Or did someone else make them, and he's just the dealer?" Darrin stared at the spreadsheets they'd created, then glanced back at the clock. "The dates are still a little off. Party at Fenway on November 5, but Parker didn't start there until November 8. Does that mean something?"

"Probably," Mason acknowledged. "I don't know what, though. Right now, I'm going to follow up with some of Alisha's friends."

"Good luck. I'm going back to hat hunting. Is there any chance you asked Maddy about the F?"

"I didn't. Maybe later. We'll see."

While Darrin was dealing with the red hat's mystery, Mason called the guidance counselor. Thankfully, Joni answered the phone right away, and even offered names without him having to go through hoops.

"Any chance you're able to see if they've registered a vehicle?" he tossed out.

"You're in luck," Joni reported. "Three of them have cars registered. However, none of them are trucks."

"Would it be possible for us to meet with these students? I'm still building a picture of Alisha's life."

"I can try. Would you like me to call you with a time?"

"That would be perfect. Thanks."

With the phone call taken care of, he searched the DMV site for the names not registered at the school. He discovered four others had cars—but none of them were trucks.

That begged the question to be asked. Where had Alisha gotten the truck? She wasn't old enough to rent one. So, did she have someone helping her?

On an offhand hunch, he looked up Brian Lloyd. His driver's license was two years old. And while he had a truck, it wasn't an old one—but a newer model.

"Where did Alisha get the truck? I know it didn't materialize out of thin air."

Darrin glanced up. "What?"

"The truck," Mason mumbled. "It's another piece, just like the Parker Turner piece, that doesn't fit."

"Do you think Turner recruits?"

It took Mason a beat to shift gears. "Recruits? What do you mean? Recruits."

"Recruits," Darrin repeated. "Like, does he recruit other kids in the schools to sell drugs?"

Mason hummed. "I guess anything is possible. Except, if Parker was responsible for the pills at the party, wouldn't he have continued to pull from the same stash?"

"Most likely."

"Then we have a hole."

"How so?"

"We know several kids ended up in the hospital after the party on November 5, right?" Mason broke it down.

Darrin nodded.

"Then," Mason continued. "If anyone pushed any pills after November 5 from the same stash, the chances of side effects should have been greater."

"But as far as we know, that didn't happen."

"There must be a connection. But I don't see it."

"The Sergeant is the one who mentioned sports," Darrin replied. "Could they be passing the pills at sporting events?"

"But who's passing them? I don't think it's the players."

"Why?"

"If it were them, then why would the girlfriends of the 'party hosts' be the ones getting the packages from Turner?"

"More to ponder," Darrin grumbled. "Are you ready to go? We can think about it on the drive."

Mason tossed his files into his drawer and followed his partner out of the precinct. He'd encourage Darrin to drive. It would allow him to ponder the question part of the way, and the rest, he'd think about Maddy.

NINETEEN

CambridgeSide Galleria
January 22, 1994
11:00 a.m.

WHEN MADDY ARRIVED AT THE TRAIN STATION, SHE DUCKED behind a pillar to wait for Tina. While she'd not seen Parker since earlier in the week, she couldn't shake the feeling of being watched. It was spooky, and not altogether comfortable.

"Maddy?"

Her heart rate spiked, and for a second, she forgot to breathe. The only thing that kept her from running was seeing Tina.

"Are you okay?"

Maddy took a deep breath and tried to relax. "It's nothing." She waved away her friend's concern. "You just startled me."

"No," Tina pushed back. "Something is going on."

They were shopping for the specific purpose of finding a formal for the fundraiser. Meaning if she didn't want to be bombarded with questions all day, she had to share. Something she really didn't want to do.

"It started with ... " Maddy gave Tina an overview of everything that had happened since they'd last spoken. When her friend gave her both sympathetic and frightened looks, she wondered which would be the strongest.

"Is this Parker the only suspect?" Tina asked.

"I know they're still trying to find Alisha's ex-boyfriend, Brian Lloyd. Mason hasn't said anything else."

"We'll just have to be careful. Since he's only approached you once, and you were alone, we should be fine."

"*We* should be fine. I hope you're right."

"I'm always right." Tina's blue eyes twinkled. "Didn't I tell you Mason liked you?"

"Touché." Maddy grinned. "I'm just not sure it's quite the same thing."

Tina smiled. "Stick with me, kid." She linked their arms and tugged Maddy toward the mall. "Do you know what you want?"

"Something long," Maddy quipped.

"Haha. I meant the style, smartass."

"No clue. You?"

They meandered through the mall, periodically stopping to look in the windows. Just like always, nothing caught their attention until they stepped into their favorite store.

Tina stopped in front of a rack and slowly pushed aside the hangers. Periodically, she studied a dress, never staying long on one, until she exclaimed, "Look at this one!"

"It's pretty."

"But?"

The dress was light pink, fitted, and floor-length. It had a thigh-high slit up one side and a plunging neckline. The thought of wearing such a dress in front of Mason sent a bolt of heat rushing through her body. Except, was the Home's fundraiser the place for that to happen?

Maddy stuck her hand under the bodice, and wasn't surprised when she could see her fingers.

"It's rather ... revealing. Don't you agree?"

Tina gave her a mischievous grin. "You don't think Blue would approve?"

"I don't think I'm going to ask her if she approves."

"Spoilsport." Tina moved to another rack. She shoved aside first one, then another, and another. Maddy didn't think she was paying attention to the dresses until suddenly ... she stopped.

"What is it?"

"This dress." Tina took it off the rack. "This is it."

Maddy glanced from Tina's enamored expression to the dress. It was ivory, floor-length, and fit tight to the knees, then flared slightly. Small cap sleeves and a round neckline completed the picture. With her dancer's frame, it would be beautiful.

"Try it on. Let's see if it looks as good on you as it does on the hanger."

Tina's eyes met hers. There was a light in them she hadn't seen earlier.

"Should I?"

"Do you like it?"

"Well, duh."

"Then go try it on."

"Maybe I should—"

"Just go, Tina," Maddy muttered. "The last time we shopped for something specific, you found what you wanted in the first store. But after we walked the entire mall, we went back so you could buy it."

Tina laughed. "True, but—"

"No buts." Maddy gave Tina a little shove toward the dressing room. "Go."

"Fine. Fine."

While Tina was trying on the ivory dress, Maddy wandered around the store. There were dresses in every color. Yet none of them spoke to her. None of them said, '*This is the dress that will knock Mason's socks off.*'

When Tina came out of the dressing room, Maddy knew she'd been right. The dress fit perfectly.

"What do you think?" Tina posed in front of the mirror.

"It looks good. What do you think?"

Tina turned in one direction to study the back of the dress, then she turned in the other. Suddenly, she froze mid-turn.

"Tina?" Maddy murmured. "What is it?"

"It's ..." Tina paused long enough to glance over her shoulder. A shadow of concern passed across her face, but gone in a heartbeat. "It's nothing."

Maddy hummed. "If you say so."

"I say so. Did you find anything to try on?"

"Nothing that screams at me like yours did."

"Let me change and pay, then we'll be on our way."

While Tina made her purchase, Maddy continued her search. She was admiring a royal blue dress when a chill raced up her spine. Her breath caught, and, like earlier, the feeling of being watched raced through her. It took several deep breaths before she was ready to look over her shoulder. As before, no one looked out of place, making her wonder if her imagination was working overtime. Or if someone was there, yet not ready to be seen.

Scott & Joy Weaver's Home
January 22, 1994
1:00 p.m.

WITH NOTHING TO DO FOR A FEW HOURS, MASON DROVE TO HIS parents' home. He'd not seen much of his mother since she'd returned from Swan Harbor and was anxious to talk to her. Mainly because he wanted to hear what she had to say about Blessed Children's Home.

When he arrived, his father was in the garage organizing the clutter.

"This, I didn't expect," Mason laughed. "Did mom send you out here?"

Scott's mouth twisted with annoyance. "Send me? No. Guilt me into it? Yes."

Mason chuckled. "How did she do that?"

"Your mother has been cleaning since she returned home," Scott humphed. "Every time she walked past me, I'd get *the eye*."

"The eye?"

"You know *the eye*. You can't tell me you and your siblings never saw *the eye* growing up."

"Of course, we got the eye," Mason murmured. "I just didn't know *you* got the eye."

"Oh, I got *the eye,* alright." Scott made a disgruntled sound. "I almost drove over to the Home. Except I didn't want to come back and find my clothes on the front porch."

"Mom wouldn't do such a thing." Mason hesitated. "Would she?"

"You never know." Scott paused as he finished clearing a shelf. "You wait. Someday, Maddy will give you *the eye*, and you'll know what I mean."

Mason wanted to tell his father he and Maddy weren't quite to that point yet. However, he knew it wouldn't do any good. Something told him his father, and the Sisters saw more than he thought.

"Where's Maddy today?" Scott came back after a bit.

"Shopping with Tina for the fundraiser. Does that mean I need to rent a tux?"

"It does," Scott confirmed. "The Kings know how to throw a party."

"Do you know them?"

"I've spoken to Leo King a time or two, but only in the sense it had to do with the Home. He's a difficult and bitter man."

"Do you know why?"

"The real reason? No. Do I have an idea? Maybe. But that's not why you stopped by, is it?"

"I haven't caught up with mom since she got home," Mason used the safest excuse. "Think I should go in? Or should I leave and pretend I was never here?"

Scott side-eyed him. "It wouldn't work. Your mother knows you're here. You can go in. I can't … yet. I'm waiting for her to lose her mad."

"You're telling me if you go back in there, she's going to give you *the eye* again?"

"No question about that," Scott retorted. "Joy will give me *the eye*."

"Sorry, Dad. I'm going inside. It's too cold out here."

"You're telling me," Scott grumbled.

Mason pushed open the back door and followed his nose. He found his mother pulling a tray of cookies out of the oven.

"Looks like I arrived at the perfect time."

"Mason!" Joy exclaimed. "It's so nice to see you. Would you like a cookie?"

"Of course."

Mason poured a glass of milk and sat down in front of a plate of cookies. He'd just taken a bite when his mother stated, "I understand you're seeing Maddy Davies."

While he chewed, he studied his mom's expression. She looked, dare he say, pleased?

"I am."

"She's a lovely girl."

Joy settled across the table from him and swiped one of his cookies.

"Get your own," Mason grumbled.

"If you want more, I'll get them," she soothed him. "It's dreadful how you two met."

Mason finished the cookie he was eating and shoved the plate aside. "Why am I just now meeting her, Mom? From what I gather, you've known Maddy for years."

Joy took a deep breath, and a look he couldn't interpret flitted across her face. "It's really not my story to tell, Mason."

"How can you say that?" he tossed back. "You were the one who told dad about the Home after he found Maddy. And that was what? Almost twenty-three years ago?"

"I can't believe it's been that long. It seems like yesterday."

"Why, mom? Why did dad call you after he'd found her? That's not normal for him, is it?"

"No, it's not," Joy agreed. "Maddy was different."

"Dad told me his first thought was to promise Maddy tomorrow," Mason kept pushing.

"She's made good use of those tomorrows, hasn't she?"

"I believe so," Mason went on. "Blue thinks dad is trying to atone for something. What do you think?"

"I think—" The phone rang, cutting her off. When she answered and immediately handed it to him, his gut started to churn.

"Hello?"

"Mason?"

"Maddy, honey, calm down," Mason tried to settle her. "Are you hurt?"

"Hurt? No," she denied. "Mad? Yes. Scared? Yes."

"Where are you? Are you still at the mall?"

"Yes."

"But you're not alone, are you?"

"No. Tina's here." Maddy took a breath, then came back with, "He's here."

Mason's heart raced, and before she'd even finished her sentence, he was out of his chair, ready to leave. "Parker?"

"No, Mason," she whispered. "Brian Lloyd. And he's following us."

"Brian Lloyd? Are you sure?"

"Yes! I'm sure. I might not have been able to describe him before. However, now that I've seen him, I know it's him."

"Tell me where you are. I'm on my way."

She rattled off the name of one of the anchor stores. "We'll be in the women's bathroom."

"I'm on my way, honey. Stay put."

Mason hung up. "I'll explain later. Do me a favor and call Darrin. Tell him to meet me at Macy's."

When he jumped into the car, he didn't waste time. He slapped the light on top and pressed hard on the accelerator.

CambridgeSide Galleria
January 22, 1994
1:45 p.m.

"Can you still see the man watching us?" Maddy whispered.

"No," Tina returned. "I think he knows I saw him."

"You don't think that's what he wanted?"

"I don't know what he wanted. What did Mason say?"

"He's on his way." Maddy nodded toward the sign for the ladies' lounge. "I told him we'd be in there."

"Come on, Maddy." Tina grabbed her arm and pulled her down the short hallway. "At least he won't follow us in here."

"You hope."

Maddy dropped her bags on the small sofa but couldn't settle. She leaned on the sink and studied herself in the mirror. What she saw surprised her. Instead of pale, there was a reddish tint spread across her cheeks, and her eyes flashed blue fire.

"You're mad," Tina murmured.

"Aren't you?"

"Well, sure, but if he's the one who killed—"

Maddy blew out a breath. "I know. I know! But yes, I'm mad." She hesitated an extra second, and her stomach swirled. "But I'm not just mad. I'm also scared."

"How did you know Mason was going to be at his parents' house?" Tina frowned. "Did he tell you?"

"Trial and error."

"Come again?"

"I called Mason's apartment. When it went straight to voicemail, I called the Home. Blue gave me Scott's number, and luckily, Mason was there. If he wasn't, I knew I could count on Scott."

"We could have called 911," Tina mumbled. "I didn't even consider it."

"Me either," Maddy answered with a sheepish grin. "Even if we had, we might not have gotten someone familiar with the name Brian Lloyd."

"Would it have mattered?"

"Do I know for sure? No. But—" Before she could finish her statement, the door opened, and a woman walked in.

"Is one of you, Maddy?"

"I am," Maddy spoke up. "Is everything okay?"

"There's a hunky guy out there asking for you. He said it's safe."

"A hunky guy?" Maddy repeated. "Tall, short dark hair and dark eyes?"

"That's him," the woman confirmed.

"Thank you."

They gathered their bags and found Mason and Darrin standing in the hallway. Maddy didn't hesitate, but walked straight into his arms.

"Are you okay?" Mason murmured against the side of her head.

"I'm fine. Did you see Brian?"

When Mason didn't answer right away, Maddy lifted her head enough to read his expression. He was keeping something from her.

"Just tell me," she snapped. "It's better for me to know."

"Let's get something to drink, and we'll talk." Mason put his arm around her and started toward the food court.

Maddy side-eyed Tina, but her friend seemed focused on putting one foot in front of the other. It had her feeling like Tina knew more than she'd let on.

They settled at a table off by itself. "Coffee?" Mason asked, but not so much in a '*Would you?*' but more in a '*You would.*' manner.

It was tempting to push back against his attitude. Except she *had* been scared. She *had* called him. And she knew he was worried about her. For those reasons, she let it go.

"Coffee works."

When he and Darrin walked away, they immediately started whispering.

"What are they saying?"

"Who knows?" Tina sighed. "I'm ..."

"You're what?"

"In a minute," Tina promised.

Mason set the coffee on the table and dumped a handful of cream and sugar packets next to it. "I didn't know what you took," he admitted with a sheepish grin.

"Just cream," Maddy murmured.

Mason sat next to her and added creamer to his coffee. He leaned on the table and glanced from her to Tina, then back.

"Who wants to start?"

Maddy blew out a breath. "While I was waiting for the subway, I thought someone was watching me."

"But you didn't see anyone?"

"No."

"I guess it's my turn," Tina took over. "When we first arrived, we were window shopping. Then I noticed someone in a baseball cap following us."

"Did you see his face?" Mason questioned.

The mention of the ball cap reminded Maddy of Alisha's killer. He'd been wearing a cap. A red one.

"No. When I turned around, he'd ducked into a store." Tina hesitated before continuing, "I didn't think about it again until I was trying on the dress I bought. That's when I saw him once more, and he was watching us."

"Is that when you stiffened?" Maddy murmured.

Tina nodded. "But when I looked again, he was gone."

At the revelation, Maddy reached for Mason's hand. Like before, the connection settled her.

"While Tina was changing, I was looking at dresses on the other side of the store. I turned to see if she was done, and there was a reflection in the mirror. I thought it was Parker, but when I looked back, no one seemed out of place. Except the man I thought was watching us didn't have a cap on."

"How did you know Brian was following you?" Mason pushed the story forward.

"He kept getting closer," Tina shivered. "We tried losing him in one of the bigger stores and by going to a different floor. It didn't work, though. For a little while, we thought we'd lost him, then suddenly, he was back."

"Detective Weaver?" Officer Jacobs, head of mall security, stopped by their table. "We couldn't find him."

"Any sign at all?" Mason tossed back.

"One of my men chased someone in a ball cap," the officer admitted. "However, by the time he reached the parking lot, he couldn't find the person."

Mason tightened his hold on her hand. "What color was the cap, Officer?"

"It was red."

"Tina, what about the cap you saw?" Mason questioned. "Was it red?"

"No."

"No?" Darrin echoed. "What color was it?"

"Navy blue?" Tina shrugged. "Or black."

Mason thanked the officer, but there was something in his voice that said more was going on.

"What did he mean, Mason?" Maddy murmured.

"I'm sure it's nothing." He squeezed her hand in what was to be a comforting move. "The man probably had multiple hats with him and kept changing them."

"I'm sure that's what was going on," Darrin added. "If you want to blend in, it's a good strategy. Just bring a few different-colored hats and periodically change them ."

Maddy was willing to take their answer at face value. Right then, anyway. After all, it made sense. However, something told her there was more to the story. And whatever it was, Mason didn't want her to know it.

TWENTY

Maddy's Apartment
January 23, 1994
11:00 a.m.

MASON PULLED HIS CAR INTO A SPOT AT MADDY'S APARTMENT complex and powered down. He brushed his hand through his hair, then let out a string of curses in frustration. Causing the woman he cared for pain wasn't high on his list of fun activities.

After picking up Maddy and Tina the evening before, the four of them had gone to dinner at Red's, located in Harvard Square. From there, they'd spent several hours at a jazz club. When he'd returned home, his answering machine light had been flashing.

The message was for him to contact Officer Jacobs from the previous night. Before he'd returned the call, he'd suspected he might need to push Maddy's memory. Afterward, though, it had become definite. He just didn't like being reminded.

Mason climbed from the car, worry for Maddy's safety weighing heavily on his mind. It took him an extra second to knock on her door, and while waiting, his nerves played havoc with his insides.

"Mason?" Maddy opened the door a little wider. "Has something happened?"

"Happened?" He shrugged. "I'm not sure what to say."

"It shouldn't be a hard question," she retorted. "All you have to say is yes or no."

A corner of his mouth threatened to curl up at the tone of her voice, but he didn't want to risk being given *the eye*, as his father called it.

"Let me in, honey."

Maddy stepped aside, and the second she shut the door, Mason tugged her into his arms and kissed her. He wanted her to know how much she meant to him. How much he hated having to ask her the questions he was going to ask.

"Mason?" Maddy brushed her fingers over his jaw. "Your kiss was really hot, but you're scaring me."

"When I got home last night, there was a message from Officer Jacobs."

"The officer at the mall?"

Mason tipped his chin.

"Did he have more information about Brian Lloyd?"

"In a roundabout way."

"Just spit it out, Mason," Maddy huffed. "What else did he say?"

"At the same time, the man in the red hat was on one end of the mall, there was an incident on the other end."

"What kind of incident?"

"An officer was in pursuit of a second man. This one wearing a dark hat."

"Black or navy," Maddy winced. "Right?"

"Right. The man in the black hat, whom we believe to be Brian Lloyd, pushed a display over on top of the officer. It delayed him long enough that while he was recovering, the person ran out the door."

"Did the officer see anything after that? Or did he lose him as well?"

"A little of both."

"Go on."

"When he ran out into the parking lot, he saw the man jump into a truck and take off." Mason hesitated and took a deep breath, then came back with, "Another one followed the man's truck ... this one old."

Mason watched Maddy's expression, waiting, wondering if she would put the pieces together.

"Wait a minute," she came back after a bit. "Another man was driving an old truck?"

"Yes."

Suddenly, it must have clicked as her eyes flared, and a concerned expression flitted across her face.

"Two men in hats and another man in an old truck, right?"

"Right."

"Who are they?"

"You said you thought you saw Parker, right?" Mason followed up.

"Yes."

"And both you and Tina saw Brian Lloyd in a dark hat, right?"

"Then who was the man in the red hat?" Maddy put together what he'd been keeping from her. "You suspected something like that yesterday, didn't you?"

"I—"

Maddy laid her hand on his thigh, cutting off his excuses. "Don't keep things from me. You can't be with me 24 hours a day," she pointed out. "I need to know what to expect. Otherwise, I'm at a disadvantage."

"My father taught you a little too well."

"Sorry," she grinned, "but not really."

"You're right. We believe Brian Lloyd had on the dark hat. One of the other two men was Parker Turner. However, the third man was a surprise."

"You have no idea?"

"No idea." Mason angled on the sofa and took both her hands. Hers were cold and had him wanting to kick himself for putting her through what came next. "I need you to try something for me."

"You need me to see if I can remember any more about *that* night, don't you?"

"I'm sorry, but yes, I do."

Maddy ducked her head for a minute. It shut out his ability to watch her expression.

"If I do this," she began. "Will you hold me when I'm done?"

"Try to stop me."

Mason gave her one of those mind-blowing kisses. The kind she never wanted to end. This time, though, she didn't have a choice.

"What do I need to do?"

"Let's try the same technique as before. Close your eyes and picture that night. You hear a sound and look up. Not at the man, though. Focus on the ceiling."

MADDY FOLLOWED THE SOUND OF MASON'S VOICE AND DID AS HE suggested. There was something there. Something that shouldn't have been. It was so out of place—it made her smile.

"What do you see, honey?" he murmured.

"A happy face stamp. It's on the ceiling."

Mason chuckled. "That wasn't the answer I expected. But if you get scared, I want you to return to the stamp. Okay?"

"Okay."

"I need you to focus on the red baseball cap. Can you do that?"

"I can try."

"Just the *hat*," Mason emphasized. "I don't want you to look at the man's face ... yet, anyway. Do you see it?"

Slowly, in her mind's eye, Maddy lowered her gaze until she could see the button on the top of the red hat. "I see it."

"You told me it had a white F on it, right?"

"Yes."

"Can you concentrate on the letter? Is the F plain white, or are there other colors on, or around it?"

It took Maddy several tries to keep her attention from drifting below the hat. If she could tell Mason who killed Alisha, maybe the nightmare would finally end.

"Focus on only the letter," Mason repeated. "Is it one color?"

Maddy pulled her focus back to the letter and studied it for a second. "It's white. Only white."

"Okay, honey. That's great. What style is it?"

"Style? What do you mean?"

"Is it script or block?"

"It's, it's block."

"That's good, honey."

Maddy didn't wait for Mason's next instruction. Instead, she stayed focused and traced the cap to the side. She'd been right the first time. The man had brown hair. There was more, though. Her gaze drifted down about an inch.

"Maddy?" Mason murmured. "Don't push it."

The image in front of her blossomed, and suddenly, the image was there.

"He had an earring on."

"An earring?" Mason repeated. "What kind of earring?"

"It was one of those that hang down."

"Can you see its color?" He led her a little farther. "Is it silver or gold?"

"It's black," she whispered. "It's a black ..." Her eyes flew open to lock with Mason's. "It was a black feather."

"A black feather? Really?"

"Yes. I'm sure."

"Anything else?"

Maddy shrugged. "It was in his left ear." She watched Mason's expression for a few seconds. "Does that help?"

"It just might." Mason kissed one of her hands. Then he kissed the other. "Are you still coming to watch my hockey game?"

It had been a surprise when she learned besides bowling, Mason played hockey.

"Do you want me to come to your hockey game?"

His dark eyes glittered, and he lowered his head just enough to brush his lips across hers.

"If I could choose, we'd spend our time doing a little of that and a little of this."

Mason kissed her a second time, and there was nothing tentative about it. He tugged her across his lap and feasted on her mouth.

Maddy's heart raced, and she couldn't get close enough. When Mason sat back, she wasn't ready for his kisses to stop.

"You go to my head. You know that, right?" he murmured, his voice huskier than normal.

She carded her fingers through his short hair, then slid her hand down to cup his jaw.

"Isn't that a good thing?"

"It's a very good thing," Mason whispered. "Except when we have somewhere to be. Perhaps later, we can explore a little more."

Maddy pressed her molars together to keep her mouth closed. When

Mason touched her, it was so easy to lose herself. She had no doubt her control would crumble very soon.

They left her apartment and made the quick trip to the rink.

"Do you skate?" he asked on the way inside.

"I used to. However, it's been a few years."

"I'll get you back on skates," Mason promised.

"Do you want me to break a leg?"

"You know I wouldn't let you get hurt," he murmured. "If you did, though, I'd kiss it and make it better."

Maddy's breath caught, and it was probably a good thing he had to leave. Otherwise, she might not be responsible for what she said, or did.

"Hi, Maddy," Graham danced up the steps toward her. "Did you come to watch Uncle Mason play?"

"I did. Is he any good?"

"I don't know." Graham shrugged. "I don't always come."

"No?" Maddy glanced toward the ice and watched the men warm up for a few minutes. "Did you come with your dad?"

"Yeah." Graham made a face. "Sierra cried a lot last night, and Mom wanted to take a nap."

"So you decided it would be more fun to watch the hockey game?"

"Well," Graham grumbled. "I didn't get to choose."

"That is tough," she consoled. "Do you play hockey?"

"I skate," Graham offered, which she took as a no. "Do you play hockey?"

"Hardly. What else is new?"

"Not much."

"How's school?"

"Oh, it's okay. Did you know my teacher is getting married?"

"I didn't. Do you like your teacher?"

Graham shrugged. "She's okay."

"Are you learning anything interesting?"

"Not really. Maybe we will next year when I'm in first grade."

"I would bet on it."

"Did you and Uncle Mason decide to get married?" Graham exclaimed.

Maddy wasn't sure she'd heard him correctly. "What did you say?"

"I asked if you and Uncle Mason decided to get married."

"Uh, no." Maddy blinked a few times. "Where did that question come from?"

"I told Uncle Mason to let me know if you decided. So, I wondered."

Don't do it! Don't do it! Except who was she kidding? The temptation was impossible to resist.

"I see." Maddy pressed her lips together, but couldn't contain her curiosity any longer. She glanced around to make sure they were still alone, then put it out there. "What exactly did Uncle Mason say?"

Ice Skating Rink
January 23, 1994
4:30 p.m.

MASON PULLED OUT HIS MOUTHGUARD, NOT SURPRISED TO SEE blood. "Son of a—"

"What happened?" Rod arrived in the middle of his tirade. "Did you bite your lip?"

"Hell, no," Mason grumbled. "I bit my tongue."

"Shouldn't have gotten in the way of my stick. You play with the big boys, you get hurt."

"Shove it," Mason growled. "I'm not in the mood."

"What put you in such a sour mood? The case? Or is it because Graham was talking to Maddy?"

"Why would that worry me?"

"You're not afraid of what he might tell her?"

"I'm Graham's favorite uncle. He won't say anything bad."

"Bad? No. However, nosy is a different story."

"True," Mason hummed. "He did ask me about my marriage plans."

"Has he gotten you married with 2.5 kids already?"

"Not quite yet. But give him a week."

Rod's brows went up, but surprisingly, he didn't pursue the topic. Instead, he came back with, "What happened earlier?"

Once again, Mason found himself in one of those situations. He could ignore his brother's question, or even try to change the subject. Except he knew his brother. If he wanted to know something, Rod wouldn't let it go.

"I pushed Maddy to see if she remembered anything else about the assailant.

"Left a bad taste in your mouth, didn't it?"

"It did."

"What did she say?"

"She gave us two new pieces of information. Now, we'll see."

He shoved his gear into his bag and slipped on his boots. "I asked mom why dad hadn't told us about his connection with the Home."

"You did?" Rod seemed surprised. "What did she say?"

"That it wasn't her story to tell."

"And you let it go."

"Not by choice. The phone rang."

"Caro and I are going over tonight for pizza. Why don't you and Maddy join us?"

Mason chuckled. "You want to gang up on him, don't you?"

"It might be the only way to force him to talk," Rod pointed out.

"Very true." Mason took another few steps. "Should we invite Brandon and Heather?" he questioned regarding his younger siblings.

"We could."

"Except you don't think we should. Why?"

"Have you said anything to them about the Home?"

"Not really. But I've not seen much of either of them lately."

"Let's wait."

"Okay. What time?"

"6:00 p.m." Rod grinned. "Caro can't wait to meet Maddy."

Mason frowned. "Why?"

"She wants to check her out."

"Great," Mason muttered. "Tell her to be nice, or I'll tell Graham where she hides the chocolate."

Rod laughed. "I'll give her the message. On your way out, Send Graham in here, will you?"

"Will do."

Mason left the locker room, only a little surprised to find Maddy and Graham waiting outside the door.

"Uncle Mason!" Graham exclaimed. "I showed Maddy how to get down here all by myself."

"Nice job! Your dad said come on in."

"Okay." Graham gave a long-suffering sigh. "He's probably going to take a shower. I wish I had my Gameboy."

"There's a blackboard in there with some chalk," Mason offered. "You could draw."

Graham shrugged. "I guess. Bye, Uncle Mason. Bye, Maddy."

Mason waited until the little boy had disappeared, then greeted Maddy properly. He kissed her with every intention of adding a little heat, but it stretched the cut on his tongue.

"Damn! That hurts!"

Maddy frowned. "My kiss hurts?"

"No, honey. My tongue hurts."

"Your tongue hurts?" Maddy's eyes twinkled. "Do I even want to know?"

Mason hooked his arm around her neck and guided her out of the rink. "Rod hit me with his stick, and I bit my tongue."

"Rod hit you with his stick? Really?"

"I've had worse." He shut her car door, then ran around to the driver's side.

"Poor baby. I wondered why there was a bruise here." She gently touched the side of his face.

"It hurts, too."

"I'm sorry." Maddy leaned a little closer. "Is there anything I can do to help?"

"Oh, honey," Mason purred. "You don't know how much I want to take you up on the offer I see in your eyes."

"Offer?" Her brows disappeared under her bangs. "What offer do you see?"

Mason cupped the back of her neck, and his mouth descended to meet hers. He'd learned his lesson, and this time, the kiss was slow and lazy. Their lips touched and held, giving permission for their tongues to dance around each other in a leisurely fashion.

"Get a room," Rod shouted seconds before slapping his hand down on the hood of the car.

Mason jumped, but he refused to let go of Maddy completely. He turned his attention to the outside, where his brother and nephew were staring at them. That was the only reason he didn't toss out a rude hand gesture.

"I'm sorry. Apparently, my brother and his son also think I'm fifteen."

Maddy snickered.

"See you two at 6:00 p.m." Rod and Graham hit the hood once more, then headed across the parking lot to their car.

"6:00 p.m.? Do you need to take me home?"

"I could." Mason told her about the dinner invitation. "However, I would really like you to go with me. Would you?"

"I sense there's a little more going on than just dinner with your parents and Rod's family. What am I missing?"

Mason tipped his chin, telling her that, yes, something else was going on.

"I need to know why dad kept the Home a secret for so long."

"Why does it matter, Mason?"

"Honestly, I don't know why it matters so much," he admitted. "I'm just trying to understand why he didn't share something so important with us."

"Blue suspects he's trying to atone for something, right?"

"She does."

"Then perhaps whatever he's trying to atone for is painful, and he doesn't want to remember."

Mason turned back to face the front and leaned his head against the headrest. "If that's true, then every time he came to the Home, wouldn't it all come back?"

"Possibly," Maddy sighed. "But don't forget you're dealing with a generation of men brought up to be the strong ones. Brought up to show no weakness. They were expected to be the breadwinners. The ones to take care of everything. I'm not saying this is the reason. Nor am I saying it to give your father a free pass. You need to remember, the male ego can be very fragile, especially for someone in Scott's age bracket."

"Maybe you're right. I ... "

"Stop right there." Maddy's eyes twinkled. "Go back to telling me I'm right."

"If I tell you some more, will you go with me?"

"Do you really want me to come?"

"I do."

"Then, of course, I'll go with you."

"Thank you."

"Thank you?" she teased. "Is that all I get?"

"What do you want?"

"I think you know."

She was leading him down the same path he'd led her on a time or two.

"What do you want, Maddy?"

"You, Mason. I just want you."

"Good answer." Then he proceeded to show her how much he liked what she had to say.

TWENTY-ONE

Scott & Joy Weaver's Home
January 23, 1994
6:00 p.m.

If someone had asked whether visiting Joy and Scott's home for the first time would make her nervous, Maddy would have laughed. But walking in as their son's girlfriend brought stirred emotions she hadn't expected.

They made it halfway up the stairs to the front porch before she froze. "Wait."

"Wait?" Mason studied her for a second. "What's up, honey?"

"I don't know."

Their gazes clashed. Maddy's heart raced, and it was a struggle to take a deep breath.

"You're scared. Aren't you?"

"Gee, ya think?"

His lips twitched, and before she could move, he hugged her.

"They don't bite."

"I know that." She blew out an exasperated breath. "Your father has seen us in the same room. Just not *together* together."

"He doesn't have a problem with us dating."

"But this is your mother!" Maddy exclaimed. "What if she doesn't think I'm good enough for her baby boy?"

"I'm not the baby boy. That would be Brandon."

She pushed his shoulder playfully. "You know what I meant."

"I do. And I appreciate the enormity of the situation. But everything is going to be fine," Mason promised. "Just hold on to me."

"Everything is going to be fine."

"Yes. Now," he murmured. "Can I have a kiss?"

"You want a kiss?"

"I do. Please."

"Well, since you asked so nicely." Maddy kissed his cheek and then skipped up the stairs before he could grab her.

"That wasn't very nice."

He stalked toward her, his intent written all over his face. When he reached the top step, Maddy pointed at him.

"You stay over there."

"You know what I want."

"I do."

"Well?"

"Lat—" was all she got out before the door opened.

"Maddy!" Joy Weaver exclaimed. "Ignore that son of mine and get in here."

Maddy tossed an impish grin over her shoulder, and as soon as she stepped over the threshold, Joy hugged her.

"I'm so happy you and Mason have found each other," she whispered. "I've always thought you'd be perfect together."

Maddy wanted to say, *'Then why didn't you tell him about me? Or about the Home?'* But she didn't want to be rude.

"You're not telling her anything bad about me, are you, Mom?" Mason teased.

Joy laughed. "Not yet."

He gave Maddy a disgruntled look. "I'll have to keep you two apart."

"Stop that." Joy shooed Mason toward the back of the house. "Go say hello to your father."

"You're a taskmaster," he grumbled.

"While you're doing that." Joy linked arms with Maddy. "We'll catch up."

There was a part of her that wanted to throw a '*Help me!*' look over her shoulder. The other part followed like it was the most natural thing in the world.

They ended up in a small reading room, and as soon as they stepped inside, the noise level decreased. Strangely enough, the room settled her.

Maddy wandered around, taking in the little personal touches and photos. It was an odd experience to see pictures of Scott with his children. An odd thought to think she was close to the same age as his daughter. To think that at the Home, there were similar photos of her with Scott. It was as if he had two families. One by blood. The other by bond.

"This space reminds me of the Home's morning room. While they're used for different purposes, the feel is similar. Which probably makes no sense, but ..."

"That was my goal," Joy replied in a slightly wistful voice. "I've always loved the Home and agree there is something special about the morning room. It's a very peaceful place."

"It's my favorite room," Maddy admitted. "I tried to convince Blue to let me put my office there, but she refused."

Joy laughed. "I don't blame you. I would want the same thing."

For the next few minutes, they talked about the children at the Home, and Joy asked about Blue, Green, and Black. Then she returned to Mason, and once again, Maddy felt like she had to be on guard.

"How are you holding up?" Joy's voice softened. "I can't imagine how terrified you must have been."

Maddy smiled, but somehow she knew it didn't reach her eyes. However, since Joy was a therapist, the question shouldn't have surprised her.

"To be honest. While it was happening, I don't remember being scared. Everything was pure reflex."

"Scott says you swing a mean skillet, though," Joy grinned. "And it brought you into Mason's life."

"Things happen when they're meant to happen," Maddy repeated Blue's favorite saying.

"You have no idea how many times my mother said those words to me when I was growing up. Or how many times I've said the same thing to one of my kids." Joy hesitated a moment, and Maddy relaxed, almost too much. "You want to know why Scott didn't tell the kids about you or the Home, don't you?"

"Not as much as Mason wants to know," Maddy admitted. "I always knew you and Scott had children, so, in a way, I had an advantage."

Before Joy could respond, a bubbly brunette bounced into the room. She was holding a baby, and the assessing look on her face told Maddy she was being sized up.

"Do you want her?" Caro held Sierra out to Joy. "Her tummy is full, and her diaper is clean."

"Give me that precious girl," Joy gushed. "Maddy, as you can guess, this is Rod's wife, Caro."

"Nah, really?" Maddy teased.

"Have you met Sierra?" Joy grinned. "Isn't she adorable?"

"Scott and Mason brought her and Graham to a birthday party at the Home a couple of weeks ago," Maddy replied.

"Oh?" Joy's brows went up. "That's interesting."

"It's nice to meet you, Maddy." Caro grinned. "Although I feel like I know you already."

"Really? From Mason?"

"Graham," Caro surprised her by saying. "He was especially excited to tell me about the kiss he and Rod broke up earlier today."

Maddy dropped her head. She could feel heat creeping up, but decided she was going to ignore it.

"He has bad timing."

Caro giggled. "You don't know the half of it."

"I'll just take Sierra to the kitchen," Joy said. "The pizza should be here any minute."

"Joy isn't mad, is she?"

"No." Caro waved away the possibility. "She left so I could interrogate you."

"You could what?"

"Gotcha," Caro snickered. "However, tell me everything about you and Mason. Inquiring minds need to know."

Maddy laughed ... just a little. Not the nervous kind she'd had on the porch, but the real kind. The one that said, *maybe this wasn't going to be so bad after all.*

Scott & Joy Weaver's Home
January 23, 1994
7:30 p.m.

MASON TOSSED HIS DIRTY NAPKIN ON HIS PLATE AND STRETCHED out his long legs. He'd decided he wouldn't put his father on the spot unless it came up. That didn't mean he couldn't give it a little nudge.

Before he could settle on what to say, he caught an exchange between his parents. One he couldn't decipher. From there, Scott's gaze drifted to Maddy, then back to his mother.

"For thirty-five years," Scott began. "Joy has been my best friend. While she might disagree, I've treasured every minute." His father's attention moved from Joy to him. "Less than a month ago, Mason found himself in a similar situation to the one I was in twenty-three years ago. It all started with a death, ... a little girl with blue eyes, ... and a promise to give her tomorrow."

There was something about the comparison of their situations that had Mason readjusting in his chair. He grabbed hold of Maddy's hand, and their connection calmed him. While he'd told her to hold on to him, it seemed their roles had reversed.

Scott told a story about being a cop in the 1950s and 60s for the Swan Harbor Police Department. Told of a fire starter who worked his way up the Maine coast. Told of how the arsonist considered it all a game.

"It was late fall," Scott's voice dropped, "and Swan Harbor General was on fire. Matt and I rushed there as fast as possible, but as you can imagine, it was chaotic. Everything seemed to move in slow motion while we helped evacuate everyone. Finally, we thought we were finished and relaxed. But then Ruby screamed a little girl's name and ran back into the fire."

Scott's gaze drifted around the table ... and landed on Maddy.

"Ruby was Ruby Blue."

Maddy's breath hitched. "Blue's grandmother."

Scott nodded. "Her son, Matt, and I had been best friends our entire lives. Which meant it was my responsibility to help her."

Mason's heart squeezed at what his father must have been feeling.

"What happened, dad?"

"I found her on the floor," Scott murmured. "A beam had hit her, and she was already gone."

"Since you couldn't save Blue's grandmother, have you been trying to make up for that?" Rod questioned.

Scott shrugged. "Did I intentionally set out for that to be true? No."

"Then what happened?" Mason followed up, even knowing he had a pretty good idea.

"Those were tough times," Scott whispered. "We were in the middle of the Vietnam War and, as a young male, fear of being drafted was never far from your mind. Not long before you were born, Mason, Blue's father—my best friend—shipped out. He left his wife and two children behind, and suddenly, there was an extra weight on my shoulders."

"Was he killed?" Rod asked.

"First, they declared Matt missing," Scott corrected. "Not knowing was worse than knowing. Until they find the person or their body, life for those who cared for them was in limbo. It was several years before they returned his remains to the States. Not long after that, your mother was offered a job in Boston. As much as I loved Swan Harbor and wanted to raise my family there, I couldn't. The memories were too heavy."

Mason had vague memories of leaving Swan Harbor and finally understood why his parents hadn't answered his questions. That even after years, his father still had scars from that time. It fit Maddy's description of men from that generation and explained why they were getting an overview of the tough times.

"We'd only been in Boston a year when I found Maddy." Scott cleared his throat. "One look in her blue eyes and, while I couldn't give her back her parents, I could give her tomorrow, and the next day. Your mother reminded me about Blessed Children's Home, and here we are."

Mason was still processing everything his father had said when a drop of water hit his hand. His breath caught when he realized tears were rolling down Maddy's face.

"Oh, honey." He hugged her, bringing her closer to his warmth. "Are you okay?"

Their eyes met and held. Hers were blue like the sky on a cloudless summer day. His heart was beating so hard it felt like it was going to jump from his chest. He was quickly learning when she hurt, so did he. In an almost unconscious move, Mason cupped her jaw and wiped away her tears. Then he kissed her.

The kiss was short and so sweet it was a struggle to move away. Then he got a good look at her face and realized what he'd done.

"Was that okay?"

A corner of Maddy's mouth lifted. "You're asking now?"

He leaned in to kiss her again, but she was too aware and held him off. Instead, her eyes made promises for later.

"Dad, it sounds like the Home is a wonderful place," Rod stepped in. "I still don't understand why you never told us." He turned his attention to Joy. "Or you, mom. You're just as guilty as dad. Why?"

Scott took a deep breath. "Pride. Stupidity. Fear. Maybe a little of all three. I kept telling myself it wasn't a big deal. It was just part of my job." He glanced across the table at Rod before moving his attention to Mason. "And when you were children, I never shared my job with you."

Mason ducked his head. That hadn't been something he'd considered. He felt ashamed. If he hadn't pressed the issue, none of this would have come out. His mother would have stayed quiet. His father wouldn't have shared. And Maddy wouldn't have cried.

"What took me a while to realize," Scott went on, "was it hadn't been a job. It was the opposite. After seeing the seedier parts of life while at work, coming home always soothed my soul. Spending time at Blessed Children's Home was different, but I'm not sure I can explain how so. Perhaps it was a way to heal the pieces of my heart I'd lost during those hard times. All I knew was I needed them, and they needed me."

Maddy brushed off her face and pressed a little tighter to Mason. Her heart ached for the man standing in front of her. He'd given her a future when she'd needed one most.

While she'd never admitted it to anyone, sometimes when she was young, she dreamed he'd take her home. Dreamed he loved her and wanted her to be a part of his family. Was that what was happening? Were Scott's two families merging?

"Maddy, dear," Scott murmured. "I'm sorry for the way it happened.

However, I'm not sorry you're here tonight. My mother used to say, '*Things happen when they're meant to happen*.' Maybe out of the sadness of Alisha's death, you've found what you were destined to find."

Her breath caught at the implication of what he'd said. She wanted to ask for clarification. Wanted to know what Mason thought of his father's comment.

"I made fresh cookies today," Joy jumped in to cover the silence. "Shall I bring a plate of them out?"

"I want cookies, grandma." Graham hopped off his chair. "Come on. I'll help."

"I'll help, too," Scott decided. "Cocoa? Milk?" everyone shouted over each other, but somehow, he seemed to know what they wanted and took off toward the kitchen.

Mason handed her a clean napkin and watched with concern while she wiped her face.

"I must look a mess."

"A beautiful mess," he whispered.

His words triggered that place inside only he could touch. She didn't initially set out to do it. Then he leaned a little closer, and his dark eyes tugged at her heart. It was a look that made it impossible to stay away, and without considering the complications, she cupped his jaw and kissed him. The kiss was soft, but very potent.

"Should I apologize?"

"For the kiss?"

"Yes."

"Only if you're apologizing because it was so short."

Maddy snickered. "Leave it to you to come up with that line."

"Is it going to get me anywhere?" His eyes flared, and his cheeks took on a rosy hue, almost as if he couldn't believe what he'd said. Especially considering where they were.

Was she brave enough to say what she wanted to say? Most likely not—at least not right then. On the other hand, if she didn't, would she regret it?

"Here I am!" Graham raced back into the room, easing the heat growing between them.

"Maddy, you get to choose first," Graham said, holding the plate of cookies for her to see.

"Oh, I do? That's very sweet of you." She pondered her choice. "What would you suggest?"

Graham studied the plate of cookies. Most of them were chocolate chip, but there were also two peanut butter and a couple with white chunk chocolate.

"How about I take one of these?" Maddy picked up a chocolate chip. "They look delicious."

"Good choice." Graham grinned. "I wanted the peanut butter."

"Hey, Graham," Mason pretend-pouted. "Don't those peanut butter ones have my name on them?"

Graham glanced up, and his expression had her pressing her lips together to keep from smiling. She looked away briefly, then went back to the exchange between Mason and his nephew.

"Well, Uncle Mason," Graham sighed. "If you really want a peanut butter one, I'll share."

"Wow, Rod," Mason chuckled. "Your son shares better than you ever did."

"Bite—" Rod began before his wife covered his mouth.

"You know what, Graham," Mason hummed. "Since you're my favorite nephew, you can have the peanut butter. I'll eat these chocolate chip ones."

"Alright!" Graham began, and then a bewildered expression crossed his face. "Hey, wait a minute." Mason had the cookie halfway to his mouth when Graham grabbed his wrist. "What did you say?"

"I said," Mason repeated. "You're my favorite nephew."

Graham giggled. "Uncle Mason, I'm your only nephew. How could you forget that?"

Mason's sparkling eyes met hers. He quickly took the platter of cookies and set it on the table. Then, before Graham could take off, he started tickling him. The sound of the little boy giggling and roughhousing with his uncle once again had tears rushing to Maddy's eyes.

"I'm going to go wash up." She turned her attention to Graham. "Would you show me the little girls' room?"

"It's not only a little girls' room," Graham exclaimed. "Little boys can use it too."

"That's good to know."

"Are you sure you don't need me?" Mason waggled his eyebrows. "I know exactly where the bathroom is."

"I know you do. However, I think Graham can handle this task."

"Yeah, Uncle Mason. I can handle this task."

Maddy snickered at Mason's expression and had to hurry to catch up with Graham. She closed the door and studied her reflection. Her face wasn't blotchy—which was good. However, her eyes felt like they were full of sand.

She splashed her face with cold water, which helped somewhat. On her way back to the dining room, she walked past the kitchen.

When Maddy glanced inside, she saw Scott with his arms looped around Joy's waist. The way they were looking at each other was so tender it took her breath. Had he been right when he'd commented about her destiny?

"Mason might not know it yet," she heard Joy say. "But his heart and Maddy's are connected."

"Why do you think I commented on her finding what she was meant to find?" Scott mused. "Was my finding her on that night so long ago part of a greater plan? Instead of just giving Maddy her tomorrows, was there a deeper meaning?"

"You're wondering if you were meant to save her because of Mason, aren't you? That maybe they're destined to be together."

"That's my dream, honey." Scott smiled. "That our family expands to include Maddy." He pulled her a little closer. "Now, before we get back to the kids, come here."

Maddy blinked back the tears that threatened. Hearing the same thing she'd been thinking earlier come out of Scott's mouth touched her. Had the family she'd always wanted been right in front of her all along?

TWENTY-TWO

South Boston Precinct
January 24, 1994
9:00 a.m.

MASON SPREAD THE FILES ON THE CONFERENCE ROOM TABLE AND added the new information. They'd learned their sergeant had been correct. Parker Turner had been a student at Newton High from October 4 to November 5. There'd also been an unreported incident on October 1. After talking with a few of the students, they'd discovered the same scenario as at the other schools.

Someone left a bag with two cases of beer for the girlfriend of the host, along with Parker's name and regrets. Just like they were with Fenway High, though, the dates were off.

He was in the middle of making notes about Saturday when his partner rushed into the room.

"I brought the red hats, folders, and a copy of Brian Lloyd's driver's license photo." Darrin tossed the picture on the table. "There's no feather earring, but can you tell if he has a pierced ear?"

"Do you have a magnifying glass?" Mason quipped. "This photo is pretty small."

"Sorry. I tried to enlarge it," Darrin sighed. "But the photo just turned grainy."

Mason spat out a word he rarely used and studied Brian Lloyd's image. The photo had been taken two years previous, and he had to wonder if the man had changed.

"We didn't ask Tina and Maddy for a description of Brian Lloyd," he suddenly realized. "Why didn't we ask for a description?"

Darrin shrugged. "Guess we didn't think we needed it. Maddy seemed pretty sure it was him."

"True," Mason agreed. "She'd seen him from a distance before. But Tina hadn't."

"Should I call Tina?" Darrin grinned. "Or do you want to call Maddy?"

"I'll let you call this time," Mason offered magnanimously. "Maybe you won't complain for a while."

"Maybe." Darrin gave him a cheeky grin and left the conference room, whistling some song Mason couldn't identify.

While his partner was busy, Mason put down the photo and went to work dividing the hats. He immediately pushed aside the ones with a multicolored letter. Then he separated the hats with block letters from the ones with script lettering.

"Okay." Darrin returned before he could move on. "Tina said Brian had on jeans and a t-shirt covered by a dark jacket. His hair was on the longer side, and he was sporting facial hair. But she couldn't say if it was only scruff or a beard."

"The long hair and possible beard are new," Mason noted. "She didn't mention the earring by any chance?"

"Hell, no," Darrin muttered. "That would be too easy."

Mason took another look at Brian's photo and focused on his left ear. When he still couldn't say for sure, he took the picture with him and grabbed a magnifying glass.

"Well?" Darrin prodded when he returned.

"You look."

It only took several minutes before Darrin glanced up, wearing a disgusted expression. "No earring."

"No earring," Mason confirmed. "That doesn't necessarily mean he didn't get one, though."

"True." Darrin nodded to the hats. "What have you found so far?"

"Maddy said the F on the red hat was block and only white," Mason shared. "Which leaves us with eight." He lined them up, facing Darrin. "Fenway High, Forest Hills High, Franklin Park, FunZone, F Street Grill, Flaherty Pool, Florian Street Cafe, and Flaming Grill & Buffet."

"That's still too many," Darrin grumbled. "Let's mark them on the map and create a grid."

Mason spread out the map they'd been using. "If we use Franklin Park as our landmark," he began. "We can put Fenway High on the northeast side, and Forest Hills High on the southwest side, right?"

"That works," Darrin murmured, already searching for the next business. "Here's the FunZone." He indicated a place not far from their precinct in South Boston.

They quickly found Flaherty Pool and F Street Grill on the northwest side of Franklin Park and marked those with an X.

"Here's Florian Street Cafe." Darrin tapped the map. "It's on the corner of Florian and Park Avenue. Should we send someone out to ask questions?"

Mason hummed and then marked off the Flaming Grill & Buffet. "We'll send patrol to both places. We deserve a break."

"We do," Darin agreed.

Mason touched the FunZone. "This one is an outlier, as it's around four miles from Franklin Park."

"It might be the only one, though."

"What about Newton High?" Mason pointed to the school in the northwest corner of the park. "It's farther away from our landmark than the other schools."

"True. But look here," Darrin went on. "While the pool and the F Street Grill are closer to Newton High, they are barely a mile away from the park.

"And the cafe and buffet are near Forest Hills High. Mason studied the map a little longer. Something was rolling around in his head. He just needed to be patient.

"Where did Lloyd live?" he exclaimed once it all coalesced.

"Lloyd? Why?"

Mason rifled through his notes until he found what he needed. After that, he located 15 Peach Street on the map.

"Here's Alisha's home, right?"

"Okay."

"We know our killer ran toward Franklin Park." Mason followed the route with his finger. "And his jacket ended up here." He touched the spot on the map.

"I'm with you."

"We also know someone saw Parker not far from where the jacket had been tossed."

Mason drew a line around Franklin Park, which had a rough diamond-like shape. He included Fenway High to the northeast, Alisha's home to the southeast, Forest Hill's High to the southwest, then added Flaherty Pool, and F Street Grill to the northwest.

"There are too many possibilities for our killer not to be inside that circle."

Darrin hummed a little before pointing to an area between the F Street Grill and Fenway High. "That's Lloyd's last address."

"Maddy said when she saw Parker, it was in an orange line station. Mason continued. "And she said she felt someone watching her, right?"

"You're thinking it would be an easy hop onto the orange line from any of these places, aren't you?"

"I am. If only—"

The day watchman knocked on the door, cutting him off. "Mason, the officer you spoke to at CambridgeSide Galleria is on line 2."

Mason exchanged looks with Darrin. "Did he say what he wanted?"

"No."

"Maybe we'll get a break," Darrin murmured.

Mason couldn't help but agree. It would be nice to have everything tied up before the fundraiser on Saturday. He'd give anything to have the weekend with nothing between him and Maddy—both literally and figuratively.

Blessed Children's Home

January 24, 1994

10:00 a.m.

MADDY HAD BEEN STARING AT THE SAME REPORT FOR ALMOST AN

hour. Once more, a member of the Weaver family had messed with her focus. She kept thinking about what she'd overheard between Joy and Scott.

"... his heart and Maddy's are connected."

"Was my finding her on that night so long ago part of a greater plan? Instead of just giving Maddy her tomorrows, was there a deeper meaning?"

What exactly did he mean? Did it mean what she hoped it meant? While she could have asked Mason, she'd chosen not to. She didn't want him to know she'd eavesdropped on his parents.

Why had she, though?

Was it because, even knowing Scott and Joy were married, she'd never witnessed anything intimate between them? Marriage wasn't something she knew much about. It was a concept she understood, but the practicality was foreign. She'd never had a role model.

That circled her thoughts back to the whole hearts connected statement. Maddy jumped up and went searching.

"Good morning, Black. Have you seen Blue?"

"She was headed to the storage closet a while ago. Why?"

"I just have a couple of questions for her. Thanks."

Maddy took the stairs to the second floor and, before she saw her, heard the older woman singing. When she poked her head in the closet door, Blue was rearranging boxes.

"Are those Tori's?"

Blue spared her a glance. "Yes. The other day, when I transferred the items you brought back into a box, I asked Scott to take me by the house. I didn't want you to have to go back."

Which shouldn't have surprised her, as that was typical behavior for Blue.

"Anyway," Blue went on. "I found three disposable cameras in one of those bags and had them developed. I thought maybe there were some photos of Tori's mom she would appreciate when she's older."

"Did you look at the pictures?"

"No. Would you like to?"

"I would, thanks."

"Once you're done, just put them in one of those boxes."

"I will." Before the older woman had gotten far, Maddy remembered why she'd come upstairs. "Blue?"

"What is it, dear?"

"I had dinner with Scott, Joy, Mason, Rod, and his family yesterday."

"That's wonderful." Blue grinned. "I'm sure you fit right in."

"Scott talked a little about his friendship with your father."

Blue's dark eyes sparkled. "From what I gather, they were always up to mischief."

"I heard Joy say something I don't quite understand."

"What's that?"

"She said Mason's and my hearts are connected. What exactly does that mean?"

"I think you know."

"Where does the saying come from?" Maddy pushed for more.

A little smile played on Blue's lips, almost as if she were remembering something. "It's a saying from where I was born," she explained. "I believe it means you're 'true loves,' just like in all those fairytales you used to read."

"That's what I thought they meant." Maddy paused. Once upon a time, she'd dreamed of fairytale endings. Maybe she still did. "But how could she know that?"

"You're going to have to ask her."

"Okay, thanks."

Of course, if she asked, they would know she'd been eavesdropping. Something she really didn't want anyone to know. Therefore, she'd wait and hope someday she'd learn.

With Blue gone, Maddy pushed the boxes back into the closet and took the photos to her office.

Her hands shook as she opened the outer envelope and pulled out three smaller ones. She took a deep breath and started through them. The first photo showed Tori as a newborn, wrapped like a mummy in a white blanket. It was clear the picture had been taken in the hospital. By whom, though? Alisha? The father? Or perhaps the social worker, Thomas Gilbert?

Tori was born in November 1992, and the roll of film ended in March 1993. With every image, her heart hurt a little more, and by the time she finished, tears were rolling down her cheeks.

Maddy picked up a pen to write a remembrance on the backs of the photos. Except the words wouldn't come, making her heart hurt even more.

She shoved them back into the envelope and moved to the second set. Most of them were of Tori, but a few were of Alisha, Tori, and Brian Lloyd.

The photo had been in a park, and everyone looked happy. It was hard to believe that less than two months later, things had gotten so bad between them, a restraining order had been necessary. A true Jekyll and Hyde situation.

Maddy closed her eyes and thought about the men she'd seen at the mall—Parker and Brian.

The man in the photos didn't look much like the man she'd seen. He appeared put together—not scruffy. However, a closer look showed her Brian had a pierced left ear. While he'd not been wearing a dangling earring, it didn't mean he wasn't the killer.

She shook the images out of her head and took out the third set. There weren't as many photos in this bunch, telling her they were going to be more recent.

For the first few, nothing stood out. Then Maddy happened upon one of Natalie carrying a box. The date confirmed it had been the day she'd moved. She continued to the next photo, and her breath caught. It was the back bumper of an old truck, complete with a partial license plate.

See, Mason, she thought. *I can be of use.*

The last few photos had been taken at Christmas. They were of Tori alone, Tori and Alisha, and Tori, Alisha, and ....

Maddy dropped the pile and reached for her phone.

CambridgeSide Galleria
January 24, 1994
10:45 a.m.

Mason and Darrin climbed from the cruiser and started toward the mall. Two officers were standing in front of a bench, one of them Jacobs.

"Detectives." Officer Jacobs stepped forward. "Thank you for coming." He nodded toward the bench. "We found the item right behind there."

"Who found it?" asked Mason.

"I did, sir," the other officer stepped forward. "I'd come out to take a smoke break and saw it."

"You didn't touch it, though, right?" Darrin questioned.

"No, sir."

"Did you contact the forensics team?" Mason asked Jacobs.

"Not yet. I thought I would wait for you."

Mason just barely kept his wince to himself. He'd rather the team was there already taking photos.

"Shall we?" Darrin handed Mason a pair of gloves. "Maybe this will narrow our red hat search a little more."

"Don't hold your breath," Mason muttered. "But you never know."

They were standing not far from the door where their 'third' male had run out on Saturday evening. Apparently, the person had cleared the door, tossed his red hat behind a bench, and faded into the night. By the time the officer made it outside, it had grown dark, allowing their suspect to get away.

Mason squatted next to the hat. It had landed on its side with the white F facing forward. From his view, there was nothing to indicate the hat had belonged to the killer.

"Do you mind contacting the forensics team?" Mason asked Jacobs. "While we can't see anything, they might be able to get DNA from it."

Jacobs disappeared, leaving Mason and Darrin alone with the young smoker.

"Do you think this will help you find the person?"

"Perhaps," Mason sighed. "For some reason, it feels like it just adds to our questions."

"Well, good luck."

Officer Jacobs returned, and with the forensics team on the way, Mason and Darrin left.

"What do you think?" Darrin murmured. "Do you think it's the killer's hat?"

"I do," Mason admitted. "Which gives me several questions that need answers. Who is the man in the truck, and why did he chase Brian? Was it Parker? If so, is he working with the third person? Is he our connection to the schools where we can't place Turner?"

"Would make sense," Darrin hummed. "Maybe we should stop by the precinct, collect our hats, and take them to the lab. Perhaps the techs can find something specific to help identify which one it matches."

"Worth a shot," Mason grumbled. "Not much else to do."

As soon as the car came to a stop, Mason ran into the precinct. He grabbed the hats and was on his way out when the day watchman called his name.

"What is it?"

"Message." She held up a slip of paper.

"Who's it from?"

"Maddy Davies. She says it's important."

He reached for the message, and a streak of fear raced up his spine.

Can you come by the Home? I found something.
Maddy

"Detour," Mason shared once he was back in the car. "We need to go by the Home."

Darrin side-eyed him, but didn't argue. He was quiet until he turned onto the highway.

"What is it?"

"Maddy found something."

"She didn't say what?"

"No," Mason sighed. "I'm just glad she didn't call to say she'd seen Turner or Lloyd again."

"Amen to that."

It took close to a half-hour to get to the Home. Before they'd even rung the bell, the door opened. "You came," Maddy whispered.

Mason took in her appearance. She was pale, and her eyes were red-rimmed. He tugged her into his arms and hugged her.

"You've been crying. What happened?"

Maddy took a breath and stepped backward. "Did you know Scott and Blue packed up Alisha's house?"

"I think dad mentioned it the other day. Why? What's going on?"

Before answering, Maddy led them to her office and tapped the photo envelopes she'd left on her desk. "Blue had these developed. Most are of Tori, but there are a few I think might help you."

Mason's gut tightened, and slowly, he went through the first roll and then handed them to Darrin. From there, Maddy gave him the second set. As soon as he saw the picture of Lloyd with the mother and daughter, it took him aback. In the photo, Brian was clean-cut, clean-shaven, and the smiles on his and Alisha's faces said they were happy. Possibly even more than happy. What could have changed between them so much she'd been forced to get a restraining order? Was it something they would ever learn?

"What do you see?" He handed the picture to Darrin.

Darrin looked at the photo for less than five seconds. "He has a pierced ear."

"Yes," Mason nodded. "His left ear."

"Here's the last set." Maddy handed him the photos, and the fact her hand shook made him curious.

"Look at these," she instructed.

The first few showed the inside of an apartment. Best guess was it belonged to Alisha or Natalie before they moved. From there, the photos became more interesting.

"I'll be a son of a ..." Mason laid the photo on the desk. "What do you see?"

"A 1974 GMC," Darrin whistled. "Boy, they don't make those anymore."

"How did—?" Maddy began.

"Darrin's dad is a mechanic," Mason explained. "He knows cars and trucks."

"Oh." She nodded toward the pictures still in his hand. "Keep going. That's not all."

Mason's eyes flared. "There's more?"

"Oh, yes."

He flipped through a few more photos until he came to the ones taken at Christmas. These were pictures Tori would appreciate someday. The last one meant something to him.

It showed Tori sitting on Alisha's lap. Next to her sat Parker Turner, the man they'd been trying to find.

"Where was the photo taken?" Darrin murmured after studying it for several minutes. "You can see the edge of a building out the window."

Mason looked at the photo again. His partner had been right. Out the window was one of Boston's tallest and most recognized buildings—the John Hancock Tower.

TWENTY-THREE

Maddy's Apartment
January 29, 1994
3:00 p.m.

Mason's kisses picked her up and carried her along on a sensual ride. She wanted more … a lot more.

"Come here."

He rolled them over and tucked a leg between hers. Their position put the pressure in the exact place she wanted … no, where she needed it.

His lips were possessive, and his hands were never still. Her heart beat so loudly she was surprised he couldn't hear it. But that didn't matter. Right then, the only thing that mattered was that build-up going on inside. It swept her up and, before she was ready, pulled her over the edge.

For a handful of minutes, she lost focus on anything but what had just happened. Seconds later, her senses began to return. Maddy buried her face against Mason's chest, both sated and embarrassed.

"Maddy, honey," Mason purred. "Are you okay?"

She wasn't sure she could form a coherent sentence, so she nodded. However, she could tell that wasn't enough to satisfy the man who was holding her.

It took another few minutes for her to work up the courage to lean back enough so their eyes met. There was a fierceness in his. One that could mean many things.

"I should ask you the same thing," Maddy murmured. "Are you okay?"

"Why are you asking?" The timber of his voice differed from any other time. It was thick with emotion and made her feel more than she could explain.

"I think you know, Mason." Maddy boldly slid her hand down to cup his hardness, causing Mason's body to jerk in response to her touch. There was a power there she'd not felt before.

"Careful, honey." He closed his hand around her wrist. "Just give me a minute."

Then, like every other night, he'd kissed her and driven back to his apartment. She knew he wanted her. Had known he wanted her for weeks. Yet, every time the opportunity presented itself, he'd walked out the door.

Their relationship had seemed complicated at the beginning. They'd worried about hurting Blue or his father. Now that they were out in the open, and her heart was *supposedly* connected to his, he was still holding back. Did it have something to do with her? Or because of him?

You won't know until you ask.

Before she changed her mind, Maddy pulled out her carry-on bag. She packed the baby doll silk nightgown she'd ordered from the *Rebecca's Fantasy* catalog. In addition, she added a change of clothes, leaving enough room for her toiletries.

With her after-the-party bag packed, Maddy took a quick shower and slipped into her black velvet dress. The moment she'd seen it, she'd known it was meant to be hers.

While she waited for Mason, she had difficulty staying still. When he finally knocked, she forced herself to count to ten before answering.

"Wow!" he exclaimed. "You look ... amazing."

"I could say the same for you." His black tux made his eyes seem even darker, and he was so handsome he took her breath. It was going to be a challenge keeping her hands to herself.

He leaned in for a kiss, but hesitated before their lips met. "Are you going somewhere?"

"That depends on you."

"Me?" Mason frowned. "What are you saying, honey?"

"I thought," she swallowed, and then rushed on, "I thought if you wanted, we could stay at your place tonight." Mason's breath hitched. "I mean, if you want to. After all, your apartment is—"

Mason kissed her quiet. It was a heady experience, and if it hadn't been important, they would have skipped the party.

"I want ... you."

"I thought so." Maddy toyed with the studs on his shirt. "But I wasn't sure why you always stopped right before ..."

"Maybe I was waiting for us to be on the same page. Now that we are, can we skip the party?"

Maddy laughed. "No. We should go."

Mason helped her with her wrap, and they made the drive to the Four Seasons. When they reached the ballroom, the Sisters were waiting.

"Did I forget something?"

"No, dear," Blue assured her. "I wanted to introduce you to the Kings."

"Oh, okay." Maddy side-eyed Mason. The smile on his face caused her heart to race. It made promises about what was to come.

Blue led her into the ballroom and stopped in front of a rather austere man. He had salt-and-pepper hair and dark eyes.

"Leo, have you met the Home's social worker, Maddy Davies?"

"I don't believe I have." Leo smiled and took her hand, but it didn't quite reach his eyes. "It's a pleasure, Miss Davies. I hope you enjoy your evening."

"Thank you."

"Maddy, dear," Blue moved her along. "This is Leo's daughter, Ava. She's the one responsible for the event this year."

Ava King was a few months pregnant and a strikingly beautiful woman. Black hair, porcelain skin, and bright blue eyes.

"It's a pleasure to meet you," Maddy smiled. "Blue speaks highly of you."

"Thank you." Ava indicated the man to her left. "This is my husband, Peter Foster. Peter, this is Sister Blue and Maddy Davies from the Blessed Children's Home."

Peter turned on the charm, and Maddy could see why he'd been such a big star. Since his marriage, though, he hadn't been in the limelight as often.

"Thank you."

It took several more minutes for them to make it through the receiving line. Then, on the way to the table, Blue introduced her to some of the big donors. By the time they sat down, she was exhausted, and the evening had just started.

***

Four Seasons Hotel
January 29, 1994
8:30 p.m.

SINCE HE'D SEEN MADDY'S OVERNIGHT BAG, MASON HAD BEEN fighting his baser instincts. His body was primed and had been for a lot longer than he was willing to admit. He'd always known their time would come, and he'd been patient ... mostly. However, with the occasion only a few hours away, his patience was fading.

After dinner, there were speeches, even more than he'd expected. He was ready to dance. Ready to hold his lady in his arms. While it might be a couple of hours of foreplay, it was definitely progress in the right direction.

Maddy glanced up, and the look in her silver-blue eyes pulled at him. It wasn't until hers flared he realized he'd almost kissed her. Something he thought she wanted, but might not be ready for, considering their company.

He needed to touch her. However, until it was permissible, Mason settled for sliding his arm around her with his hand resting on her shoulder. Almost unconsciously, he began a rhythmic motion with his thumb.

A delicate shiver raced through her. She pressed closer and laid her hand on his thigh. His muscles jumped, and other parts of his body begged for attention.

"You're playing with fire," Mason whispered for her ears only.

Maddy's response was to use her fingers to create little circles on the inside of his thigh. With each time around, his body tensed a little more. Finally, he decided he was going to embarrass both of them if she didn't stop, and covered her fingers with his hand. She gave him a mischievous grin he wanted to kiss off.

If everyone hadn't started clapping right then, he might have done just that. Instead, he turned toward the front in time to hear Blue say a few words. Then the lights dimmed, and a video started playing.

Mason tried to pay attention to what was going on in front of him, but the pull from his left was too strong. He squeezed Maddy's hand and settled for kissing her fingers.

"Is it time to go yet? We've been here forever."

Maddy snickered. "Not yet. Relax."

How was he supposed to do so when every fiber of his being knew what lay ahead?

Once again, he forced his attention back to the speaker. Ava King, the one Blue claimed was responsible for the party, had just stepped behind the microphone to thank everyone for coming.

Mason sighed. "Do they always have so many speakers?"

"Oh, this was nothing," Joy whispered. "Last year, there were more."

"I was sick," Maddy answered before he could ask her if she'd been there.

"So, you missed the festivities?"

"I did. Wasn't I lucky?"

I'm the lucky one, floated through his head. It so stunned him, he stiffened.

Maddy pressed a little closer. "Are you okay?"

"Perfect."

"Really?"

He tapped his ear. "Do you hear that?"

"The music?"

"Yes. Would you dance with me?"

"I would like that."

When he took her in his arms, it settled him. "I've been waiting for this moment for hours."

"You were awfully impatient during the speeches." Maddy's sparkling blue eyes met his. "What could be the reason?"

Mason smiled, but it felt wicked. "I'm very impatient."

"Oh? Is there something going on later?"

"Going on? No, honey. It's most definitely coming off."

"Mason, Mason," Maddy sighed. "Don't put those images into my head yet."

"You're telling me you've not already had a few of them today? I don't believe you."

"No?"

"Oh, no." Mason kissed her, but it was way too brief to be satisfying. "How many times have you relived last night?"

"Mason!"

She pressed her face against his chest, giving him the perfect opportunity to whisper, "Feeling you come undone in my arms was hot. You have no idea how much I wanted to rip your clothes off and love you all night long."

"Why didn't you?"

"Stupidity? Fear? Or a little of both," he repeated, similar words he'd heard his father say. "Instead, I went home and took a cold shower."

"I'm sorry." Her words were so soft, he wouldn't have heard them if he hadn't been looking at her.

"Don't be sorry, honey. I made good use of the memory."

"Really?"

"I would have much rather had your hands on me ... in a pinch, mine worked fine."

Maddy tilted her head back, and her mouth dropped open. Her shock at his statement was evident—somehow, that turned him on even more.

"You didn't," she apparently recovered her voice. "Did you?"

"Do you want me to show you exactly how?"

Once again, her surprised expression appeared. In his eyes, he had no other option than to kiss her.

He'd just tucked her a little closer when, from the corner of his eye, he saw his father approach and knew he was going to lose her.

"Damn."

"Mason, I'm here to steal your partner. Go dance with your mother."

He bit his tongue to keep the words he really wanted to say quiet and exchanged Maddy for his mother.

"I'm sorry." Joy smiled. "I told him to leave you alone."

"It's okay, mom. We'll have more dances."

"Yes, you will, son. Yes, you will."

Something told him his mother was referring to more than just the next few hours.

"Maddy's the one you've been waiting for, isn't she?"

Mason leaned back enough to meet his mother's eyes. "Why do you say it like that? I've had girlfriends before."

Joy's eyes sparkled. "You were never serious about them, though."

"And you think I'm serious about Maddy?"

"When your hearts connect, Mason," Joy reminded him. "You no longer have a say."

He'd heard her mention hearts connecting before, but he'd been a nonbeliever until he'd experienced it. Lately, though, the concept made much more sense.

Unconsciously, his gaze drifted to Maddy. His heart felt as if it was reaching for her. Was what he felt for her love? Or was it just his need to protect mixed in with a bit of lust?

"MASON IS GIVING ME *THE EYE*," SCOTT CHUCKLED. "I DIDN'T expect that."

"The eye?" Maddy repeated. "What's that?"

"It's *the eye*," Scott emphasized the last two words. "I told him to watch out for *the eye* from you. For some reason, I didn't expect him to use it on me."

Maddy laughed. "Are you telling me you've never used *the eye* before, Lieutenant? I would bet you've used it plenty."

"I admit to nothing."

For a few minutes, neither of them spoke. Maddy could have said several things, but she was content to let him direct the conversation. Somehow, she knew eventually he'd work his way around to what was on his mind.

"How are you feeling?"

"Fine, why?"

"You went through an ordeal the night Alisha died. And since then, you've had some other encounters. Are you okay?"

Maddy let go of a dry laugh. "I won't lie and say I don't have moments when I want to run and hide. But mostly, I'm okay."

"You're being careful?"

"I'm being careful," Maddy assured him. "You taught me well."

Scott's nod was small, but proud. "I meant what I said the other night," he went on. "In fact, you'll never know how many times over the past twenty-three years I considered talking to Joy about adopting you. About making you one of ours."

Maddy's breath hitched. "I used to think about the same thing."

"Do you know why I didn't?"

Her throat was so tight it was impossible even to consider forming words. She finally gave up and shook her head.

"I had a dream."

"You had a dream?" Maddy echoed. "How did that stop you?"

"Because in my dream, I was walking you down the aisle," Scott began. "Your husband-to-be was standing at the altar. It was Mason. He was the one waiting for you. It felt like I'd been given a message. One saying I'd promised you tomorrow to be a part of our family. Not as my daughter, but as my son's wife. I couldn't take that away from you ... from either of you."

Maddy tried to blink away the tears, but it was a challenge. Several spilled, and when she glanced sideways and caught Mason's eye, she could tell he'd noticed.

"Connected hearts."

"You've been talking to Blue, I see. But yes, connected hearts."

"Does Mason know this? I would think he would have a thing or two to say about it."

"Well, I've not shared my dream with him ... yet," Scott admitted. "Only Joy knows—and now you."

Her thoughts from earlier in the week circled back. "I know nothing about marriage, Scott. It's not something I've ever considered."

"What about those fairytales we used to read? Most of those ended with a wedding."

"But a wedding and a marriage aren't the same thing," Maddy gently pushed back. "I think in my head a wedding was a party. A marriage, though, that's very different."

"A marriage is so many things," Scott murmured. "It's knowing that someone is going to be there for you, no matter what. Knowing someone is on the same journey that you're on. Knowing that while there might be bumps along the way, you're not alone. It's when you're near that person, your heart literally reaches for theirs."

"I never knew you were such a romantic, Scott," Maddy grinned. "But thank you for that answer."

"You'll know when you're ready to take that next step, Maddy. Don't let that son of mine bully you."

"He wouldn't do that."

"Just ask if you have more questions, alright?"

"I will."

"Also, I have a gift for you." He led her back to their table and pulled something out of his pocket. "I have a friend who's a prison guard, and he makes these in his spare time."

Scott handed her a piece of lightweight metal shaped like the head of a cat. It had a mouth, two holes for its eyes, and pointed ears. Hanging from the bottom was a key ring.

"It's a keychain." Maddy held it so it dangled from her finger.

"It's not just a keychain, Maddy." Scott showed her how to put her fingers through the eyes, which essentially turned the cat's head into a weapon. They worked like brass knuckles, but the ears were sharp. "Anytime you're out alone, have this handy. You might not have a skillet available next time."

Maddy laughed. "I hope I never need a skillet again. Thank you. I will carry this with me."

Mason and Joy returned to the table as she was putting it into her evening bag.

"Your dad gave me a gift."

"I hope you never need it." His dark eyes dove into hers, and she read what he was thinking. His patience had run out.

"Are you ready to go?"

"I am. Let's say our goodbyes."

They said goodbye in record time, and Mason hustled her out of the party and into his car. He turned on soft music and linked their fingers. It made her wish the car didn't have a center console. She wanted to be closer.

As soon as he'd parked, Mason cupped her face and kissed her. It was potent and sent a rush of excitement racing through her.

"Are you sure?"

"Mason," Maddy teased. "Maybe I need to ask if *you're* sure?"

His response was to hop out of the car, grab her bag and hand, then rush her upstairs.

"Hold on. You're going too fast."

"Sorry." When they reached his apartment, Mason backed her against the door and kissed her. It consumed her, making her want to climb onto him.

She was vaguely aware when the wall behind her moved, sensing a difference in the environment. Maddy pushed off her wrap and stepped out of her shoes. Their eyes clashed. The look in his was hot, intense, and every time he moved forward, she took a step backward, prolonging the anticipation. Her legs hit the sofa, and the phone rang.

"Ignore it." Mason returned, giving his attention to her neck.

After three rings, the machine picked up, and she heard a beep. Maddy thought it was a wrong number until she heard the message.

"Mason, it's dad. I'm sorry to do this, but I got a call from the night watchman. Someone delivered an anonymous message. It's a map showing where the knife is hidden. I'll meet you and Darrin at the precinct."

She could feel Mason's frustration. It poured off him in waves. Then, because she had to, Maddy took a step backward.

"Go change. I'll be here when you get back."

Their gazes met and held for a long minute. It was several heartbeats before he kissed her.

"I'll be back as quickly as I can."

"I'll be here. Now, go."

He kissed her again, leaving her lips tingling. She hated the fact he had to go, but when he returned, she'd be waiting.

TWENTY-FOUR

South Boston Precinct
January 30, 1994
12:00 a.m.

By the time Mason arrived at the precinct, he'd exhausted his vocabulary of swear words—and then started over. He'd once told Maddy there was a conspiracy to keep them apart, and tonight only reiterated those thoughts.

Of course, the conspiracy to keep them apart bounced up against his mom's words about connected hearts.

"When your hearts connect, Mason. You no longer have a say."

Was what she'd said about no longer having a say true?

"Maybe, in the sadness of Alisha's death, you've found what you were destined to find."

Sitting around the dining room table with Maddy next to him, his parents and married brother, had felt right. Even more right than he'd thought possible. In the past, anything close to that way of thinking would have sent him running. It had him realizing his mom had been correct. Maddy was the woman he'd been waiting for.

What was next, though?

"Mason!" Darrin knocked on his window. "Stop woolgathering and get inside!"

Mason threw open his door. "I'm coming, I'm coming." It was a fight not to take those words down another hole. One involving only him ... and Maddy.

They found his father in the conference room, looking over a map. When their eyes met, he saw the apology there—just acknowledging it might embarrass Maddy. Something Mason would never do.

"Are you feeling alright, son?"

That he'd referred to him as son didn't escape Mason's notice. Usually at work, he was Detective or Mason. The familial connection was another sign of his father's thoughts on the timing.

"Fine, why?"

"Just making sure."

Mason bit his tongue, not wanting to dive into his frustration. Instead, he pulled back his emotions and put on his detective's hat.

"Why are we here?"

Scott pushed the piece of paper across the table. "Someone left that at the night watchman's desk a little over an hour ago."

"He didn't see anyone?"

"No. He'd stepped away to deliver a message. When he returned, a large envelope was lying on the counter."

"The night watchman opened it?"

"I'm afraid so. And no, he didn't have on gloves."

"Was it examined for fingerprints?"

"Only a cursory examination."

"And nothing stood out?"

"No."

Mason blew out a breath. "They didn't want to make it too easy for us."

"They never do," Scott sighed. "Why make our jobs easy?"

"What do you need from us?" Mason thumbed between himself and Darrin.

"While someone recognized the park from the crude drawing," Scott answered. "No one can figure out how the symbols on the map connect to the case. Since you two have spent time in the park lately ..."

Mason pulled on a pair of gloves and unfolded the drawing. He had to agree with his father. The crude picture was of Franklin Park. It took him several minutes to orient himself to the squiggles on the paper. Once he did, though, he immediately knew what they were looking at.

He slid the paper toward Darrin. "Look familiar?"

Darrin studied the image for several seconds before nodding. "The knife isn't far from where we found the jacket."

"I still don't understand how our perp made it from Alisha's home to Franklin Park, with no one seeing him," Mason grumbled. "It doesn't feel right."

"You canvassed?" asked Scott.

"We did." Mason almost pointed at something on the map his father was looking at, but at the last minute, he changed his mind. "I'll be right back."

He went after the map he and Darrin had been using to label what they knew. When he spread it out on the table, he quickly explained what the marks meant. Then followed up with, "Darrin and I were in Franklin Park and happened upon Maddy."

"Maddy? She was in Franklin Park? Alone?"

"She was," Mason sighed, unwilling to say more. "I walked her back to the Home. We took this route." He traced one thin line and then pointed to where 15 Peach Street was located. "The officers chased the perp for seven blocks before losing him."

Scott was quiet while he studied the map. "You think when the perp disappeared, he ducked into the alley and found someplace to hide, don't you?"

"It's the only thing we could come up with," Darrin replied. "We've been up and down that road multiple times. No one saw anything, and there are no exterior cameras anywhere."

"Damn," Scott snapped. "It's almost like the perp knew exactly what he was doing, isn't it?"

"Our thoughts, as well." Mason traced the path they'd walked through Franklin Park. "Since both the jacket and knife were found in the park, maybe we need to canvass."

"All 527 acres?" Darrin winced. "Remind me why we didn't become accountants?"

"Was our killer smart, desperate, or both?" Mason tossed out. "Was he prepared or impulsive?"

"If he was smart, then he knew exactly where to run and why."

"True."

"And if he was prepared, he had to have left a change of clothing somewhere."

Mason agreed. "Is the person who drew the map our killer?"

"Why would a killer tell us where he'd tossed the weapon? I don't think he wants to get caught."

"I don't either. But who would have found these items and not contacted us directly? While those teachers didn't stay and talk, they didn't hide their identity."

Darrin hummed. "That's true."

"Which brings us back to the question. Who is this person? If they aren't the killer, then how did they find the knife?"

"And why all the secrecy?"

"The forensics team is on their way to the park," Scott stated. "By the time you get there, they should have the lights set up."

"What about Fremont?"

"Fremont?" Scott's brows rose in question. "Fremont, the dog?"

Mason nodded. "We have the jacket. Maybe a dog could find more."

"Worth a try," Scott hummed. "Let's wait for daylight. Right now, see about the knife. After all, you don't want to be here all night, do you?"

Mason looked at his father. While his expression was innocent, the look in his eyes said he was fishing.

"A good night's rest is important. Isn't it, Darrin?"

"Very," Darrin confirmed. "We'll see you later, Lieutenant."

Mason's Apartment
January 30, 1994
1:00 a.m.

"I'll be here when you get back."

Her promise to Mason. Except when he'd left, she'd not had any concept of how long it might take him. He'd been gone for over an hour, and she wasn't sure how to spend her time. She was afraid that if she sat still, she'd fall asleep and miss the moment they'd both been waiting for.

Maddy found her overnight bag in Mason's bedroom and hung up her dress. She pulled on the baby doll, and the silk material glided across her sensitive skin. It sent a rush of awareness zipping up her spine, causing her breath to catch. *Soon. Very soon.* But it left too much bare skin, especially without someone to keep her warm.

Mason's bathrobe temporarily served the purpose. It was well-worn, soft, and carried his scent. Several times, she caught herself burying her face in the lapels and taking a deep breath. It smelled like him, and for a few minutes, made her feel closer. She brushed out her hair, and the photo album on the nightstand caught her attention.

Initially, she thought it was something Joy had created for him. Then she looked closer. The album wasn't of Mason's childhood, but of hers.

"... Your husband-to-be was standing at the altar. It was Mason. He was the one waiting for you. It felt like I'd been given a message. One saying I'd promised you tomorrow to be a part of our family. Not as my daughter, but as my son's wife. I couldn't take that away from you ... from either of you."

Mason didn't know about his father's dream. If he did, what would he say? Did he believe in 'connected hearts?'

Maddy flipped through several pages. They were photos of when she'd first arrived at the Home. She'd been so young those memories weren't readily available.

On the next page, there was a picture of her sitting on Scott's lap. He was reading the book *Goodnight Moon,* and the sight had tears rushing to her eyes. Looking back, there'd been multiple moments like that. Those times made her the person who looked in the mirror each day. If anything had changed, Maddy Davies would have been someone completely different.

She turned the page again and found a note. One written by Blue the past Wednesday.

Mason,

I know you probably have more questions than I
have answers regarding your father and his connection to

Blessed Children's Home. While it started with Maddy, it didn't stop with her. He's been important to many who've come through our doors over the past twenty-three years. Try not to judge him too harshly for not sharing this part of his life with you. 'Things happen when they're meant to happen,' a saying I'm sure you've heard from Joy a time or two in your life. Believe those words to be true.

If you have any more questions, my door is always open.

Blue

Had Mason gone looking for answers about Scott's connection to the Home? About his father's visits when she'd been a child? What had he thought when he looked through the album? Had it confused him—or clarified everything?

Maddy couldn't help but think that didn't feel right. In fact, it was almost the opposite. Since Wednesday, his behavior toward her had been *more.* His kisses hotter, his hands bolder. Every time he touched her, he pushed the intimacy a little farther. Could the combination of hearing Scott's story, as well as seeing hers, have clarified things in his mind?

"Mason might not know it yet, but his heart and Maddy's are connected."

"Is your mom, right, Mason? Are our hearts connected?"

"It's a saying from where I was born," Blue explained. "I believe it means you're 'true loves.' Just like in all those fairytales you used to read."

Scott had used the same example as Blue. Were they right? Was having her heart 'connected' to someone else's the same thing as finding her true love? Or was it a deeper connection?

When Mason got home, they were taking a giant step. One she didn't take lightly.

Did Mason see marriage in their future? Did *she?* Was what she felt for him love—or something deeper?

From the moment she'd heard his voice in the hospital, he'd affected her like no other. He'd held her when she cried, and every time he took her hand or wrapped his arms around her, he filled those spaces inside she'd not known were empty. Mason settled her one minute and revved her up the next.

"A marriage is so many things," Scott murmured. *"It's knowing someone is going to be there for you, no matter what. Knowing someone is on the same journey you're on."*

Was that where they were heading? Could she imagine spending the rest of her days with Mason?

Her answer didn't appear in words, but in a feeling that started deep inside. It warmed her, filled her, and whispered the truth she hadn't dared admit aloud—but already knew. Blue had always been right. Things really did happen when they were meant to happen.

Franklin Park
January 30, 1994
2:00 a.m.

WHEN THEY ARRIVED AT FRANKLIN PARK, THE FORENSICS TEAM was still working on the lighting. With the temperature in the single digits, Mason and Darrin waited in the cruiser.

"How much longer do you think we'll be here?" Darrin sighed. "I'd rather be home."

"Me too," Mason murmured, not realizing how he sounded.

"Oh?" Darrin pounced. "Is there any reason *you* want to be home?"

"Right back at you."

"Yes. Tina is waiting for me."

"Has she moved in? It seems she's there more often than at her place."

"Moved in?" Darrin sighed. "I've tried."

"What did she say?"

"That she likes what we have. That she doesn't want to mess it up."

"Do you believe her?"

"I don't know." Darrin blew out a breath. "There's a part of me that thinks she's right. We do have a good thing, and I don't want to mess it up. Other days, though, I look at her and think I want to marry her."

"Wow! That's a big step. Do you think you're ready for marriage?"

"What about you and Maddy?" Darrin turned the tables. "You two seemed pretty close at the fundraiser."

"A little more so each day," Mason replied. "I just—"

The generators kicked on, cutting him off.

"Shall we?"

They followed the tech person to a marked-off area. It had him making a mental note to chat with Natalie again. She'd seen Parker Turner standing next to the pond. Exactly where, though?

"Let me take some photos," the tech said. "Then you can have a look before I process it."

From where they were standing, the jacket had been found in some trees off to their left. An area just before the path turned north. The knife was on the opposite side of the path, ten feet farther east, and another fifteen feet closer to the water.

"The perp ran into the park, holding the knife the entire way?" Mason questioned. "I can't see that."

"I can't either. Could he have tossed it while the officers were chasing him and returned a day or two later?"

"Possibly. Especially if he knew his way around."

"Look where it was found, though." Darrin pointed to an area of high grass next to the pond. "If he was running along this path, there's no way he could toss it from here."

"Not only that," Mason added. "But if he had tried to get closer, and snow covered this area, I'm not sure he could have maintained traction."

"Why didn't he throw it off the bridge?"

"He wasn't trying to hide it," Mason muttered, almost to himself.

"Say that again."

Mason let the clues bounce around in his head for several seconds. Somehow, no matter how he arranged them, they still didn't fit.

"Neither one of us can figure out how the officers could have lost the perp after seven blocks, right?"

"Okay."

"Plus, we can't figure out how no one noticed him running through neighborhoods wearing bloody clothing, right?"

"Right."

"I don't know how or where, but somehow, our perp found a place to lie low. Then, after a few days, he returned, collected everything, and has been leaving them for us."

"But why?"

"Looking to frame someone else?" Mason tossed the comment out, not sure he really bought what he was saying.

"A definite possibility. Which could be where the third person came from."

"It could also explain why the third person tossed the red hat," Mason added. "They knew we'd find it."

"Except we haven't identified the DNA," Darrin reminded him.

"It adds to the thrill?" Mason murmured. "He's pitting his smarts against ours."

"Damn. As much as I hate the idea, it makes sense. Who, though?"

"That, I can't tell you. We need to know who the third person is. Did you ask the lab if they'd matched the hat found at the galleria to any of the others?"

"They said Monday."

"Okay, Detectives," the tech called. "Do you want to come down?"

Mason stepped carefully, staying in the already visible footsteps as he walked closer to the water. The grass was slippery, even without snow and ice, but manageable if he moved slowly.

"That's definitely the knife from 15 Peach Street," Mason murmured. "I remember the black handle. And there was one missing from the butcher block."

"It's the slicer," the tech responded. "The blade is around 10" long and fits the coroner's findings."

The image of Maddy lying in the hospital bed returned in glaring color. Mason shivered at how close she'd come to ....

"There's no blood on it," Darrin pointed out. "Did the snow wash it off?"

The tech grunted. "Maybe. More likely, the perp wiped it off." He sprayed something on the knife, focusing on the area where the handle met the blade. It immediately turned pink. "The pink means there's blood present, and it's human. We'll compare it to the other items back at the lab."

"Thanks," Mason replied. "How long?"

"Monday."

Mason glanced at Darrin. "Ready to go? Or do you want to hang around a little longer?"

Darrin started toward the car without responding. The ride back was quiet, both men focusing on who was waiting for them at their apartments. They stopped by the precinct, signed out, and then were on their way home. Everything else could wait until Monday.

Once home, Mason took the stairs to his apartment two at a time. He opened the door, tossed his jacket in one direction, and kicked off his shoes. Maddy was asleep on the sofa. His breath caught at how beautiful she looked.

Almost reverently, he knelt in front of her and feathered a kiss across her soft cheek. "Maddy," he whispered. "You have no idea what you do to me."

He gently brushed back her hair, then, ever so slowly, kissed her sweet mouth. When she opened her silver-blue eyes, he was lost.

TWENTY-FIVE

Mason's Apartment
January 30, 1994
3:30 a.m.

THE HEAT IN MASON'S EYES STOLE WHAT SHE WAS GOING TO SAY. No one had ever looked at her the way he did—the way he always had. A part of her wanted to throw herself into his arms, while the other side was content to just bask in the feeling.

"Mason," she whispered. "It's you."

"You weren't expecting anyone else, were you?"

"You, Mason. Only you."

"Good answer."

He kissed her. One of those all-consuming ones where the only thing in her world was him. When he lifted his head, his dark-eyed gaze was alight with an emotion she could only guess at. It melted her heart and had her leaning into him for one more kiss.

"Did you miss me?"

"You know I did."

"Good answer." Mason trailed his finger down the center of her chest and pushed the robe lapels aside. His eyes flared, and everywhere his gaze touched, her body sizzled. "I like this. Is it new?"

"Is that your way of asking me if I've worn it for anyone else?"

"Well …" He ducked his head and looked back up from under his brows. "I didn't mean it that way, but now that you mention it. Is it?"

Maddy carded her fingers through his hair and decided talking could wait. She wanted him—and with a slight tug on the belt, the robe pooled around her waist.

His breath caught, but his full attention never moved from the bodice of her gown. While it wasn't sheer, she knew he could see her nipples through the gossamer fabric—even more so when they hardened.

"You are so beautiful."

There was a reverence in the way his fingers glided across her skin. In the way he stroked her sides, each pass taking him a little closer to where she wanted his touch.

He leaned forward slowly, so slowly, she had to fight not to help him along. Her body felt like it was hanging off a ledge, waiting for someone to catch her.

"So beautiful."

Mason pressed to her mouth, then to her breastbone. He laved her nipple, then blew across it lightly, causing the tip to harden even more. Before she'd caught her breath, he'd repeated the process on the other side.

"Mason," she groaned. "Mason."

"You never gave me an answer," he whispered. "Am I the only one who's seen you in this?"

"I bought it for you, Mason. Only you."

He growled and, in a single motion, wrapped his hand behind her neck, tugged her forward, and covered her mouth. His hands, lips, and tongue worked together to see how much pleasure they could wring from her.

The feelings he pulled from her were unlike anything she'd ever felt. She reached for him, but each time she did, he chuckled. It was a dark and dangerous sound and caused her pulse to skyrocket.

A kiss on her cheek, another on her lips, until with a groan, he latched on to a sensitive place on her neck.

She never knew where he would go next, but each time, just before it stung, he backed off, leaving her breathless. With every stroke, she wanted another. With every brush of his fingers, she offered him more.

"Come here," Maddy pleaded.

"Don't be so impatient, honey. We have all night."

Mason leaned back on his heels. He undid one shirt button and then another, revealing more and more of his smooth chest. His pace was slow—almost too slow—causing her to squirm, to ache for his touch.

When he still had half of the buttons to go, she lost patience.

"Let me show you how it's done."

Maddy fisted his shirt and tugged it apart. Buttons flew to the left and right, but neither noticed. Her only focus was on unwrapping the man in front of her as if it were Christmas.

She pushed his shirt off, tossed it aside, and pressed her chest against his. The feeling of being so close to him, with very little between them, was indescribable.

"Do you know how good you feel?" Mason murmured, tightening his arms around her.

"Oh, I have some idea."

"Do you know what would feel even better?"

The boldness she'd felt several nights before returned as, once again, Maddy cupped his hardness.

"Didn't you promise to show me how you made good use of a memory?"

Mason hissed and pressed his hand against hers, holding her still.

"Careful, honey."

There were a million things she wanted to say. A million things she wanted to try. But as soon as their gazes met, she got lost in his dark, dark eyes.

"Let me." Mason lifted her gown up and over her head, leaving her in a pair of barely-there panties. "Heaven. Pure Heaven."

He dropped a kiss on her breastbone. Another on her right shoulder. Then on her left. He nibbled his way down the slope of her breast and sucked the hard tip into his moist mouth.

Maddy couldn't sit still. She carded her fingers through his hair and held him in place. Pleasure rushed through her, and every time his thumb glided across her nipple, her pulse jumped.

Suddenly, Mason stood up. Maddy started to complain, but his look said, *Watch this.* He unzipped his pants, tucked his thumbs into the waistband, and gave her a look that said, *What do you want? Should I leave a layer or expose everything?*

The tension between them climbed, ratcheting up her need even higher. Her fingers itched to add a little effort to his mission. But when she tried to help, Mason took a step backward.

"Now, honey, don't be so impatient."

His delay gave her the perfect opportunity to toss his robe onto the floor. She leaned back and thrust her chest forward, drawing his attention back to her breasts.

What did he see when he looked at her as he was? What was he thinking?

Goosebumps crawled across her skin, causing her nipples to pucker and her body to tingle. Awareness zipped around inside, and excitement raced up her spine.

"What are you waiting for?" Maddy murmured in a sultry voice. "I want your hands on me now."

A corner of Mason's mouth curled up, and when he continued to hold her at bay, she did the only thing a girl could do. She cupped the bottom of her breasts and brushed her thumbs back and forth over her nipples. With every pass, the tips hardened a little more, leaving taut peaks, begging for his touch.

Mason silently groaned. What was he waiting for? Every fiber of his being said, pick her up and carry her to bed. Yet, he hesitated. Not because he was unsure of his feelings for her—or hers for him. His pace was slow, meant to stretch out the moment. Meant to make it one neither would ever forget.

His heart stuttered, their eyes locked in confrontation. Every time her thumb brushed over her nipples, he ached to touch, ached to taste. Then she licked her lips, and he about lost it. His patience was gone. He needed her, and he needed her right then.

Mason pushed down his pants, taking his boxers as well. Her gaze was like a laser, focused on every piece of skin he uncovered. When she touched him, the feel of her soft hand wrapped around his hardness almost brought him to his knees.

"Careful there, honey. We don't want it to be over before it begins."

"Having difficulty with your control? Huh?"

"Where you're concerned? Yes," Mason growled. "There's just one problem."

"Oh?" Maddy's gaze dropped, making his body throb, then right back up. "Looks like everything works exactly as it should."

"Oh, it's working all right. Except I want to feel you ... all of you." Mason picked her up, kicked aside his pants and carried her down the hall.

It was dark in his bedroom, forcing him to feel his way across the floor. "It's a good thing I didn't make my bed today, isn't it?"

With every step he took, Maddy's sexy body rubbed against his. Once his shins hit the side of the bed, he covered her mouth and followed her down.

"Mason." She tightened her arms around him. "Mason."

"What is it, honey?"

"Kiss me, Mason," Maddy whispered. "Love me."

He dove in, his intent to get acquainted with every part of her body. With each new spot he loved, another one called to him, until she wouldn't stay still.

Mason memorized those places that turned her on the most. Memorized those places that caused her to shiver, moan, and swear. His goal was to see how many times he could bring her to the brink before backing away.

Her sighs were just the beginning. They encouraged him to suck a little harder. To push a little deeper. When she groaned, Mason let go of the nipple he'd latched onto and switched sides.

His body throbbed, begging him to give in, but he refused to listen. Instead, he pushed a little more. Took a little more from her.

"Mason!"

"Hold on, honey."

He trailed kisses down her torso and nipped one hip bone, then the other. For every move he made, her body telegraphed precisely what she wanted. All he had to do was listen.

Sometimes, the end justifies the means, he thought, sucking a little harder. Flicking his tongue a little faster. Then he felt what he'd been waiting for. The tremors started. *Not much longer. Just a little more.*

Again, he latched onto that place that took her higher than any other. Finally, she could no longer fight. Finally, Maddy screamed his name and came apart in his arms.

Mason reached for one of the foil packets from his nightstand and, with trembling fingers, slid it into place. Before he was completely ready, Maddy tugged him over onto her.

"Am I too heavy?"

"Who cares? I'm tired of waiting."

"What is it you want, honey?"

"I'll show you." She wrapped her hand around his length and showed him precisely what and where she wanted him. "How's that?"

"If it were any better, I'd be crying," he whispered.

Mason cupped her head and stared down into her face. It was too dark for him to really see her. Somehow, though, he knew how she was looking at him. The longer he hovered, the more the words on the tip of his tongue begged to be shared.

It wasn't the right time, though. He wanted it to matter, and not just because he thought it was expected.

Maddy hooked her legs around his flanks and dug her fingers into his ass.

"Move, Mason."

"Your wish ..." Then move he did. While he set the pace, that didn't mean he'd stopped listening to her body. In fact, the opposite was true. With his sight hindered by the darkness, all he could do was react.

The way she made him feel was something brand new. Something he'd never even considered. She completed him. His mother had been right. Their hearts were connected.

Mason kept up the pace, bringing her along with him, until she cried out his name again. Her sudden tremors pulled him over the crest with her.

They lay there safe in each other's arms until their pulses slowed and their breathing returned to normal.

"Are you okay?" he murmured softly.

"Don't I feel okay?"

"Honey, you feel more than okay." Mason gently kissed her lips, and then rolled them onto their sides.

"Thank you, Mason," Maddy murmured, lethargy obvious in her voice.

"No, honey." He kissed her again. "Thank you."

She snuggled a little closer. His heart felt full—more full than it had ever felt in his life. "I love you, Maddy." But he knew she hadn't heard him, as sleep had pulled her under.

Mason lay still for another second, then quietly slipped out of bed to clean up. When he returned, she reached for him, giving him the chance to wrap around her once again. He wanted to savor the feeling, but she felt too good, and he was too tired. In a matter of minutes, his body betrayed him, pulling him under.

❧

Mason's Apartment
January 30, 1994
11:00 a.m.

MADDY HUNG IN THAT PLACE BETWEEN SLEEP AND WAKEFULNESS. She'd slept better than she had in forever. In her slumber, there were delicious dreams, gentle kisses, and a ride that put all other rides to shame. It was only the soreness in her little-used muscles that assured her everything hadn't been a dream.

He touched her again, and her heart beat a little faster. When his talented mouth joined in and demanded she respond, she couldn't hold back the groan of pleasure any longer.

"I knew you were in there." He kissed her. "I was beginning to wonder."

Slowly, she opened her eyes to see Mason leaning on one elbow, watching her. It left one of his hands free to explore. At one time, she'd worried that she'd feel embarrassed in the light of day. But there was none of that—only a deep ache inside for more.

"How are you feeling?"

"How are you feeling?" she countered.

"Like I'm ten feet tall." Mason dropped a quick kiss on her mouth. "Now, your turn to answer."

Maddy scooted closer and pressed against his bare skin. His body hardened, almost begging her to touch. A feeling washed over her—one that was new and exciting. She had questions, but wasn't sure how to bring them up.

"Are you hungry?" he asked.

"I could eat, but we'd have to get up, right?"

"We would."

"Can we wait?"

"Sure."

"Did you ask Blue for that photo album?" She hesitated. "Or did she volunteer it?"

"She volunteered it."

"Why? She said nothing to me."

"When I arrived on Wednesday to pick you up, she told me you mentioned dinner with my parents." Mason grinned. "Then she asked if I'd spoken to my mother about my father's secrecy."

"Did you tell her why your father kept the secrets?"

"No."

"Why not?"

"I'm with my mother on that one. The story is my dad's to share. Especially since it involves Blue's family members."

"I agree." Maddy tilted her head back to read his expression. "Was that when she gave you the book?"

"It was." He frowned. "Did you say anything else to her?"

"Well ..."

"Maddy, honey." Mason tipped her chin up and gave her one of those short, but potent kisses. "What?"

"I just asked her what something meant," Maddy replied, trying not to feel defensive. "That's all."

Mason stared at her for so long she wanted to bury her face against his chest, but he wouldn't let her.

"What did you think when you saw those photos?" she switched to an easier topic.

"That you were adorable." He kissed her again. "That many of the photos reminded me of ones with my dad and Heather, my sister."

"We're close to the same age, aren't we?"

"You are."

Maddy wasn't sure what pushed her forward, but she confessed, "Scott used to talk about you, your sister, and brothers. I wanted to be a part of his family."

Mason tightened his arms around her. "I'm sorry."

"It's not your fault, Mason. Besides, that was then."

"And now?"

Maddy squirmed against him, more than pleased to feel the power she had over him.

"I'm glad I wasn't raised as your sister."

He kissed her, making it obvious he felt the same way. When their eyes met, there were emotions in his she'd never seen before. Whatever they were, they made her heart race.

"Do you have hockey this afternoon?"

"I do."

"Do you want to take me home before you go?"

"Do I want to? No, that's not the question, though."

"No? Then what is?"

"The question is, do you want me to take you home?"

Did she? Did she want him to take her home to give her time to think? While there was some merit to that, she really wasn't ready to be apart.

"Maddy, honey?" Mason murmured. "Do you want me to take you home?"

"Well, I guess that depends."

"I already told you I didn't want to take you home," he reminded her.

"That wasn't what I was referring to. It depends on what you want to do afterward."

"Oh?"

"If you want to go out afterward, or even to see your parents, I need to go home."

"Why?"

"I don't have anything to wear."

Mason laughed. "I'm sure we could find you something."

"Stop!" Maddy exclaimed. "I have a pair of sweats and a shirt. That's it."

"I've made no plans for after the game. Do you have any ideas?"

"Maybe afterward, we can go by the store, then cook at my place."

"I like that idea."

Maddy leaned over Mason to look at the clock. "Do you know what time it is?"

"9:00 a.m. or 10:00 a.m."

"Try almost noon. We should get up."

"I'm getting there." A devilish grin flitted across Mason's face. "And I know just how to *get up* a little faster *and* save time."

"Eat?"

"Not yet."

"Kiss me?"

He kissed her but didn't stay around, leaving her to pout.

"Oh, I think you'll like what I have in mind."

Mason threw the covers aside and hopped out of bed. His heated gaze raked down her body, and then right back up. Even after spending the entire night with him, she wanted more.

"Are you sure about that?" Maddy crooked her finger, hoping to get him back into bed.

"Positive." He picked her up and started toward the bathroom. "We're going to take a shower."

Maddy swallowed. "A shower? Together?"

"Together." Mason wiggled his brows. "I'll even wash your ... parts."

"I'll allow that if ..."

"If?"

"If I can wash your parts as well."

"I'm pretty sure we can work something out."

Then he kissed her, and suddenly, she decided that talking could wait until later, especially when there was kissing to do.

TWENTY-SIX

South Boston Precinct
January 31, 1994
9:00 a.m.

MASON PRESSED HIS LIPS TOGETHER TO KEEP HIS SMILE FROM flying free. After spending the weekend with Maddy, it had been more difficult than he'd expected to go their separate ways. He felt like he was forgetting something and needed to find it. Was that the whole connected hearts thing at work? A question he really wanted to have answered. But who could he ask without embarrassing Maddy? That was more difficult.

"Anything?" Darrin dropped into his desk chair.

"What?"

"Those interviews." Darrin nodded at the papers on the desk. "Did anything stick out?"

"Not yet."

Darrin glanced over his shoulder, then rolled his chair closer. "Weaver, it's obvious you spent the weekend with Maddy."

"How?"

"You have that glow," Darrin snickered. "However, it's also obvious you're feeling a little guilt."

"Guilt? Where did that come from?"

"Because you're feeling like you slept with the boss's daughter, aren't you?"

Mason winced. "Is it that obvious?"

"You mean I'm right?"

"Yes. No. Maybe." Mason blew out a breath. "I'm an adult. Maddy's an adult. Where our relationship goes is our decision."

"But?"

"But now we've," Mason hesitated because he was not one to kiss and tell, "now we've …"

"Had sex?" Darrin supplied.

"Spent the night together," Mason came back with. "What if I say the wrong thing? But not to Maddy—to my dad."

Darrin nodded sympathetically. "I can see that. However, as corny as it sounds for a man to say, follow your heart."

"Wow, Anderson," Mason smirked. "I didn't realize you were so in touch with your feminine side."

"Hello, four sisters here," Darrin reminded him. "They scrutinized every relationship I've ever had. So, while it might not be the same as your situation with Scott, I get the pressure."

Mason mulled over his friend's comment. Somehow, hearing he wasn't completely nuts about the way he felt, took a little weight off his shoulders. It allowed him to look into his heart and realize the truth. It was for him and Maddy to decide where they went. No one else.

"Now, do you think you can read those interviews?" Darrin grumbled. "I would like to solve this case before we're old and gray."

"Bite me."

"Looks like Maddy did that for me. Did your dad notice?"

"What?" Mason adjusted his collar and realized Darrin had tricked him. "You dickhead."

"Sorry. I'm going for a donut. Read!"

Mason blew out a breath and refocused his attention on the forms in front of him. After the Sergeant's comments regarding the coaches, they came up with a few questions, and then they sent an officer out to complete the interviews. The responses were what he'd been trying to make sense of all morning.

If he focused on just the coaches—football and basketball—from all five schools, nothing stood out. None of them had ever seen their players acting differently. None of them had ever seen anyone with pills. None of them knew who Parker Turner was—even the coaches from the two schools he'd attended.

It wasn't until he expanded to other sports, something caught his attention. Not because it had anything to do with his case, per se. It was more about the unusualness. That was what made it interesting.

"You've been staring at the same four pages for five minutes," Darrin grunted. "What are you looking at?"

Mason pushed the papers aside with frustration. "Nothing stands out from the interviews, implicating the coaches."

"But something bothered you?"

"Bothered? I'm not sure I'd use bothered. I would say—intrigued."

"Just get on with it. You rarely let me ramble."

Mason tossed the pages onto Darrin's desk. "You look."

Darrin spread the pages in front of him. "These are the questions from Newton High, Fenway High, Dorchester High, Franklin High, and Forest Hills High."

"Go on."

"They questioned the track and tennis coaches."

"Keep reading," Mason grumbled. "We don't have all day."

Darrin was quiet for several minutes while he read over the forms. When he looked up, his expression said he had noticed nothing amiss.

"The names," Mason hinted, knowing those would get him somewhere.

"There's a Coach Hines at both Newton High and Fenway High," Darrin noted. "A Coach Lloyd at Dorchester High. And a Marsh at Franklin, but she's not a coach. She's the principal."

"Marsh's wife?" Mason guessed.

"Possibly." Darrin frowned. "What about Hines? Is it the same coach shared by two schools?"

"Aren't the first names there?"

"First initial. It's the same. K. The sport is different, though."

"So, probably not the same person."

"What did the Hines at Forest Hills teach?"

Mason checked his notes on Gerry Hines to verify his memory. "He teaches chemistry. What about Lloyd? Think they're related to Brian?"

"Could be," Darrin agreed. "Could also be a coincidence."

"Lloyd isn't as common as Smith or Williams, though. But I guess it wouldn't shock me. After we fill in the blanks for these coaches, we're supposed to meet Fremont and his handler at Franklin Park."

"Oh, joy," Darrin muttered. "Just how I want to spend my day. Following a dog running through the snow in hopes he'll lead us somewhere."

"Quit grumbling," Mason retorted. "There are worse things to be doing."

"Name one."

"Following a dog running through a landfill," Mason tossed back.

Darrin winced.

"See what I mean. Better to be cold than go home smelling like a dumpster."

"Point." Darrin tossed two of the pages on his desk. "You take two, and I'll take two. Go!"

They reached for the same phone, but Darrin got there first. "Fine, I'll go use the conference room phone."

Blessed Children's Home
January 31, 1994
11:00 a.m.

Maddy grabbed the phone on its first ring. "Hello!"

"Just hello?" Mason tsked. "What happened to your 'Hello, this is Maddy Davies?'"

"Mason!" Maddy exclaimed breathlessly. "Hi. Is everything okay?"

"Everything is fine. Why?"

"Well, you usually don't call me when you're at work."

"True. I needed ... "

"What is it you needed, Mason?"

"Oh, I think you know." Mason's voice dropped into the low register that did things to her. "But since I can't have that right now, I needed to hear your voice."

"Oh, Mason. I miss you too."

"Good."

"Is there anything new going on with the case?"

"Fremont, our K-9, and his handler are in Franklin Park," he told her. "Darrin and I are getting ready to head in that direction."

"What are they looking for?"

"Clothing."

"Clothing the killer wore? Right?"

"Yes."

There was something in his voice she couldn't put her finger on. But she knew he wouldn't tell her, especially over the phone.

"What time do you finish today?" she asked. "I have an idea."

"An idea? Is this an idea I'll like?"

Maddy grinned. "I think so."

"Is this an idea that involves no clothing?"

"Mason! What if someone heard you?"

He chuckled. "They won't. I'm in a conference room with the door closed."

"Oh? Where's Darrin?"

"Stole the desk phone," Mason grumbled. "I had to leave to make a few calls."

"Poor baby. What would make it all better?"

"You know what would make it all better," he purred.

"Later."

"Maddy, honey, now who's the one starting something she can't do anything about?"

"Sorry," she giggled. "How about this? I'll go by the store on the way home and cook dinner for you before bowling."

"And you'll go to bowling with me?"

"Maybe." She pressed her lips together to keep from laughing at his pouty voice. "You'll have to see if you can convince me."

"It would be my pleasure," Mason assured her. "As for now, I'd better go."

"Okay. I'll see you later."

"Bye, honey."

Maddy sighed. Her concentration had been off all day. It vacillated—from memories of her weekend with Mason to questions she wasn't sure how to answer. How did she define them? Did they even need a name?

After trying to refocus another handful of times, she gave up and called Tina.

"Hello."

"Tina, it's Maddy. Do you have time for lunch?"

"It depends."

"On?"

"On whether you're going to tell me about your weekend?"

"I'll tell you about some of it."

"Then I'll see how much more I can get out of you."

"Where shall we meet?"

"Well, duh. Where do you think?"

"Fritz's?"

"Yes, please."

"See you there."

When Maddy hung up, she felt only a bit of guilt about her plans. Since she'd arrived at the Home, she'd worried Blue would notice something different about her. Or ask what she'd done over the weekend.

"We're adults," she repeated a few times. "We're adults."

Didn't mean it was comfortable, though, did it?

Maddy grabbed her bag and started toward the front door. When she walked into the kitchen, Green was jabbing at the air. Her stance resembled that of someone fencing.

"Do I even want to know?"

Green jumped. She whirled around, and the sight of her frightened face made Maddy take a step backward. That was when she saw what the other woman's 'fencing' weapon was.

"Did Scott give your weapon to you?"

Green studied the 'keychain' in her hand. "I was practicing."

"Practicing?" Maddy raised a brow. "Why?"

"You can never be too safe," Green murmured. "Look at that poor Alisha."

"I'm sorry, Green. You're right. Did Scott show you how to use it?"

"No. But how hard can it be? You just do this." Green punched up, hitting herself in the chin. "Ouch!"

Maddy grabbed a napkin and shoved it into Green's hands. "You're bleeding."

"Bleeding? Oh, dear!" Then she smiled as if it were the best thing that had ever happened to her. "It works. I'd better go clean up."

"Maddy?" Black came from the opposite direction Green had disappeared. "Is everything alright?"

"Green cut her chin," Maddy supplied. "She went to clean up."

Black shook her head. "Let me guess. She was playing with that keychain."

"How did you know?"

"Do you see this?" Black held out her arm and pointed to the angry-looking scratch on it. "She was practicing then, too."

"Oh, dear. Maybe Scott shouldn't have given it to her."

"Or maybe it will get misplaced." Black chuckled. "I'll go check on her."

"Okay, I'm off. I'm having lunch with Tina. Afterward, I have a home visit. I'll see you tomorrow."

"Bye, dear."

Maddy rushed to the train station. It wasn't until they were on their way that she realized she hadn't paid attention to who was around her. Instead, her thoughts were on what lay ahead.

"Not cool, Maddy." She took a quick look around. "Not cool at all." When she got off at Haymarket Station, Tina was waiting. "Have you been here long?"

"Not too long. Did you get hung up?"

"It's nothing."

"While I'm happy to have lunch with you," Tina murmured. "I can tell there's more going on."

"It's nothing bad."

Tina side-eyed her. "Okay, spill."

Maddy sighed. "I have a question."

"Go on."

"It's about Mason."

"Well, duh."

She couldn't believe she was doing this. However, when she needed answers, she didn't have many choices. Especially without a crystal ball.

"How do I know if my feelings for Mason are love or lust?"

Tina stopped walking and stared. Then she smiled, and her eyes sparkled.

"You called the right person. My PhD is in *just enough bad decisions to know the differences.*"

"I'm glad to hear that," Maddy muttered tongue-in-cheek.

"Just you wait," Tina offered as they slid into a booth at Fritz's.

After ordering, Tina dug around in her bag and pulled out a wrinkled magazine.

"What's that?"

"*Cosmo.*" Tina gave her a cheeky grin. "There's a quiz in here. We can both take it."

"A quiz? Really?"

"Sure. It's called 'Love or Lust?' First, we need to answer these questions. Are you ready?"

"I guess."

"Good. Okay. The first question is ...""

Franklin Park
January 31, 1994
1:00 p.m.

WHEN MASON AND DARRIN ARRIVED AT THE PARK, THEY FOUND the 'command center' set up in one lot. Two people, a tech and an officer, were standing around.

"Fremont found something." Mason pointed to several bags on a table. "What happened?"

The tech blew out a breath. "So far, Fremont has found a pair of black pants and one shoe."

"Any thoughts?"

"I'm leaning toward your idea of the assailant—or someone else— spreading out the items recently."

Mason unfolded the map and had the tech point out the two locations. They'd just finished when the call went out—the dog had found something else.

"What was it?" the tech called.

The officer thumbed over his shoulder. "A glove.""

Mason and Darrin followed the officer into the park. They found the dog and his handler just west of the path where the jacket had been located.

"How did the perp get those pieces down here and tossed around with no one seeing anything?" Mason muttered. "When were they spread around the park? I don't believe they've been there a month."

"I don't either. But if not, where have they been?"

"Shall we?" Mason nodded toward a path that, once in Dorchester, led farther west. "If our assailant found a place to hide that night, it has to be in plain sight."

They crossed several roads—both business and residential—before happening onto a quiet neighborhood. "What do you see?"

"The homes are older, but there's been very little upkeep," Darrin answered. "They remind me of my grandparents' home. No longer nice and shiny, but it has a lived-in look."

"Agreed. Anything else?"

Darrin side-eyed him before glancing in both directions and asking for the map. He spread it out, and the next time he glanced up, Mason realized they'd arrived at the same place.

"It's parallel to Peach Street."

"And?" Mason pointed to a thin line that ran horizontally to the road. "See this?"

"It's probably an alley." Darrin traced the line east toward 15 Peach Street. "It dead ends on the next street over."

"Or does it?" Mason took one side of the map and studied. He pointed to where the thin line dead-ended. "Is it possible the killer didn't head west to escape, but circled back east?"

"Yes."

"The officers chasing the killer lost him after seven blocks, right?" Darrin hummed, pushing Mason to ask, "If the perp turned a corner and was gone, could he have ducked in and out of alleys and turned back west?"

Darrin grunted. "Lead on."

They were halfway down the street before locating an alley. While it didn't go directly to Peach Street, if you knew the route, it was possible.

"Now, we look for someone who's lived here a long time and knows all.

They ended up knocking on several doors before a curmudgeonly man north of eighty answered.

"Who are you?" he shouted.

Mason and Darrin introduced themselves, then showed the man their badges.

"We'd like to ask you a few questions," Mason began.

"Name's Walter."

"Walter," Mason tried again. "Can I ask you some questions?"

The man cupped his right ear. "Say what?"

"Questions," Mason repeated a little louder.

"Come in. Come in." Walter waved them inside. "Let me get my hearing aids."

Mason side-eyed Darrin. Had his idea been totally off?

"Okay." Walter adjusted his hearing aids. "Now, what would you like to ask?"

"How long have you lived on this street?"

"Oh, sixty years or so," Walter replied. "Moved here with my bride."

"There was a woman killed in December on Peach Street," Mason began.

"Yeah. It was the Kennedy's home." Walter nodded. "Nice people."

"Do you know who owns the house now?" Mason tossed out a hunch.

"I think it stayed in the family. In fact, I'm sure of it."

"They had a daughter, right?"

"Yes."

"Any idea whom she married?"

"Sure do. I owned a bakery then. In fact, I baked their wedding cake."

Mason's heart pounded a little harder. "Really? Who was it?"

"Rich fella," Walter murmured. "Victor Gilmore."

"Gilmore?" Mason repeated. "Attorney?"

"That's the one." Walter shook his head. "Between you and me, I think the mob got him."

"The mob? Really?"

"Oh, yes. Victor was involved in a big case against the mob when he died."

"We'll look into it when we get back to the precinct." Mason circled back to the original topic. "Have you noticed anything different this past month? Seen anyone you haven't seen before? Or heard sounds that don't fit?"

Walter frowned. "Now that you mention it, a few weeks ago, there were footprints in my yard. But it was too cold for me to go look."

"Where did they lead?"

Walter thumbed over his shoulder. "Around the corner to the basement apartment."

"Does anyone use the apartment?"

"Haven't for a long time. My grandson used to, but he hasn't been around lately."

"Would you mind if we looked?"

"Go right ahead."

They left Walter inside and traipsed around the side of the house. Before they'd taken the first step down, Mason knew they'd found the assailant's hideout.

He stuck the map into his pocket and tried the door handle. It turned easily. Something he hadn't expected.

"Do we go inside? Or do we call the forensics team?"

"Let's open the door, then decide," Darrin suggested.

What they saw when they opened the door decided for them. Just over the threshold, rust-colored drops littered the floor. Several bloody rags, the second shoe, and a black feather earring were nearby.

"What's Walter's last name?" Mason grunted.

"And who's his grandson?"

"Did you fellas find anything?" Walter called.

Darrin and Mason shut the door and walked back to where the older man was standing.

"Did you find anything?" Walter repeated.

"We did," Mason answered. "Let's go back inside. While my partner uses your phone, I have a few more questions. Would that be alright?"

Walter hesitated a second, then beckoned for them to follow him. With Darrin on the phone, it was Mason's turn.

"Walter, what was your last name again?"

"I didn't tell you," Walter frowned. "Could have sworn I did."

"No, sir."

"It's Turner. Walter Turner."

"Turner?" Mason echoed. "Is your grandson Parker Turner?"

"Oh, no," Walter denied. "My grandson's last name is Lloyd. Eric Lloyd."

Mason took a step backward. "Eric Lloyd? Don't you mean Brian Lloyd?"

"I believe he's one of the twins," Walter murmured. "Never could tell those boys apart."

"Twins?" Mason exclaimed. "Brian is a twin?"

"Let's see," Walter hummed. "My daughter, Tammy, is married to Conrad Lloyd. They have one son, Eric. Are you with me so far?"

"I'm with you," Mason assured the older man. "But where does Brian come in?"

"Conrad's twin is Roger, who has the twins Brian and Jason. Those boys were just alike, but their temperaments were night and day."

"Was Brian the one with the temper?"

"You know, I'm not sure. Would you like to see a picture?"

"You have a photo of Brian Lloyd and his twin?"

"Sure." Walter picked up an 8" x 10" framed photo from the mantle and handed it to Mason. "Someone took this at my daughter's sixty-fifth birthday party last July."

One look at the photo, and Mason knew his case had just blown open.

TWENTY-SEVEN

Faneuil Hall Marketplace
January 31, 1994
2:00 p.m.

"What's up, Maddy?" Tina questioned. "Since you took the quiz, you've been quiet."

"It's nothing," Maddy assured her. Though really it was everything. Her mind had been spinning since that last question. "I was trying to decide what to have for dinner."

Tina laughed. "Maddy, we just had lunch."

"I'm cooking for Mason and realized I don't know what he likes."

"You'll be fine. Really."

Maddy hummed that she'd heard her friend, but many emotions were rolling around inside—many she still didn't understand.

"Listen, do you have to get back right away? I want to walk around Faneuil Hall for a little while."

"What about your home visit?"

"It will wait."

"You just want to think about Mason."

"Guilty."

"While you're walking 'around,'" Tina made air quotes. "You should stop in PINK."

"Why should I stop in PINK?"

"Sexy lingerie, of course!" Tina exclaimed. "Trust me, Mason will appreciate it."

"We'll see. Thanks."

"I'd love to stay, but I have a class. Next time."

Maddy waved goodbye and wandered toward the candy store—IT'S SUGAR. After choosing an assortment of candies for the Home, she left the store and turned left. When she did so, a movement in her peripheral vision sent a chill racing up her spine.

Her pulse slammed into overdrive. What should she do—run? Or pretend she didn't see him?

She took a deep breath and casually glanced around.

Was someone watching her?

Was he watching her? Maddy continued down the mall, but the farther she walked, the more her sixth sense kicked in. While she might see no one ... she could certainly *feel* see them.

She passed a few more stores, and slowly the feeling went away. Once again, her thoughts drifted back to the quiz.

The first time your partner hugged you in public, you felt ...

On the one hand, her heart had raced. Whereas, on the other hand , he'd settled her.

When you and your partner are together, you often ...

They talked about any and everything. There were even moments when she just wanted to look at him.

When you met his family, he treated ...

He'd treated her like she were precious to him. In that situation, she was the one who'd been more nervous.

The first time you made love was ...

Heavenly and still made her feel all tingly.

According to *Cosmo's* quiz, she was indeed in love with Mason. Did she tell him? Or keep it inside?

Tina's suggestion had been to share. Except, was she brave enough to put it out there?

A half-hour later, Maddy stopped in front of PINK. She opened the door, and before entering, glanced over her shoulder. What she saw had her rushing inside, ducking behind a display, and looking out the window.

Had she seen what she thought she'd seen?

A man wearing a dark baseball cap was standing next to a display, looking her way. She pressed her hands against her stomach and leaned against a wall.

Was it Brian Lloyd? Was it Parker? Or, worse, was it the third person? Someone they didn't know.

Her fight-or-flight reflex kicked in, but rather than run toward the exit, Maddy took several deep breaths to center herself. Slowly, she relaxed, but was it because of her breathing, or the bright colors and satin?

Whichever it was, she didn't care and took her time choosing a few things she liked ... and thought Mason might, too. Once she'd completed her transaction, though, her nerves returned.

Maddy stepped behind a display and looked out the window. The man was still there, but this time, he was talking to another man—both similar in size. Their only difference was, one had on a red baseball cap, and the other a black one. But they were too far away for her to tell if they had letters on them.

She was considering her options when the bell over the store door rang, and a familiar face walked in, pushing a stroller.

"Maddy?" Caro questioned. "Why are you hiding over there?"

"Who said I was hiding?" Maddy answered, fighting to calm down.

Caro raised a brow but didn't pursue the topic. "How are things?"

"Things?" Maddy grinned. "Are you really asking about things?"

"I am. How are things?"

"They're good."

Before Caro could say more, the baby began to fuss.

"Sierra is hungry. Any chance you could join me for a treat?"

"A treat?"

"Ben & Jerry's?"

"Ice cream sounds good."

On the way to the ice cream store, Maddy kept hoping she'd been mistaken. However, once she'd ordered and started back to the table, she chanced a look out the window.

It's him!

"Maddy," Alisha cried. "He found me. I can hear him outside yelling. He's trying to get inside."

Fear zipped up her spine, and her thoughts raced. She hated being scared. Hated the fact that someone was doing his best to frighten her. Why? Was it because he'd killed Alisha and worried she'd recognize him?

She hesitated when a woman, holding a toddler's hand, stopped next to the two men. A short time later, the man in the red hat left with the woman. But not the man in the black hat—Brian, she thought.

"Maddy?" Caro frowned once she'd sat down. "Are you okay? You're as pale as a ghost."

Maddy hummed. She didn't want to say anything because she didn't want Caro to worry.

"Maddy?" Caro repeated in a no-nonsense voice. "Did you see one of those men who've been following you?"

"How did you know?"

"How do you think?"

"I know it wasn't Graham," Maddy replied. "So, I'm guessing indirectly from Scott."

"Rod told me. Was I right?"

"Yes," Maddy whispered. "I think it's Brian Lloyd and someone else."

"The third man?" Caro asked. "Or Parker Turner?"

"I'm surprised you know so much." Maddy grinned. "Is that normal?"

Caro gave a quick shake of her head. "No. But since this involves family, I asked. I just had to wait until Graham wasn't around. He has big ears."

Maddy laughed. "That, I've experienced."

"Oh my," Caro groaned. "What did my son say?"

"It wasn't much. He asked if Mason and I were getting married."

"He didn't?"

"He did. Of course," Maddy put her finger over her lips, "I used the moment to see what I could learn."

"Good for you." Caro paused long enough to put Sierra's bottle down and eat some of her ice cream. "You know he loves you, right?"

"Graham?"

"Him too." Caro came back without missing a beat. "I'm talking about Mason."

Hearing his name made Maddy feel gooey inside. Even more so because of the person saying it.

"How long have you and Rod been married?"

"Six years. Mason had just graduated from college and was dating Ginger."

"Ginger?" Maddy hummed. "Was she a long-time girlfriend?"

"She wanted to be more than just a girlfriend."

"What happened?"

"I think she pushed too hard. It sent Mason running in the other direction."

"Bad for Ginger, good for me," Maddy retorted.

"Exactly. Listen, call and leave a message for Mason about what you saw, then tell him you ran into me, and I'm taking you home."

"Oh, you don't—"

"I know, I don't," Caro assured her. "But you did me a favor today, so I owe you one."

"What favor did I do for you?"

Caro took another bite of her ice cream, and her dark eyes sparkled. "Gave me an excuse to eat Ben & Jerry's. Now, go."

Maddy glanced out the store window again. Brian was sitting on the same bench facing the ice cream store. It sent a shiver up her spine and had her wishing she was inside her apartment with the door locked.

South Boston Precinct

January 31, 1994

2:45 p.m.

ONCE THE TECH TEAM ARRIVED AT WALTER'S, MASON AND Darrin returned to the precinct. The second they walked in, Gail, the day watch, waylaid them.

"The Lieutenant wants to see you."

"Both of us?" Mason questioned.

"Both of you." Gail nodded. "It's important."

Her expression made him curious. It was apparent she knew the why behind the request.

"No hints?"

"Don't act like you're being sent to the principal's office," Gail teased. "Get up there. He's expecting you."

They dropped their coats over their desk chairs and took the stairs. His father and three others were waiting in the conference room.

"Detectives." Scott waved them over. "Come join us."

Mason studied his father's expression for an extra second, then he and Darrin stepped into the room. His case files were spread across the table, and three men were watching him closely.

"I'd like you to meet Section Chief Lance Diamond," Scott began. "And Special Agent Tommy Gilmore. They're from the Agency based in DC. And this is Special Agent Brian Lloyd. He's with the DEA."

"You're Parker Turner." Mason stared at the man introduced as Tommy Gilmore, his face battered. Not the ghost in the background anymore—flesh and blood—and hiding something.

Gilmore nodded. "Guilty."

From there, he scrutinized Brian Lloyd and compared him to the picture they'd brought back from Walter's. While the man standing in front of him had longer hair than in some of his photos, Mason could say one thing with certainty. "You weren't the one following Maddy."

"No," Brian sighed. "That's my brother, Jason."

"Your twin brother, Jason," Mason murmured.

"My identical twin brother," Brian clarified, "in everything but temperament. Except, how did you know?"

Mason showed him the picture. "We met Walter Turner today."

"Is he okay?" Brian asked.

"He's fine," Mason mumbled. "But would someone fill us in?"

"Sit down, Detectives," Scott instructed. "Lance, Tommy, and Brian arrived an hour ago and have already gone through your case files."

Mason clenched his teeth to keep from saying something that might embarrass his father. He pulled out a chair and made eye contact with the Section Chief, giving him the floor.

"Last summer," Diamond began. "I'd taken my family to Swan Harbor, Maine, for a vacation. One afternoon, the Sheriff, Robert Prince, mentioned some rather odd behavior. It struck a memory chord."

"How so?" Mason pushed.

"A similar scenario had been playing out across the south," Brian picked up the story. "I'd been following the trail up the coast when I met Alisha."

His voice cracked, reminding Mason of the photo in the park. They'd looked happy. Yet, less than two months later, Alisha filed a restraining order. Was he finally going to learn the reason behind the transition?

Brian took a breath and continued, "Last July, I took Alisha and Tori to a party."

"Tammy Lloyd's birthday?" Mason murmured.

"Yes. Jason was there. From the time we were small, my brother couldn't keep his temper under control."

"Hence Walter's comment about you two being like night and day," Mason murmured.

A little smile crossed Brian's face. "That about sums it up. My parents did everything they could. Then, when we were teens, Jason's temper spun out of control, and he hurt someone. They put him in an institute that promised he could be 'cured.'"

"Didn't happen, though, did it?" Mason sighed.

"Sadly, no," Brian murmured. "When I introduced Alisha to Jason, he immediately took an interest in her. He'd done it before, though. I wish ..."

Mason caught an exchange between Tommy and Brian. There was empathy and understanding in it. The look had him curious and wondering where they were being led.

"What happened next?"

"I was a fool to trust him," Brian spat. "But trust him, I did. One evening, he invited me over to 'shoot the breeze.' The next thing I remember, I was in a locked room. It wasn't until yesterday Tommy and I escaped."

Mason exchanged looks with Darrin and his father before giving his attention back to Brian.

"We'll get to how Tommy was involved in a minute," he grumbled. "Do you really expect me to believe that for the six months Jason held you captive, no one missed you?"

Brian shrugged. "My family is used to my coming and going. They know if I'm gone, I'm probably undercover. Jason knew that, too."

"And used it to his advantage?"

"Yeah," Brian acknowledged. "To the world, he was me. When he was with my parents, he was himself."

"Where was he keeping you?"

"In the house's basement where he's renting."

"You know about Alisha?"

Brian closed his eyes and dropped his head. His shoulders sagged, and empathy for him washed over Mason. He couldn't imagine how he would feel if anything ever happened to Maddy or his sister.

"Tommy filled me in."

"Which brings us to how the Agency got involved," Lance continued. "After speaking to a friend of mine in the DEA, we went after the dealer from multiple angles."

"How so?" Mason questioned.

"When school started in September, they sent me undercover at Swan Harbor High," Tommy picked up. "My task was to blend in and see if I could discover where the drugs were coming from."

"And did you?" Darrin jumped in. "Did you find out where they were coming from?"

"In Swan Harbor? No," Tommy denied. "But after four weeks, they pulled me out and sent me to Newton High. That was October 4."

"Did you choose the name Parker Turner?" Darrin followed up. "Or did you find out that was the name of the person leaving the drugs and took it over?"

"The latter," Tommy admitted. "As soon as we had a name, we built him a troubled past."

"So, besides you, there's no Parker Turner?" Mason frowned. "Where did the name come from?"

"I haven't figured that one out," Tommy admitted. "It took me until after the Dorchester party to find a connection and a name. That was when I heard the name Brian Lloyd."

"Then what happened?" Mason questioned. "Why didn't you come to us for help?" He turned to Section Chief Diamond. "Why weren't we notified?"

"DEA wanted us to wait," Diamond replied. "Yes, it was against my better judgment. But they do more drug busts than we do."

"What happened, Gilmore?" Mason demanded. "Where did everything go south?"

"My family got in the way."

Mason tilted his head and studied Tommy Gilmore. He was young, possibly around Maddy's age. Something still wasn't adding up. What that was, he didn't know.

"You knew Alisha Chapman, didn't you?"

"I did."

"You loaned the truck to her, didn't you?"

"Yes," Tommy nodded. "She was a horrible driver, but I couldn't tell her no."

"Why didn't you help the girls move?"

"I couldn't risk anyone seeing me," Tommy replied. "I'd established my cover. Or at least, I thought I had."

His voice shook on the last part, and somehow, Mason knew the worst was yet to come.

"You spent Christmas with her and Tori, didn't you?"

"I did." Gilmore smiled, except it didn't quite reach his eyes.

"They stayed with me from December 23 until early on December 30." Tommy blew out a breath. "I really wanted her to stay longer. But she refused."

"Are you Tori's father?"

Mason hadn't wanted it to come out harshly, and as soon as it was out of his mouth, he regretted it. Especially when Gilmore's jaw tightened, and he had to look away to compose himself.

"No."

"Then how ...?"

"She was my sister." Tommy took a deep breath before continuing, "Her name was Allison Gilmore."

❧

Maddy's Apartment
January 31, 1994
3:15 p.m.

After Maddy waved goodbye to Caro, she realized she'd forgotten about going to the store. Meaning, if she planned on cooking, she had to use what was in her kitchen. Or she could order out, which sounded like the better idea. It would give her a chance to show off her purchases. Something told her if she did, food would be the last thing on Mason's mind. A not altogether bad thing.

On her way upstairs, Maddy stopped by her mailbox. She left her bag right inside the door, kicked off her shoes, and carried the mail to the sofa. A bill, clutter, and a letter with a return address she didn't recognize.

The envelope was manila, measuring 4" x 8" and of average thickness. Bold black letters were scrawled across the front. The handwriting wasn't familiar. But the sensation in her stomach, and the nerves racing around inside, reminded her of what she'd felt earlier.

It didn't stop her, though, and with a deep breath, she ripped open the letter.

> *January 26, 1994*
>
> *Maddy,*
>
> *I'd hoped to tell you in person. But circumstances prevent me from doing so.*
>
> *My name is Thomas Gilmore, but you know me by the name of Parker Turner. You also know my sister Allison by another name— Alisha Chapman.*

Maddy's eyes immediately filled with tears. She reread the last two lines several times. The letter was from Tori's uncle. Did that mean he was interested in giving her a home?

> *I'm a special agent with a US government agency. My assignments are primarily undercover. For the past six months, I've been working on a drug case in multiple high schools. Since last October, Boston has been my home.*
>
> *I was lucky enough to spend Christmas with Allison and Tori. During that time, she spoke highly of you. It was how I knew you were the person who could help me.*
>
> *My parents were Victor and Angela Gilmore, and Allison was four years younger than me. Our father was an attorney, our mother a nurse, and we grew up in Burlington, Massachusetts. I started college in the fall of 1984. That December, my grandfather*

called to tell me my parents and Allison had been involved in a car accident. That call changed my life completely.

My parents were dead, my sister's life was on the line, and suddenly, I had to make decisions I didn't quite understand.

Months went by before Allison was ready to be released from the hospital. Our grandparents, Frank and Beatrice Kennedy—my mother's parents—took her in. However, the good situation didn't last forever.

During Allison's senior year in high school, my grandfather became very ill. He died right after her graduation, then six months later, my grandmother followed. My sister needed me, yet I was out chasing my career.

By then, I was in full-time training for the Agency. In the fall of 1990, I had limited communication with the outside world. Without help, Allison's behavior quickly spiraled out of control.

When I returned to Boston in early 1991, my sister had disappeared. For over a year, I searched for her, yet came up empty. It wasn't until after Tori's birth that Allison called and left a message.

Once again, I wasn't there when my sister needed me. Tori was six months old before I saw her for the first time. By then, you had stepped in to help. For that, I will be forever grateful. Allison was happy and excited about starting over.

From February to September 1993, our contact was sporadic. Allison's emotions were all over the place. Initially, she was her usual bubbly self. Toward the end, she was abnormally quiet, and sadness had crept back into her voice. Unfortunately, she didn't confide in me right then. It wasn't until I returned to Boston I learned about her situation with Brian Lloyd. Again, you had saved my sister.

That was when I helped Allison and Tori move to 15 Peach

Street. The house belonged to our grandparents and where our mother lived as a child. It was always meant to be Allison's.

Hindsight is always better, and if I had it to do again, I would have moved Allison out of the state, but she refused. Ultimately, Lloyd found her because of me.

Somehow, there's a connection between Allison's death and my case. I've just not discovered the how or why. Until I do, I must remain undercover. In the meantime, I need your help.

In the envelope, there's a letter for Natalie French. Allison spoke highly of her, and I want to thank her.

The second favor involves Mason Weaver and his partner. Since I arrived in Boston, I've been collecting evidence. As I write this, it's in a safe place. However, I'm hoping they can help.

I pray daily this assignment will be over soon. That we'll catch Allison's killer and the dealer. Until then, give Tori a kiss from her Uncle Tommy. Tell her I love her, and as soon as I am able, we'll move forward together, as a family.

I'll be in touch. Stay safe.

Fondly,
Tommy Gilmore

Maddy tossed the letter on the table, and sorrow rose inside. Four weeks ago, Alisha ... no, Allison had been killed, leaving Tori without a mother.

Her heart cracked a little, then a little more, as sobs crept in. The more she tried to push them back down, the bigger they grew. Eventually, she couldn't hold them back any longer. Tears rushed up and, like a wave, washed over her. Only then did she give into the pain, bury her face in a pillow, and cry.

TWENTY-EIGHT

MASON HAD KNOWN THE PHOTO WALTER HAD GIVEN HIM MEANT his case had blown open. He just hadn't expected it to happen in quite the same manner.

Tommy Gilmore had filled in many of the holes about Alisha's, or rather Allison's, life. That he was carrying a ton of guilt was obvious. He blamed himself for leading Jason Lloyd to his sister. But the guilt going around wasn't only his.

Brian had his own. After all, he'd been the one to introduce Alisha to Jason, who most likely had been her assailant. Between the two men, the guilt was almost all-consuming. Guilt that would forever remain until justice had been served.

With Tommy's family history winding down, Mason pulled out his notebook. A few holes needed to be filled, one of which involved the ownership of the home on Peach Street.

Walter had been correct in saying the family still owned the home. Their will left everything to their daughter, Angela. However, because she died prior to her parents, ownership transferred to her children, Tommy and Allison.

"My father's old law firm manages my parents' estate," Tommy explained. "With Allison's death, her money will go to Tori."

Mason could have asked more questions about the estate. But since he basically had the information, he moved on.

"Were you the one responsible for helping Allison become Alisha?"

Tommy shook his head. "That story goes back to my father's clientele."

The memory of Walter's comment had Mason asking, "Did it have something to do with the mob?"

"Yes. But how did you know?"

"The man who told us Brian was a twin."

"After my grandparents' death, Allison thought someone was following her. She dropped out of sight and became Alisha Chapman. I didn't know until after Tori was born, which was why I couldn't find her."

"I'm sorry for what you walked into," Mason murmured. "But let's see if we can get your sister's killer off the street."

"I want nothing more," Tommy whispered. "I thought I had it all figured out until ..."

"Until?"

"I'm the one who left the map with the knife's whereabouts."

"That was you?"

"Yes."

"Why didn't you just turn yourself in?"

"I wasn't done," Tommy murmured huskily. "However, that was a huge mistake."

"How so?"

"Lloyd was waiting for me when I left," Tommy shared.

"You're saying suddenly the hunted had become the hunter?"

Tommy pointed to his black eye. "Worked me over pretty hard. Then he threw me into the basement with Brian. We finally compared our stories and escaped."

"They called me," Lance offered, "and here we are."

"You've done a good job helping us understand your sister," Mason assured Tommy. "Now, let's turn back to the reason you're in Boston. Do you believe Jason Lloyd is involved with the drugs?"

"I know he is," Tommy retorted.

"Okay. I can buy that," Mason answered. "Now, help us build the case."

"I'd been at Newton High for four weeks with nothing to show for my time," Tommy explained. "Then there was another incident at Fenway High."

"That's when I transferred him to Fenway High," Lance Diamond spoke up. "When the next incident occurred at a different high school, Tommy and I decided it would be easier for him to investigate from the outside."

"What did you find out?" Mason tossed the question back to Tommy.

"That was when I heard the name Brian Lloyd for the first time," Tommy explained. "It took a few more days for me to find the man I thought was Brian."

"Which we now know was Jason Lloyd," Mason filled in one blank.

"That was in early December, and I saw my sister and her friend at the mall. The only problem was—so did Jason. But I didn't know it."

"Where did you hear the name Brian Lloyd?" Mason asked.

Tommy side-eyed Brian. "From some high schooler. One of them offered me ecstasy. I bought one pill from him and pushed him for information."

"What's Lloyd's role?"

"I think he's a go-between." Tommy frowned. "Where he's getting it, though, I'm not sure."

Darrin stepped in to ask, "Do you think he recruits at each high school?"

Tommy shrugged. "I'm not sure."

"Gut feeling?" Darrin prodded.

"Then no."

Mason glanced at Darrin and could tell they were thinking along the same lines.

"How do you think the drugs are getting from school to school?" asked Darrin.

"I've come up with a few options," Tommy offered. "Either there's a partner, a connection to the schools, or a commonality between them."

"Did you ever see him with anyone?" Mason questioned.

"Did I see him selling drugs to any of the high school kids?" Tommy reworded the question. "No. I did, however, see him with another man about his age and an older man. The only other time I saw Lloyd was at the arcade."

"Any ideas, Brian?" Mason posed.

"I didn't even know my brother had any friends."

"None?" Mason hummed. "Really?"

"Like I said," Brian reminded them. "My brother spent much of his life in an institute."

"Habits?" Mason came back with something else.

"Video games," Brian responded. "It was almost as if his development stopped when he was fourteen."

"So, perhaps he met someone in an arcade," Mason murmured, almost to himself.

"Very possible," Brian agreed.

"Tommy, where were you when you bought the pill?" Darrin asked the same question that Mason wanted answered.

"At a park," Tommy murmured, and the look on his face said he was connecting some dots. "The kid mentioned he could get more from 'Brian Lloyd.' From there, I kept searching until one night, when I was at the arcade, I heard Brian's name. That's when I started following Jason."

"Once you located Lloyd," Mason moved on. "Did you ever see him make a buy?"

"No."

"What about the supplier?" Mason kept prodding. "Any ideas there?"

"Definite?" Tommy shook his head.

"Meaning, you heard something?" Mason questioned.

"Only that someone local is 'making' them."

"Making their own supply?" Mason exclaimed. "Really?"

"It's easy, as long as you have a little knowledge of chemicals," Brian jumped in.

That news triggered Mason to ask, "You mean like a chemistry teacher?"

"Exactly like a chemistry teacher."

"Well, well," Mason side-eyed Darrin. "That certainly opens up new questions, doesn't it?"

"Plenty," Darrin grumbled.

"What?" Tommy asked.

"The teachers out for a little hanky panky during their lunch discovered the jacket worn by the assailant," Mason began.

"And one of those lovebirds teaches chemistry," Darrin added.

"Not only does he teach chemistry," Mason jumped back in. "But his brothers are coaches at both Newton and Fenway High."

Tommy's expression had Mason making eye contact. "What are you thinking?"

"I mentioned I'd seen Lloyd with two other men, right?"

"Go on," Mason pushed.

"There's a possibility he was picking up or dropping off." Tommy smiled, the first genuine smile Mason had seen. "While I couldn't hear them, I did, however, take photos."

"Photos?"

"Yes," Tommy confirmed. "I also have notes."

"Where is everything?"

"In a storage unit," Tommy replied. "No one knows where it is."

"No one?"

"Just me." Tommy hesitated, and then offered. "I was afraid to have the film developed. I couldn't be sure who to trust."

"We need to get hold of your evidence," Mason stated. "Can we go now?"

"Sure." Tommy nodded.

"Lieutenant?" Mason turned to his father. "Would you like to come?"

"I'll hold the fort down here." Scott grinned. "Lance, you're welcome to ride along."

"I'll stay here as well," Lance replied. "I need to make a few phone calls."

The other four headed downstairs, and while Mason signed them out, Tommy, Darrin, and Brian started toward the car.

Seconds later, the first shot rang out. Mason pulled his gun and raced outside.

Maddy's Apartment
January 31, 1994
4:30 p.m.

MADDY ROLLED OVER ON THE SOFA AND STARED AT THE CEILING. Her thoughts were sluggish, and her head pounded. A part of her wanted to stay exactly where she was until Mason knocked on her door. Then, when he arrived, she'd sink into his arms and let him make everything alright. The other part, wanted to run right out and take care of everyone.

A cup of tea, something for her headache, and a notepad helped organize her thoughts. Then, she changed into more comfortable clothing.

When Maddy walked back into the front room, she'd already decided in what order she'd accomplish everything. She picked up the phone to call Natalie.

"Blessed Children's Home," Blue answered.

It took her several extra seconds to put together what she'd done. Once she'd connected the dots, though, it made sense. The Sisters at the Home were *her* family.

"Hello," Blue tried again. "Is anyone there?"

"It's me," Maddy murmured, but there wasn't much weight behind her words.

"Maddy?" Blue questioned. "Are you alright? What's going on?"

"I'm fine," Maddy assured the older woman. "I'm ..." Her voice cracked, and she had to take another breath before she could continue, "I got a letter today. It was from Tori's uncle."

"Tori's uncle? Really?"

"Yes." She briefly shared what was in the letter.

"This is wonderful news, Maddy. Are you worried about Tori?"

"No. I'm happy. More than happy, really. It's just ..."

"You're feeling the pain Tori is too young to feel regarding the loss of her mother, grandparents, and great-grandparents, all in one day?" Blue guessed. "Am I close?"

Hearing it laid out for her in those terms made her feelings seem more normal—less strung out.

"I think so. Anyway, I just wanted you to know. I'll see you later."

Blue hesitated, then came back with, "Maddy, if you need to talk, call me."

"Thanks, Blue."

After she hung up, Maddy called Natalie and left a message that she had something for her. She'd just decided to order pizza when the phone rang.

"Hello."

There was a brief hesitation before anyone responded, but what she could hear tied her stomach in knots.

"Hello," Maddy repeated. "Who is this?"

"It's Scott, Maddy."

It didn't take long for panic to set in, as she couldn't think of any good reason Scott would call her in the middle of the day.

"What's going on, Scott? Are you okay? Is Mason?"

"He'll be fine. There's been an incident, and, just in case you had on the TV, I didn't want you to worry."

"An incident?" Maddy asked, her voice rendered weak by emotion. "What kind of incident?"

"A shooting," Scott sighed. "The guys were ambushed right outside our precinct."

"Ambushed? Who, who was it?"

"We're still piecing it together," Scott side-stepped the question.

"Scott," Maddy pushed back. "You said Mason would be okay. Where is he? Where are you?"

"We're at King's Castle General."

"What about Mason?" she tossed back almost before he'd completed his answer.

"Mason's getting stitched up. Like I said. He'll be fine. I do, however, need a favor."

"Anything, Scott. How can I help?"

"Darrin was shot."

"No!" Maddy cried. "Is he?"

"No, he's alive," Scott assured her. "But they rushed him into surgery, and well ..." he hesitated. When he returned, his voice was huskier, thicker. It reinforced the seriousness of the phone call. "Well, it's pretty bad. Can you reach out to Tina?"

"Reach out to her? What are you asking, Scott? Do you want me to call her? Or should we come there?"

Scott sighed. "I think it would be best if you brought her here."

Maddy's stomach somersaulted, and for a minute, she thought she was going to be sick. She swallowed hard to push down the bile.

"Bring her there? Okay. I can do that."

"We'll wait for you inside the emergency department."

"King's Castle General Emergency Department," Maddy echoed. "It might take a while, depending on the trains. But we'll be there."

"Mason and I will watch for you."

"Is there anything else I can do?"

"Hurry."

The phone went dead, and for a good minute, she couldn't move. Her hands were shaking, her head was spinning, and tears threatened.

Maddy grabbed the phone to call Tina. Before she punched in the last number, she had second thoughts. If the roles were reversed and something had happened to Mason, face-to-face would be preferable.

From there, it was a matter of functioning on autopilot. Maddy slipped on her coat and boots, then grabbed her bag and ran.

In the back of her mind, she realized she'd let down her guard. Realized that even after she'd seen Lloyd at the mall, she'd pushed any danger to herself away. Her only thoughts were of being there for her friend and getting to the hospital.

For the first two stops, she ended up hugging a pole. Finally, after the third stop, she found a seat. Before she'd gotten comfortable, a man crowded in next to her and jabbed something into her side.

Maddy's breath caught. Slowly, she turned in his direction. When her eyes clashed with the man's, she couldn't decide what she was seeing. Anger, fear and ...

"You're Brian Lloyd," she whispered.

"We'll go with that for now," he replied mockingly.

"What?"

"Never mind," Lloyd hissed. "You have something I need, and I want it now."

King's Castle General Hospital
January 31, 1994
6:00 p.m.

As soon as the nurse finished stitching his side where the bullet grazed him, Mason went searching for his father. He found him pacing in the emergency department waiting room.

"Dad?"

"Mason!" Scott exclaimed. "How are you feeling?"

"I'll be fine," Mason replied. "What about Darrin, Tommy, and Brian?" Scott shut his eyes, and Mason imagined the worst. "Are they—?"

"Hold on," Scott murmured. "Darrin's in surgery. I just spoke to Maddy. She's going to tell Tina and bring her here."

"Is, is it bad?" Mason asked, even though he wasn't sure he wanted to hear the answer.

"Bad enough. The Doc said his age and health are on his side, but ..."

Mason dropped his head. He'd been friends with Darrin for years. If anything happened to him ...

"How about Brian Lloyd?"

"Surgery. That's all I know."

"What about Tommy? He was the first one hit."

"Tommy isn't doing well," Scott gave him the answer he'd expected. "I've heard nothing in the last ten minutes, though."

"Have you spoken to the sergeant or anyone else from the office?"

"I talked to her first," Scott explained. "They have one suspect in custody."

"Is the other one dead?"

Scott frowned. "The other one?"

"The other one," Mason repeated. "There were two shooters."

"Are you sure about that?"

Mason blew out a breath and thought back. "When I ran outside, I saw Tommy go down. Based on the direction he fell, the shooter was on the right."

"And the other one?"

"I'd taken a step forward," Mason remembered. "That's when the bullet grazed my right side. The angle is all wrong for the shooter to be on the same side."

"Damn," Scott snapped. "I'll call the sergeant. Why don't you go see about Tommy?"

Mason waited outside Tommy's cubicle until a nurse stepped out. Her grim expression told him more than anything else.

"How is he?"

"He's a fighter," she murmured. "Are you Mason?"

"I am."

"Mr. Gilmore refuses to allow us to take him to surgery until he speaks with you."

"Is that all he said?"

"Yes. Are you ready?"

"I'm ready."

"Go on in." She paused for a second. "But don't stay long."

Mason nodded and pushed aside the curtain. The sight took him back to the first time he'd met Maddy. However, there were considerable differences—Tommy had multiple monitors attached to him.

"Tommy, it's Mason. I was told you have something for me."

The younger man opened his eyes, and the look in them wasn't one Mason saw often. There was pain, sorrow, and so much regret, he could almost feel it.

"Muh, Mason," Tommy sighed. "I'm, I'm sorry."

His labored breathing made speaking difficult, and his voice was barely above a whisper.

"It's not your fault, Tommy," Mason tried to soothe him. "This is all on someone else."

"I, I wanted to get him."

"To get Jason?" Mason questioned. "Is that who you mean?"

"And the others," Tommy breathed out.

"We'll get them. I promise you. They won't get away with anything."

Tommy's eyes closed, and for several minutes, Mason wasn't sure what was going on. He wanted to think, whatever message he was meant to receive, he'd not heard yet.

One nurse came in and traded out an IV bag, then quietly disappeared. Mason debated with himself for several more seconds before he decided what to do. Tommy had more to say, namely, where he'd put the evidence, and the combination to retrieve it.

He took a step backward. When he did, Tommy's eyes fluttered open. The spark he'd noticed earlier was fading.

"Tommy?"

"S-S-Storage," Tommy forced out. "Get the evidence."

"I will," Mason promised. "Where? Do you remember the combination?"

"Com-Combination?"

"For the storage, Tommy."

"Maddy knows."

"Did you say Maddy knows? What does she know?"

"Pink cat," Tommy whispered. "Maddy knows."

"Maddy? How do you know Maddy?"

"Tried, tried to call …"

Mason took a step back, trying to connect everything he'd just heard. He took another look at Tommy, then left to find his father.

"Did he give you his information?" the nurse asked.

"He did," Mason hummed. "Now, I just need to put it together."

"Good luck," she replied. " We're taking him to surgery soon."

"If he asks, tell him I'm handling it. Okay?"

"Thank you."

He left her with Tommy and went looking for his father. He found Scott finishing a phone call.

"Any word on Darrin?"

"None."

"Dad? What's going on?"

Scott glanced at his watch. "Maddy and Tina were supposed to be here fifteen minutes ago or so."

"Okay," Mason hummed. "It's rush hour. I'm sure they're just running late."

"I wish I could be as confident as you."

"Dad? What is it?"

"I called Gail to check on everything," Scott explained. "She told me she had a message for you from Theo."

At the mention of the teen's name, Mason's heart rate immediately doubled. "A message? From Theo?"

"I don't know where he called from," Scott replied. "But his message was, 'Tell Mason the bad man is pushing Maddy.'"

Mason's first inclination was to sprint out of there. Except until he knew what that meant, he didn't know where to go.

"Did you try to call Maddy?"

"I did. No one answered."

"So, then, where would Theo have seen Maddy?"

"I don't know, but I know someone who will." Before he'd completed his statement, Scott was already dialing.

"Blue, listen," Scott began. "Is Theo there?"

It was quiet for a second, then Scott tossed out. "Where? Okay. When?"

Mason wanted to take the phone from his father. And he would have if it could have helped.

"Okay. Theo and Jimmy had Taekwondo. Black was with them."

"They were on the subway?"

"Yes." Scott spat out a word Mason rarely heard his father use. "Blue thinks they were on the Orange line."

Mason brushed his hand through his hair, and Tommy's words whirled around.

"Dad! Tommy said Maddy knows. Pink cat."

"The bad man?" Mason repeated several times. He'd heard that before, and then he remembered—Theo!

"Last night, when I looked out my window, I saw a bad man standing out front."

"The Home," Mason exclaimed, "and Tori. Could the bad man be our second shooter?"

"Go!" Scott tossed his keys to Mason. "You know where my spare gun is. I'll call for backup and warn Blue."

Mason didn't wait for any more instructions. Before his father picked up the phone, he was running toward the cruiser.

TWENTY-NINE

To Blessed Children's Home
January 31, 1994
7:00 p.m.

MADDY WAS TIRED OF BEING PUSHED. TIRED OF BEING PRODDED. At the fourth stop, it was only his threat to kill as many as possible that kept her from running. Instead, she went along like a good little girl and followed Brian Lloyd to the other side of the tracks, then back onto the train.

"Where are we going?"

"To get the combination," he grunted.

"The combination? What combination?"

Brian jabbed the barrel of the gun a little harder into her side. "You know exactly what combination."

"What's the combination to?" Maddy prodded for a little more information.

"The stuff," Brian snapped.

Maddy frowned. *The stuff?* "Drugs?"

She felt him shrug.

"I'm not sure if the drugs are in there or not. I just told him I'd get it."

"But—"

"I said wait!" he snapped.

Maddy clamped her lips together and let Brian drag her off the train. One side was hoping she'd see someone she knew. Or that she'd see Mason driving by. The other side kept remembering Scott's words, '*Remember, girls. While you can hope someone will be there to help, you can't always depend on that. Sometimes, you need to take responsibility for yourself. To do that, be prepared to use anything possible.*'

They left the station, and Maddy put up with being manhandled until they were away from people. Then she dug in and tugged on her arm.

"Loosen your grip. You're cutting off my circulation."

He tightened his hand a little more, causing her fingers to tingle. *See*, his look seemed to say. *I can do whatever I want, and you can't stop me.*

"I said, loosen up," she snapped.

"And I said, let's go," he tossed right back. However, his grip relaxed slightly.

It gave her an opportunity to pay attention to where he was taking her.

"We're going to Alisha's house, aren't we?"

Brian spared her a glance. "I told you we're going to get the combination."

He dragged her up the back steps of Alisha's home and kicked the door. It didn't budge the first time, but while he was focused on that, Maddy pulled her keychain from her bag and slid it into her pocket. *If* the opportunity presented itself, she would be ready.

On the third kick, the door budged enough for Brian to push it open and drag her inside. The house smelled like a mixture of chemicals and, to her imagination, blood. The scent was so overwhelming that for a few minutes, she worried she might pass out.

"Now find it." Lloyd shoved her toward the island.

Maddy glanced around the room in search of something that might help her out of her situation. The skillet she'd hit him with was missing, but the knife set remained. However, it wouldn't help her in this fight. The gun would still win every time.

"Look," she aimed for a reasonable tone. "I want to help. I really do. But you need to help me."

"Help you?" Lloyd's lips twisted with disdain. "Why would I do that?"

"Because apparently, you think I know where something is that you want, right?"

"I know you do."

"How? Who told you that?"

"Her." Lloyd glanced toward where she'd found Alisha lying in her blood. "She told me."

"Alisha told you I had it?" Maddy whispered. "Really?"

"Told her I'd let the kid live if she told me," Brian smiled. "I did, too. Didn't I?"

"You did. But why did you have to kill Alisha? Didn't you care for her?"

Lloyd turned hate-filled eyes in her direction. "*She* didn't care for me."

"How can you say that?" Maddy tossed back. "I've seen the photos of you two with Tori. Alisha liked you."

He was quiet for a minute. Then, when she least expected it, Brian whirled around, ripped a knife from the butcher block, and stabbed it into the bar. However, while the bar was made of wood, there was a substance covering the top, making it impenetrable.

The knife blade snapped, and the broken piece kicked up, puncturing his forearm.

"Damn!" Brian tugged out the steel piece and tossed it aside, leaving behind a bleeding wound.

"Why don't you let me wrap it?"

Brian glanced down, and while his arm was oozing, it wasn't bleeding heavily.

"Forget it. Now, where is the combination? I couldn't find it when I looked."

His statement rang a bell in Maddy's head. The man standing in front of her had searched the house, but his comment also reminded her of something else.

"By any chance, was the combination written on a piece of paper and stuffed into a book?"

"Written, yes."

"It's not here."

"Where is it?"

"With Tori's things."

"At the Home," he stated, rather than asking.

Which told her he wasn't in the dark about Tori's whereabouts.

"I guess we're in the wrong place, then." Brian grabbed her elbow and pulled her out the door. "Take me there."

On the way up Peach Street, she thought about running multiple times. She knew the area. Then again, so did he. Possibly even better than she did. After all, he'd evaded capture the night of the murder.

When they reached the Home's grounds, something caught Maddy's attention. She glanced up in time to see a curtain move. It was quick and caused her heart rate to speed up.

Right before she opened the door, Brian grunted, "No funny stuff."

"You have the gun," she retorted.

"I'm watching you."

Do it, she thought. *That way, you'll never know what hit you.*

Maddy opened the door with her left hand, keeping her right one out of the way. Once they were inside, she tightened her hold on the keychain, waiting. Somehow, knowing what came next.

"Where to?" Brian growled.

It happened so quickly, she almost forgot her part in the action. Black stepped from the dining room and hit him with a baseball bat. Simultaneously, Maddy rammed her keychain into Brian's neck, and Green jammed hers into his hand. He dropped the gun, and someone shouted, "Get it!"

Blessed Children's Home
January 31, 1994
8:00 p.m.

Mason ran into the Home in time to see Theo kick Lloyd in the stomach, while Jimmy kicked him in the knee. A part of him wanted to stand back and watch what was going on. That was until he saw Maddy on the floor, going for the gun.

"I've got him!" he shouted over the melee.

The sea of bodies parted, allowing him to push Lloyd against the wall. He'd snapped the cuffs around one wrist when backup arrived.

"Read him his rights." Mason shoved Lloyd toward one officer. "Then take him to the precinct."

"Here, Mason." Theo handed him the gun. "Did you see what I did?"

"I did, Theo." Mason's gaze drifted to Maddy. He wanted to haul her into his arms and never let her go. However, ... "You were a big help, Theo."

"I think you deserve a treat." Blue gave Theo and Jimmy each a little nudge. "Don't you think so, Black? Green, do we have some fresh cookies?"

For five or ten seconds, there was absolute silence. Then, the Sisters moved as one and hustled the boys into the dining room. On her way by, Blue winked. "Thank you."

Mason's gaze met Maddy's. Determined to let her make the first move, he clenched his fists and stood his ground. His gaze drifted around her face and down, making sure she was indeed in one piece.

"Are you alright?"

Maddy took a deep breath. Her eyes were glassy from unshed tears, and her breathing was ragged. One second, she was five feet away, then the next, she launched herself toward him.

He wrapped his arms around her and buried his face in her sweet-smelling hair. "I've never been more scared in my entire life."

"I'm sorry," she whispered. "I didn't—"

Mason cut off whatever she was going to say with his mouth. The kiss was hard and possessive. His fear for her was still there, simmering just beneath the surface.

Gradually, he released her lips and relaxed his hold. There was something he needed to do, and it couldn't wait.

"Mason, what did Brian want?" Maddy frowned. "He kept talking about a combination."

"We'll get to that in a minute." Mason cupped Maddy's jaw and got lost in her silver-blue eyes. Just as they had the first time he'd looked into them, they mesmerized him.

"What is it?"

He placed a butterfly kiss on her cheek. "Maddy."

"Yes, Mason."

"I love you." He kissed her again. "I should have told you before, but I—"

"Shush." She placed her finger on his lips. "It happened when it was meant to happen."

"Oh?"

"Yes. And Mason?"

"What?"

"I love you too."

Mason couldn't stop smiling, nor could he keep from kissing her once more. Long seconds later, he took a step backward, leaving only their linked fingers touching.

"Now, back to business. Temporarily, anyway."

"Okay."

"That wasn't Brian Lloyd."

"Oh, but—"

"It was Jason Lloyd, Brian's identical twin brother."

"When? What?"

"I promise I'll fill you in. For now, though, where's Tori's pink cat?"

Maddy frowned. "I'm sure it's in her crib. Why?"

"The combination is inside."

"Inside?" Maddy's eyes flared. "Really?"

"Until we look, it's only a guess."

"Then let's go look."

They retrieved the cat, and as soon as Mason touched it, he could feel something inside. After Maddy split the seam, he pulled the card free.

"This combination opens a storage unit that holds answers to many questions," he explained. "However, we'll deal with it tomorrow. I should get you home."

"Mason, what about Darrin?"

"Darrin was in surgery when I left the hospital. Same for the real Brian Lloyd and Tommy Gilmore."

"Tommy?" Maddy's eyes filled with tears. "Someone shot Tommy?"

"Yes."

"Can we?"

Their eyes clashed for several seconds, and multiple thoughts rushed through his head. He wanted to be strong. Wanted to be professional. However, what he felt for her wouldn't allow him to keep her at arm's length.

He crushed her against his chest and held on. How long they stood there —he wasn't sure. When he relaxed his hold, their hearts were beating as one.

"Do you really want to go?"

"Yes."

"I need to talk to the Sisters first."

"You're going to ask them about their ragtag army, aren't you?"

"I am."

"You know where that came from, right?"

"Let me guess," Mason sighed. "From the same person who taught you to swing a skillet."

"Good guess, Detective."

"I'll have to thank him." Mason kissed her once more. "However, it's not a sight I hope to see again. Shall we?"

They found the Sisters, Theo, and Jimmy, sitting in the morning room. Mason snatched a cookie and shoved it into his mouth before saying anything.

"I gather my father got through to you." He looked pointedly at Blue.

"Yes, he did." She beamed. "Once Black, Theo, and Jimmy were back, I just rallied the troops."

Green held aloft her 'keychain.' "Do I need to submit this for evidence?"

"I think you're good. Just be careful with that thing."

"You're telling me." Black tapped her arm. "She's dangerous."

Mason pressed his lips together, biting back the words that threatened. It would probably sound better coming from his father, anyway.

"If I need anything else, I'll let you know. Maddy and I should get back to the hospital. When I left, three men were in surgery."

"We'll say a prayer for them." Blue smiled. "We're glad you were here." She turned her attention to Maddy. "You're not hurt?"

"I'm fine. But one of those men is Tori's uncle. I want to be there."

"Then be there, you must." Blue walked with them to the door. She hugged Maddy, then did the same to him. "Stay safe."

Mason slid his arm around his reckless spitfire and guided her to the car. It felt much like things between them had come full circle.

"Do you need some clucking around?" he teased.

"What?"

"The first night we met, you told me the Sisters were going to cluck around you," Mason reminded her. "So, I ask. Do you need me to cluck around you?"

Maddy giggled, and before she climbed into the car, kissed him. "You can cluck around me later."

That was one task he couldn't turn down.

"It would be my pleasure."

"Good."

King's Castle General Hospital

January 31, 1994

9:00 p.m.

WHEN THEY REACHED THE SURGICAL WAITING ROOM, MASON caught up with Scott, and Maddy headed for Tina.

"Have you heard anything?"

Tina's eyes watered, and when a few tears spilled over, she brushed them away almost angrily.

"No. And because we're not married, I can't get anyone to give me a straight answer."

Maddy glanced over Tina's shoulder to where Mason and Scott were involved in a serious discussion.

"Did you ask Scott?"

"He's been busy. Do you know anything?"

"Not much. What about Darrin's parents?"

A panicked expression flitted across Tina's face. "I've never met them. Nor have I met his sisters. But this isn't how I'd planned on doing it, either."

Maddy squeezed Tina's arm in support. "Let me see if Scott or Mason can pull some strings."

"Thanks, Maddy. That would be great."

She started across the room, and before she could interrupt, Mason took her hand and pulled her close.

"How's Tina holding up?"

"No one will tell her anything." Maddy gave both Weavers a pointed look. "Do you think you can find out how Darrin is doing?"

A corner of Scott's mouth curled up. "I think I can do that."

"What about his family?" Maddy pushed a little more.

"They're on their way," Mason answered. "Including his four sisters."

"Tina hasn't met them." Maddy murmured. "She's nervous."

"She'll be okay."

Maddy poked him playfully. "She'd better be, or they'll have to answer to me."

"I'll tell them."

"What about the real Brian? How is he?"

Scott sighed. "Brian's out of surgery and in recovery. I believe his superior is en route and has already contacted his parents."

"And Tommy?" Maddy asked hesitantly. "How is he?"

"The last time I spoke to his Chief, Lance Diamond, Tommy was still in surgery," Scott explained.

"That's it?" Maddy arched a brow. "Your voice says there's more."

"See there, Mason," Scott grumbled. "She's gearing up to use *the eye*."

Mason smiled down at her. "My dad warned me about that."

"When we danced at the fundraiser, he talked about *the eye*. I think he made it all up."

"You just wait, Mason," Scott muttered. "Don't think you're immune to *the eye*. Now, if you two will excuse me, I'll see what I can find out about Darrin."

"Thanks, Scott."

Scott squeezed her hand. "I'm glad you're alright. Mason filled me in."

She leaned her head against Mason's chest for an extra second before answering, "It wasn't fun. But I'm happy it's over."

"Amen." Mason tightened his hold on her. "With a little luck, we can clean out the storage tomorrow and round up all of them."

Scott agreed, then excused himself to go see what he could find out. She could feel Mason watching her. When she looked up, and their eyes met, there was so much love in them, it took her breath.

"Are you hungry?"

"A little. You?"

"If I remember correctly, you promised to cook for me." Mason kissed the tip of her nose. "What did you plan?"

"I forgot to go by the store."

"Really?"

"Didn't you get the message?"

"Message?"

Mason shoved his hands into his pockets and eventually pulled out a crumpled slip of paper. Before he could open it, she snatched it out of his fingers and shoved it into her bag.

"Why did you do that?"

"Because it's over and done with now."

"Meaning?"

Maddy blew out a breath. "It's nothing now. Really. But the fake Brian—"

"Jason," Mason supplied.

"Alright, Jason, and another man were at the mall today," she explained. "I ran into Caro at PINK, and she took me home."

"You were in PINK?" Mason smiled, the one that was a little crooked, and a lot sexy. It took her breath. "Did you buy anything?"

"I may have."

"What?"

"You'll have to wait and see."

He pressed a kiss against the side of her head. "You're killing me, honey."

"Here's what I found out," Scott interrupted. "They're closing Darrin as we speak. Then they'll move him into recovery until he wakes up."

"How's Tommy?"

The expression that crossed Scott's face gave her the answer before he said anything.

"They removed one bullet," he said. "Before they could remove the other two, he crashed. The surgeons opted to leave those alone for a few hours. Tommy is in the ICU."

"Mason, I ..."

"We'll check on him." Mason read her mind. "We'll be back."

On the way to the ICU, Maddy's stomach tied itself into knots. After everything, surely ....

"Chief Diamond," Mason greeted Tommy's superior. "Is there anything new?"

"It's not good," the Chief murmured. "The nurse said if he makes it through the night, his chances of survival increase, but ..."

"This is Maddy Davies," Mason introduced her. "Would you mind if we checked on Tommy?"

"Go on." The Chief took a deep breath. "Maybe it will give Tommy something to live for."

She clasped Mason's hand as tightly as she could and followed him into

Tommy's room. There were so many machines around him, she was hesitant to get too close. Then she thought about the letter he'd written to her. About how Tori had lost everyone, and she wanted to see if she could give the little girl's uncle some hope.

Maddy moved against the railing and gazed down at the man lying on the bed. He was so still and lifeless she could feel her heart cracking into tiny pieces.

"Hi, Tommy, it's Maddy. Mason told me you tried to call me. I'm so sorry we didn't connect. Until you're ready, Tori can stay at Blessed Children's Home. Fight, Tommy."

Maddy squeezed his hand. When she took a step backward, it was in Mason's arms. She tightened her hands on the lapels of his jacket.

"He's not going to make it, is he?"

Mason pulled her a little closer and pressed his cheek against her temple.

"I don't know, honey. We just wait and see."

They turned to go, and an alarm went off. Suddenly, the room was full of medical personnel pushing Maddy and Mason out the door.

They hadn't been standing there very long when she could no longer hear the machines. In her heart of hearts, she knew what that meant.

"Oh, Tommy."

The door opened, and two nurses walked out. "I'm sorry. He was too weak."

Maddy tried to keep from falling apart. Tried to be strong. But it didn't matter. For the second time that day, she gave in to her emotions and cried.

"I've got you, honey. Just hold on to me."

That one was easy. She was holding on and didn't plan on letting go anytime soon.

THIRTY

South Boston Precinct
February 3, 1994
2:00 p.m.

THREE DAYS LATER, MASON WAS STILL SORTING THROUGH everything they'd collected since Monday. Every time he caught sight of Darrin's empty chair, his gut twisted. His partner would be fine ... eventually. In the meantime, he was in excellent hands, leaving Mason with a multitude of '*if only*' thoughts.

The real Brian Lloyd was one of those. He would heal, but '*if only*' they'd dug a little deeper into his past. Instead, they'd chased after Parker Turner—someone who only existed in the minds of his creators.

Which brought him to the shooters. They'd captured a Hines, related, but not the son of Gerry Hines, the chemistry teacher from Forest Hill's High. The younger Hines had challenged his uncle to make ecstasy. An issue on many levels, but especially when it involved experimentation with chemicals. That seemed to be how they explained the variances in side effects.

It also answered a few questions, regarding the man who'd followed Maddy—the younger Hines. He and Jason had taken turns following her, hoping she would lead them to the combination.

Tommy's film and notes verified much of this, dating from September to mid-January. In addition, there were photos of the arcade where he'd seen Jason Lloyd. There were also pictures of the younger Hines tossing the evidence randomly throughout Franklin Park.

The last piece of information the younger Hines shared was where the name Parker Turner came from. He and Jason created it one afternoon when they were at a cafe on the corner of Florian Street and Park Avenue.

Hines came up with the first name—Parker, and Jason, the last name—Turner, which was Tammy, the birthday person's maiden name. They'd discovered early on that by leaving the bags with beer and pills on porches, customers often returned.

The smudged design on the blue pills was a Pac-Man. Information that led them to the FunZone and the red hat. Yet, another '*if only*' in his mind for not looking into the arcade as a high school hangout.

While they made connections between the five high schools, the pills, and the Hines family, they couldn't say the same for outside of Boston. Those were cases for either the Agency, the DEA, or both to pursue.

Mason took out the photo Walter had given him and set it aside. He'd return it the next day or so.

Finding out about Jason's involvement had proven easier than expected, as he'd answered the questions himself.

He'd not gone to Allison's home, intending to kill her. After following her from the mall, he'd returned to the house several times. However, she'd been at Tommy's apartment. On New Year's Eve, Lloyd had taken a chance and stopped by her house. When she wouldn't let him in, he'd become angry, then forced his way inside and grabbed a knife.

While the younger Hines was the one who encouraged Jason to 'get' the combination, he wasn't aware of what the storage unit held. That had been a bonus for Mason and his team. Without it, their case would have been much more difficult.

Mason tossed the last folder aside, and a piece of paper slipped out. It was Blue's note from speaking with Sister Margaret.

"TG," he murmured. "Not Thomas Gilbert. But Tommy Gilmore, the brother. That had him dialing the number he'd copied from the address book. When the answering machine clicked on—'*Hello, this is Tommy. You know what to do,*' he had his answer. Another one of those '*if only*' moments.

With it taken care of, Mason shoved the folders into his bottom drawer. Sometime the following week, he'd go back through them and double-check everything. He was determined there would be no surprises, especially if the case went to trial.

Until then, there was something he needed to do. And it worried him the most.

Mason took a deep breath, then ran up the stairs and paused right outside his father's office.

"Mason?" Scott questioned before he'd knocked. "Did you need something?"

"Got a minute?"

"Sure, come on in."

Mason stepped inside and closed the door. When he turned back around, his father was watching him closely.

"Is everything alright, Mason?"

"Everything's good," Mason said. "Better than good, even."

"Okay," Scott stretched out the word. "Is it Maddy? Is she okay?"

Mason's smile blossomed. Then he reminded himself to 'be cool' and tamped it down, slightly, anyway.

"Actually, Dad, Maddy is the reason I wanted to talk to you."

Scott's brows rose, and he leaned back in his chair. There was an expression on his face that Mason wasn't sure how to read. It had him proceeding with caution.

"You know Maddy and I have been seeing each other, right?"

"Of course."

"Well, hell," Mason muttered. "I'm just going to spit it out."

"By all means," Scott murmured.

"I'm going to ask Maddy to marry me."

Five seconds passed. Then ten. Twenty. Thirty. The entire time, Scott held his stare, refusing to look away. He'd decided to say, '*Forget it, I don't need your permission anyway,*' and leave. Yet something held him still.

Then his father started laughing. "Had you going there, didn't I?"

Mason blew out a breath and dropped into a chair. "What the hell was that?"

Scott smirked. "I'm practicing my approach for when some boy comes asking for your sister's hand. How was it?"

"I survived, didn't I?"

"When are you going to ask her?" Scott surprised him by following up.

"If I can find the perfect way, maybe tonight. I just don't want it to feel contrived."

"Good luck with that."

"Meaning?"

"Oh, my dear boy." Scott shook his head. "You have so much to learn about the female mind."

"I'm aware of that."

Scott laughed again. "I can't wait to tell your mother." He hesitated a bit, then came back with, "You haven't told her, have you?"

"No. I thought I'd wait until afterward."

"Do you have a ring?"

"I plan to let Maddy pick it out."

"No, no, no." Scott tugged his phone closer and dialed a number. "Stuart," he said after a second. "My son, Mason, is ready to propose to his girlfriend. Can you help him out? Excellent. Thank you."

Scott tossed a card across the table. "Stuart at PiZaZZ will help you. Trust me, he knows the right questions to ask."

"Okay." Mason glanced at his watch. "When am I supposed to go see him?"

"Now. You'd better hurry. You don't want to get stuck in traffic."

Mason stood to go, surprised when his father hugged him.

"Congratulations, son. I couldn't have picked anyone more perfect for either of you."

"Connected hearts?"

"Your mother will be pleased she rubbed off on you." Scott laughed. "Bring Maddy by tomorrow so we can welcome her to the family. Now, hurry, Stuart's expecting you."

Mason left his father's office feeling much lighter than when he'd arrived. On his way out, he grabbed his coat. His future was waiting.

Natalie's Apartment
February 3, 1994

2:45 p.m.

Maddy knocked lightly on the door, just in case Natalie's little boy was sleeping.

"Maddy?" the younger woman greeted her. "Is everything okay? I'm sorry I haven't called—"

Maddy tapped the envelope she held. "I was in the area and wanted to talk to you about this."

Natalie glanced at the envelope, then back. "Is that why you left a message?"

"It is. Do you mind?"

"No, come on in."

Like before, they settled in the living room. Maddy took a deep breath and began. She explained about Tommy's letter, Alisha's real name, and the house. Then, she ended with, "Allison's brother wanted me to give this to you."

Hesitantly, Natalie took the envelope. "Should I open it now?"

"You can. Or you can wait until I'm gone."

"No, you're fine." Natalie ripped open the envelope and took out the letter. When she opened it, a check fell onto the floor, landing face-up.

As soon as Maddy saw the check's amount, her heart lightened. Tommy had given Natalie enough money to start afresh.

"He says Alisha ... I mean, Allison talked about our friendship every time he saw her. Tommy thanked me for being there for his sister. He wants me to use the money to finish my education. Then have enough to start over anywhere I want." She sniffed, and her eyes were glassy. "It doesn't seem fair, does it?"

"No, it doesn't," Maddy sighed. "But now, nothing is standing in your way."

Natalie glanced down at the check. "This is a lot of money."

"It is. Spend it wisely." While Tommy's death may have slowed the process, Maddy knew eventually Natalie would get the money. "Have you decided where you want to go after you graduate?"

Natalie smiled. "I've been talking to Blue. I think I'm going to move to Swan Harbor."

"I'm happy for you, Natalie. You have my number if you ever need anything, right?"

"I do."

When they reached the door, they hugged goodbye. "Thank you for everything," Natalie whispered. "You've been wonderful."

The younger woman's words brought tears to Maddy's eyes. "You're very welcome. Good luck."

She'd taken only a few steps when Natalie asked, "Maddy, what's going to happen to Tori? Did you find her family?" She paused a beat, then came back with, "I mean—besides Tommy?"

"Sadly, no, but Tori's going to be fine. She'll grow up in the Home, just like I did, and someday, she'll be a very rich young woman."

Natalie blinked several times. "Can I still visit her?"

"Of course. You take care of yourself, okay?"

"I will. Bye Maddy."

With that last task taken care of, she turned her attention to the evening ahead. She'd cook for Mason, then show off her purchases from PINK.

Maddy raced to the store and got home with little time to spare. She started the pasta water, then hurried to change clothes. Once she'd set the table and put on soft music, she turned her full attention to the meal.

The casserole had just gone into the oven when the doorbell rang. Maddy wiped her hands on a towel, then rushed to the door—and froze. The sight that greeted her rendered her speechless.

"You look ..."

Mason smiled, that sexy smile of his that took her breath. He raised a brow. "I look?"

"Good."

"Just good?" He took a step closer. "Honey, you can do better than that. Can't you?"

"Well ..."

Very slowly, Maddy circled Mason. He was wearing a dark gray suit with a bright blue shirt and a multicolored tie. In one hand, he was holding a bottle of champagne, and in the other, a bouquet of roses. She brushed her hand down his back, across his very fine butt, and up his chest to cup his jaw.

"Okay, you look very sexy. But aren't you a little overdressed?"

"No."

"Then what am I missing?"

"Nothing."

She side-eyed him. He was up to something, but the heated look in his eyes said she would like it.

Mason handed her the flowers, then pressed a hard kiss to her mouth. "These are for you."

"They're beautiful."

"Just like you." He winked. "Something smells good."

"I hope you like lobster macaroni and cheese."

"It's my favorite."

"Really?"

"Really." He nodded toward the flowers. "Now, put those in water, and I'll put this on ice."

"Champagne? Are we celebrating something?"

Mason didn't respond until she stuck the roses in water, then he pulled her into his arms.

"Mason?" Maddy came back again. "You didn't answer me."

"I didn't?" Mason kissed her lips, then continued nibbling his way down her neck. "What was the question again?"

His kisses made it difficult to stay focused. Every time his mouth touched a new piece of skin, her knees threatened to buckle. But she was holding back, unable to rest completely against him.

"Maddy, honey." He lifted his head and glanced down to where she'd pressed her hands against his chest. "Why are you pushing me away? Did something happen?"

"No!" Maddy waved her hand over the front of her clothes. There were cheese bits and a few other things clinging to her black sweater. "I don't want to get you dirty."

Mason's smile turned wolfish. "I can fix that." And before she could react, he tugged her sweater off and tossed it over his shoulder. "There."

The heated look in his eyes warmed her all over. As if it were the most natural thing in the world, she flowed against him and offered him everything.

MASON FOUGHT TO KEEP THE IMAGE OF MADDY IN A BRIGHT green lace bra out of his head. It was sheer, sexy, and made his mouth water. She was beautiful, and he wanted nothing more than to rip it off.

The second their lips touched, and she pressed her chest against his, he dove in and took what she freely offered. Her kiss was wild—unpracticed but perfect, as if made just for him.

He slowly lifted his head and held on. Her breath was just as ragged as his. For a handful of seconds, he debated with what to say. Should he wait?

"How much time until dinner's ready?"

Maddy glanced over her shoulder. "Fifteen to twenty minutes. Is that okay?"

Mason kissed her again. "I think I'll survive … barely."

"Barely, huh? I need to get another shirt."

"Don't do it on my account." His dark eyes raked down her body, and then right back up. "Only if you think you should."

"Won't it be distracting while we eat?"

"Oh, it will be very distracting while we eat." Mason kissed her again. "Or we could skip dinner and go straight to dessert."

"We could …"

"On second thought, honey." Mason turned her toward her bedroom. "Go cover up, or I won't be responsible."

She giggled and practically skipped down the hallway.

Mason slid his hand into his pants pocket and fingered the ring. He'd thought about proposing all day. Even knew exactly what he wanted to say. Seeing the scene, though. It just wasn't there.

"Go with the flow, Weaver. You'll know."

"Did you say something?"

"I'm talking to myself." Mason dropped a quick kiss on her mouth. "What do we need to do?"

She glanced around the kitchen. "Are we supposed to drink champagne with dinner?"

"Do you have something else?"

Maddy wrinkled her nose. "I forgot the wine. I could make some tea, or we could have sparkling water."

"Do you have a lime?"

"Probably."

As if they'd done it before, they worked well together, and soon it was time to eat. She set the plates on the table, leaving him to light the candles and adjust the music.

"Are you hungry?"

Mason dropped his gaze, landing on certain pulse points up and down her body. "I think you know the answer to that."

"Now, Mason." Maddy wagged her finger at him. "You know how I feel about you starting things you can't finish."

He chuckled. "Who said we can't finish them?"

"It's time to eat. Sit."

"No, honey. You sit."

Mason pushed her chair closer to the table, then seated himself. It was a struggle to stay in the moment. There were words that begged to be said, and he wanted to find the perfect opportunity.

"Everything smells wonderful."

"Don't praise me until you taste it."

"I'm sure it will be delicious."

Maddy grinned. "How can you say that?"

He captured her hand and kissed her fingers. "Because you made it. Everything you make is delicious."

"You're such a sweet talker."

"Only for you, honey."

"Oh, Mason."

"Oh, Maddy."

She lifted her head, and their eyes met. It was a struggle not to drown in those blue, blue eyes.

"Don't look at me like that."

"Sorry." Then, thankfully, she changed the conversation, allowing the temperature to lower slightly. "I saw Natalie today."

"You gave her Tommy's letter?"

"I did." She hesitated for half a second. "Tommy gave her money."

Mason frowned. "Did you say Tommy gave her money?"

"A lot of money."

"How much is a lot?"

"$100,000."

He whistled. "That's a nice chunk of change."

"She's thinking of moving to Swan Harbor. Blue has been talking to her."

"I've not been to Swan Harbor for several years. We should go visit."

"*We* should visit?"

"*We* should visit." Mason squeezed her fingers. "I love you, Maddy. Of course, I want you with me."

She smiled, and the way the candle bounced off her skin caused it to glow. Her eyes glittered with secrets, and her bottom lip glistened. It told him he'd found the moment he was looking for. Without second-guessing his actions, Mason reached for the ring and knelt next to her.

Maddy's eyes flared, and awareness jumped between them. "I love you too, Mason."

"Good. That's very, very good."

"It is?"

"It is." Mason held the ring where she could see it. "When we had dinner at my parents' house, my father said something about you finding what you were destined to find."

She nodded.

"I'm not sure he was right," Mason murmured. "I think it's the other way around. If it hadn't been for Alisha's death, I wouldn't have found you."

"What about the whole connected hearts thing? Doesn't that mean we were destined to meet at some point?"

"Perhaps. I want to believe my father saved you and promised you tomorrow for one reason, and one reason only."

"What's that, Mason?"

"So I could promise you forever. Maddy, honey, will you marry me?"

Maddy closed her hand around his fingers and the ring. "You want to marry me? Really?"

"I do."

"I know nothing about being married."

"We'll learn together."

"Mason?"

"Yes, honey."

"I love you."

"And?"

"I want to marry you very much."

Mason's hand shook as he slid the ring onto her finger. He reached for her, but she acted first and pushed him backward, then followed him down. With her on top of him, he no longer had to wait, but took advantage of the position.

The kiss was unlike any they'd ever exchanged. It was an affirmation of their connected hearts. One that spoke of love, longing, hope, and shared dreams. Most importantly, it was a promise. A promise he didn't plan on holding her for just today. Nor did he plan on holding her for just tomorrow. He planned on holding her forever.

YOU ARE CORDIALLY INVITED TO ...

Blessed Children's Home
May 21, 1994
12:30 p.m.

"I, Maddy, take you, Mason, to be my husband ..."

They held their wedding in the backyard of the Home. She'd wanted something small. He'd not cared. Tina, Mason's sister, Heather, and Caro were bridesmaids. Darrin, Rod, and Mason's younger brother, Brandon, were the groomsmen.

Scott walked her down the aisle. Abby and Tori were their flower girls. Theo and Jimmy were the ushers.

She was wearing a white velvet wedding dress, and, for most of the day, Maddy felt like she was floating. Her wedding hadn't been something she'd thought much about. But being in the middle of it had her wondering why. Perhaps it was because she hadn't met Mason. Perhaps, as he liked to think, his father had given her tomorrow so he could give her forever.

"Do you have rings?"

"With this ring, I thee wed." Mason slid the gold band onto her finger.

He brushed his thumb over the back of her hand, and his touch had her heart racing. The way he was looking at her stole her breath.

"Maddy?" the minister murmured. "The ring?"

Maddy gave Mason *the eye*, not surprised to see his flare. "With this ring, I thee wed." She slipped the gold band onto his finger.

"I now pronounce you husband and wife. Mason, you may kiss your bride."

"Finally," he whispered.

Before she could catch her breath, Mason crushed her against his chest and kissed her like there was no tomorrow. When he finally let her go, she opened her eyes—and saw him watching her.

"I love you."

"I love you too."

He dropped a last kiss on her nose and stepped back, although she could tell he didn't really want to.

"Ladies and gentlemen, Mr. and Mrs. Mason Weaver."

She side-eyed him, as it wasn't the introduction they'd agreed upon. However, when she saw how he was looking at her, she decided it didn't matter. He was hers, just as much as she was his.

"Shall we, Mrs. Weaver?"

Maddy tightened her hand around Mason's and practically floated up the aisle. She was the princess who'd married her prince.

The music started, and Mason pulled her close. "Happy?"

"Who? Me? What do you think?"

Mason smiled. "You look beautiful."

"Thank you. I feel beautiful."

He twirled her around a few times, then pressed her a little tighter against his chest.

"Are you packed for our honeymoon?"

Maddy laughed. "Are you?"

"I have my swim trunks and a toothbrush."

"Your swim trunks and a toothbrush?" Maddy repeated. "Don't you need a few other pieces of clothing?"

Mason kissed her again, this one short and sweet. "I guess that depends."

"On?"

"If we have to leave the room."

"Mason! Be quiet." But she couldn't deny how good that sounded. "Tell me again where we're going?"

"We're going to Key West."

Maddy rolled her eyes. "That much, I do know. Are we staying in a hotel?"

"We're staying in an old Victorian Home that's been turned into a Bed & Breakfast. I requested their corner room that looks out over the water. For the five days we're there, we'll only have to focus on each other."

"It sounds perfect."

"Wherever I am," Mason purred. "As long as I'm with you, that's perfect."

"You're such a romantic."

"Not always. But I'm trying to do better. I never want you to feel neglected."

"Never." Maddy pressed her cheek against Mason's chest and let him lead.

It had been a long time coming, but Scott had been right—she had found what she was meant to find. A man who loved her unconditionally. He'd also been right when he'd shared his dream with Joy. The Weavers had welcomed her with open arms.

"A penny for your thoughts," Mason murmured when the song ended.

"I was thinking about how much I love you."

"Good answer. That, however, wasn't what you were thinking."

"No?"

She'd not told him about overhearing Scott and Joy talking. Therefore, the actual answer might require too much explaining.

"I was thinking it's about time for—" and right on cue, the music stopped, and Scott tapped his glass. "See?"

"We'll talk about this later." Mason kissed her, then led her across the room and handed her a glass of champagne.

"I'd like to make a toast." Scott cleared his throat and reached for Joy's hand. "Joy and I just want to say we couldn't be happier you two found each other. 'Things happen when they're meant to happen' is a saying we heard growing up more times than we could count. In this instance, though, it couldn't be more true. However, falling in love with someone is the easy part. It's what comes next that requires work, bringing me to several important rules for a healthy marriage." He paused and pulled a piece of paper out of his tux jacket. "I even wrote them down so you wouldn't forget. Some of these rules are for both of you, ... and others are only for you, Mason. Sorry, son. Never go to bed angry. Never criticize her cooking. Never forget the love you're feeling right now. Never expect her to do something for you that you can do yourself—unless she volunteers. Never take each other for granted. Never try to change each other. And, Mason, when you do something and end up getting *the eye*, don't go back in the door empty-handed. Figure out what makes her happy and put a smile on her face. To Maddy and Mason, may you always be as happy as you are today."

Maddy blinked several times, but a few tears still escaped.

"Hey now." Mason brushed his fingers across her cheek. "Where did these come from? My father gave you only two or three rules. Whereas I have ..."

"I'm sorry," she laughed. "You're right. We'll have to hang that piece of paper on the refrigerator."

Mason took her champagne flute and set it next to his. "Come, they're playing our song."

"No, they aren't."

"If it's the only way to keep you to myself ... it's our song." Mason tightened his arms around her. "This is where you belong today, tomorrow, and forever. I love you, Maddy."

A brutal message written in blood.
A body left behind.
A name she hadn't heard in years—spoken like a threat.

NOTE FROM THE AUTHOR:

Thank you for spending time with Maddy and Mason. Somehow, I knew from the moment she answered the phone in Chapter 1 and ran out to help without a coat that she'd have a mind of her own. Watching them circle each other has been a lot of fun.

If you're familiar with my Swan Harbor series, did you catch a touch of Captain Jack's "knowing" in Sister Blue? And what about Scott's connection to Maddy in the past? Were you surprised where I got the title?

If you enjoyed this story and are curious about Scott & Joy's beginnings—and their move to Boston—you can step back to 1959 in *The Promise of Home*, a story set in Swan Harbor that explores the roots of the promises made decades before Maddy and Mason ever met.

Join my newsletter and you'll receive a complimentary copy here: The Promise of Home.

Different time. Same heartbeat.

The **Promise of Tomorrow** has a playlist you can find on my website. Maddy and Mason had three songs.

The Promise of Tomorrow Playlist
Keys to Your Heart by Wet, Wet, Wet
Hold on by Jamie Walters
How Do You Talk To an Angel from The Heights

Moving along ...

If you'd like to be the first to know when the next **Love's Promises** book releases, I'd love to have you join my newsletter. I send notes a few times each month with updates on new releases, book sales, giveaways, and a few behind-the-scenes tidbits.

When you join, you'll receive a complimentary copy of **The Promise of Home**—Scott and Joy's Swan Harbor beginning.

Join my newsletter and you'll receive a complimentary copy here: The Promise of Home.

I hope to see you there.

Sophie

P.S. *The Promise to Dance*

Tina thought she'd buried her past. Now it's clawing its way back—darker and more dangerous than before. Trust is a luxury she can't afford when the price could be her life. But as the shadows close in, the one man she keeps pushing away may be the only one who can help her survive.
The Promise to Dance
Summer 2026

THE PROMISE TO DANCE BLURB

Even broken wings remember how to fly.

A brutal message written in blood.
A body left behind.
A name she hasn't heard in years—spoken like a threat.

Tina thought she'd buried her past. But now it's back, darker and more dangerous than before. She's done relying on others. Trust is a weakness she can't afford—not when the cost could be her life.

But Darrin Anderson isn't going anywhere.

Not this time.

She keeps pushing him away, but the man who once swore to protect her is willing to risk everything to keep that promise—even if it means breaking through the walls she built to survive.

Read on for an excerpt of Tina's book.
Love's Promises Book 2 coming summer 2026
Check Sophie's website for updated information
The Promise to Dance
www.sophiebartow.com

THE PROMISE TO DANCE - EXCERPT

Roslindale, Mass
June 15, 1976
6:30 p.m.

Chrissy pushed the window open, crawled onto the fire escape, then closed it behind her. She leaned against the wall and studied the book she'd gotten at the library.

The cover had faded with age. The corners, tattered and taped, showed signs of wear. But the ballerina on the cover looked like she was flying. Someday that would be her. Someday she would be the one to fly.

Ballet Shoes.

She'd only just started it, but she already liked the youngest sister. Posy moved without fear, almost as if her feet knew where to go even when she didn't.

Chrissy opened the book to chapter 2 and smoothed out the pages. She was halfway down the page when she heard it.

The sound.

The car.

Her hands shook, and her stomach began to churn. She glanced up, and from her vantage point could see when it turned the corner.

Chrissy was already on her way inside when her mother ran into the room.

"Hurry, honey," she whispered, already moving the boxes out of the way. "Go on, now."

"But, but mom. You too."

"Not this time, honey. Billy's here. I'll be fine. Go on now."

Chrissy glanced at her mom again, but her expression said her mind was made up.

"Go now. I'll put the boxes back."

"Okay," Chrissy whispered in a shaky voice.

"Don't forget, honey. No matter what you hear, don't come out for anyone other than me or Billy."

"Okay."

Chrissy pressed into the corner of the hiding place Billy fashioned for her and her mother. He'd left pillows, a blanket, snacks, and a flashlight for them. But most importantly, there was a phone. One very few knew about. One she could use if she needed it.

"I love you Chrissy. Be brave."

"Okay, momma."

"I'll see you real soon."

When her mother slid the door shut, the darkness closed around Chrissy. Tears immediately sprang to her eyes, and for a minute she wasn't sure if she could breathe.

"*Close your eyes,*" Billy's words played in her head. "*Take a deep breath and let it out slowly.*"

"*But what if there's no air?*"

"*Don't worry, Chrissy. There's plenty of air for you.*"

Her conversation with Billy, her mother's boyfriend, came back around.

It hadn't been that long ago when she'd come home from school and found him working in her mother's closet. He'd created a space for them to hide. If you didn't know where to look, it was invisible, especially with the boxes stacked in front of it.

But when he'd told her about it, her mother had been there. When he'd talked about it, she'd understood it was a place to hide for her ... and her mother. Instead, her mother shoved her inside—alone.

Chrissy searched for the flashlight and turned it on. She pushed aside the blanket, wanting to find her book, but realized she'd forgotten it. Could she go after it?

Before she could open the panel, she heard a door slam. The sound sent a chill up her spine and caused her heart to race.

"Loraine," her father barked. "Stop hiding behind that pussy you call a boyfriend. Where's Chrissy? I told you I wanted to see her."

Chrissy's breath caught, and a memory of her mother's expression after hanging up the phone one day floated by. After that, she'd heard her mother and Billy whispering. But they'd never been loud enough for her to hear what they were saying. It was then, the safe place came to be.

"I told you to stay away, Mitch. Get out of here."

"Give me Chrissy."

"Now Mitch," Billy's voice came across calmly. "Let's talk about this like adults."

The next thing she heard were five loud shots, and her mother scream. Chrissy covered her ears and pressed closer to the wall.

She knew the sound. Had even heard it once or twice when she'd been on the fire escape. Knew from the sound of her mother's crying it meant trouble.

Carefully, she moved around, feeling for the phone. When she knocked something off the shelf, the noise reverberated loudly in the small space.

Don't let him find me. Don't let him find me. were on repeat inside her head.

Finally, she found the phone, tugged it closer, and with her heart in her throat, lifted the receiver. Using touch, she found the zero. It was the last hole, just below the silver piece.

With a shaking finger, Chrissy slid the dial around as far as possible, then let it go. She held the phone with both hands and waited as it returned to rest. It didn't ring—just a pause and a click.

"Operator. What number, please?"

Chrissy opened her mouth, but nothing came out except for a small whimper.

"Hello, operator," came across the line. "How can I help?"

"Po-police," Chrissy whispered. "Please. It's—bad."

"Just one minute."

While she waited, Chrissy tuned into what was happening in the other room. Her mother's screams had her pressing the phone tighter against her ear.

"Hello," came through the line. "How can I help you?"

"Is this the police?" Chrissy whispered.

"Yes. Who is this?"

"Chrissy."

"Hi, Chrissy. My name's Dan. How old are you?"

"I'm seven."

She heard several sounds at once on the other end of the phone, before Dan returned.

"Where's your mother, Chrissy?"

"She's crying."

"Do you know why she's crying?"

"I, I think Mitch is hurting her."

"Mitch? Who's that?"

"My dad," Chrissy cried. "I think he hurt Billy."

"Okay, honey," Dan went on. "Let me get you some help. Can you tell me your address?"

"My address?"

"Yes. Where do you live?"

Chrissy froze. Her mother had tried to teach her their address several times. But every time she'd learned it, they'd moved again.

"I, I don't know the number."

"That's okay. There are other ways to find you," Dan went on. "Do you know the street?"

"Beech Street."

"And the building color?"

"Yellow," Chrissy murmured. "But not bright, more dirty."

"Dirty yellow?"

"Yes. Like old mustard."

"Okay," Dan replied. "When you're outside, what do you see? Are there any parks, signs, or stores you can tell me?"

"There's a park by the library," she exclaimed. "I like to sit there by the flower beds."

She could hear Dan say something in the background, then he asked, "Does Adams Park sound familiar?"

Chrissy shrugged, even though she knew he couldn't see her. "Maybe."

"Okay, honey. Is there anything else you can tell me?"

"Like what?"

"A sign. A smell. How big your building is."

"I remember seeing a sign when I'm in the car."

"That's good, honey. Is it big or small?"

"It's big and red," she whispered.

"Is there a picture on it?"

"A soda." Chrissy grinned. "I like that soda, but I don't get to drink it very often."

"That's very good." He paused. "Is there anything else you can tell me?"

"It always smells in the hallway outside my house."

"Smells?"

"It smells like food. Mrs. Duffy always shares with us."

"Mrs. Duffy?"

"She lives across the hall."

"That's good, honey. Can you do one more thing Chrissy, for me?"

"What?"

"What can you hear outside your hiding place?"

Chrissy slowly lowered the phone and listened. For a heartbeat, she heard nothing—just silence. That only lasted a second until her father started screaming her name.

"He's coming," she whispered. "I'm scared."

"Someone's on the way," Dan assured her. "Can you tell me when you hear the police sirens?"

"I'll try."

She heard a crash, and then her dad's voice nearby.

"I'm scared."

"Just stay with me," Dan murmured. "Listen for the sirens."

"I'll try."

"I know you're here, Chrissy," her dad yelled, sounding like he was right outside the door. "Come on out, honey. You can tell me about your new book."

"He has my book," Chrissy whimpered. "I have to go."

"No, Chrissy. Stay with me."

"But my book ..." Her voice cracked. "Momma always said I could fly someday."

Chrissy pressed on the panel, but just before she slid it open, she heard the police sirens.

"I hear them," she whispered.

"Good girl. Now, listen ..."

Love's Promises
Broken paths. Fierce hearts. Unbreakable promises.
Each story in the *Love's Promises* series stands alone—united by powerful emotions, layered mysteries, and the strength it takes to heal.
In this next installment, meet Tina.
Coming summer 2026.
Check Sophie's website for updated information
The Promise to Dance
www.sophiebartow.come

Love's Promises

THE PROMISE OF HOME - Magnet

THE PROMISE OF TOMORROW

THE PROMISE TO DANCE

coming in summer 2026

Other books by Sophie

<u>SWAN HARBOR</u>

<u>HISTORICAL HOPE & HEARTS</u>

<u>CONTEMPORARY HOPE & HEARTS</u>

<u>MYSTICAL WATERS CANYON</u>

ABOUT THE AUTHOR

Sophie crafts small- town mystery romances that weave intricate plots with richly developed characters. Her female leads are intelligent, resourceful, and resilient, while her male characters, often stubborn, exude sexiness, wit, and a protective nature. She delights in building slow-burn romances, savoring the tension and delaying that first kiss for as long as possible. No matter the trope, every story she writes has a happy ending.

After a fulfilling 30-plus-year career as a speech-language pathologist, working with adult post-stroke and Parkinson's patients, she is enjoying her new journey. With their four children spread out, Sophie and her husband live in South Florida. They share their home with a spoiled cat named Irma.

You can find her on her website: **https://sophiebartow.com/** *Sophiexo*

facebook.com/SophieBartowAuthor

x.com/SophieBartow

instagram.com/sophiebartow

goodreads.com/sophiebartow

bookbub.com/profile/sophie-bartow

pinterest.com/sophiebartow